RISE OF EMPIRES

The Roman Empire never fell.
It became Byzantium.

The Walls of Byzantium

The Towers of Samarcand

The Lion of Mistra

Praise for RISE OF EMPIRES

'A stirring tale of the struggle for Byzantium. Heneage brings to life both the tragedy and the heroism' *Tom Holland*

'One hell of a fine book. Fascinating historical mysteries and vivid colourful characters. It's a page-turner fast enough to make its own breeze' *Conn Iggulden*

'A compelling narrative of intrigue, love and war' *Bookseller*

'An electrifying historical novel that will keep you awake deep into the night' *Good Book Guide*

'James loves history and communicates that love with enthusiasm, bathing us in an era and world that I didn't know much about. The insights into the Turks' Islamic culture are fascinating ... Enough excitement and riveting history to keep me going through to the end and enough loose ends and intrigue for me to eagerly anticipate what lies ahead' *Bookbag*

'Like all the best first volumes, it ends in a cliffhanger that will leave you panting for the next installment . . .' *We Love This Book*

THE LION OF MISTRA

RISE OF EMPIRES

JAMES HENEAGE

HERON
BOOKS

First published in Great Britain in 2015 by Heron Books
This paperback edition published in 2016 by Heron Books
an imprint of

Quercus Publishing Ltd
Carmelite House
50 Victoria Embankment
London EC4Y 0DZ

An Hachette UK company

PB ISBN 978 1 78206 122 9
EBOOK ISBN 978 1 78429 199 0

10 9 8 7 6 5 4 3 2 1

Typeset by CC Book Production
Printed and bound in Great Britain by Clays Ltd, St Ives plc

For Timothy

CONTENTS

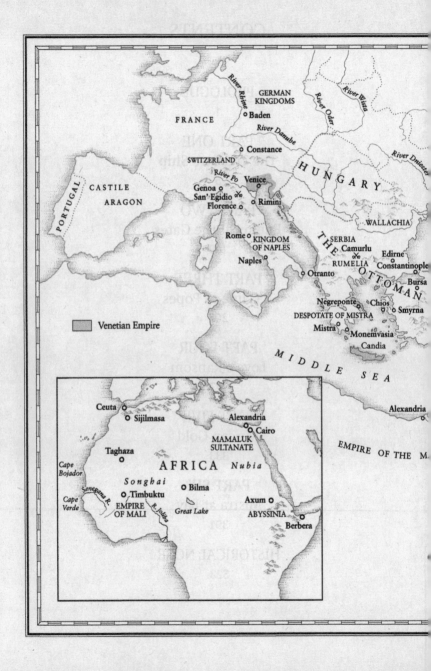

FRANCE

GERMAN
KINGDOMS

River Rhine

River Oder

River Wisła

River Dniester

● Baden

River Danube

○ Constance

SWITZERLAND

H U N G A R Y

PORTUGAL

CASTILE
ARAGON

River Po

Venice ○

WALLACHIA

Genoa ○
San' Egidio ○
Florence ○

● Rimini

SERBIA

Rome ○

KINGDOM
OF NAPLES

Camurlu

Edirne ○

Naples ●

RUMELIA

Constantinople

THE   OTTOMAN

○ Otranto

Bursa ○

Venetian Empire

Negreponte ○

Chios ○

Smyrna ○

DESPOTATE OF MISTRA

Mistra ○   Monemvasia ○

M I D D L E   S E A

Candia

Alexandria ●

Ceuta ○

Sijilmasa ○

Alexandria ○
Cairo ○

EMPIRE   OF   THE   M.

MAMALUK
SULTANATE

Taghaza ○

A F R I C A   Nubia

Cape
Bojador

Songhai

Bilma ○

Cape
Verde

Senegana R.

Timbuktu ○

Great Lake

Axum ○

R. Joliba

EMPIRE
OF MALI

ABYSSINIA

Berbera ○

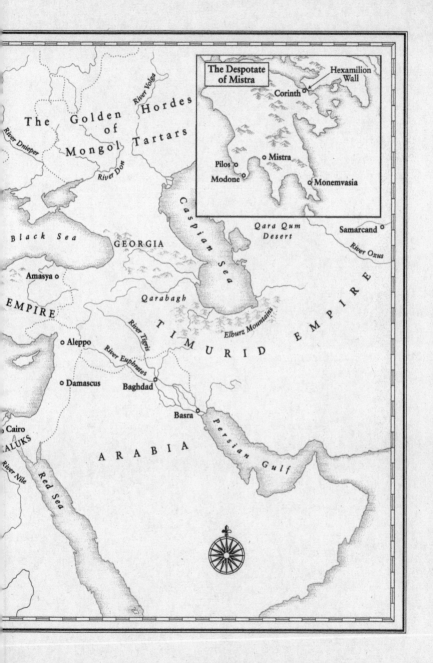

PROLOGUE

THE CHINESE BORDER, WINTER 1405

Tamerlane's eagle was in the sky and his leopard in the snow, free from their chains at last.

The woman on the tower couldn't see them. Nor could the Mongol soldiers huddled around their fires; they could hardly see each other for the blizzard. Their breath froze in their beards and their spit was ice when it reached the ground. Fingers and toes had been lost on the march, then hands and feet. Men had ridden without nose to smell or ears to hear. When hunger came, they'd hacked meat from the horse in front without pain to the animal. At the Syr Darya River, they'd dug the height of a man to reach water.

The Horde had left Samarcand bent against a driving wind that came in from the steppe. They'd rocked slowly in their saddles, gathering what warmth they could from their animals, hoping this adventure would be Tamerlane's last.

His generals had begged him not to march. The Ming army numbered more than a million and the victory at Ankara had been costly. But the Sword of Islam was seventy-two and felt the Angel Izrail at his shoulder. He wouldn't wait until spring to begin his final, greatest task: the conquest of China.

And hadn't the astrologers found fortune in a new celestial conjunction?

So the army had marched and was now camped around the border town of Otra. Beijing was three thousand miles away and the scouts had ridden in to say that the mountain passes between held snow deeper than two spears joined. It waited to hear what Tamerlane would decide.

The woman on the tower stood next to a brazier, stamping her feet and warming her hands. She was hooded and dressed for riding and steam rose from her clothes. She heard a sound behind her and turned.

Another woman stood in the doorway holding her cloak tight to her shoulders. She walked over to the first and kissed her. She put her palms to the fire. 'It seems I'm too late. What did it?'

'A cold, nothing more. He was old.'

Khan-zada nodded. 'The army will be thankful for it. They can go home.' She paused. 'China was always a reckless plan.'

Mother and daughter were silent after that, both considering the capricious reach of fate. Tamerlane was dead, leaving a world in chaos. They said that twenty million had died over his two decades of slaughter; that whole cities, from Delhi to Damascus, had become towers of skulls. But the storm that Tamerlane had unleashed had been sucked back into hell. At last.

Khan-zada said what she'd come to say. 'Come back with me to Samarcand, Shulen. Don't go west.'

Shulen looked out into the night and saw only confusion. She heard something and turned her head. An enormous bird had landed on the wall, its wings beating against the snow: Tamerlane's eagle. She watched it as it watched her, tiny fires dancing in its eyes. Then it rose into the night, snowflakes scattering in its path. The blizzard lifted the bird and swept it away.

He has gone at last.

And Shulen, who'd long waited for the day when Tamerlane would go and she'd be free to go too, nodded. She'd return to Samarcand.

PART ONE

THE TREASURE SHIP

CHAPTER ONE

SAMARCAND, SUMMER 1407

Samarcand.

In the garden of Tamerlane, beyond the suburb they called Cairo, four men stood beneath a night made festive with stars. They'd ridden through desert to come to this city of blue and gold, arriving as the evening sun set fire to domes that floated over walls five miles around. They'd come to meet the man who now ruled from Samarcand: Ulugh Beg.

They stood before an open tent lit by braziers set against stone *tuqs*, their carved horsetails moving with the flames. Inside, they could see men talking, and one of them break away. He shuffled over to them in slippers, his thin frame stooped beneath his *thoub*.

'Luke Magoris.' He kissed the cheeks of one. 'They made you Protostrator of Mistra. Is that a prince?'

Luke Magoris crossed his hands to his heart and bowed. 'Majesty. Not a prince, something less.' He straightened to look at the man in front of him. He saw thin hair sprung from a neck that seemed too thin to hold a head. The eyes that studied him were reserved, uncertain; too young to rule. Luke looked around him. 'You still use your grandfather's garden?'

Ulugh Beg pointed to the sky. 'I come here to look at the stars. There's too much light in Samarcand.'

Luke Magoris gestured to the men behind him. 'My friends. You will remember them.'

Matthew, Arcadius and Nikolas were dressed in the armour of the Varangian Guard and were as tall and fair as Luke. They bowed.

Ulugh Beg dipped his head. 'Varangians are difficult to forget.' He looked back at Luke. 'Prince Mehmed is here already.'

'Alone?'

'No. He's brought Murad.' He paused. 'And Yakub.'

Luke saw two men and a boy approach. The first was Yakub, *gazi* chief of the Germiyan tribe, more centaur than man. He was short, middle-aged, and had legs curved by the saddle. He held Luke hard to his chest, rising on tiptoe to whisper into his ear: 'We have some work to do here, old friend.'

Luke kissed him, then turned to the Ottoman princes: father and son. He'd met Mehmed as he'd been led in chains from the battlefield at Ankara. He saw how little he'd changed from his two years with Tamerlane. He had the flat face of the steppe, but something of the court in his dress. The boy at his side was a scowl beneath a turban. Luke bowed. 'Prince Murad. We are to teach you in Mistra.'

The boy's frown flooded its banks. 'Against my wishes. My tutor is Bedreddin.'

Mehmed put a hand on his son's shoulder. 'Greek philosophy is no bad thing for a prince. Bedreddin teaches only the Koran. It is agreed you will go to learn from Plethon in Mistra.' He spoke to Luke. 'Will Suleyman march on Constantinople? I hear he expects cannon from Venice.'

Luke shrugged. 'Your brother is unpredictable these days.'

8

The Prince nodded. 'All that effort to bring Tamerlane to fight us and we are back where we were. Was it worth it all, Luke Magoris?'

Was it? Was all that blood worth a dying empire? A memory of a child came to him, a child with a toy amidst a ruined city: four dead eyes staring up into his. Luke turned away.

Ulugh Beg gestured to chairs. 'We should sit.'

When they'd sat, when the sherbet had been poured and the pastilles lit against the first night raiders, Prince Mehmed turned to Ulugh Beg. 'You will know why we're here.'

Ulugh Beg nodded. 'You are here, Prince Mehmed, because your older brother Suleyman is winning his war against you.' He turned to Luke. 'The Protostrator of Mistra is here because Suleyman may attack Constantinople. You both want my help to defeat him.'

Mehmed said: 'As you are obliged to do. Tamerlane released me to rule over all the Ottoman lands. And he meant for Byzantium to survive.'

Ulugh Beg was grave, apologetic. 'He did. But after Ankara, Suleyman took half the army to Europe, while you were captured.' He spread his hands on the table. 'Our time of war has passed. We seek peace now: peace with the Chinese, peace with Byzantium, peace with you Ottomans. Tamerlane's armies are dispersed. Can you not divide the Empire between you?'

Mehmed shook his head. 'Suleyman has invaded Anatolia and taken Bursa. It's too late for that.'

Ulugh Beg shook his head. 'But we have nothing to give you.'

Luke said: 'You still hold Musa.'

Ulugh Beg turned to him. 'We thought you considered Musa dangerous. It's why Tamerlane kept him here after Ankara.'

'And we are grateful,' said Mehmed. 'But my brother can raise the faithful against Suleyman, especially if we put Bedreddin at his side. They are both fanatics.' He paused and glanced at Luke. 'And Suleyman is not what he was.'

Luke nodded slowly. Suleyman was debauched these days, they said, but he still had the army. Musa and Bedreddin were risks they'd have to take if Byzantium was to be saved.

'My Varangians will go with them,' he said. 'They'll watch them.'

When Ulugh Beg had finally agreed to release Musa, when they'd feasted on horse, drunk toasts to Tamerlane and mostly gone to their beds, Luke went alone out into the garden. He walked on a path between tall grasses that breathed garlic and mint. Around him, the air danced with winged creatures and above shone a thousand diamonds set in velvet. In the distance, he heard the cry of an elephant.

There was a torch approaching as he knew there would be, moving with her walk. It stopped in front of him.

'You've come.' Shulen reached up to touch his cheek. The torchlight made her face a landscape of hidden valleys. 'You've come and you've changed.'

Luke bent to kiss her forehead, then drew back to look at her. Shulen, the shaman's daughter whom he'd brought from the steppe to meet Tamerlane; Shulen, who'd turned into the daughter of princes. She was wearing a collared tunic of white silk and her hair was gathered above a neck that was longer than he remembered.

Had he changed? He was older now, certainly: over thirty. He had a wife and two sons. He'd governed Mistra for four years and worked hard to do it well. Was there grey in his hair?

He said: 'You haven't.'

'Did you hear the elephant?' she asked, looking round. 'They live here now that the building's stopped.'

Luke had heard. Samarcand had fallen silent with Tamerlane's passing; the builders gone home. Weeds grew in these gardens where he'd once set his tents, and his elephants took their ease among ostriches, gazelles and, quite possibly, a snow leopard to hunt them all.

'Ulugh Beg will not build?'

'Observatories perhaps, one day. He is not like his grandfather. He doesn't destroy.'

They were silent after that, both thinking of a man who'd nearly ruined the world.

'But he couldn't destroy China,' she said. 'It destroyed him.' She paused and looked up at him. 'How was your journey?'

'It was the same as we made, this time by caravan.'

She smiled, remembering Arcadius falling from his camel in a night of no stars. They'd crossed the desert of Kara Kum on their way to Tamerlane and it had nearly killed them. 'Well, we got here, and we brought Tamerlane back to fight Bayezid.' She paused. 'And he returned to Samarcand. Eventually.'

'And you went with him.'

A bat skittered by and they heard the elephant again, fainter now, for the garden was very large. The air was strummed by tiny wingbeats and Luke felt the secret life of the night all around him.

'Tell me about Ulugh Beg.'

'He likes astronomy,' she said. 'He doesn't think Ptolemy counted the stars properly.'

Luke looked up into the heavens and thought of nights above a caravan. 'There's comfort in the stars.'

'Because they're constant? But some fall and die.'

Luke smiled. 'And will he rule well, Ulugh Beg?'

Shulen thought for a moment. 'He is young but he's already wise.' She paused. 'He wants peace with everyone.'

Luke took her arm and they walked on. 'Shulen, we brought Tamerlane to fight Bayezid but it only bought us time. Suleyman is preparing to march on Constantinople. And he's getting cannon from Venice.'

'So your two-thousand-year empire might finally fall?' She glanced at him. 'Can some part of it not be saved?'

She knew him so well, better than anyone, perhaps even Anna, his wife 'Perhaps Mistra can be saved. Plethon thinks so.'

'And your Varangian oath to the Empire?'

He didn't answer.

'So what will you do?' she asked.

'Stop Suleyman getting the cannon, I suppose. I have a new army of Varangians, a hundred giants brought from England by Matthew. And Yakub is lending me some gazis. They'll go with Musa to attack Suleyman in Europe. Do you know Ulugh Beg has agreed to release Musa?'

Shulen nodded. Beneath the moon, her long, dark beauty had an alchemist's touch. 'Mehmed is playing a risky game, letting Musa loose in Europe with Bedreddin. And even if Mehmed wins his war, we both know who'll be his heir. Did you see Murad tonight? Bedreddin has made a holy warrior of the boy.'

Luke remembered the stubborn silence, the unrelenting scowl. He said: 'I have a plan for Murad. My price for helping Musa is for Murad to be tutored by Plethon at Mistra.' He stopped and looked at her. 'But you're right. No peace with the Turks will last forever and they won't rest until they've taken Constantinople. So perhaps I will make Mistra into a fortress: build a wall at Corinth and a navy to stop people going round it.'

12

'And how will you get the money?'

'How will *we* get the money, Shulen. Matthew, Nikolas, Arcadius . . . we'll do it together.'

They'd come to a stone bench beside the path, bordered by tall grass. They sat and Shulen took off her shoes, curling her toes into the dew. Luke said: 'Matthew will train our Varangian army with Arcadius. After it helps Musa, it can go to Italy where they pay well for mercenaries. And Nikolas will go to China.'

'China?'

Luke nodded. 'If Ulugh Beg will allow it, Nikolas will stay in Samarcand and join the next mission to the Ming Emperor. I want to trade with them.'

'And what will you trade?'

'Alum, mastic, horses.' He looked at her. 'The Portuguese have a new ship that will take them round Africa one day. Then China will be open to all. We must get there first.'

Shulen considered this for a while, her eyes on his. Luke saw the doubt in them.

He said: 'You'll be against it, as Matthew is. You'll say we're soldiers, not merchants. But if we're to save Mistra, we'll need money. Look at the Mamonas family, look how rich they've got through being merchants.'

'But you're not a merchant, Luke.'

'You never knew me on Chios,' he said quietly. 'Marchese Longo taught me the business of trade and I became rich. I can do it again.' He paused. '*We* can do it again. We'll become a Varangian brotherhood of merchants or we'll see our homeland disappear.'

Shulen leant forward. 'And me? Am I not a sister to your brotherhood? After all, I came to get Tamerlane with you. You couldn't have done it without me.'

13

It was true. But they'd been soldiers then, the best in the world and, in a way, she'd been a soldier too. She studied him for a time, seeing the same resolve that he'd brought to the business of Tamerlane. She'd followed him there and would have followed him further had things been different. She bent down to find her shoes. 'I'll go to China with Nikolas. Why not? I'm bored here.'

There was a rustling from the grass behind them. They heard the crack of wood splitting. Something big was coming towards them, something hidden by the night. Luke rose and put his finger to his lips. 'Stay here.'

He thought it might be an elephant or roebuck or even ostrich. Then he remembered the snow leopard. He looked around for a weapon and saw a stick lying next to the bench. He picked it up.

'Luke.'

But he was already walking away, feeling the grass wet against his thighs. He glanced back at her, his hand raised.

He heard the sound of branches pulled from trees, more cracking. It was too big for a leopard. He crept forward, the stick before him.

Then he saw it.

He turned and called to Shulen and she came. She took his hand and they both looked. Fifty paces to their front, they could see a long neck and, above it, the shape of a head pulling leaves from a tree. The head had little horns that glowed under the moon.

'Tamerlane's jornufa,' said Luke.

14

CHAPTER TWO

AMASYA, ANATOLIA, SPRING 1409

The city of Amasya hardly needed walls to defend itself. High in the mountains of northern Anatolia, it was perched astride the Iris River, which wandered down its valley like a sailor ashore, bumping the mountains as it went. It had always been a cussed, dogged place, made so by its geography. It had been where Prince Mehmed had spent his youth; now it was his sanctuary.

A shelf of rock split the city in two and on this rock sat the citadel. It dominated the valley, and the steepness of the slopes, before and behind, made it impregnable. In a courtyard over-looking its walls, Mehmed was talking to Yakub, chief of the Germiyans and one of the few people he could trust.

The two men were sitting on a bench too far back to see anything but colour. The sky was awash with it, fierce blue sur-rendering to night and leaving bloody claw-marks in its wake. Below, out of sight of the sitters, was a torrent of lava spilling out from the dying sun. The only sound was the drone of insects come up to carouse.

Mehmed had just finished reading a letter from his son. 'Murad writes that he's unhappy in Mistra and wants to come

15

home,' he said. 'Or better still, go and fight with Musa. He hates Plethon and wants to learn from Bedreddin again.'

'That would be dangerous.'

Mehmed didn't reply. Had Bedreddin really turned his son into a fanatic? And would the calm logic of a Greek syllabus change him?

Yakub rose, his hand on Mehmed's shoulder. His long hair was greying with his beard, but his chest was broad and his neck clustered with muscle. He was dressed in the *deel* of the gazi chief and his boots were worn. 'Let's worry about Murad later. It's Suleyman we should concern ourselves with. He has the army: the janissaries, *sipahis*, *bashibozouks*.'

'But not the hundred gazis you've lent to Luke.'

Yakub looked out at the tenuity of pink that was still the day. Soon they'd hear the muezzin's call and shuffle of prayer in the castle's corridors. Soon it would be night.

'No, not them. And not cannon.' He paused. 'Yet.'

Far to the west, a hundred Varangians and an engineer from Chios were waiting in ambush on a hill. They were lying on their fronts on grass still warm from the day, overlooking the main road that linked Edirne to Constantinople. The hill fell steeply to the road and then a wide river, too deep and fast to cross. It was a good place for an ambush.

They were waiting for an army to arrive with wagons. They expected it to be about a thousand strong and made up of sipahi knights, janissaries and wagons with cannon in them, cannon recently bought from Venice by Suleyman. Luke was lying between Matthew and the engineer Benedo Barbi, who was holding wires.

Matthew said: 'They won't be expecting anyone to attack such a large force, especially at night.'

16

'It won't be night when I've pulled my wires,' said Barbi. 'Where are the gazis?'

Luke shrugged. 'Don't ask me, ask the general. Matthew, where are they?'

'Waiting down the valley with Arcadius.'

'And our guns?'

Matthew pointed. 'In front, behind that stockade.'

Luke could feel tension in the air between them. This was the Varangian Company's first battle. They were outnumbered five to one but they had surprise and Benedo Barbi on their side. Luke rolled on to his back. 'Tell me again how you recruited them.'

Luke liked the story. Three years before, Matthew had travelled through Europe, part of an embassy sent by the Emperor Manuel to raise money for Byzantium's cause. In England, they'd been entertained by the English King at his palace at Eltham.

'They were bodyguards to King Henry,' said Matthew. 'It was after a feast on Christmas Day and the King asked what gift we'd like since he was unable to part with money. I suggested his bodyguard.'

Luke smiled. 'The first Varangian business. Should we call it a *campagna* as we do on Chios?'

Matthew glanced along the line of soldiers, all with longbows and axes by their sides. He pointed to one kneeling behind them. He wore the same uniform as the others: a scaled cuirass over a green tunic. 'That is Peter of Norfolk. Call it a campagna and he'll desert. No, we're the Varangian Company, descendants of the men who came from England with your ancestor Siward after the Normans took their country. Peter's good. He was with John Hawkwood's Company for the Italian wars.'

Luke knew how useful Peter had been. He'd organised the

men into thirty lances; two bowmen and a man-at-arms in each. He'd mounted the lances so they could deploy quickly in battle. He asked: 'Have you thought how we'll use them in Italy? I'm told that the *condottieri* change sides, sometimes in the middle of battle if the bribe's big enough.'

'So we'll swear our Varangian oath and be loyal.'

Matthew thought for a while. Then he turned to Luke and lowered his voice. 'Is all this wise, Luke?'

Luke propped himself up on his elbows. 'Do you mean taking Suleyman's cannon? We're going to destroy them.'

Matthew was silent for a while. 'I meant this trade with China. Nikolas should be here with us, not acting the merchant.'

They'd talked of it before and would do so again. Matthew's idea of Varangian brotherhood did not include trade. Luke said: 'A hundred men cannot save Mistra. Only a wall and a navy can do that. We need money.' He took hold of his friend's arm. 'Matthew, Mehmed is losing this war. If Suleyman wins, he'll attack Constantinople. And when Constantinople falls, where will he go next?'

Six hours later, the trip wires were still intact. The three men had stopped talking and one was asleep, nudged awake whenever his snores got too loud.

Matthew put a finger to his lips. 'Shh! I heard something. Squeaks.'

There were lights in the darkness. The squeaks came from wheels; the lights from torches held by riders. There was the jangle of harness and the ring of hoof on stone and the blow and neigh of horses. The lights went on forever.

Luke could just make out the outline of Barbi's helmet. 'How long until they trip the wire?'

'Any moment.'

Luke drew his sword and ran his thumb over the dragon head. He curled his hand around the scales of its neck, finger by finger. The sword had been his ancestor Siward's: the first English Varangian.

Then, suddenly, it was day. The wires had been tripped and little fountains of flame sprang up all down the road. Horses reared and the air was full of shouts. Luke could see sipahi cavalry at the front and back and, in between, janissaries guarding three long wagons. Matthew lifted his arm.

'Now!'

There was the swoosh of arrows in flight. The range was good and the targets bright. Arrows parted mail and fifty sipahis fell to the ground.

'They're going to deploy,' shouted Matthew. 'Aim low to bring down the horses.'

The sipahis were spreading out across the bottom of the hill, readying their horses to charge. The slope was steep and they could see nothing above it, blinded by the light all around them. They'd lost a quarter of their men and dead horses were getting in the way. Then a man raised his sword and kicked his horse up the hill.

'Aim low!'

The next volley was more lethal. The sipahis were silhouetted by fire and more horses fell, some on top of their riders. It was mayhem but still they came on. It took two more volleys to stop them and by then half their number were on the ground. An order was shouted and the sipahis turned back down the hill.

About half a mile distant, Arcadius was sitting on his horse in front of a line of Germiyan tribesmen. It seemed an unlikely pairing, but Arcadius had learnt how to ride and shoot in the service of Tamerlane and it wasn't very different from what these men did.

He saw the glow ahead. The night was still and the sound of escape wafted down the valley to him.

It took some time for them to come. The retreating janissaries were on foot and the wagons slow. At last there were torches.

'Now!'

Arcadius kicked his horse and leapt forward, the rest following. They were invisible to the men below but the janissaries heard their hooves and fired into the night at whatever was coming towards them.

The gazis fell on them like jackals. There was hatred between the Anatolian tribes and the men who'd come to their land to crush them into obedience. They attacked them with swords that parted heads from shoulders, heads that only saw their attackers for an instant before they fell. They got close to the wagons but their momentum had stalled and the janissaries were fighting hard. Arcadius yelled his orders and the gazis fell back, ready to charge again.

There were shouts and the sound of hooves. A group of sipahi knights came out of the darkness and dismounted. Covered by the janissaries, they turned the wagons back the way they'd come. Arcadius watched them go.

At the ambush, Barbi's incendiaries had burnt themselves out. Half of the Varangian Company had advanced with Matthew down the hill, driving the sipahis back to the road. The Turks now were few in number but they knew what they must do: wait for the wagons to come up and then try to ride them out through the barrier ahead.

Luke was still on the hill with Barbi, Peter of Norfolk and the bowmen. He saw torches on the road and heard the rumble of the wagons. There was an explosion and, in its sudden light, he saw the smoking barrels of two ribaudekins between tree trunks laid across the road. The little guns had poured grapeshot into the sipahis and a dozen men and horses lay on the road, their bodies ripped open. The men in front were trying to get away but those behind were still advancing and there was a river to one side and a hill to the other.

They chose the hill.

But Luke was on the hill and the archers, led by Peter of Norfolk, were lined up beside him, bows at the ready.

The sipahis came on. They'd left the cannon on the road and were now charging up the hill, most on foot. But they were surrounded. They stopped and formed themselves into a square and fell to the arrows and grapeshot that came at them from every direction. At last they broke and ran and Matthew's men parted to let them through.

When it was over, Luke walked down to where Matthew stood amongst the bodies. 'How many dead?'

'Theirs? Most of them. Ours, three wounded, I think.' Matthew stooped to pull an arrow from a sipahi and give it to an archer. There were cheers behind them and they turned. The Varangians were on top of the wagons.

'So Suleyman won't get his cannon.'

Matthew nodded. 'And Constantinople gets another reprieve. Should we take the cannon to Mistra?'

Luke rubbed his eyelids between his fingers and thumbs. He felt the exhaustion of relief. He was alive, his friends were alive, and the battle was won. 'We're needed here,' he said. 'It's as I said: we throw them in the river.'

CHAPTER THREE

EDIRNE, SUMMER 1409

The surgeon Şerafeddin Sabuncuoğlu had already made a name for himself in Amasya when Mehmed sent him to cure Suleyman of his headaches. That had been when the brothers were still talking to each other. Sabuncuoğlu prescribed opium for the pain. In time, Suleyman's migraines were joined by melancholy and Sabuncuoğlu prescribed opium for that too. By the third year of the war between Bayezid's sons, Suleyman was addicted. So Mehmed brought the doctor home.

Now, smoking no fewer than ten pipes a day, Suleyman had become more degenerate, even, than his father. He spent most of his time in the harem, surrounded by creatures who were as addicted as he. He'd replaced his father's concubines with women of every age, size and colour. There were some too fat to stand, some young enough to be his offspring, and even an amputee. He'd become addicted to cleanliness, wearing gloves to eat. His food was tasted a dozen times before it reached his table and he ate beneath gauze. He dreamt, once, that all the figs in the palace garden had been coated with poison and decreed that every fig tree in the Empire be felled.

The Grand Vizier, of course, had ignored the decree. Both

he and Suleyman's greatest general, Evrenos Bey, had watched Suleyman's decline with concern, doing what they could to conceal it from the court and, especially, the army. But Suleyman had taken to wearing make-up to hide his pallor, sometimes applied clumsily. The army didn't like it.

Zoe Mamonas was sitting with Suleyman in a room in the basement of the palace, connected by a secret corridor to the harem. Its walls were decorated with coupling men and women. There were low tables and cushions around the walls and on each table stood a pipe with a funnelled lamp beside it. The air was thick with smoke and Zoe felt sick. She thought of Mehmed.

How clever you've been.

'You will die of it,' she said. Her face had hardly changed over the years. It still held the langourous beauty that had driven men to do things they shouldn't, in bed or with a knife. Her long hair, black as jet, travelled to her waist over a body still shaped by the contours of youth. 'Either it, or the army, will kill you. It's been Mehmed's best weapon.'

She studied him. He'd just finished a pipe and his eyes were bloodshot and unfocused, his hands shaking. He was very different from the man she'd tried so hard to marry. Then, he'd been a slender spear of a man, pointed of nose, beard and intellect. He'd been a compact and subtle vessel of ambition and she had, in her way, admired him. Now he was old before his time.

He coughed. 'It helps me rule. Anyway, I have Rumelia and most of Anatolia; he has Amasya. I have an army of fifty thousand; he has some gazi tribes. You exaggerate, as usual.'

'You also have Musa on these shores,' she said, waving the smoke away. Her eyes were stinging. 'And some Varangians who've stolen your cannon.'

Suleyman frowned, trying to focus on the woman in front of

him. Why did she always want to talk about bad things? 'We'll get more.'

'Not for a long time. Venice takes six months to cast them.'

'I intend to take Constantinople.'

Zoe laughed. 'Take Constantinople? How? You've got two brothers fighting you now.'

Suleyman used a distant part of his mind to ponder this. It was true that the *akincis*, the Anatolian tribesmen on the frontiers of the Empire, were rallying to Musa, liking the sound of his jihad. But Constantinople was Suleyman's destiny.

'I will take Constantinople when I have defeated Mehmed and Musa,' he said. He looked up at her. 'Why don't you go and poison them? It's what you're good at: whoring and poisoning.'

Zoe coloured. Suleyman knew that she'd been Tamerlane's mistress after Ankara, but he didn't know that she'd only stayed with Suleyman because she wasn't welcome anywhere else. She might be heir to Pavlos Mamonas, Venice's richest banker, but few cities would welcome the woman who'd so nearly brought Tamerlane into Constantinople. Not even Venice.

'Be nicer to the army, Suleyman,' she said quietly. 'Evrenos Bey told me you punished the janissaries: beat them and confiscated their cauldrons. That wasn't intelligent.'

'They didn't bow to me when I passed. How could I not punish them?'

'They didn't know it was you, fool. Their aga told me you were wearing make-up. Now they hate you, as does everyone else.'

'As you do?' Suleyman stood unsteadily, kicking over a table, sending its clay pipe to the floor. 'Why don't you leave then?'

'Because, Suleyman,' said Zoe, standing too, 'if I went there'd be no one left you could trust. Think about that before you insult me again.'

Suleyman stared at her. He was breathing hard, his chest rising and falling, his fists clenched. So often he'd wanted to hit her. But she was right: he needed her. He sat down. A servant began to gather the pieces of the pipe but Suleyman waved him away.

'Why are you here?'

Zoe remained standing. 'Because my father is here.'

Upstairs, Pavlos Mamonas was striding up and down, his shoes squeaking on the turn. He was in his late fifties and wore his little remaining hair short. His face was handsome but lined with care and cowled by a second chin. He was pale and tending to portliness, the result of hibernation inside his Venetian *fondaco*. He'd never got over the death of his son eleven years earlier and blamed himself every day.

Zoe blamed him too. She'd been Damian's twin and had loved her brother. His death had secured her sole inheritance of the vast Mamonas trading empire but that had not stopped her speculating as to how he'd died – and who was responsible.

The man she suspected was standing in front of her now, his hat in his hands. Beside him stood the Grand Vizier wearing a white housecoat and a tall hat that brushed the ceiling. The two bowed low as she and Suleyman entered.

Suleyman went unsteadily to the throne and sat down. He called for wine. Zoe intercepted the cup and put it down beside him.

'I hear that you are richer than ever, Pavlos,' said Suleyman. 'Tell me, why is banking so profitable?'

Mamonas thought for a moment before replying. 'Because the Catholic Church doesn't like it and doesn't understand it, lord. So there's little competition and what there is makes up its own rules.'

25

Zoe watched Suleyman summoning the effort to absorb this, his fingers to his temples. He said: 'I have to talk to you about getting more cannon.'

Pavlos Mamonas glanced at Zoe. They'd not spoken since Damian's death. 'In the matter of the war between you and your brothers, lord,' he said, 'I regret the Serenissima must now remain neutral.'

'Is that because she thinks Mehmed might win?'

Pavlos Mamonas remained silent, knowing it to be the reason.

The Grand Vizier spoke. 'It is understandable that Venice is reluctant to provoke Mehmed, but sending Musa to Europe has unsettled the whole frontier. He has the Sufi Bedreddin with him who is inciting the akincis to raid across the borders of Wallachia and Serbia. Venice is not so far away.'

Pavlos Mamonas spread his hands in apology. 'The Serenissima seeks peace between the sons of Bayezid.'

Suleyman lost his temper. 'Peace? Venice would like nothing more than for us to destroy each other!' He looked at Zoe. 'Is this your father? He doesn't sound like the Pavlos Mamonas I used to know.'

Zoe looked at her father for the first time. 'What is it that worries Venice?' she asked quietly. 'Suleyman will win this war because he has the army. So why won't she support him?'

Pavlos Mamonas stared back at his daughter. If he thought of Damian daily, he thought of her every hour. He had agreed to this meeting in the hope of seeing her, but he looked into eyes filmed with indifference.

The vizier began to speak but Suleyman raised his hand. He was getting bored. 'Without cannon, Pavlos,' he said, 'my army cannot take Constantinople. What should it do instead? It wants me to lead it somewhere.'

'It can defeat Musa.'

'But many in its ranks admire Musa. I need to do something more popular first.' He glanced at Zoe, malice in his eyes now. 'What about Mistra? There's plenty of gold in Mistra, gold to buy cannon from somewhere other than Venice.' He paused. 'And Mistra doesn't have walls.'

Zoe looked hard at Suleyman. She saw the red, dilated eyes, and the pallor of a sickness too far gone to return. His madness would kill her too. She wanted to be somewhere else. 'If you march on Mistra, Musa will be free to take Edirne.'

Suleyman shrugged. 'Let him. I'll create a new kingdom out of the one you and your father left.'

As Pavlos Mamonas was leaving the palace, he was stopped by his daughter. She led her father into a small room with a fountain at its centre, tiled in blue majolica. The water played over coral, making a music that might have soothed. She stopped with the fountain between them, trailing her fingers in the water, moving them to make little currents, before looking up.

'Suleyman cannot take Mistra.'

Pavlos Mamonas stared at his daughter. He'd not seen her for an eternity and only water separated them now. He could almost touch her. He said: 'With Luke and the Varangians away, it would not be difficult.'

Zoe turned to one side so that her father saw only profile. 'I mean that he cannot be allowed to. It's directly on the trade route to Alexandria. Imagine what Turkish corsairs would do to our shipping.'

Pavlos knew it well. Generations of Mamonases had been Archons of Monemvasia until they'd been expelled for siding

27

with the Turk. His ancestors, and Zoe's, had been pirates; it was how the Mamonas fortune had been founded. He nodded.

She glanced at him. 'It is also the gold route from Africa to Venice and the basis of Venice's wealth. It would be a disaster for Venice, for us.'

Us.

'You wish to come back to Venice?' asked Mamonas, still staring at his daughter. 'It may be too soon. People remember your adventure with Tamerlane. But . . .'

Zoe was shaking her head. 'I wish to leave Suleyman but I will make my own arrangements. I know it's too soon to return to Venice.' She looked into the water. 'I will come back when I'm pardoned and when you're dead.'

Pavlos felt the blade go deep into his heart. His knees weakened and he put a hand out to the fountain's wall. His daughter had turned away and begun to walk towards the door.

'Venice must get to Mistra before Suleyman,' she said. 'You must persuade her to attack Monemvasia. It'll bring home the Varangians and might allow Suleyman to win his war.' She paused at the door and turned. 'Venice has always wanted Mistra. Now she must take it.'

Later that night, Zoe was walking through the back streets of Edirne. She was dressed head to toe in the blackest of garments with a veil drawn across her face so that only her eyes were visible. She couldn't see further than a few paces ahead but there was no one to bump into. The streets were empty of people and the only living things she met were dogs scavenging outside a butcher's shop. She thought of a night in Venice when she'd walked through streets noisy with crime on her way to buy poison from a man with a viper on his door. That was in

Christian Venice, a city full of churches and cats. Muslim Edirne had no crime or poison and dogs instead of cats. It was a place of infinite dullness and she loathed it.

A dog emerged from the night, offal in its mouth. It growled and she kept close to the wall.

She came to a door. It was identical to others in the narrow street and she checked to left and right before knocking. It was opened by a big man she knew: Yusuf, once a janissary and now her slave. She kept him in a house in the city for meetings of any private kind.

Inside the room there were candles but no wine on the table, this being a Muslim house. A man rose from the table as she entered. He was tall, middle-aged and bearded. He wore the clothes of a Sufi theologian, plain, long and with beads hung from its belt. His face was serious and his mouth had the curve of the ascetic. Zoe disliked him on sight.

'Sheikh Bedreddin,' she said, removing her cloak and passing it to Yusuf. She sat.

The man bowed from the neck and remained standing. Nothing in his face indicated pleasure to meet her.

'Please sit,' sighed Zoe, gesturing to the seat from which he'd just risen. 'I can't talk to you standing up.'

The sheikh sat so stiffly that Zoe wondered that his joints had allowed it. He glowered at her from beneath eyebrows as thick as hanging gardens. She noticed beads of sweat above them; the sheikh had not been here long.

'I was thinking, on the way here,' said Zoe pleasantly, 'of how remarkable it is that Muslim and Christian can live so peaceably together in this city.'

'It is the wisdom of Muhammad,' murmured the sheikh. 'Conquest, then peace.'

'You yourself', continued Zoe brightly, 'came from a Christian mother who continued to practise her religion after marriage. I can't imagine that happening in Rome.'

Sheikh Bedreddin remained silent, not liking any mention of his mother. Zoe could hear the clack of fingered beads from below the table. Was he praying as he spoke to her?

'Anyway,' Zoe said, placing her palms on the table. 'I am pleased that you agreed to come. I want to talk about Suleyman.'

'Whose creature you are,' said Bedreddin nastily. The scowl had never left his face.

'Whose friend I have been, yes. Until another usurped me.'

'The opium?'

Zoe nodded. 'Sent by Mehmed to cure his headaches. A form of warfare better suited to us Byzantines, you might imagine.' She composed herself, bringing her hands to her knees. She leant forward slightly. 'Suleyman is powerful but vulnerable. The opium makes him erratic. People no longer love him – they fear him.'

'Did they ever love him?' asked Bedreddin.

It was a good question. Probably not, but at least they'd feared him. She heard a creak at the door. Yusuf was listening, as he always did. She didn't care; her body kept him loyal.

'You will need help to destroy Suleyman,' she said quietly. 'My help.'

For the first time the Sufi showed some surprise. 'You are here to betray him? Why?'

Zoe looked at her hands. 'That is my business. What you will want to know is what I want in return. I want Musa's friendship and protection after I deliver Suleyman to him.'

'Will you kill him?'

'No, I won't kill him, I'll persuade him. When the time is

right, I will tell you to bring Musa's army to the walls of Edirne.' She paused. 'But I'll want Musa's word first: his word on the Koran that I will have his protection.'

Zoe rose. She had noticed for some time that the man before her smelt. She wished, suddenly, to be outside. She walked to the door and stopped. She thought of something and turned. 'I wonder how Murad is getting on?' she asked. 'It will be interesting to see which genius finally nourishes the young mind: yours or Plethon's.'

CHAPTER FOUR

MONEMVASIA IN THE GREEK PELOPONNESE, SUMMER 1409

The little party stood in the square of Monemvasia and looked out to sea. It was a summer morning of some bluster and the ships below were bobbing like apples at a Lenten fair. There were square-rigged round ships from Italy, galleys and carracks from the Levant, picards from Normandy and a brand-new lateen-rigged caravel flying the flag of Portugal. Some had bunting pitched between bowsprit and rudder that flew like washing in the breeze. It was a carnival afloat and it was there to celebrate the enthronement of a new despot: Theodore, a boy of fourteen.

By Luke Magoris's side stood his wife, Anna, clamping her tunic to her front with one hand while holding her son's hand with the other. The boy was her six-year-old image and bored. Next to him stood a stout man dressed in a toga: Plethon, disciple of Plato and, with Luke, co-ruler of the despotate these past two years until Theodore's coming of age.

The small square was bordered by the bell tower of the Elkomenos Church, the Patriarch's palace and a balcony that looked out over a million terracotta tiles down to the deep blue of the Mirtoon Sea. Beneath was the maze of house, step and alley that made up Monemvasia, second city in the Despotate of Mistra. Behind, a wall of red rock soared up to palaces, churches and gardens where the rich lived, of whom there were many. The city, perched like a jewel on the forefinger of the Peloponnese, was on the trade route from Europe to the East.

Luke was studying a round ship flying the flag of Chios, an island he knew well. He turned to his son. 'Hilarion, tell me again why we're here.'

The boy was staring up at the tower wondering when the bells would ring again. He looked up at his father, blinking in the sunlight. 'We're here to meet the Lord and Lady of Chios and take them to Mistra.'

'Who've you missed out?'

The boy thought for a while. 'Giovanni, my cousin, who is to be your page. I will be friends with him.'

Anna glanced at her husband. 'He's not really your cousin and he might think you too young to play with. He's twelve.'

'Does he speak Greek?'

Luke nodded. 'He speaks Greek, Latin, French and Italian. He has a gift for languages, it seems.'

'Like you.' His wife stared ahead, the phantom of a smile on her lips. 'Just like you.'

Luke frowned and turned to the philosopher. 'Plethon, what do you think of these?' He gestured to a hundred giants who ringed the square, dressed in the blue and gold armour of the Varangian Guard. Each had an axe strapped to his front.

'I've never seen such monsters,' said the philosopher. 'Can they talk?'

'Hush, old man, or they'll cut off your head. They're no bigger than I am.' This was true. But then Luke Magoris was a Varangian himself. 'Did you hear they stole Suleyman's cannon?

33

As soon as Mehmed becomes sultan, I'll send them to Italy to be mercenaries.'

'And what will you call them?'

'The Varangian Company, of course. They'll make us rich, Plethon.'

There was a blast of trumpets and Hilarion jumped. A man and woman had walked into the square. He was dressed in black and she in a tunic of red damask embroidered with flowers. Behind them walked a tall boy with long, fair hair above a doublet slashed to reveal two colours of silk. The sword by his side seemed too small for him.

'Marchese Longo, Fiorenza.' Luke's arms were wide. 'You are most welcome.'

The woman kissed him, raising herself on tiptoes to see beyond. 'Ah, Hilarion. Of course.' She came back to earth. Two dimples had appeared on either side of a smile as she tilted her head. 'He has his mother's looks, lucky child.'

Anna came forward. 'You are without shame, Fiorenza.'

Marchese Longo was looking up at the rock behind, his eye travelling up the zigzag steps that joined the lower town to the upper: an acropolis perhaps. He looked at Plethon. 'They say you've started a school.'

Luke put his arm around the philosopher's shoulder, 'The best in the Empire. But I could wish the teaching more Christian.'

Longo said: 'I'd heard that Prince Murad had joined it.'

Plethon nodded. 'His father wanted it. He is difficult.'

They heard shouts below them. People had stopped in the streets and were staring out to sea, crowding the balconies, pointing. Luke looked out and saw that a new island had risen from the deep.

Bang!

The island had disappeared, exploding in fire and smoke. Monemvasia shook between its walls and its citizens sank to their knees. Hilarion's hands were too late for his ears.

Luke walked forward to the balcony at the front of the square, lifting his hand to the sun to see. Far out, well beyond the round ships and galleys and carracks, with its decks still smoking from the discharge of twenty-four cast-bronze cannon, was the biggest ship he'd ever seen.

On its aft-deck, emerging through the smoke, were two men in long robes: one tall, one short. They seemed to be looking back at him.

The larger of the two men was dressed in a red silk *zhiju* that fell to his ankles. On his head was the black cap, the *jin*, worn by senior functionaries of the Ming Dynasty of China. He had high cheeks and forehead and good teeth. He was in his late thirties and looked used to command. The shorter man was perhaps a decade older. He was long-bearded, slightly stooped and had the look of learning about him. He turned to the other. 'We have their attention.'

Admiral Zheng was used to his flagship commanding attention. The ship had nine masts with twelve sails before them. At 444 *chi*, it was many times larger than any ship in the sea around it.

The smoke was clearing and the city came back into view. They could see a square ringed by giant statues. There was a tall man in front looking at them. Zheng gave the order to lower the sails. Soon the colossal ship had dropped anchor and come to a stop. The sailors cheered, some swinging their pigtails. The admiral had brought them to their journey's end.

Admiral Zheng said: 'What a lot of ships. Why are they so decorated, Chen Cheng?'

The smaller man shrugged. 'Who knows why the barbarians celebrate?' He brought a handkerchief from his sleeve and dabbed his forehead. The day would be hot. 'Did you see the giants in the square?'

'Barbarians.'

'But clever barbarians,' said Chen Cheng. 'They brought the Mongol Tamerlane to fight their enemy.' He lowered his arm and stared at the city to their front. 'And they brought us here.'

It was entirely coincidence that Admiral Zheng and Chen Cheng had arrived at Monemvasia the same week as guests for the Despot's coronation. They considered the coincidence propitious. From Luke's point of view, it was inconvenient. He'd not counted on envoys arriving from the Middle Kingdom. He sent riders ahead to the city of Mistra to arrange rooms.

The party that set forth on a day of sun and scent was about two hundred strong and contained an emperor, a dozen kings, emirs, sheikhs and scores of ambassadors. They came from the Holy Roman Empire, Hungary, England, France, Burgundy, Portugal and both Spains. The Lusignan King of Cyprus rode beneath a palanquin with a young leopard on his lap, the English royal duke with a barrel of Malmsey on his. There was silk from the East, damask from the West, and the Papal Legate wore a ring the size of an ostrich egg. Behind it all marched a hundred fair-haired giants with axes and longbows. It was the Journey of the Magi and children came to the doors and were told to watch and not speak. They'd not see its like again.

The day smelt of lemon and liquid. The winter rains had been heavy: the rivers were full and the air alive with the sound of water. There were birds that swept out of nowhere in flapping swarms, lizards on the road and butterflies in between. God looked down on the little Kingdom of Mistra and made all fair for its new despot.

Luke rode at the front between Marchese Longo and Matthew. He glanced at the two Chinese behind, sitting beneath their sunhats like things embalmed. He leant towards Longo. 'I want to discuss trade with you, Marchese. Trade with China.'

Longo smiled. He was a good man who'd been a father to Luke since his own had died. He and Fiorenza had given him a home on Chios, an education and the foundation for his fortune. 'I hear Nikolas is there now.'

Matthew said: 'Where he shouldn't be. We're Varangians, not merchants.'

'Except that Luke has proved himself good at being both,' said Longo. 'And you'll need money to save Byzantium.' He looked at Luke, his head to one side. 'I assume it is still Byzantium you want to save, or has Tamerlane changed things?'

Luke didn't answer. Tamerlane had so nearly taken Constantinople, had shown how weak this Empire now was. Of course he'd changed things.

Matthew brought his horse closer to Luke's, leaning across him to talk to Longo. 'Luke's listening to Plethon now,' he said. 'He wants to turn Mistra into a fortress and call it Sparta. He wants a wall at Corinth and a navy.' He paused and bent further forward. 'He thinks we should save what can be saved.'

'And you agree?'

Matthew drew back and shrugged. 'Suleyman could threaten Mistra but we have our oath to defend the Empire, our oath to the Emperor.'

Luke was frowning. 'It makes sense to defend Mistra in case Constantinople falls,' he said. 'Which is why we need money.' He turned to Longo. 'How much have I on Chios?'

'Not enough for your wall. And certainly not enough for a navy as well.'

Luke nodded. 'So I've been thinking of starting a bank. The nobles are fleeing from Constantinople to Mistra with their money. Someone needs to look after it.'

They rode on for a while in silence. Then Longo said: 'The Medici of Florence are the people to talk to.' He paused and lowered his voice. 'They have a plan to buy the papacy, did you know that? It might be a good time to talk to them.'

'How do you buy the papacy?'

'Well, first you find a rogue to be pope. In their case, he's a pirate called Baldassare Cossa whose cardinal's hat has already cost them ten thousand florins. Then you spend whatever it takes to put him on the throne of St Peter. It'll be worth it to get the banking.'

'And how do we gain from this?'

Longo leant forward in his stirrups to wave flies away from his horse's ears. 'All new popes need money and Cossa will need more than most. The Medici might want some of your nobles' gold.' He straightened up again. 'And the beauty of it is that the Curia's debt is the safest investment in the world.' He paused. 'But what about Venice?'

'Venice?'

'I stopped at Negroponte on the way here. Something's happening there. They're assembling a fleet.'

Luke pondered this. 'Against the Turk?'

Marchese shook his head. 'They have no reason to fight Suleyman at present. And if they wanted to attack Musa they'd not do it from Negroponte.'

'Do you think they're coming here?' asked Matthew. 'But they have no pretext.'

'Oh, they'd find one if it mattered enough,' said Longo. 'And it would matter to them very much if they thought that Mistra might be threatened by Suleyman.'

Luke stopped his horse. Tamerlane had bought them time against the Turk, not Venice. 'Venice might *invade*?' He shook his head. 'But they're a Christian ally.'

Longo had stopped too, as had Matthew. He looked from one to other of the Varangians. 'Venice's only true ally is gold,' he said quietly. 'If she thought her trade route to Alexandria might become prey to Turkish corsairs, she'd do whatever was necessary to prevent it.' He paused. 'Venice may be your enemy, Luke, as much as Suleyman.'

They heard the sound of hooves behind them and Giovanni came level. Luke saw that he sat his horse well.

My page. My son.

He knew it, Anna knew it and, of course, Fiorenza knew it. But did Marchese Longo know it?

They reached Mistra early the following evening. The day had been jovial, the translators working hard. Even the Ming envoys had smiled at the cat that had jumped up to sit behind Hilarion like King Janus's leopard. As they'd ridden down into the Vale of Sparta, not one of them wasn't happy to be alive, and Mistra caught their mood. It was a city in carnival. The streets and houses had been washed clean and flowers bloomed from every balcony. They walked up the steep, stepped streets and people crowded at their sides and threw petals. Wine was passed and toasts made in a score of tongues.

Longo turned to Luke. 'I've never seen anything like it!'

Luke laughed. 'It's not every day they see such a sight.'

'No. I meant the building.' He pointed up the hill. 'There must be a hundred palaces being built. Think of the money coming in. A bank makes sense.'

They arrived at the palace square to find the Varangians there before them. They'd formed two lines of shimmering mail at the end of which stood Manuel, Emperor of Byzantium, with his wife and son: the new Despot of Mistra. Matthew went to stand next to them; Luke, Anna and Plethon behind.

Manuel II Palaiologos was, at this time, in his sixtieth year and the pressures of keeping up appearance had told heavily on his spirit. His empire may have started with Romulus and once ruled much of the world, but now all that was left was Constantinople and this little Despotate of Mistra that his son would rule. Appearances were hard to keep up for an emperor with no money. His wife, Helena Dragaš, was daughter to the King of Serbia and her jewels were in pawn in Venice.

Manuel watched his guests approach and spoke to Matthew from the corner of his mouth. 'King Henry of England has written to me, *Akolouthos*. He's offered money for the return of his bodyguard.'

The Empress intervened. 'Which we'll not accept. If he didn't have money when you asked for it, then it's not worth having now. Besides, they look splendid. Look at them, Anna.'

'They'll need wives with ladders, Matthew,' said Anna. 'Had you thought of that?'

The coronation passed without complication. The morning was hot and an awning had been set above the colonnaded courtyard of the Cathedral of Agios Demetrios.

Luke, Anna and Hilarion walked down from the palace behind the Ming envoys. Word had travelled and people stared from every window, too amazed to throw petals.

When the guests were seated beneath the awning, the Patriarch led Theodore and his parents into the cathedral for prayers, Luke and Plethon following. Theodore knelt in the vaulted aisle while the Patriarch lifted psalms and incense to heaven. Then Theodore was led to the narthex. He received Holy Communion, had his forehead anointed with oil and placed the jewel-studded diadem on his own teenage head. Finally he rose, pulled the cope tight to his shoulders and heard hosannas from the choir outside.

Afterwards, there was a feast in the palace square, the guests carried there by garlanded litter. Twelve courses of meat, fish, vegetables and fruit were served beneath a trellis of twisted vine, orchids and pimpernels, with lemon cut for its scent. The afternoon sun played its delicate fingers across the tables beneath, scattered with flowers and every colour of wine. By the time dinner was served, the guests were merry.

Afternoon turned to evening, then night, and candles were lit the length of the tables. Between the vines, the stars emerged one by one, tiptoeing into the sky like late guests. A beacon was set aflame on the citadel tower high above the palace and everyone raised their glasses to it. Other beacons would be lit across the hills, jumping like fireflies until they reached the sea and Monemvasia.

The Emperor was seated between Luke and Admiral Zheng and the translator behind was telling the story of their voyage.

'We left China and travelled west to the port of Malacca in the Empire of Singapura. From there, it took two months to reach the Kingdom of Kotte in Ceylon where we were becalmed for a month. Then we sailed round India to arrive at Calicut where the rest of the fleet stayed to trade spices. The admiral brought only his flagship further.'

Luke asked: 'And how did you get to us?'

'We sailed up the Red Sea and were towed to the Nile by canal. We came up the Nile to Alexandria and from there into your Middle Sea.'

Luke frowned. 'But the Mamluks of Egypt have never allowed such a thing.' He turned to Plethon. 'Is it not so?'

But Zheng had risen. The translator asked: 'The admiral wonders if you doubt his account?'

There was a moment of silence when the sound of the feast around them seemed somewhere else. Luke stared at the admiral.

Chen Cheng, sitting on Luke's other side, had also risen. He glanced at the admiral. 'We have a gift for the new Despot,' he said. 'Not here but out there.' He gestured towards the square's balcony that looked over the city.

Manuel had already risen and was moving towards the side of the square. Soon the balcony was full of spectators staring into the darkness. Luke walked over to Anna, who had taken Hilarion on to her lap. He looked down and kissed his son on the forehead, his cheeks between his palms.

'What is it, Father?' Hilarion asked, looking up. 'What have the Ming brought our emperor?'

'We'll go and see. Giovanni, will you come?'

Giovanni picked up Hilarion and swung him on to his shoulders, holding on to his hands to keep him steady. He looked up at the boy. 'You'll need my height to see over the heads. Hold on.'

The boys left and Luke asked: 'Did she bring it?'

Anna nodded.

He whispered: 'We may have to watch him now.'

They'd reached the end of the balcony where it met the palace wall in a little alcove where Plethon taught his school. They stood on either side of Hilarion who was above the crowd with both hands on Giovanni's head. Anna reached up and squeezed his hand.

She did so just in time.

There was a deep thud to their front, far out in the valley, that seemed to rise from the ground. Then another and another. A giant was stamping his way through the night up to the city walls and the crowd gasped and backed away.

Now bangs came out of the sky, loud bangs that could have been the stars exploding, and a thousand cats shed their skins. The night, quite suddenly, became a garden. Flower after flower exploded into bloom. There were peonies and chrysanthemums, willows and palm trees. Colour flashed and cascaded in waterfall and rain, throwing silver across the Evrotas River and turning it into a dragon.

Luke heard Hilarion's scream. He looked up to see his son's hands clamped to his ears, his face streaked with terror. Giovanni fell to his knees and Anna lifted Hilarion off his shoulders and carried him into the alcove. Luke looked at the crowd to their front. No one had seen. He turned to Giovanni. 'Come with me.'

Luke led Giovanni to the alcove, turning him to face the crowd. Behind came the sound of struggle. 'Don't look.'

The screams went on for a while, then became moans. Anna came out to Luke. 'I'll take him home.'

'I'm coming.'

She took his arm. 'No you're not,' her mouth next to his ear. 'Nothing has happened and if nothing has happened, there's no need for you to come. You're needed here.' She turned to the older boy. 'Giovanni, please bring your mother to the Laskaris house. Quickly.'

43

The firework display continued, pulling blossom from the night until, with one final explosion, the garden became a wilderness. Then all was silent.

Much later, when most of the guests had retired, Luke and Plethon were sitting on the square's balcony, looking out into the night. They hadn't spoken for a long while and Luke was frowning.

At last Luke said: 'They came round Africa, didn't they?'

'Yes they did,' said Plethon. 'And if it can be done from the east, it can be done from the west, which makes your plan to trade with them wise. You can make Mistra rich.'

'And safe.'

'And safe.' He glanced at Luke. 'We both know that we can no longer look to Manuel for our protection. He has barely enough money to repair Constantinople's walls, let alone build one for us.' He paused and turned. 'The time is coming when you'll have to make a choice, Luke: do you work to save Byzantium or Mistra? The Turk won't disappear.'

Luke nodded slowly, still frowning. 'Marchese says we may be in danger from Venice too, and soon. He saw a fleet assembling at Negroponte.'

Plethon stroked his beard. 'Most likely. They'll not want to see Suleyman take Mistra, which is what he might do now he's lost his cannon. It would threaten their entire trade route to Africa.'

'So we need a navy as much as a wall. And quickly.'

They didn't speak for some time and Plethon began to hum softly. In the square, people were standing together in small groups, talking in low voices as if anything louder would diminish the wonder that had come from the sky. At last

Plethon put his hand on Luke's arm. 'Hilarion's sleeping,' he said. 'Fiorenza's draught worked.'

He received no answer and glanced sideways. Luke was staring at the ground. 'Plato had it,' he said gently. 'So did Caesar. They called it *morbus comitialis* in Rome, "the disease of the assembly". God knows why.' He paused. 'One of our emperors had it too, Michael the Paphlagonian, I think. It goes with greatness.'

'Michael wasn't very great. He usurped the throne and imprisoned his wife.'

'Well, yes. But Plato? Now there's greatness. I mean to tell you that it needn't get in the way of a good life. Anyway, the mixture worked. He's sleeping peacefully.'

They heard a cough and looked up. Standing in front of them was Chen Cheng. They rose.

Chen Cheng said: 'May I talk with you? We leave tomorrow. The admiral is consulting his maps.'

Luke saw servants approaching with chairs. The Ming envoy had assumed they would talk.

Chen Cheng sat very upright and spread silk over his knees with his palms. 'You know that we didn't come for the enthronement. The fireworks were hastily prepared.' He looked from Plethon to Luke. 'You sent a man and a woman to us to enquire into the possibilities of trade. Why?'

Luke studied the man in front of him. Whoever he was, he wasn't a merchant. 'Because the time is right – for you, for us. But then you know that.'

Chen Cheng tilted his head. 'Do I?'

'Yes,' said Luke. 'Because you came round Africa to get here. The admiral misled us.' He paused. 'If you can do it, others can too, from the west. Your command of eastern trade looks suddenly precarious. We can help.'

45

Chen Cheng stared at Luke. His hands were now lost somewhere deep within his sleeves. 'The Portuguese have a new ship. I saw it in your harbour.'

'The caravel, yes,' said Luke. 'It can sail into the wind.'

Chen Cheng dipped his head. 'In time, that is the ship that will go round Africa from the west.' He looked towards the square where the lights were being extinguished one by one. There was no sound beyond the clearing of chairs and the cicadas reclaiming the night. He turned back. 'May we talk of Venice?'

'Venice?'

'A great trading city that seems to us like a ravenous sea animal with tentacles thrust anywhere likely to contain money. No?'

It seemed accurate to Luke. 'You are well informed.'

'Venice has an agreement with the Mamluks of Egypt that gives it a monopoly over trade with Africa and the East, nearly all of which comes through Alexandria.'

Luke nodded. 'Endorsed by the Pope, who allows only them to trade with the heathen.'

Chen Cheng continued: 'It seems likely to us that your kingdom of Mistra will always be coveted by Venice since you are a vital link in its trade route to Alexandria.' He passed his eyes from Luke to Plethon and back again. 'But what if we were to make that route irrelevant?'

Luke frowned. 'You mean create a new trade route that links the East to Europe without using Egypt?'

Chen Cheng inclined his head. 'Yes, one that brings our ships as far as the Persian Gulf. From there it is only seventy days by caravan to Constantinople.'

Plethon was frowning now. 'But that would mean taking it through Mongol and Ottoman lands.'

'Yes,' said Luke, speaking as much to himself, 'which would be possible if Mehmed wins his war. Ulugh Beg would certainly allow it for Mongol lands.'

Chen Cheng withdrew his hands from his sleeves and placed them back on his knees. 'And Mehmed might win his war with your help.'

Luke stared at the Ming envoy. Chen Cheng must have spoken to Nikolas. What was being offered was nothing less than a realignment of world trade to the benefit of those that might arrange it. It was a dazzling prospect. But there was still a question.

'Why us?' he asked.

Chen Cheng smoothed the silk over his knees. 'There could be many reasons. Because you know the Turks and the Mongols, and now us? Because you need to find a place in the world for your empire? Because I have come to like Nikolas and Shulen?' The Ming envoy looked hard at Luke. 'Most of all, because you need to get rich, Luke Magoris. Rich enough to save Mistra from those who covet it.'

Luke nodded slowly. He'd sent Nikolas and Shulen to China to trade horses and mastic: this was a much greater opportunity. But was it real? 'And your emperor? Does he know of this thinking?'

Chen Cheng smiled. 'My emperor wishes to bring the whole world into Confucian harmony. To do this, he is creating great fleets and an encyclopaedia of all human knowledge that is nearly complete: the *diadan*. The fleets will bring it with them. With trade comes harmony.'

Plethon sat up. '*All* human knowledge? Not just Chinese?'

'All that we have gathered; all that we will gather.'

Luke glanced at the philosopher, knowing where his mind was travelling.

'And might it include certain papers brought to you by Nestorian Christians many centuries ago?' Plethon asked, leaning forward. 'Papers from Constantinople relating to their heresy?'

'Assuredly.' Chen Cheng's eyes were studying Plethon carefully. 'There is some legend of a treasure here at Mistra, one brought out of Constantinople when it was taken by the Franks. It is said it may save your empire one day. We have speculated what it might be.'

But Plethon had risen quickly and was already arranging the folds of his toga. He bowed to Chen Cheng. 'It is late and you have far to travel. You should rest.'

Luke rose too. It was not so long ago that he'd seen the Varangian treasure for himself and felt it touch every part of his world. But it was not a conversation to have now. He said: 'We will discuss this trade further tomorrow before you leave and I will give you letters for Shulen and Nikolas.' He paused, waiting for Chen Cheng to rise. 'We are grateful to you for coming.' He smiled. 'Perhaps we will change the world together.'

CHAPTER FIVE

NANJING, AUTUMN 1409

Shulen stood on the aft-deck of a ship wondering if it was the smell of new paint or its motion that made her feel so dizzy. She held Nikolas's arm to steady herself.

The mandarin Min Qing was pointing with his hand, chopping as he spoke. 'Each of the shipyard's basins can hold three ships. They are filled with water once the ships are ready to be towed into the locks that join us to the Yangtze. Then it's two days to the Yellow Sea.'

Shulen glanced over the shipyards, counting seven basins with quays between, piled with logs of pine and teak, stripped of bark and numbered each for their place. Beside them were heaps of iron staples, nails, hemp and barrels of *tung* oil. There were windlasses, rope mats, pitchers of caulking material and, further down, fields of hemp and tung trees between pools stocked with fish. Everywhere, smoke was rising from kilns and furnaces. Her eyes went back to Nikolas, quite liking the way he bent his head forward when he listened.

'It's extraordinary,' he was saying. 'I've seen the Arsenale shipyards in Venice but they're nothing like this.'

'What's that?' Shulen was pointing to the statue of a strange beast in the middle of it all. It was sitting on its hind legs and had a long neck and a head with horns.

'That,' said Min Qing, 'is a *qilin*.' The mandarin was dressed in his usual long red tunic with a stork on its front and tall black hat. Wisps of hair had escaped to tickle his forehead and he pushed them into place with his delicate fingers. 'It is a mythical beast said to appear in the reign of great emperors. We have not seen one yet in this Emperor's reign.'

Min Qing was frowning, which was what he usually did. He'd been their constant companion since Chen Cheng and Admiral Zheng had left with the fleet. They had no idea who'd arranged it and Min Qing wouldn't say. He was silent and aloof and neither Shulen nor Nikolas liked him much.

'Well, I'm sure you will,' said Shulen. 'Your emperor is a great man.'

Min Qing made no comment. He was one of the Confucian scholar class that had always run China. Always, except now. This Emperor preferred the eunuchs, like Admiral Zheng, who'd put him on the throne. The eunuchs had the Emperor's ear and the mandarins didn't like it.

The ship had stopped rising and Shulen asked a question she'd been meaning to ask for some time. 'Why are they called treasure ships, Min Qing?'

'Because they are sent out to collect tribute for the Emperor, which is sometimes treasure.'

She looked down at the vessel below her, nearly two hundred feet across, four storeys high, its teak decks gleaming in the sunshine. Her eyes travelled up the nine masts, yet to carry their sails. It didn't seem possible there was much in the world the Emperor didn't already have.

'But the ships also carry a different kind of treasure,' the mandarin continued. 'Below us are sixty state rooms for envoys, scientists, artists and other scholars.'

'So the ships collect tribute and dispense knowledge?'

Min Qing inclined his head. 'The Emperor wishes to bring the whole world into Confucian harmony,' he said without enthusiasm. 'He wants to do it by displaying China's supremacy in every area of human endeavour.'

Nikolas patted the handrail. 'But this ship will carry horses. There they are.'

He pointed beyond the lock gates to the banks of the canal where two horses were waiting to come aboard with their grooms, their coats shining. They were the offspring of Luke's horse, Eskalon, and had come with them from Samarcand.

It was a year ago that Nikolas and Shulen had travelled by caravan to from Samarcand to China with emissaries from Ulugh Beg. On arrival at the Ming court, they'd asked for an audience with the Emperor and been politely handed over to Chen Cheng, who spoke Greek and was deemed suitable to judge all things foreign. But it had only been when Nikolas had talked about Plethon that he'd shown any interest.

'Ah, Plethon. Now, I have heard of *Plethon*.'

'He is a brilliant man,' said Nikolas.

'He is a *scholar* and, if he's a follower of Plato, halfway to being Confucian. I shall put it about that you are his disciple. The mandarins don't like foreigners, especially merchants.'

Shulen asked: 'But are you not yourself a mandarin, sir?'

Chen Cheng delivered a wink with no trace of the scholar in it. 'Indeed I am, but my best friend is Admiral Zheng, chief among eunuchs. Unlike my class, I see trade as the way to exchange knowledge with the world for the improvement of mankind. Tell me about your horses.'

So Nikolas told him of the wonder of Eskalon, *Escrivo* to a new dynasty. Shulen, meanwhile, thought about the man who'd tamed Eskalon, spoken to him, made him into the best of horses. She thought about Luke.

Chen Cheng smiled. 'You will have an easy time of it. We Chinese love horses above all animals. We've even designed boats to carry them. Look.'

He produced pages from a drawer. He placed them on the table and leafed through them until he came to one with ship designs.

Nikolas whistled softly. 'What is this?'

'It is one small part of the diadan, the greatest encyclopaedia ever created and nothing less than the sum of all human knowledge. It has taken two thousand scholars six years to make. Admiral Zheng and I will take some of it on the next voyage, unless the mandarins get their way.'

'And where will this voyage go?' asked Shulen.

'Perhaps round Africa, perhaps into the Middle Sea.' Chen Cheng glanced at Nikolas and winked again. 'I should like to meet Plethon.'

'But why will the mandarins try and stop you?'

'Because they disapprove of sharing the diadan with foreigners. In fact, they disapprove of foreigners completely. They see you as bringers of things that the Middle Kingdom doesn't need, the first of many. They'd like to see you banished or, better still, dead. What else do you have?'

Nikolas stared at him. They'd arrived in the middle of what sounded like civil war between the ruling classes. 'Mastic from

Chios,' he said at last. 'A substance with a hundred different uses. Can you get us an introduction to the harem?'

'Is it an aphrodisiac?'

'When mixed with certain herbs that I know of,' said Shulen. 'But it can help earlier in the transaction. It is a breath-sweetener.'

'Ah!' Chen Cheng slapped his knees with delight. 'Excellent! I'll arrange a meeting with the concubine Zhu Chou. She speaks your language.'

Nikolas and Shulen had met Zhu Chou the next morning. They'd been housed in the palace compound in Nanjing next to the Emperor's harem and met her in a library that separated the two buildings. She rose as they entered, leaving a book open on the table.

Chen Cheng walked over, bowed and took her hands in his. He kissed them each in turn. 'Zhu Chou, I have brought you some people to speak Greek to. And they have something to show you.'

Nikolas stared at the woman. She was a flawless china doll with the longest fingernails he'd ever seen. Her face was chalk white with crimson lips painted into a smile. Her hair was gathered in black waves on her head with jade birds holding it in place. She was dressed in a blue zhiju embroidered with gold kingfishers perched above pools. It was impossible to know her age.

He bowed. He'd met the *cortigiane oneste* in Venice and imagined the Ming Emperor's concubines to be women of similar refinement. This one was looking at him with curiosity and her smile was unsettling. She tilted her head a fraction, her eyes not leaving his.

'I shall enjoy that.'

Nikolas glanced around him. He'd not seen so many books before, even in Venice. 'Have you read all these?'

She followed his gaze. 'Most, not all.'

His eyes came back to hers. 'Is that how you learnt to speak Greek?'

'I learnt Greek from the diadan. It was not difficult.'

Nikolas nodded slowly, unsure of what to say next.

Shulen glanced from one to other of them. 'We have mastic to show you,' she said. 'You'll find it useful in many ways.' She took a small bag from her pocket and tipped its contents out on to the table. There were a dozen pieces of resin, yellow and opaque. 'The "tears of St Isidore", we call it. He is the saint of Chios where it is harvested.'

The concubine picked up a piece and brought it to her nose. 'It has a strange smell.'

'Taste it,' said Shulen. 'Bite some off.'

Zhu Chou looked at her, then did so. 'It tastes of nothing.'

'Yes, but your breath will smell sweet. See.' Shulen picked up another piece and bit into it. She walked up to Zhu Chou. 'May I?'

The concubine nodded and Shulen leant forward and breathed.

Zhu Chou smiled. 'Good,' she said. She turned to Chen Cheng. 'I shall inform the Emperor.'

A message had arrived from the harem the next day, saying that the Emperor wanted mastic as well as horses. A week later, Chen Cheng had left with the fleet and Min Qing had arrived to shadow them.

Now, at last, the ship to bring horses back from Mistra was ready. A whole deck had been converted into two hundred berths, each on its own gimbals to keep the animals upright in rough weather. A clever system of drainage would keep them clean, and holes in the prow would fill with water during storms, lessening the ship's motion. It would join Admiral Zheng's fleet when it returned and sail in its next expedition.

The gates were opening and tugs coming to pull them through. Skeleton poplars lined the banks and the waiting horses stamped their feet among russet leaves, crisp as parchment. People stood four ranks deep and gazed up at the colossus. Shulen saw soldiers using pikes to barge their way through them.

'Min Qing, why are there soldiers?'

The mandarin was looking at the gates behind them. Not moving his head, he said: 'They are my men. They are here to protect the horses.'

'From who?'

Min Qing turned now, his head always erect. 'From the people. The horses are valuable.'

A horn sounded and the ship bumped the canal's side. The soldiers pushed the people back as a gangplank with rails was lowered on ropes.

It took some time to coax the horses aboard, the process interrupted by clapping from the crowd When it was done, the soldiers came on board too. There were eight of them, all dressed in the same red as Min Qing, all with storks on their fronts. Shulen noticed that each had an unsheathed dagger tucked into his belt.

She leant in to Nikolas and whispered, 'Are the people so dangerous?'

But the ship's engineer was beckoning to them. The deck hatches were being opened and the horses strapped into canvas supports that would lower them down into the gimballed berths. The foreigners were to go below and watch them descend.

Shulen followed the man down some steps, Matthew and Min Qing behind her, until they came to the deck set aside for the horses. They walked between the berths to one beneath the hatch and looked up to see the horses being lowered side by side. The animals looked ridiculous. Their legs were splayed either side of their supports and their bodies jerked with each release of rope. One of the horses was becoming agitated.

Nikolas stepped out to call up to the men. He was directly below the animal and held a hand up to his eyes. 'Slow down!'

The animal's hooves were twenty feet above him and getting closer with every release of the rope.

Shulen felt suddenly uneasy. Something was wrong. 'Nikolas . . .'

Too late. There was the smack of broken rope and the horse was falling through the air.

'Nikolas!'

Shulen threw herself forward and pushed him to the floor as the horse landed beside them in an explosion of splintered wood and bone. The animal's screams rang through the ship's hull. Its hooves were flailing inches from where they lay. Shulen looked across at Nikolas beside her. His eyes were staring at the open hatch above.

Oh no.

There came the same sound of snapping rope and she looked up. The second horse was about to fall and there was nowhere left to roll. She screamed.

'Nikolas!'

She saw him shield his face as the horse fell on to him. It had pitched forward and landed on its head, its legs spreadeagled.

56

There was a terrible crack and the animal lay still, its neck broken.

Nikolas's head and shoulders were free of the horse, but his eyes were closed and he wasn't moving. Shulen reached out her hand.

'*Nikolas.*'

CHAPTER SIX

FLORENCE, SPRING 1410

Against the wishes of Anna and Matthew, Luke travelled to Florence to meet the Medici in the spring, taking with him Giovanni as his page. They'd tried hard to stop him. Mistra was where the Protostrator should be, helping the young Despot to rule. But Luke had left Plethon behind and any doubts he might have had about leaving had been dispelled by the letter from China.

It had arrived at Christmas, having taken two months to travel the five thousand miles from Nanjing. Luke had read it aloud to Anna, Matthew and Arcadius.

'Well, he's not dead.' He'd lowered the letter. 'We should be thankful for that.'

Matthew had nodded slowly. 'And she says that the Chinese doctors know what they're doing. But it'll take time for him to walk again.'

Anna had frowned. 'I suppose this makes it certain that you'll go to Italy.'

She'd been right. The letter had made clear that Shulen blamed Min Qing for the accident. The mandarins had wanted to send the strongest warning to Chinese merchants not to do business with the foreigners and they'd succeeded. Shulen had done no further trade in China and it would take all of Chen Cheng and Admiral Zheng's influence to mend things. And they were still on their way back from Mistra.

So Luke's banking idea was more vital than ever. It was why he was meeting Cosimo de' Medici in Florence.

They were crossing the Ponte Vecchio, beneath which the brown waters of the Arno churned, passing butchers' shops and the smelly carcasses of animals. The air was speckled with flies and sawdust. The sky above them was without cloud and the morning sun beat down like God's furnace. Giovanni would have killed to lose his doublet.

'We'll go to the Orsanmichele, where the city's granary is,' said Cosimo, stopping to put money into a beggar's hands. 'You'll see bankers there.'

Cosimo was in his early twenties and blighted with the looks of his father. He was short, prematurely bald and of poor complexion. His eyes were uneven and the skin around his mouth flaked. He was plainly dressed in an ankle-length gown that was buttoned down the front like a cassock. If he was one of the richest men in Florence, he didn't look it, and this had much to do with his father's advice: avoid the public eye.

'We are a city of trade,' he was saying to Giovanni, nodding to left and right. 'A Florentine who is not a merchant enjoys no esteem. The Medici are, above all, merchants.'

This was nonsense, of course. Luke had described the precarious place bankers occupied in Catholic Italy. They were usurers, really, whom the poet Dante had placed alongside blasphemers and sodomites in his seventh circle of hell. But everyone needed them, not least the Church, which was why they were allowed to lend money at interest and pretend to do otherwise.

They left the bridge and came to a church with statues in alcoves outside. Under shaded porticos were tables with men behind them writing in large ledgers. Piles of coin sat on green cloth: some gold, some silver. Cosimo stopped at one and picked up a coin.

'This is the florin, minted by us with fifty-four grains of gold from Mali inside. It is used across the world.' He turned it over to show Giovanni. 'See, no king's head on it, only the lily. We have no kings or queens in Florence.'

Luke looked around him. The streets were crowded with men and women who looked very much like kings and queens. The women had pale, powdered skin and fair hair, often wigged, and were dressed in silks scattered with jewels. The men wore scarlet ankle-length gowns with wide sleeves and hoods attached to the neck. Some had slaves trailing behind them in livery.

'I see plenty of Tartars here,' he said.

'They make the best slaves,' replied Cosimo, turning. 'They work hard but the Circassians are better-looking and better-tempered. They're bought in Venice and Genoa. We don't sell people here.'

Luke smiled. It was as Plethon had said: Florence's chief export was its hypocrisy. They walked on, past the unfinished Duomo and into a square.

'This', said Cosimo, sweeping his hand through the air, 'is the Mercato Vecchio, where the Roman forum used to be.'

It was so full that Luke wondered if they'd even get across it. There were stalls with every kind of produce beneath their shade: fishmongers, drapers, fruit- and vegetable-sellers, silk and feather merchants. There were animals everywhere: dogs with silver collars, geese and pigs rooting in doorways. There were painted prostitutes talking to men waiting to have their beards shaved and bakers pushing trolleys of dough to the communal ovens. It was pandemonium.

They walked on into another square where men and women sat eating on a raised loggia, as if on stage. Their children played at their feet and threw food down to the beggars on the street outside.

'It's how the city's business is done these days,' explained Cosimo as they passed. 'People like to be seen.'

They came to a quieter part of the city where men walked faster and spoke less. Everywhere on the walls were gold shields with six balls on them: five red, one blue.

'This is our quarter,' said Cosimo. 'This is where the Medici live, pray and do business.' He gestured to a shield. 'That is our sign. The balls represent dents on my ancestor's shield when he fought a giant.'

They entered a building that seemed more monastery than palace, with no adornment on its walls and only the Medici crest above the door. Inside was a lawned courtyard bordered by gravel with statues in niches around it. There was a wide flight of steps that led up to a balcony with ancient busts on its walls. A man was coming down them.

He was shorter than Cosimo but, thought Luke, even more ugly. He was roughly shaven and had thin wisps of hair wafting above his dome like grass. His clothes were fine but plain and had not a trace of vanity about them.

'Did Cosimo show you the city?' His voice had the hiss of a reed. He stopped in front of Luke and bowed. 'So young. But you saved an empire, I hear.'

Luke gestured to the other Giovanni. 'Your namesake, sir, son of Marchese Giustiniani Longo of Chios and his wife, the

Princess Fiorenza, with whom I think you've done business. He is my page.'

Giovanni de' Medici looked at the boy, then back at Luke, a question in his eye. 'Of course, what could be more fitting?' He smiled at Giovanni. 'Page to the Protostrator.'

They walked up the steps and entered a room with white-washed walls, a fireplace and no other decoration. A bed, twelve feet across, stood behind tapestries on a dais at one end. At its foot was a long chest with wedding scenes on its sides and a jug and cups on its top. The floor was bare stone with reed matting on it. Three dogs lay beneath a window, asleep in the sunshine.

Giovanni de' Medici walked over to the chest and poured wine. 'You have written asking us to help you start a bank in Mistra,' he said, bringing cups to Luke and Cosimo. He spoke with precision, nothing wasted. 'You have told us that the wealth of Byzantium is coming to Mistra on every tide. The nobles need somewhere safe and productive for their money.'

Luke sipped his wine. It was cool and fragant. 'I am interested in your connection with the Curia.'

'Ah, the Pope's banking. It is lucrative and it's safe. Everyone is interested in that. But we have no connection.'

Luke glanced at Cosimo. 'But you have a plan, perhaps?'

Cosimo nodded. 'Baldassare Cossa is our plan. He is cardinal at Bologna. He is ambitious and ruthless and will make a perfect pope.'

'And when he becomes pope,' said Luke, 'you'll become his banker. I hear he is extravagant.'

Cosimo smiled. 'None more so.'

'Which may mean you need more money to lend him. I can help with that.'

The two Medicis glanced at each other. The father said:

'There is some attraction to sharing the debt, particularly with someone outside the city states of Italy.' He was watching Luke closely. 'But it occurs to me that you'll need to make a great deal more money if you are to save Mistra.' Giovanni de' Medici paused to drink, then continued: 'There is a bigger plan. If Cossa becomes pope, we'll get his banking, yes. But the prize is for him to become the *only* pope. Did you know we have three?'

Luke knew. The Catholic Church had been in schism for more than thirty years with one pope in Italy and another in France. It had split Europe asunder and a Church council had been called at Pisa to resolve things. But the two popes had refused to step down and a third had been created: Alexander V.

Cosimo took up the theme. 'If three popes become one, the banking will be very great indeed. Certainly enough for two. *That* is the prize.'

'And how might that happen?' asked Luke.

'By calling another council, forcing all three popes to attend, and then persuading the cardinals to vote for ours. If Cossa becomes one of the three, he will call that council.'

It sounded difficult but this was Italy and Luke knew that anything was possible with the right bribes. He felt some unease but this Church was not his and rotten to the core. Mistra was more important than any pope.

Giovanni de' Medici looked at him. 'You can leave us to arrange the Pope and his council,' he said. 'You must concentrate on gaining the trust of your potential depositors. I suggest you start a fair in Mistra so that the nobles learn to trust you with their money. Cosimo will help you. Then we'll talk more. But now' – he smiled – 'you should meet our candidate for pope.'

*

Not much later, Luke found himself walking through Florence dressed as Hermes, messenger of the gods. He wore a short tunic and a hat with wings on it. There were more wings on his ankles and one at the end of a wand that he'd tucked into his belt. Giovanni was Poseidon, all scales and seaweed. Cosimo was Cupid with a bow.

It was some Saint's Day and the streets were full of song. In the Mercato Vecchio, the stalls had been replaced by floats waiting to be pulled through the streets with different guilds aboard, each with its own liveried musicians and theme. He saw the perfume-makers sniffing tiny vials of scent and the Arte della Lana sitting amidst sheep cropping grass.

Luke adjusted the wand, which was sticking into his thigh. 'Why are we dressed like this to meet the cardinal?'

'Cossa is at a feast given by the Albizzi. It is to be held on Mount Olympus.'

'And which other gods will be there?'

'Ah, now that is the question. The three Malatesta brothers certainly, who are all condottieri. They and Venice support Benedict, a rival pope to ours whom they guard in their city of Rimini. We must make sure they don't poison our candidate.'

Luke was warming to Cosimo. He asked: 'Why are the Malatestas in Florence?'

Cosimo shrugged. 'Why indeed? It might be to do with Cleope, daughter of the one who writes sonnets. She is of marriageable age and lovely, they say. Italy is all about marriages these days.'

Luke had been instructed by Plethon on the complicated politics of Italy. There were six major states more or less permanently at war with each other. In the south was Naples. Halfway up were the Papal States, stretching from sea to sea. In the north were Florence, Milan, Genoa and Venice. They were all rich, ambitious and jealous. Some of the smaller states' princes had become mercenary generals, condottieri, enriching themselves and protecting their borders at the same time. The most famous were the Malatestas of Rimini. There were three brothers: Carlo, Pandolfo and the man they called Malatesta dei Sonnetti.

Giovanni asked: 'So is Venice the enemy of Florence?'

Cosimo put his hand on the boy's shoulder. 'Often, but not now. We support different popes and we worry about Venice's ambitions, particularly with regard to the Byzantine Empire.' He turned to Luke. 'We hear she has a fleet sitting at Negroponte. Do you know about it?'

Luke wondered how much he should tell this man. He said: 'We think it might be waiting for a pretext to attack Mistra. We have ships watching the straits.'

Cosimo nodded. 'They want to stop Suleyman getting to Mistra first. We have a branch of the bank in Negroponte. I'll get them to find out what they can.' He slowed his pace, taking his hand from Giovanni's shoulder. 'Isn't there supposed to be a treasure buried somewhere in Mistra? If you need gold quickly, shouldn't you try to find that?'

Luke changed the subject. 'You talked of a fair.'

Cosimo took the bow from his belt and tested the string. 'Ah yes, like they have in Champagne, but for the Peloponnese. I can help bring the merchants.'

'How will that prove anything?'

'You'll organise it; the nobles will invest in it. They'll trust you when it works and give you more to invest. Suddenly you'll be a bank.'

They were approaching a large building bearing a shield above the gate with a yellow target on it.

Cosimo stopped and looked up at it. 'I should be Daniel.'

Luke looked up too. 'This is the lion's den?'

Cosimo nodded. 'The Albizzi family are one of the oldest in Florence, and those are their arms. They don't like the Medici – they think we're upstarts.' He aimed his bow. 'Still, I bring the arrow of love and it's a difficult target to miss.'

A stream of people were flowing in and out of the gates, some dressed for the occasion, some not.

'They have opened their palace for the feast day,' Cosimo continued. 'It's how republics work: wine and votes.'

Inside were tables laden with food and jugs of wine with slaves behind, all dressed as myths. People were queuing to take away bread and meat in every pocket. A man was lying beneath a barrel with his mouth open.

Cosimo used Luke's wand to point their way through the crowd to a central courtyard raised as a stage. Upon it were low tables with couches set around, each with a god or goddess reclining, sometimes two. Around them were poles supporting a pergola woven with fruit and flowers and, suspended, candles within clouds of different sizes. At the back was scenery of mountains and blue sky. Mount Olympus had been transported to Florence. A Bacchus on stilts plucked fruit for the gods.

'Cosimo!' A man had risen with a jug in his hand. 'Come and share some nectar. Are you Plutus tonight?'

There was laughter but Cosimo seemed unperturbed. The man climbed down from the podium and brought Cupid to his bosom.

Cosimo, detaching, said: 'Rinaldo, may I present the Protostrator of Mistra, Luke Magoris, and his page Giovanni Giustiniani Longo of Chios?'

Rinaldo degli Albizzi bowed. He was a man of middle years, shining with the gloss of wealth. He was dressed as Zeus. 'Well, we must make room for you. The Malatestas are with us.' He winked. 'And your candidate for pope.'

They climbed on to the stage and walked past the *trombadori*: eight trumpets, a drummer and a cenamella player. Rinaldo put his arm round Cosimo's shoulders and nodded at the trombonist. 'Their leader is German,' he said, sotto voce. 'He hasn't managed to put Malatesta's sonnets to music and I don't blame him.' They approached the head table. 'Still, we must all be poets in this Rinascimento, mustn't we? Even condottieri. Do you write?'

'Only ledgers,' replied Cosimo, stopping to greet the god of the underworld. He straightened and turned to Albizzi. 'Oh, and letters of credit. Do you need any?'

Rinaldo laughed. He turned back to Luke. 'This man', he said, 'can make money copulate. Ah, we have arrived.'

Luke saw three men lying next to each other who looked related. They were all dark, thickset and had handsome noses. They looked like men you'd want on your side in a battle. Rinaldo introduced the Malatesta brothers, each in turn. Then he turned to two men who lay apart, one dressed as a prince of the Church. 'Now, these men you know: Cardinal Cossa and his scribe, Poggio Bracciolini.'

Luke looked at a man in cardinal's red. His thin face was dominated by a smile not matched in his eyes. His cheeks had the flush of wine and his hair the tincture of dye. He was, thought Luke, not a serious man of the Church, whatever he wore. The other wore the plain gown of the secretary. His body was slight and he had a face pointed by intelligence.

The cardinal had presented a hand banded with rings. Cosimo knelt to kiss the biggest. Luke and Giovanni followed.

Cosimo rose. 'Your eminence has not come as a god.'

Cossa looked up at him, no hint of a smile on his smooth face. 'We like, at all times, to be reminded of our mortality.'

Luke wondered if he was including his secretary or already adopting the papal 'we'. He heard a Malatesta snort behind him.

Cosimo turned to Poggio. 'I'm told that you have an interest in finding ancient manuscripts?'

'And copying them when they're found,' replied the secretary.

'You find them often?'

Poggio shook his head. 'It takes time and money, master. Everything in the Italian monasteries has been found and most in France. Germany and Switzerland are the places to look now. Some of the monasteries are remote.'

Albizzi had taken Luke's arm. 'You've arrived in time to eat. We have chicken, guinea fowl, spiced veal, tench and eel to begin with, then partridge and peacock to follow.' He counted them off on his fingers. 'Please sit.'

They sat and Carlo Malatesta turned to Luke. 'They say you have an army for sale.'

Luke studied the condottiere. He was half-bull, half-man, with small, bulging eyes beneath a forehead flattened, perhaps, by helmets. His face was fringed by a thick, wiry beard that failed to hide its scars. His lower lip jutted out from his jaw and he looked dangerous. Luke nodded. 'Perhaps in the future. It is engaged by the Turk for now.'

'The Turk? You'd hire your company to the heathen?'

Luke smiled. 'If he pays, yes.'

Carlo Malatesta grunted. 'You think to teach us our business? What can Greeks teach us?'

An awkward silence fell until Cosimo broke it. 'Perhaps', he said, 'we could hire your army after the Turk. What do you call it?'

'The Varangian Company,' said Luke. 'It is made up of men taller than myself who come from England and fight with the axe.' He glanced at Carlo. 'And who don't change sides.'

Carlo snorted. 'Well, it depends on whether you mean to make money. Loyalty can be expensive.' He waved his cup at Cosimo. 'Why don't you go into banking like your friend here? There's no honour in it but it can make you rich.'

Giovanni leant forward on his couch. 'Why no honour, sir?'

Malatesta glanced at him, his tight forehead creased in a frown. 'It dislodges a man from his station in life. Work without toil is unnatural. Like sodomy.' He drank and turned to Cosimo, wine cup poised on his lower lip. 'If his army's coming to Italy and you're going to hire it, Pope Alexander won't need your condottiere any more, Medici. Braccio da Montone can go and guard someone else.'

Cardinal Cossa was peeling an orange with some concentration. He stopped and looked up. 'Braccio da Montone will continue to protect the rightful Pope. He is a condottiere with conscience.'

The barb was sharp and all three Malatestas rose to their elbows to answer it. Carlo was first: 'You should worry more about your pope's conscience, not his bodyguard. What if Pope Alexander doesn't recommend you to be his successor?' He turned to Cosimo. 'Or have you bribed him too?'

Cossa remained calm, his black eyes fixed on Carlo. He spoke quietly. 'We all want the same thing, Malatesta: reform of our Holy Mother Church. If I am chosen to succeed Alexander, I shall call the council that will do it.'

There was a sound from the scenery behind and they turned to see two new gods descend from Olympus. They were Apollo, god of the sun, and Gaia, goddess of the earth, and their beauty was astonishing. The old gods stopped their talking and turned to look at them.

Pandolfo Malatesta leant over and whispered. 'My son Sigismondo and my niece Cleope. Is she not lovely?'

She was, perhaps, the loveliest person Luke had ever seen. Her face was like snowdrops and poppies – a face unused to the sun. Her hair, almost white, was gathered above her brow in a plaited diadem scattered with flowers. She was dressed in a long dress of white that showed no curve of her body. She was a perfect symmetry of grace. He glanced at Giovanni. His son was transfixed.

The dance was performed, a carol measured out by teenage feet. It was solemnly done, with neither god looking up. They held hands as gods do, their fingers hardly touching. While they performed their artistry, not a breath was released.

At length it was over and the mortal world intruded. Hands were clapped and goblets thumped and Luke looked at Cleope, still smiling with her hands clasped at her front. He glanced at Giovanni, also smiling but in a dream. He saw that they were looking at each other.

Oh no.

Just then, the first drops of rain began to fall on Mount Olympus.

Far to the south, the rain was heavier.

Murad lay in his bed in the Laskaris house and heard the storm outside. He was thinking of something Plethon had said earlier.

When we know what makes the thunder and lightning, then there'll be no more need for God.

It was a strange thing to say. How could anyone not need God?

Allah was everywhere. It was like saying they didn't need air.

The lightning lit up his bedroom. He listened to the rain beating against the shutters and counted for the thunder. A crack rolled around the night in one rumbling echo, coming and going. He put his hands behind his head on the pillow. He liked storms.

He thought about his lessons. He'd tried to do as Bedreddin had told him: not speak and not listen. But Plethon had said something that afternoon that he'd heard. He'd said that Islam, Christianity and the Jewish faith were all flowers from the same root, that each needed watering with new ideas to grow. But he knew the Koran from cover to cover and it contained everything he needed to know.

The lightning struck again and the shutters rattled with thunder. The storm was above them. He heard a scream.

It came from Hilarion's bedroom across the hall. He'd heard it before. The Ming fireworks.

He'd been standing with his father, wishing Mehmed had put him on his shoulders as Giovanni had with Hilarion. When the first fireworks had exploded, he'd seen Hilarion clamp his hands to his ears and scream that scream. He'd seen him lowered to the ground and taken somewhere. He'd quietly slipped away to see what was wrong with the boy.

But there'd been nothing to see except Hilarion's father and Giovanni standing before an alcove. He'd heard the sounds of struggle, though, and then Anna had appeared with her son in her arms. A firework had burst and he'd caught a glimpse of Hilarion's face: open mouth, tongue lolling on his lips, eyes wide with madness.

The Devil.

Bedreddin had told him of this. The Devil enters humans to

do his evil on earth unnoticed. Only sometimes he can't help but show himself.

The scream came again and he heard footsteps outside in the corridor and the sound of a door opening. He heard Anna's voice, soothing.

He rose, tiptoed to his door and turned the handle. He opened it fractionally, then some more. He could see straight into the room opposite. Hilarion was lying on the bed with Anna's arms held tight around him. He was jerking to left and right, kicking and kicking.

Murad closed the door and got back into bed. He looked up at the ceiling and smiled.

Hilarion has the Devil inside him.

CHAPTER SEVEN

BOLOGNA, SPRING 1410

Cardinal Baldassare Cossa of Bologna was in bed with a nun when the condottiere Braccio da Montone came to call. The cardinal was uncertain if she was a true nun, suspecting that the procuratress might have dressed another for the part, but so long as she acted the nun he was happy.

He'd been expecting Braccio. The two were old acquaintances and had met often to discuss the business of extortion. Now the condottiere's army was bringing Pope Alexander to Bologna and Braccio had ridden ahead to check the accommodation.

The cardinal's palace was in the centre of the city, not far from the university where he'd received his doctorate of law. It was a magnificent building, more fortress than palace, and Cossa, as ambitious in cultivating flowers as his career, had created an unusual garden within its walls. The condottiere was waiting in it when the cardinal came down to receive him.

'I saw a sister escape to the street,' he said as Cossa approached. 'Was she going to confession?'

The cardinal ignored him. 'Do you like my garden?'

Braccio looked around at the shaded paths bordered with low hedges, ornamental parterres, fountains and bushes shaped as animals. There was a miniature meadow of wild flowers around the kiosk where they stood. He was a soldier but he appreciated beauty. 'It's impressive.'

Cossa nodded, bending to the smell of honeysuckle climbing a trellis. 'Pliny called it *otium*, the place to think. I like to pray here.'

Or scheme, thought Braccio, enjoying the charade. He went over to a bench to sit. He was a powerful man in his early forties with a neat beard and lips in a permanent pout. He wore his hair to his shoulders above expensive clothes. He'd been partially crippled at the siege of Fosombrone and preferred conversation from the horse. He watched Cossa spread crimson across the bench opposite and finger a rosary above his cassock.

'I have the means to make our army stronger, Braccio,' said Cossa. 'Assuming, that is, that the Medici can afford it.'

Braccio looked up. 'You have a platoon of nuns?'

Cossa smiled. 'Not nuns, Varangians. Quite different. They are fighting Turks at the moment but expect to be free soon. I met one of them in Florence. The Malatestas were there.'

Braccio grimaced. Carlo Malatesta had been his rival for years. 'I hear he's been seen in Negroponte. Is he fighting for Venice again?'

Cossa shrugged. 'I care more about the Pope he keeps at Rimini. He'll need to be persuaded to bring him to the council I'll call when I'm pope.'

They were silent for a while, both looking for a way into the subtle business of inference. At last Braccio said: 'Alexander is seventy-one. Did you know that? He gets tired. Don't keep him up too late.'

'He doesn't drink,' said Cossa, putting the rosary to one

side, 'unlike the other two. There'll be nothing to keep him up for.'

'He is a man of God.'

'As am I. And where would we men of God be without wine and the sacrament of confession, Braccio?'

Braccio began to remove his gloves, finger by finger. 'Has it occurred to you that he might prefer someone else to be his successor?'

Cossa looked up. 'The next pope will be decided by the cardinals, Braccio, not Alexander.'

Braccio folded his arms, leaning back on the bench. They both knew that the Pope's opinion counted for half the cardinals' votes, particularly if he was respected, as Alexander was.

'And there seems to be another problem obvious even to a simple soldier,' said the condottiere. 'Your claim to succeed Alexander is based on your readiness to call a council to reform the Church. But what if that council were to choose one of the other popes to unite behind?'

Cossa spread his hands on his satin knees, allowing his emerald ring to catch light in its many sides. He turned to Braccio. 'Let's deal with one thing at a time.' He picked honeysuckle and held it to his nose, breathing in. He threw it away, rose, and arranged the crucifix resting on his chest. 'Let's just make me pope, and quite soon, I think.' He folded his hands in front of him like a priest. 'Now, shouldn't you be inspecting my kitchen for poison?'

Pope Alexander rode through the palace gates as its garden was being eclipsed by the shadow of its walls. But the flowers were still breathing the evening air and the pontiff lifted his nose to their scent. He was riding a young grey draped with velvet and gold, and on his head was the episcopal mitre littered with pearls. He wore the white cassock of chastity and his finger bore the Ring of the Fisherman.

The cardinal was there to meet him, Poggio on one side, Braccio on the other. Cossa wore the habit of a mendicant order, his head bare and sandals on his feet.

Alexander stopped his horse and looked down. 'You are fasting?'

Cossa had fallen to his knees. 'I have just finished, Holy Father. Lent.'

The Pope frowned. 'But Lent's long over, Baldassare,' he said, extending his hand for the kiss.

'Never for me,' said Cossa, his voice muffled in the kiss. 'But tonight we'll eat fish.'

The Pope studied him for a while then dismounted into the arms of one of Braccio's men. He lifted Poggio from his knees. 'When do I succeed in bringing you back into the Curia, Poggio?' he asked. 'Your talents are wasted in Bologna.'

Poggio kissed the ring. 'The Lord sends me where he will, Holy Father. Perhaps the Curia next.'

Alexander glanced at Baldassare Cossa, one eyebrow raised. He turned to Braccio. 'You've found lodging for your men? They've ridden hard today.'

The mercenary dipped his head. 'No harder than the Holy Father. They are here to guard you.'

Alexander shook his head. 'You exaggerate the threat from my fellow popes, Braccio. They follow in the path of St Peter, which is the path of peace.'

The condottiere glanced at Cossa. 'Assuredly, Holy Father. But they keep company with men unfamiliar with that path.' He glanced up. 'And your mitre alone is worth a prince's ransom.'

Alexander raised him to his feet, kissing him on each cheek. He followed his host up the steps to the loggia where there were servants on their knees, dressed also for fasting. Each received a blessing. They walked into a room without furniture except for a table and two chairs. The night was warm but there was a fire burning at one end.

The Pope took off his mitre and set down his crozier. He gestured to the mitre. 'I want you to look after this, Baldassare,' he said. 'It's too heavy for an old man and too valuable to be out on the road. Can we eat? I am hungry and tired.'

Alexander sat on a chair and closed his eyes in prayer. Cossa sat across from him and did the same, praying for something different. The food arrived as promised: a flat fish from Ischia, coated with almonds, cinnamon and sandal, with ravioli set around it. The servants attended them, then disappeared.

The Pope ate. He said: 'The fish is good.'

'It is from Ischia, Holiness. Where I was born.'

Alexander nodded. 'You have come far, Baldassare.'

Cossa didn't think he referred to geography. 'I have gone where God has sent me. I have been blessed.'

'Then why', asked Alexander, sipping his water and wiping his lips with the napkin, 'did he make me pope and not you? You cannot pretend that you weren't surprised.'

Cossa had not expected this. They both knew he'd been surprised, given the breadth and depth of the Medici bribes. He gathered his thoughts. 'He may think I want experience still. I am young after all, Holy Father.'

The Pope smiled. 'Or perhaps He thought you wanted the *right* experience, Baldassare.' He looked up at the walls. 'Where have you put your paintings?'

Cossa looked surprised. 'Paintings, Holy Father?'

'Yes, paintings. There are squares around the walls where paintings have been removed.'

Cossa frowned. He'd hoped that the candle light wouldn't reveal the spaces. 'They have gone for cleaning, holiness.'

Alexander shook his head. 'One qualification for pope is an ability to lie, Cossa. The paintings were of different saints, all women, and all in different stages of torture. Is that not so?'

'It helps me to remember my mission, holiness.'

The Pope rubbed his eyes. He seemed suddenly tired from the conversation. He said: 'Your mission, Baldassare? What has the rape of St Catherine got to do with your mission?' He looked down at his food. 'The Cardinal of Bologna has robber bands on the roads around his city, in alliance with the chief of my bodyguard. They extort money from people in exchange for their protection. When he's not robbing them, the cardinal sells his flock a variety of ways to escape purgatory, most of them unknown to his Mother Church.' He paused, looking up. 'Baldassare, you inspect the local convents only to find nuns you can bed. Is this the work of God?'

Cossa began to reply but the Pope raised his hand. 'The Medici have preferred you, paid for you, because you get things done. But such a man cannot be *pope*.' Alexander let out a long sigh. 'I am here to tell you, Baldassare, that I am on my way to the cardinals to recommend Cardinal Colonna to succeed me. I am old and may not last the year.' He paused. 'I'm sorry.'

There was a long silence, punctured by the arrival of servants bringing rice cooked in milk and honey. It gave Cossa time to think.

When they were alone again, the Pope continued: 'There is also the politics to think of. Always the politics, Baldassare . . . Colonna has connections. His brother is the Prince of Salerno and his niece is the lovely Cleope Malatesta who can be useful with the right marriage. You just have bankers behind you.'

By this time, Cossa was nodding, his chin in his hands, no longer sipping his wine. He said: 'You are right, Holy Father, and the Almighty speaks through you. Cardinal Colonna is much better suited to the task of uniting this Church and I thank God that you have shown me this.'

He rose and moved to the wall where a bell-pull hung beside the space for St Anne. He pulled it.

'You are tired,' he said, coming back to the table. 'I will call for chocolate and Poggio to draw up something on the mitre you're leaving behind. We will go and sit and talk of something other than politics. Come.'

Cossa extended his hand and led the Pope over to the fire and chairs placed on either side for its warmth. They sat and a servant appeared with a tray, handing one cup to the Pope and the other to Baldassare Cossa. The cardinal asked for Poggio to be found. He raised his cup. 'To our Holy Mother Church.'

They drank their chocolate and sat in silence for a while. There was a knock on the door and Poggio appeared. Behind him was Braccio da Montone. Cossa turned.

'The Holy Father wishes to leave his mitre in my care, Poggio. Please draw up the necessary papers.' He glanced at Alexander, who was sitting with his eyes closed, his head nodding. He lowered his voice. 'Braccio will help you. Something along the lines of: "trusting to the honour of the cardinal, I hereby entrust the holy mitre of the office of pontiff . . ." et cetera, et cetera.' He looked up, but not at Poggio. 'You know the sort of thing?'

Braccio nodded. He said quietly: 'I'm sure we can manage.'

*

It was as Cossa, Braccio and Poggio were having breakfast that they heard the news.

The servant was ashen-faced and trembling in every limb. 'I passed a glass before his mouth, then took his pulse.' He shook his head. 'There is no doubt.'

Braccio was first up the stairs, the other two close behind. They ran into the papal bedroom. Poggio went to the bed, sat and pulled back the sheet. He put his head to Alexander's heart, his ear next to the crucifix.

'There's no beat,' he said, 'no beat at all.' He placed his hand on the Pope's forehead. 'He's cold.' He sat up and looked at the cardinal. 'The Holy Father is dead.'

Baldassare Cossa was shaking his head, holding the side of a table. 'No,' he whispered. 'Not in my house.'

Braccio glanced at him. 'Why not? He had to die somewhere. He was old.' He walked over to a table in the middle of the room with a scroll on it. He picked it up, undid it and read. He looked up when he'd finished.

'This says that Alexander entrusts the holy mitre to your care,' he said. 'What do you think that means?'

'Its meaning, I think, is clear,' replied Cossa.

Poggio was frowning. Its meaning was clear to him as well but he judged it prudent to remain silent.

Braccio read the paper again, then nodded. He folded the paper and put it within his doublet. He looked at Cossa. 'I think I will take this to the cardinals,' he said quietly. 'Will you come too?'

Cossa shook his head. 'No,' he said. 'The cardinals will do their duty better without me.'

CHAPTER EIGHT

NANJING, WINTER 1410

Shulen had been surprised to survive the attempted murder of Nikolas. The cutting of the ropes had been so obvious that she'd assumed Min Qing's men would come down and kill her too. But instead they'd lifted Nikolas's twisted body and carried it gently to the riverbank where a litter was waiting to take him to the palace. Shulen had seen Min Qing watch it all from the ship's deck.

So much had been broken in Nikolas's body that it was difficult to know which bone joined to which. But the palace surgeons were the best in China and Chinese medicine the best in the world. Nikolas was opened and reorganised and given herbs to transport him somewhere else while it all happened. Shulen sat by his bedside and watched his every breath. She was there when he awoke.

'Will I live?'

'Oh yes,' she said, smiling and taking his hand. 'It's the walking that's in doubt.'

'Was I meant to die?'

Shulen gave a little shrug. 'Probably. Anyway, Min Qing's warning worked. I've not seen a merchant since it happened.'

'So what have you been doing?'

'Waiting for you to mend and for Chen Cheng to get back with the fleet. I won't feel safe until he's here.' She took his hand and smiled. 'At least not with you on your sick bed. What use is a Varangian who can't fight?'

That had been the start of a deeper friendship between them. With Nikolas in bed and no merchants to trade with, they'd talked. And they'd talked.

Shulen found Nikolas very different from the man she'd thought him to be, and very different from her. He'd been brought up embraced by the cosy walls of Monemvasia, she on the limitless steppe. He longed for the certainties of home and family; she didn't long for what she didn't know. He saw China as the temporary means to an end, she as an end in itself, perhaps. They were both impatient to sail.

'Chen Cheng is back,' she said one morning as she lifted the blinds in his room, 'and Min Qing has been arrested. You need to start walking.'

And he had. Day by day, with Shulen's help, Nikolas had coaxed his big frame back into motion. Inch by inch, he'd relearnt how to walk. And all the time they'd learnt more and more about each other.

'Have you ever loved?' he asked her one day as they walked by the river. He had a stick in one hand and the other rested on her shoulder.

She paused before answering. 'Yes. You know that, I think.'

'And do you still?'

She didn't answer, busying herself with the view. The river was full of junks and there was ice melting at its banks. The landscape was brushed with snow.

He glanced at her. 'Will you stay for a while when we go west?'

Shulen stopped and turned to him. 'What is the point? He is married and happy.'

Nikolas brushed a snowflake from her hair. 'Is it painful?'

She looked away. 'I just want to sail. He needs our gold.'

Nikolas nodded. They'd had a letter from Luke. They knew of the threats from Venice and Suleyman. Luke needed money for his wall, quickly.

Shulen looked up beneath a palm. The winter sun gave no heat but had sown diamonds into the landscape. Through her breath, her eyes had a question in them. 'And you,' she asked, 'have you ever loved?'

He didn't say anything for a while; he just looked out over the river. Then he turned to her. 'I do now,' he said.

In a way, it had been Shulen's fault. Nikolas had had little to do while he'd been bed-bound, then confined to a wheelchair. So Shulen had taken him back to the library where they'd met Zhu Chou. She'd leave him there to read.

Most days, Zhu Chou would arrive and sit at the other end of the table. She and Nikolas would read in silence. One day, they talked.

'What are you reading?' he asked.

She looked up from a pile of papers. As before, her skin was powdered to a porcelain white and she wore her hair in a double bun with a cobalt-tasselled pin pushed into it. There were blue flowers pinned to its sides above her temples.

'An excerpt from the diadan,' she said. 'It's about Monemvasia, added recently by Chen Cheng. Your home.'

Monemvasia. Nikolas missed it with an intensity that didn't wane. 'Can I see it?'

She rose and brought the papers over to him. She sat down

next to him and the smell of jasmine filled his senses. They were almost touching.

'See, he's had it painted.'

There was a map and pictures of Monemvasia and Mistra, coloured woodcuts that showed their walls, the Goulas, the sea, and his heart ached with the missing of it. There was writing below that he couldn't read.

'What does it say?'

She read to him, slowly, as she pointed out each word. Chen Cheng described their journey around Africa, their arrival in Monemvasia, the fireworks at Mistra. There were pieces about the Ottoman civil war, about the Byzantine Empire, about the Portuguese caravel, also illustrated. There was a description of Plethon and his thinking.

When she finished, he asked: 'Can I tell you about Monemvasia?'

She smiled. 'I'd like that.'

Soon afterwards, just when Nikolas was beginning to walk without a stick, Zhu Chou disappeared. The Emperor had left Nanjing and his harem had gone with him. That was when Chen Cheng came to see them.

'I am sorry about Min Qing,' he said as he came through the door. 'He was tortured to the eighth degree but still didn't tell us whose orders he was following.'

'*Eighth*?' Shulen had been shocked. '*Eight* removes of his family tortured? Was that really necessary?'

But Chen Cheng had been certain. 'His warning was strong; ours had to be stronger. I assume the merchants have returned?'

They'd returned with the proclamation of Min Qing's arrest, pasted to the palace walls where every merchant in Nanjing would see it.

84

'Yes,' said Nikolas, 'all anxious to see the horses you brought back from Mistra. They want as many as can be brought by the next fleet.'

Shulen turned to Chen Cheng. 'So when can we sail?'

'There will be delays. The mandarins will still find all manner of ways to thwart a project they dislike and exchanging gold for foreign goods they dislike absolutely. Taxes will be withheld, paperwork delayed, the boats subjected to pointless inspection. You'll see.' He turned to Nikolas. 'You have been meeting the concubine Zhu Chou.'

Nikolas wondered if there was anything this man didn't know. 'We read together, yes.'

'You read the diadan.'

Nikolas nodded. 'But no longer. She's disappeared.'

Chen Cheng brought the tips of his fingers together in one elegant movement and rested them at the point of his chin. 'She has gone with the Emperor. She goes wherever he goes.' He looked at Nikolas. 'She will never leave the harem, you know that.'

Nikolas felt the familiar pang. 'Yes, I know that.'

Chen Cheng lowered his hands. 'Good.' He paused. 'She has persuaded the Emperor to let you see more of the diadan. I am to take you.'

They left immediately. Chen Cheng led them through a blizzard of cherry blossom to the other side of the palace compound. They came to a vast building, passing men with wooden carriers on their backs piled high with scrolls. Chen Cheng strode into it, Shulen shuffling to catch up, her zhiju too tight to run in. Nikolas hobbled behind.

The room was big enough to hold two of Zheng's treasure ships. It was filled with long lines of shelves with corridors in between. Everywhere were men in black silk with emblems on their fronts, all wearing gloves, all in a hurry. Apart from the hiss of slipper, there was absolute silence. In the centre were lecterns and chests of drawers and a long table, piled high with books and scrolls and tablets of clay.

A man was approaching them. He was bald except for the pigtail that rose like a palm tree from the top of his head and coiled round his shoulder. He looked obsequious.

Chen Cheng's voice fell to a whisper. 'The Emperor is compiling the diadan, building fleets to sail around the world and the greatest palace the world has ever seen. There are many who would like him to fail. You are about to meet one.'

'Excellency,' whispered the man as he came up to them, 'you have brought guests. We are fortunate.' He bowed to Shulen, then Nikolas.

'They are here to see the diadan, Bao Zhi,' said Chen Cheng, 'as I told you.'

'Ah yes,' said the man. 'Of course.'

Shulen studied him. He had a blandness in his manner that was there to divert. He was clearly intelligent, sly and dangerous and she could feel the enmity between him and their friend. They walked on and came to a table with a single book on it, bound in calfskin and the size of a small child. Shulen went up to the table and ran her fingers over its cover. It was cool to the touch. 'Can I open it?'

Bao Zhi slid gloves from his sleeve like a magician. Shulen put them on, untied the string and opened the book. The smell of must, fibre and ink came and went. Inside were row upon row of Chinese characters, each exquisitely crafted by pen, some in coloured inks. She turned the pages. Every one seemed identical and their symmetry was a thing of beauty in itself. 'It's extraordinary,' she said.

'Yes, extraordinary,' said Chen Cheng. He turned to Bao Zhi. 'You may go.' He turned to Shulen. 'Continue.'

She turned more pages and came to some full of diagrams. There were contraptions with gear wheels and pinions and buckets, all powered by water. There were machines for threshing and weaving and printing. There were ships without sails but paddles on each side. There were guns with many barrels and a man with wings on his arms.

Nikolas whistled softly. 'Do we have such things in the West? I don't think so.'

'No, you don't. Nor would you without this Emperor. Some of the diadan will go with the fleet you will sail on.' He turned the pages until they came to one without pictures. The script was not Chinese but something else. 'Ancient Hebrew,' he said, his finger running down the lines of words. 'It is part of the Nestorian codex. Plethon asked me to look it out for him.'

'What does it say?' asked Shulen, leaning forward. 'Do you know?'

'Oh yes,' said Chen Cheng.

She turned to him. 'And will you tell us?'

'It relates to a Varangian treasure said to lie somewhere in Mistra.' He glanced at Nikolas. 'Your duty has been to guard it, I think. I expected you to know what it was.'

The Varangian shook his head. 'Only Plethon and Luke know what it is,' he said, 'And Anna. The rest of us are not allowed to know.'

Chen Cheng closed the book. 'Then I will not be the one to tell you.'

CHAPTER NINE

MISTRA, SPRING 1411

Baldassare Cossa took the name of John for his papacy. He became John XXIII and the Medici became his bankers. In the spring, Cosimo came to Mistra.

On a calm afternoon, Luke stood with him on the walls of the city, looking down at the Peloponnese's first fair. Beyond the Jewish and Albanian quarters, past the stink of the tanning yards, a new city of canvas and anchoring hemp had risen from the ground to spread like weed. Cosimo had promised to use the many branches of the Medici Bank to pass the word and merchants from Bruges to Prague had made the journey south to sell to the Byzantines. Luke had provided the site, the police force, a court to settle disputes and a system of weights and measures. Cosimo had provided the investment. Together, they would use the fair to launch the Magoris Bank.

But Cosimo had brought bad news as well. 'My agent has confirmed it, I'm afraid,' he said. 'There are at least forty galleys, most with cannon. And the quartermasters are looking for billets in the town for three thousand soldiers.'

Luke's frown creased his forehead. Up until Cosimo's arrival an hour ago, he'd been enjoying the spectacle of the fair, relieved that it had all worked so well. He turned to Cosimo. 'When will they sail?'

'When the last troops arrive at Negroponte, I suppose.'

Luke's gaze went back to the fair. He could just see Anna standing beneath the silk awning of the most splendid tent of all. It had the Medici and Magoris arms over its entrance and gold tassels on every rope. She was talking to a group of nobles and there were more entering and leaving the tent. Business was as brisk as it had been all week.

'You may need to act soon, before it's too late. Where are your Varangians?'

'At Corinth, helping build the wall. I'll go and join them tonight. Can you manage here without me?'

Cosimo nodded. On arriving at Monemvasia at dawn, he'd ridden straight to the fair and had been briefed by his factors. The new bank was attracting many depositors. 'From what I've heard, you seem to have done it all without me.' He put his hand on Luke's shoulder. 'I'll stay until the fair's over, then take the money to Rome,' he said. 'You must do what you have to do, then meet me there. We need to remind Cossa of the second part of the plan: a council to unite the Church. We can make any further loan from the Magoris Bank dependent on him calling the council.'

They parted and Luke made his way towards the city gate. These days Mistra was a jumble of cranes and scaffolding as every week a new palace opened its doors, its frescoes still wet to the touch. They were all in the Chinese style now, people remembering the Ming and wanting lotus leaves for their walls. The price of land was soaring.

He left the city and crossed the open fields to the fair, arriving at the Magoris Bank tent as Anna was waving off another flattered noble. He watched an elderly couple emerge from the tent behind her, clutching a scroll embossed with the Medici and Magoris seals. He looked around him. The fair was packed with people spending money, people who'd come from as far away as Corinth.

Corinth. This would be the difficult part: telling Anna that he was to leave again.

'There you are.'

She was smiling but the smile was uneasy. He knew she worried about this bank, but it all made sense: the papal debt, backed by the vast revenues of the Curia, was the safest investment you could find. They'd discussed the logic of it many times. They needed money to finish the wall and build a fleet against the Turk, or perhaps Venice. There'd been no word from China since Shulen's last letter and it looked unlikely that gold would come from there any month soon. So banking made sense. But that meant absence, and Luke's last long absence had involved a woman they never talked about.

'I have to go to Corinth,' he said, coming up and kissing her. 'Tonight.'

The smile faded. 'But Cosimo has just arrived.'

'I know. It was he who told me. The Venetians are preparing to sail out of Negroponte.'

'It was to be Hilarion's first grown-up dinner. You promised.'

Luke suddenly felt irritated. 'Anna, Mistra may be about to be attacked. I have to go.'

'Can't Matthew do it without you? He commands the Varangians, after all.'

Luke took her hands in his. 'I must go to Corinth and then to Rome. I must talk to the new Pope.' He looked around him. 'Now, where is Hilarion?'

Hilarion was making his way down the hill of Mistra with Plethon and Murad. The two boys looked as though they might be taking part in the mystery play: Hilarion tall, fair and dressed in white; Murad short, dark and dressed as a junior Magus.

Plethon walked behind the two boys and spoke in bursts as he tried to keep up. 'They have these fairs in Europe, especially France. Merchants from all over Europe are here. It will make money to finish the wall.'

'What wall?' asked Murad. They'd come to a steep part of the street and he'd quickened his pace.

Hilarion took Murad's arm to slow him. 'The Hexamilion Wall at the Isthmus of Corinth.'

'To stop us?' Murad shook himself free. 'It won't stop me.'

They reached the city gate and joined the throng of people on their way out to the plain. It was early evening now, and a light stretched across the Evrotas Valley that touched everything it met with gold. It had been a long, hard winter and the exhausted ground had only recently thawed. They entered the fair and Hilarion saw his father and mother standing at the entrance to a tent. He heard a shout and saw Giovanni approach from another direction. He'd hoped Giovanni would be there.

Anna came forward to meet them, bowing to Murad and embracing Plethon, then her son. Hilarion watched Luke talking to Giovanni from over her shoulder. Anna released him and turned. 'Sir, your son is here.'

Luke and Giovanni looked round. Their smiles were identical. 'Hilarion!' said Luke, walking over. 'What would you like to see? Giovanni can take you.'

Anna frowned. 'You cannot take him yourself? It may not be safe.'

'Giovanni can look after them,' said Luke.

A bear and its keeper had wandered over. Hilarion stared up at it. 'Does it dance?'

Giovanni walked over to him. 'It can hardly stand, poor animal, let alone dance. Don't waste your money.'

Murad turned to him: 'It's taller than you.'

This was true, although Giovanni seemed to grow an inch every month and showed no sign of stopping. He was nearly Luke's size now and his fair hair tumbled to his shoulders like florins from a banker's board. He ignored Murad and put his arm round Hilarion's shoulders. 'What would you like to do?' he said, walking away. Murad followed.

They came to merchants selling everything from leather, wax and spices to several kinds of fur. The air was full of the sound of coin on wood. They reached the area colonised by the spice merchants, a landscape of indigo, ochre and violet. A cough came from behind them and they turned. A man of oiled rotundity stood there, hands joined and fingers pointed to his chest. He wore a straw hat against the sun and cotton to shield his neck.

'Excellency,' said the man to Giovanni, 'I have a message for you at my stall.'

Giovanni frowned. 'A message? From whom?'

'That I don't know,' answered the man. 'It was put into my hand as I was leaving my home in Rimini.'

Hilarion watched Giovanni go with the man. He looked for Murad and saw him wandering towards a stage on which two men were shouting at each other. He followed him.

The two men were monks and they stood on either side of a large crucifix. One, whom Hilarion recognised, was from the Peribleptos Monastery in Mistra. The other was a mendicant of the Dominican Order. He was tonsured, pale, badly shaven and dressed in a black habit that was frayed and torn. Hilarion pushed his way to the front of the crowd and found Murad staring up at them. He looked around him. The audience was a mix of Greeks and merchants from the fair: Orthodox and Catholic. The monk from Mistra was laughing.

'Your Catholic Church has a hydra of popes! Every time you lose one, another jumps up! How many do you need to sell you the way to heaven?'

The crowd roared at this. There were more Orthodox than Catholic and they were backing their champion. The monk drew encouragement. '*And*,' he shouted above the cheers, 'the latest one is a whoremonger and a pirate! He robs his flock and takes the clothes off their backs, especially if they're nuns!'

The Dominican was the smaller of the two and had the face of a rodent. He shouted through the laughter: 'And yet . . .' He raised his voice. 'And *yet* . . .' The noise subsided a little. 'Your Emperor Manuel, and your patriarch, are willing to prostrate themselves to Rome to save their empire! Why not bow to the Sultan as well?' There were shouts of anger from the crowd now. 'Yes . . . *yes* . . .' continued the Dominican, turning to his audience, his hand cupped to his ear. He saw Murad and his rat face widened into a smile. 'Look! We have the Sultan here!'

The Dominican knelt, raised his arms, then fell flat to the stage. 'Suleyman! You grace us with your presence!'

Murad took a step backwards. 'I am the son of Mehmed,' he shouted, 'not the usurper!'

The Dominican looked up, apparently surprised. He raised his hand for silence and gradually it came. 'Ah,' he said, rising to his knees, 'then can you tell us why Muhammad is so great?'

Murad was angry now. He knew he was being mocked. 'Because he does not tolerate priests such as you!' he shouted.

The Dominican got to his feet. He shouted over Murad's head.

'And why do the followers of Muhammad not have priests? Because they'd be too busy driving out their devils!'

The crowd roared. They might disagree over the Pope, but they could unite in their loathing for the Turk. Hilarion saw Murad look around him at the pointed fingers, the waving fists.

'Let's see,' shouted the Dominican, 'let's see if we can remove the Devil from this one, shall we? Pass him up to me.'

Hilarion watched it all and felt the press of the crowd around him, felt its heat, its anger. The drumming began in his temples and a wave of dizziness stole up him.

No. Not here.

His eyes weren't really focusing but he could see Murad being lifted on to the stage, his arms flailing. He could hear his screams of fear. The drumming got louder.

Please. Not here.

He forced himself to look up at the stage. Murad was being held to the floor, his face to the wood. One man had a knee to his back. The Dominican held his palms flat on his head, forcing his face down. He was chanting in Latin: *'Exorcizamus te . . .'*

Hilarion shut his eyes, and then opened them. He had to focus. He turned to a man beside him. 'Lift me up there.'

The man looked surprised. He turned to another. 'He wants to join him!'

They laughed and lifted him on to the stage by his armpits. The Dominican was three paces away, his eyes shut, his face lifted to heaven. Hilarion shook his head, his palms to his temples.

He rushed at the monk and pushed him with all his strength. The man toppled over and Hilarion fell with him. He got to his knees. He felt dizzy and sick but he had to get Murad away from here. He turned.

Murad had shaken off the two men holding him down. He was pointing at Hilarion, his face twisted with rage. 'You want a devil?' he was shouting. '*There's* your devil! He has the Devil inside him! Watch him now!'

Hilarion knew that he was shaking all over his body, his arms waving in every direction. He fell on to his back and screwed his eyes shut.

NO!

But he was beyond the point of return. The convulsions were upon him and there was nothing he could do to stop them.

NO! NO! NO!

'No!'

A new voice, one he knew. He felt the stage rock as something heavy landed on it. Then arms were beneath him, lifting him: strong arms. His head was next to a chest that smelt of home and safety. Every part of his body was shaking but the arms that held him could control it. He heard a shout.

'You, too, Murad.'

There were faces coming and going as Luke pushed their way through the crowd. He closed his eyes and felt terror and relief and something else.

Shame.

Luke hadn't spoken a word as he'd left the fair, carrying Hilarion and pulling Murad up the empty streets of Mistra. He'd arrived at the house, given Hilarion a draught of Fiorenza's mixture and put him to bed. Then, silently and relentlessly, he had beaten Murad.

It had been done across his knee. Murad had struggled and screamed but Luke's cold fury had been deaf and blind to anything but retribution. It was only when Anna arrived that he'd stopped.

'*What are you doing?*' She was standing in the open door, her face stricken. 'What are you *doing*, Luke?'

Luke looked at her as if she was a stranger. Murad managed to get a foot to the ground, then broke free. He ran to Anna.

'I thought you'd ridden to Corinth,' she said, Murad's face in her tunic. 'You said it was urgent.'

Luke was still staring at his wife, opening and closing his hands. 'Hilarion had a seizure.'

Anna was shaking her head in disbelief. 'Is it Murad's fault that our son had a seizure?' Her voice was rising. 'Where was Giovanni? Wasn't he supposed to be looking after them? If anyone should be beaten, it should be Giovanni. This is his fault!'

Murad turned. He was shaking with anger, his face blotched by tears. 'Giovanni left us. He went off with a merchant.' He pointed at Luke. 'You have beaten me.'

Luke tried to speak but the rage had left as quickly as it had come and he felt empty of everything. He slumped in the chair.

Murad saw it was safe to step out from behind Anna's skirts. He was trembling with outrage. He walked up to Luke. 'You have beaten the future sultan. No wall will save you once I come to rule.'

CHAPTER TEN

NEGROPONTE, SPRING 1411

The letter Giovanni had received at the fair had been shy but insistent: Cleope wanted to see him again.

Their first sight of each other had lasted five seconds, no more. Then she'd gone; left the stage to go beyond the mountains from where she'd come. Giovanni had risen, excused himself, and gone to find her.

She'd been waiting for him behind Mount Olympus, holding a kerchief in fingers linked at her waist. Her young cousin had disappeared and it seemed to Giovanni that Malatestas, Albizzis, popes, fathers were in some other world, the hum of their conversation distant and obscure. He'd looked only at her face: her eyes, nose, lips and the spaces between, marvelling at an arrangement that seemed to him without flaw. He felt no urge to speak or touch, as if any sound or movement would pierce the membrane of a happiness that he'd never felt before. Then she'd given him the kerchief, walking forward and tucking it into his open shirt. It had been next to his heart ever since.

And it had been his secret until Luke had found it. It had been while they were waiting, becalmed, on the round ship.

'What's that?'

They'd been sitting with their backs to the ship's side. Luke had been sharpening the dagger that he was now using to point.

Giovanni had looked down to see red silk peeping between the buttons of his shirt. 'It's a gift.'

'From whom? Cleope?'

Giovanni nodded. 'It was she who wrote the letter at the fair.'

Luke went back to sharpening. 'No wonder you abandoned the boys. How old is she?'

'Thirteen. I'm going to marry her.'

Luke saw nothing strange in this. 'Does her father know?'

'No, but he'll say yes when he knows how much we love each other. He's a poet.'

Luke had looked up. 'He's a condottiere, Giovanni; one who writes bad sonnets. Let me tell you something.'

And he'd told him. It had been said kindly, but it had been said. Cleope Malatesta was intended for better things. Where she married would depend on where the Malatesta brothers saw advantage, and Chios was unlikely to be on the list. 'But who becomes pope next will be important. Her uncle is Otto Colonna, Cardinal-Deacon of San Giorgio al Velabro. If it's him, then her value rises even further.'

Now Giovanni sat with giants below decks in a round ship and forced himself not to be sick. He was between two men who smelt badly. The swell of the sea made him press against one, then the other.

There were a hundred of them crammed into the hold, sitting with their backs to the hull, crossbows in their laps. It was midday and stiflingly hot and the only light came through the gap around the hatch. There was no sound, just the slap of waves and the voice of the man talking to them from above: Peter of Norfolk.

'Not much longer,' he heard through the wood. 'Not a sound now. As we planned.'

Despite his surroundings, Giovanni was happy: he was with Luke and the Varangian Company and they were about to see battle. He heard shouts from the deck above. Luke's voice. He was calling: 'Our mast's broken. We need a pull.'

Now he spoke more quietly. 'They're coming aboard, the bastards. They just couldn't resist it.'

He didn't sound displeased; but then Giovanni knew the plan. The Varangian Company had sailed in a round ship from Corinth and were now wallowing with a broken mast between the islands of Andros and Negroponte. It was where any Venetian galley making for Negroponte could not fail to find them. They just had to wait.

Now it seemed that a galley was coming alongside them.

He heard Peter's voice close to the hatch. 'Steady, lads. They're coming aboard. About twenty of the brutes. On my word.'

Giovanni held his breath. There were the thumps of men landing, then footsteps, heavy. He heard the knock of steel.

'We are a merchant ship out of Chios.' This was Luke, plaintive. 'You've no need to bring weapons on board – we are unarmed. We need a tow.'

Then a new voice. 'You are Genoese and no Genoese ship belongs here. These are Venetian waters. We're taking your ship, or at least its cargo. What is it?'

Now Luke was outraged. Outraged and informative. 'You come on to my ship with twenty crossbows, stand against the rail pointing them at us, and think you can just take my cargo?'

There was the sound of a safety catch released. 'What's in the hold?'

'Alum. We are on our way to Pisa. You'll have to answer to the Florentines.'

A laugh. 'Not if you're all dead.' A pause. 'Show us.'

Footsteps approached the hatches. He heard an order, the slip of a bolt. Then daylight as the hatch doors crashed open. And Peter's face.

'*Now!*'

Ten men leapt to their feet, sandbag in one hand, crossbow in the other. Ten more crouched to make platforms. The crossbowmen climbed on to them and threw the sandbags forward. Giovanni heard a thud as Luke fell to the deck. The Varangians fired their volley.

There were screams from the rail and the sound of bolts hitting wood. Then ten more Varangians had taken their comrades' place and fired another volley. More screams and splashes as men hit water. Giovanni itched to get up and see. But he'd promised to stay below.

What he'd have seen was a deck strewn with Venetian corpses and those still alive surrendering.

'You can come up.'

Giovanni climbed out of the hold to see Luke taking the sword from a tall man in armour.

'I have two hundred men on my ship,' said the man.

'And we', said Luke, throwing the sword to one side, 'are in a round ship. Are your men mountaineers?'

Giovanni could only see the tops of two masts from where he was standing and knew they were at least twenty feet above the galley's *rembata*. The Venetians might have bombards on the fighting stage, but they'd be pointing the wrong way.

The Varangians had gone to the rail and were now lined up along it, their crossbows aimed below. Matthew and Arcadius, not fluent in Italian, had just emerged from the aft cabin with Benedo Barbi. They were smiling.

'Well, that went better than I could have hoped,' said Matthew, joining Luke. 'Not a single casualty.'

'No, but there's a lot of them,' said Luke.

'They'll all fit in the hold, I'm sure.' He turned to Giovanni. 'Was it hot in there?'

Giovanni was moving towards the rail. Luke caught his arm. 'No.'

The boy turned, frowning. 'I wanted to see how many oars it has.'

'It's a trireme,' said Luke. 'One hundred and seventy rowers, three to a bench.'

'So how will we sail her?' This was Arcadius.

The Venetian *sopracomito* had overheard. 'How indeed? We don't use slaves in Venice. Every man down there is a volunteer. They won't row for you.'

'Oh, I'm sure they're not all volunteers,' said Luke. 'I should think some are prisoners of war. I'm sure they'll row for us.' He smiled genially. 'Now, we can do this calmly or otherwise; it's up to you. I want every man on your galley who is not a prisoner of war up here. They can leave their weapons behind.'

The captain was thinking hard. His men were down there with crossbows pointing at them and the round ship was impregnable. On the other hand, like every other sopracomito, he was a gentleman of Venice. And half his fortune was invested in that galley.

Benedo Barbi helped him make up his mind. He shouted to the forecastle. 'Take them off.'

Four sailors removed tarpaulins from two bombards that, unlike the Venetians', were pointed in the right direction.

'Grapeshot in one barrel,' said Barbi, turning to the captain, 'and ball in the other. The first will kill most of your men, the second will drown the rest.'

Luke was still smiling at the man. 'So what is it to be?'

The captain had no choice. He walked to the rail and shouted orders. From below came the clatter of arms and the thud of wood as men laid down their weapons. Rope ladders were thrown over the side and the Venetians started arriving on deck, some angry, some scared. Then the rowers emerged, half-naked, their hair stiff with salt.

The Varangians herded them into the hold, kicking them when they went too slowly. Last in was the sopracomito. Giovanni watched him go below and wondered how he'd fare down there with his men. The bolt was slid shut.

The Varangians were already climbing over the side, their swords and axes strapped to their backs. Giovanni went to the rail to stand beside Luke. The galley below them was hard against the side of their ship. Its oars had been stowed and ropes were attached to the round ship at bow and stern. There was a parapet along the side of the ship where the rest of the oarsmen sat, the prisoners of war. Some were waving up at them, men who'd be going home.

Within the hour, everything they needed had been taken from the round ship, including two large lighters, and it had been cut loose to drift. The Venetians would find a way out of the hold but the ship had no mast and had been intended for the scrap yard anyway. Their best hope was rescue.

The Varangians stripped to the waist and Matthew arranged them on the rowing benches, three to an oar: two sitting, one standing. The prisoners of war were from Genoa and Milan and they distributed themselves to show how it was done. Luke placed himself on the gangway behind a drum to beat out the tempo. The galley turned circles for a while, then got under way, the two lighters in tow. Giovanni patrolled the gangway dispensing water and encouragement. The Varangians liked him.

They were headed for Andros, the northernmost island in the Duchy of Naxos, where the prisoners of war would be set free. It was only six miles south-east of Negroponte and had many natural harbours. It was the perfect place to rest and wait.

That evening, as the sun was putting its first toe in the water, Luke was joined by Benedo Barbi, Matthew and Arcadius in the sopracomito's cabin. The room was low and beamed and had a cot in one corner. A wide window looked over the rudder and two bombards were stowed beneath it. In the centre was a table with a map on it.

There was a knock on the door and Peter of Norfolk came in with two men. 'The lightermen, sir.'

Luke looked up from the map. 'Good. Please join us. You too, Peter.'

'Gentlemen,' continued Luke, an arm around each of the lightermen, 'may I introduce Marco and Zeno? They know these waters and our lives will be in their hands tonight. Please be nice to them.'

He released the men and came back to the map. He pointed to the island and his finger came to rest at what looked like a castle. 'The fortress port of Negroponte is where this galley was making for when we intercepted it. In its harbour lies the Venetian fleet. The harbour is outside the city walls and open to the south.'

He traced his finger down the island's long coastline. 'You'll see that Negroponte Island is separated from the mainland by this narrow channel. It is the Strait of Euripus and it has extraordinary qualities.'

Luke leant over the map, still pointing. The strait narrowed as it went north, so that the island was almost touching the mainland where the fortress was. He continued: 'You'll know that our Middle Sea has very little tide, especially here in the east. Not so with this strait. The tide is strong, faster than the best speed of a galley. And it changes four times a day.'

Arcadius whistled. It was a torrent.

Luke pointed at a promontory at the entrance to the strait. 'This is Styra where we'll start from tonight at the moment the tide changes to flow north. It's fifty miles from there to Negroponte and if we make five knots and the tide beneath us another seven, we'll be sailing at twelve knots. That means we'll get there in four hours, which is when the tide reverses.'

Luke walked over to a table where a model of the galley sat. He brought it to the table and set it down. 'Now, this is the difficult bit.' He pointed at the ship. 'You'll have guessed by now that we are going to make a fireship of this galley and that Barbi here is going to load it with enough Greek fire for it to burn its way into the Venetian fleet. The challenge for us will be not being on it when it does its work.'

Matthew was shaking his head. 'But how? We'll be going faster than a horse at gallop.'

Luke gestured to Marco and Zeno. 'That's why you must be nice to Marco and Zeno,' he said, smiling. 'The two lighters will be fixed hard to our stern with these men in them. As the galley approaches the fleet, our oarsmen will fill the lighters, row by row. When we're certain of hitting the fleet, we'll cut loose.'

'But on that tide, won't the lighters just follow the galley into the inferno?' asked Arcadius.

'Not with these men in charge. They'll take us into the shore to wait for it to turn. Remember, if we've timed it right, we'll be casting loose just before that happens. Then we'll come back.'

There was silence after that. It seemed possible but dangerous.

At last Matthew spoke. 'It should work. We know the tides, we know our speed and we know the distance. But how will we ignite the ship?'

'The galley's hull will be laced with Greek fire in flammable canisters,' replied Luke. 'There will be a gunpowder trail that will be lit by fire-arrows shot by the Varangians. The ship will burn slowly enough to still be alight by the time it reaches the fleet at anchor.'

'Well, there we are,' said Arcadius. 'What could possibly go wrong?'

'I was coming to that,' said Luke quietly. 'Unfortunately there is something else. Marco?'

The lighterman leant forward. He swept his hand down the channel. 'It's a strange place, this strait,' he said. 'Many I know won't even go in it, experienced pilots too. It does funny things.'

'Like?' asked Matthew.

'Like whirlpools,' he said. 'The change in the tide is so sudden that sometimes it creates whirlpools. I've seen whole ships sucked under.'

'But it's rare,' said Luke. 'We'll be unlucky if it happens. We just have to look out for them.'

'And what if the Venetians give chase?' asked Arcadius.

'They won't have time,' said Luke. 'With that current we'll be back in Andros by the time they've worked out what's going on. There'll be a ship to meet us there.' He spread his hands on the map and looked at the men, each in turn. 'This, gentlemen,' he said, 'will be the Varangian Company's finest hour.'

When it was dark and the sky sprinkled with stars, a full moon shuffling its way up to join them, Giovanni was standing by the rail of the stern deck next to Luke. On his other side, Barbi had an hourglass balanced on his open palm. Luke was bent over the rail with a string in his hand. Something heavy was at its other end.

The galley was entering the channel, having left Styra on its starboard side ten minutes before. Giovanni looked down the gangway to where Matthew had taken over the drum, Arcadius running up and down with the water. He could see the inner oarsmen standing behind their oars, rising and falling with the rhythm of their pull. Peter of Norfolk was on the rembata looking out into the night, his arm raised. Giovanni lifted his head and filled his lungs with the smell of salt and spray. He looked back to the stern, seeing one of the lighters strapped to the ship's side. The wake behind it sparkled with phosphorescence. They were going fast and every moment their speed was increasing.

He turned to Luke. 'What are you doing?'

Luke pointed over the side. 'This is a chip log. Do you see the string it's attached to?'

Giovanni nodded.

'It has knots tied in it every fifty feet.' Luke pointed at Barbi. 'Using the hourglass we can measure our speed.'

Giovanni didn't understand but didn't much care. He had absolute faith in this man to get them to where they had to be, with or without whirlpools.

'You shouldn't be here,' said Luke.

'I'm fourteen' said Giovanni, 'and almost as tall as you are.'

Luke turned to Giovanni. 'Yes you are, but you'll be first into the lighter when it's time to board, am I clear?'

Three hours later, when the moon was racing above their masts and the wind loud in their ears, Luke said to Giovanni: 'Go and tell Matthew to slow the beat by a fifth.'

Giovanni dropped to the gangplank and told Matthew. When he returned, Luke was talking to Barbi. There were two men straining against the rudder behind them.

Luke said: 'We're getting close to Negroponte. We need to start putting men into the lighters.'

Barbi nodded and swayed his way down to give the order. The galley was lurching from side to side and spray was exploding over the rails, soaking the rowers below. Giovanni looked out at the shoreline and saw mountains marching past like black camels.

'Slower!' yelled Luke down to the rowers. 'Matthew, slow the beat!'

It was done but the boat hardly slowed. Luke had reeled in the chip log and was holding on to the side. The first of the Varangian Company were passing him to get to the rope ladders.

'Hurry!' shouted Luke against the wind. 'Get the next men up!'

Giovanni looked down to see Matthew and Peter pulling men from their oars, two at a time. Only the outer oarsmen would stay until the last moment to keep the ship on course.

'Quick!'

Luke was pushing men past them to the rope ladders. The Varangians were doing their best but few of them had been to sea before. Giovanni doubted whether many could even swim.

He looked out ahead, beyond the rembata. There were lights in the distance, coming and going behind the mast. It wasn't five miles.

The Varangians were running past him now and he could hear shouts from the lighters below.

Luke had turned to Barbi and was yelling in his ear. 'If we're this close then the tide must be about to turn, right?'

The engineer nodded, shielding his eyes from the spray. 'We've got to release the boats!' he shouted. 'Otherwise the galley won't get there before it turns. They're holding us back!'

Giovanni glanced down at the rowing deck. The last of the oarsmen were coming up now. Matthew and the other two Varangians were pushing them on. They might reach the boats in time.

Luke saw him. 'What are you doing here? Get into the lighter!'

Giovanni was pulled to the front of the Varangians and two of them lifted him over the side. He climbed down and found himself in a boat crammed with men, bouncing in the wake of the galley. He looked up to see the last Varangians come down, Luke not among them.

The lighterman shouted from the other end. 'Let loose!'

The men at the front pulled a rope. The lighter stayed where it was.

'Let loose!' he shouted again.

'It's stuck, sir! Must be snagged at the other end!'

Giovanni heard a shout from beyond the galley's stern. He saw the other lighter separate itself from the big ship with Zeno at its back pushing against a giant paddle to take it out of the wake. Immediately, the galley increased its speed, veering to the side. It was going off course.

The lighterman yelled: 'Which of you swims? Someone's got to climb the rope to pull it free.'

Giovanni saw the men look at each other. It was as he'd suspected.

'I'll cut it, sir,' shouted Peter.

'No! We'll spin. It has to be played out!'

Giovanni got to his feet. 'I'll go.'

The lighterman nodded. 'You'll be all right. Just hold on to the rope and we'll pull you in. Go!'

Giovanni turned but Peter of Norfolk was in front of him. 'No.'

Giovanni looked up at the giant. 'Do you swim, Peter?'

'Not you.'

Peter had his feet astride, keeping his balance between two benches. Giovanni pushed him hard and he fell back into the boat. Then Giovanni was on the rope, one leg hooked around it, pulling himself up to the rail. It was wet and slippery and the angle was steep. Spray was lashing his body and his leg was hitting the side of the galley and he felt the sting of salt in his palms. But he was nearly there.

Then he was. He climbed over the rail and dropped on to the rolling deck. The rope was jammed in a ball between two of the railings. He looked around for something to prise it free. Nothing. He kicked it, driving his heel into the knot to force it out. It didn't move.

He looked to the front of the ship and saw many lights much closer now. They came from stern lanterns and were rising and falling. But the galley was going off course with the boat still attached to its side. He backed away, then launched himself, feet first, at the rail.

There was a loud crack and it gave way before him. Giovanni

found himself in the air, splinters all around him. Then he was falling and the rope was escaping with the lighter, which was bucking and turning with the sudden release. He hit the water on his side and felt his shoulder move. A scalding pain ripped up his body and he screwed his eyes shut.

There was no question of swimming. Without the rope, the current was carrying him after the galley and he'd have to fight to keep his head above water. The sea was buffeting his shoulder and the agony was beyond bearing. He opened his eyes and saw the sky full of little flames.

He heard an explosion and turned his head to see the galley catch fire. It was headed straight for the harbour. But something was happening. The galley was pulling away from him and he was going sideways not forwards. He felt the current had become ten times stronger but it was beneath him, sucking him down.

A whirlpool.

He clamped his loose arm to his side with his good one and kicked hard, trying to propel himself away. But the current was too strong and now there was a roaring in his ears as if some monster from the deep wanted to swallow him whole.

He closed his eyes and kicked with all his strength. If he could just get himself free of the monster's jaws, he might live. But he was spinning and spinning and the circles were getting tighter and faster. He was going down.

'No!'

There was something on his collar pulling him away, something perhaps stronger than the monster. He looked behind him, sweeping the spray from his eyes.

It was Luke. He was next to him in the water, fighting the whirlpool with one hand, holding his collar in the other. Slowly,

110

slowly, they were moving away from the centre of the churning vortex. Giovanni used his last strength to kick and kick, ignoring the pain in his shoulder.

Then they were free, and Luke had his arm around Giovanni's chest and they were swimming towards the bank.

'Hold on!'

Giovanni ground his teeth to stop himself from crying out. The pain was worse than anything he'd ever experienced. He opened his eyes to see the galley ablaze and heading straight down the channel. There was an explosion as another canister ignited.

'Your shoulder!' Luke was blinking from the spray, looking down at Giovanni's arm. 'Is it loose?'

'Yes!'

'Shut your eyes, hold your breath!'

Luke took Giovanni's elbow and pushed and twisted it once, kicking to keep them afloat. A piercing pain shot through Giovanni's body and he cried out.

'There,' shouted Luke. 'Don't use it.'

The pain lessened but Giovanni felt sick from the shock. He took another deep breath. Luke's arm was beneath his chin and he could feel the muscle flex against his skin, wet hair scratching his cheek. The water was racing past: filling his eyes, his nose.

Luke's voice was in his ear. 'Hold on to me. I've got to let go of you!'

Giovanni hugged Luke's middle as he was released. Then he was in the air. Luke had grabbed a branch fallen across the water.

'Can you climb on to it? Use my shoulder.'

Giovanni pulled himself on to the branch and crawled his way to the bank. Luke followed and lay next to him, staring up at the stars. Neither of them could speak, their chests rising and falling, their breaths coming in rasps.

Luke laughed. 'We made it. We actually made it!' He turned to Giovanni and hugged him. 'You're a brave boy.'

They heard an explosion and sat up. The end of the channel was an inferno, the walls of the fortress lit up as if it was day. The fireship had struck the galleys and the flames were spreading from ship to ship. They could hear shouts of panic and the screams of the burnt. Men were jumping into the water.

Giovanni watched it all, the fire flickering in his eyes. Water ran down his cheeks and broke over a first growth of beard. He turned to find Luke staring at him. Was it water on his cheek or tears?

Luke wiped his face with his palms. He rose and swept a branch from his tunic. 'We need to find the others.'

He pulled Giovanni to his feet and together they stumbled over the rocks until they came to a path. The night was clear and the moon almost full but it was the fire in the harbour that lit their way. As they walked, Giovanni watched it play over the back of the man who'd saved his life.

They found the lighter half a mile further up the coastline, Marco at its stern, six of the Varangians holding it to the shore. The tide had turned and the boat was straining to be on its way.

Giovanni was leaning against Luke as they approached, his good arm round his shoulders. The Varangians helped him aboard and got in themselves. The current picked up the boat and it left the bank so fast that men fell back on their benches.

Peter's face was in front of Giovanni. 'Did you see it? A whole Venetian fleet destroyed!'

'I pushed you over.'

Luke laughed: 'I dare say worse has happened to him.' He turned back to Marco, who was working the rudder, his brow crossed with concentration. 'How long to Andros?'

'The current will last to the start of the straits,' he shouted. 'Then we'll hoist the sail. Four hours.'

Giovanni suddenly felt more tired than he'd ever felt. He lay back and began to drift into sleep. He forced his eyes open to find Luke staring at him as he had before. He looked sad but he was smiling.

'You're a brave boy,' he said quietly. 'I'm proud of you.'

CHAPTER ELEVEN

ROME, SPRING 1411

'Who is she?'

Luke was looking at a naked woman being scourged by Roman soldiers. Her face was gazing to heaven but was not unhappy. The papal secretary Poggio stood next to him, wilting; the day was hot and his robes heavy.

'St Agnes,' answered Poggio, his fingers loosening his collar. 'She was thirteen at the time, I believe.'

'And this one?' Luke had turned to another painting of a girl strapped to a spiked wheel. Her bare flesh was awash with blood but she had the same ecstatic look on her face.

'Ah, now that's St Catherine. The Holy Father has a particular affection for her. He'll stand and contemplate her for hours.'

Luke exchanged glances with Cosimo de' Medici. They were standing with Poggio outside the private apartment of Pope John XXIII, awaiting an audience. They'd been there some time.

'He's still in session?' asked Luke.

Poggio shrugged. 'Ask them.' He gestured to two guards playing dice outside the apartment doors.

Luke and Giovanni had arrived in Rome the evening before. They'd ridden up from Taranto, having taken ship to Italy from

Mistra. They were still bruised and exhausted from Negroponte and they'd slept their way across the Ionian Sea. Their sleep last night had been more broken.

Luke had not imagined Rome to be a city of such stench and destitution. It had once boasted a million citizens who took their leisure in marbled baths. Now grass grew in the forum and sheep grazed on the Palatine Hill beside headless gods. They'd ridden along the banks of the Tiber with cloths held to their faces. They'd circled the giant hulk of the Colosseum and found it a place of thieves and beggars. They'd come to Nero's Circus and seen prostitutes calling their trade from the steps of St Peter's Basilica, a stork's nest crowning the bell tower above. That night, they'd lain awake and listened to a city without law, the sounds of fights started suddenly in dark streets, of violence and despair.

Giovanni had finally fallen asleep with the coming of dawn and Luke had crept out alone to meet Cosimo. They'd break-fasted together and discussed how best to persuade Cossa to call the council. In the end they'd settled on bribery.

'It usually works with popes,' Cosimo had said as they'd left the inn.

Now they were waiting to see a pope who didn't seem in any hurry to receive them. There was the sound of hammering from a nearby room, then a curse. The palace was full of builders, painters and plasterers. Coming in, they'd passed men carrying marble tiles, statues and brocade from Bruges: luxury for the new Pope.

Poggio kept his voice low: 'I had hoped he'd become more restrained in office.'

'Does it matter so much provided he calls the council?' asked Cosimo. 'It will not only unite the Church, it will reform it. And he'll have to reform with it.'

Poggio shook his head solemnly. 'But I don't know that he wants to call a council any more. He certainly doesn't want to reform.'

Luke turned to Cosimo, frowning. 'Why do we need to risk a council that may work no better than Pisa did? What if it doesn't produce a single pope? What if it does, but he isn't Cossa?'

Cosimo shook his head. 'There's little risk. Cossa has the majority of cardinals behind him. He's created at least a dozen since becoming pope.' He glanced at Poggio. 'Isn't that so?'

Poggio nodded. 'It's the cardinals who vote and he has more than Benedict and Gregory combined.'

'So the prize is worth going for,' said Cosimo, turning back to Luke. 'The banking of a single pope who has the whole Christian world's obedience. Think of it.'

One of the giant doors opened slightly and a woman slithered through, crouched low. She ran past them, not looking to left or right. She had the dress of an abbess but not the age. Her wimple was askew.

One of the guards nodded to Poggio. They walked in and down corridors lined with bowls of herbs to catch draughts from the city outside. They found the Holy Father in his bedroom, reclining on a chair with soap on his face, his barber leaning over him. Far above, seraphim played amidst the clouds and a Virgin, circled by stars, looked down without disapproval. The air smelt of lavender.

'To allow a man so near your throat in Rome might seem optimistic,' said Cossa as they fell to their knees beside the chair, 'but the Pope must be shaved.' He extended his arm from beneath the towel for the Fisherman's Ring to be kissed. 'Have you heard what happened at Negroponte? A whole fleet destroyed, I hear.' He looked delighted. 'And Malatesta was there!'

Luke looked up. 'Malatesta?'

'Yes, Carlo Malatesta. He commanded the fleet for Venice. They say he nearly drowned.'

Luke glanced at Cosimo. It had been rumoured; now it was confirmed.

Poggio rose. 'There is the issue of the council to be discussed, Holy Father.'

'Ah yes, the council to make three popes into one and reform the Church,' said Pope John, turning his chin for the barber's attention. His eyes were closed. 'Rome, I think.'

Poggio nodded in a way that suggested the opposite. 'There are those who would have it outside Italy. They prefer Constance.'

Cossa opened his eyes. 'Constance? Who prefers Constance, Poggio?'

'The German kings,' said Cosimo. 'The heretic Jan Hus is inciting their people to rebel against the Church, telling them not to pay their tithes until it is reformed. They want a council in Germany to which Hus is invited.'

The Pope began to shake his head and thought better of it; the blade was at his throat. He frowned instead. 'A few German kings cannot dictate to the Pope.'

'But what of your bishops in Germany?' asked Cosimo quietly. 'Their flocks complain of being shorn too close to the skin, about the rising cost of reaching heaven. Jan Hus tells the people to ignore them and they love him for it.' He paused. 'The cry is general, Holy Father. The people want a single pope and they want reform. The council needs to happen soon.'

Cossa waved away the barber and applied the towel to his face. He sat up to face his visitors. 'Why have a council at all? It will only encourage dissent.' He signalled for the barber to leave. 'Anyway, I can't afford it.'

117

Cosimo glanced at Luke. He said: 'Holy Father, if you call the council you will win it. You have the vast majority of the cardinals behind you. You will lead a united Church.'

Cossa turned to him. 'And you will have a united Church's banking. Is that why you're here?'

Luke decided to speak. 'I am here to lend you money to pay for the council and, once you become the only pope, to lend you money thereafter.'

'And if I refuse?'

'Then,' said Luke, 'we will be unable to lend you money for anything.'

It was blunt and Cossa stared at Luke, then Cosimo for some time. He looked down to his slippered foot and traced tesserae on the floor. 'How do you know that the other two popes will attend?'

'The French King will make Benedict come from Avignon,' said Cosimo. 'As for Gregory at Rimini, we need to agree incentives to put in front of the Malatestas.' He glanced at Luke. 'Could you go to Rimini?' He paused, waiting for the assent. 'Ah, of course, Carlo was at Negroponte. But no one knows who sent the fireship.'

Luke considered this. How could they know?

'I'll go,' he said.

Three hours later, Luke and Giovanni were riding hard towards Rimini.

It was two hundred miles from Rome to Rimini and though the road was Roman and straight, there were mountains in the way. They reached Arezzo as the sun was setting. The city rose from the floodplain of the Arno River like a hand pointing to heaven, the cathedral its middle finger. They rode through ancient streets to a place that would feed them and their horses.

They lay down side by side in a room high in the inn with windows flung open for air. Above them were low beams etched by generations of restless guests and Luke heard the breathing of one unable to sleep. He turned his head to Giovanni.

'She may not be there,' he said quietly. 'Or she may be unavailable. You may be disappointed.'

Giovanni moved his head, the straw crackling. 'You married better than you could have hoped, didn't you? I just have to prove myself.'

'Which you'll do,' said Luke. 'I'll help you.' He looked back at the rafters and closed his eyes. 'Remember you start from a better place than me. Your father rules Chios and your mother's a princess from Trebizond.'

They were silent after that, Giovanni thinking of Cleope and Luke of how he might help his son. Fourteen was not too young to love. He'd not been much older when he'd first met Anna.

He thought back to his parting from her on the night of the fair. Murad had been taken shouting from the scene of his humiliation and they'd been left alone.

'Why not take Hilarion to Corinth?' she'd asked, her anger everywhere in her face. 'Did you know he thinks you don't love him as much as you love Giovanni?'

'He's told you this?'

'He doesn't have to. I'm his mother.'

The next morning, they rose early and rejoined the road to Rimini. The fields around were tall with wheat and had wide-hatted men at their sides waving flags to scare away the crows.

The road was full of dust and wagons carrying the last of the year's grain, birds hopping behind.

They rose into hills, then mountains with deep forests of pine and chestnut, coming down into valleys with orchards and vineyards. The people were happier, fatter, friendlier here, screened by nature's ramparts from Italy's violence. They were in Malatesta lands, the family's chequered coat of arms carved into fountains in village squares. They stopped for the night and fell asleep as soon as they lay down, too exhausted to talk.

The next day they saw the sea. It was evening and they stood on a low hill overlooking the city of Rimini, which sat between brown fields and blue water, fringed by beach. There was smoke rising from the fields and lines of fire where the stubble burnt. The air smelt of salt and cinders.

Giovanni asked: 'What do I say to her?'

Luke waved a fly away from his horse's ear, leaning forward to pat its neck. 'What does she say in her letters?'

'That she thinks about me.'

'And what have you said in yours?'

Giovanni had put his hand to his breast, feeling the fabric beneath. 'That I love her.'

'Ha! So you've said all there is to say.' Luke smiled at his son. 'From now on it's easy. Just be kind.'

Had he been kind to Anna? Luke kicked his horse and started down the road. 'Come on, we must get there before the gates close.'

They were expected. A messenger had been sent ahead and there was a welcome awaiting them. Pandolfo and Malatesta dei Sonnetti were standing in their palace courtyard, a chequered servant behind holding a tray of wine.

'From Chios,' said Pandolfo as they dismounted. He handed them both a cup, then lifted his. 'To popes and panders! I hear this one has work for them.'

Their horses were led away and they entered through big studded oak doors. They came into a second courtyard, enclosed by the five floors of the palace and open to the sky. Everything was supported by an arched colonnade that had busts on plinths in the spaces between. It was cool and dark and Luke saw Giovanni look around, then up. She wasn't there.

Malatesta dei Sonnetti had taken Luke by the arm. 'You have entered my home, which means good food and perhaps some song after it. I have borrowed the trombadori from the Albizzi for the summer.'

They began to climb the steps. Luke glanced up at the balcony. 'Your brother is away?'

Pandolfo was at his other side. 'He is recovering in the spa at Baden,' he said shortly. 'He was at Negroponte when the fireship struck. He got burnt.' He looked at Luke. 'You'd heard of this?'

Luke nodded. 'I'd heard. Was he hurt badly?'

Pandolfo grunted. 'He's a soldier and a Malatesta. We mend quickly.'

On the balcony they met ten men in hats who bowed low as they passed. Giovanni noticed paint on their hands.

'Artists,' said dei Sonnetti, without further explanation. They entered a big room with herringbone tiles and a lofty ceiling of painted beams. The windows were high in the walls and had heavy shutters on either side. There were coloured roundels in them that let in little light. A long table with majolica plates on stands ran down the centre, tapestried chairs on either side. At the end was a fireplace with a hood and a coat of arms on it. It looked like a giant mouth, the ironwork its teeth.

121

Dei Sonnetti pointed to a line of little trapdoors cut into the tiles beneath them. 'They let us see who has arrived and pour oil on to the ones we wish hadn't,' he said, stooping to lift one for Giovanni to see into the courtyard below. 'We are condottieri, so we have enemies.'

'But you are protected by your pope's blessing,' said Luke. 'Where does the Holy Father stay?'

'I have given him my palace,' said Pandolfo, putting his cup down on the table. 'Which is not convenient.'

Luke nodded. 'The world has too many popes,' he said. 'There's not enough space for them all.'

'A trinity,' agreed Pandolfo. 'An insult to the one above.'

'But', said Malatesta dei Sonnetti, 'the superfluous one is the scoundrel in Rome. He's making a laughing stock of the Church.'

'No,' said Luke. 'What is making your Church ridiculous is the existence of three popes. We need a council to make them one and reform the whole edifice. We need your pope to attend.'

'And you have a proposal?'

Luke had a proposal that he'd agreed with Cosimo and Cossa before leaving Rome. It involved the grant of certain papal lands and titles to the Malatestas. But such a discussion should have a limited audience. Luke asked: 'Is there someone who might show Giovanni the castle? One of your pages, perhaps?'

Perhaps a little bell had been rung, for, almost immediately, there was the sound of a door opening behind him. He turned.

Cleope was standing in the doorway. She was wearing a cotton gown without pattern that reached down to bare feet. Her hair was loose and finer than spun silk. Beside her stood a woman who looked like a childhood nurse: plump, bosomed

122

and secure; she wore a headscarf. Cleope was looking at Giovanni and smiling.

Luke saw that Giovanni was smiling back and that his hand had gone to the small piece of fabric next to his heart.

'Ah, Cleope,' said her father. 'Giovanni needs entertaining while we talk. Perhaps you can show him round the palace?' He nodded at the older woman. 'With Isabella, of course.'

Cleope's eyes hadn't left Giovanni's. 'It will be a pleasure, Father.'

Giovanni rose and went to the door; he followed Cleope through it and they walked in silence along the loggia until they came to stairs. They went up and along and up again and came to a door. Cleope opened it and they entered a room. Isabella stayed outside. Cleope closed the door, took his hand and turned.

'Your letters,' she said. 'I have them under my pillow. Always.'

Giovanni undid the top button of his doublet and brought out her kerchief. 'And I have this next to my heart. Always.'

He lifted her hand and kissed each of its fingers. They smelt of spring flowers. He looked around the room. It was as busy as the one below had been empty. There were *cassoni* – wedding chests – lining the sides, decorated with garlanded animals pulling chariots. On the walls was a mural of a columned loggia looking out over a garden, with parrots everywhere, flying, resting, opening their beaks to speak. There was a chair in the centre of the room and ten easels placed around it, each with a stool. A table stood to one side with small piles of coloured powder and the stuff for mixing. The air smelt of paint.

She let go of his hand and went to sit on the chair, arranging herself. She lifted her chin in pose, smiling. 'They are painting me,' she said.

'Why?'

'For churches. I am their Madonna.'

Giovanni walked behind the easels. Each held an image of her at a different stage of completion. In every one she was smiling.

'Are you paid to do it?' he asked.

She laughed. 'Perhaps my father is. He says it will help me be married.'

Giovanni frowned. Ten paintings of perfection. Ten suitors, all worthier than he, to consider them. He looked down. 'This one has stars.'

'Sometimes I am queen of the universe, sometimes of the manger. I am flexible.'

He went to a chest and sat and she came to join him. She put her head on his shoulder and he felt her hair against his cheek. He closed his eyes and breathed in.

'I'm told I must marry soon,' she murmured. 'It will be that or the convent.' She found his hand. 'What should we do?'

Luke opened his eyes. Her scent was all around him like her Madonna's stars. 'They'll say we're too young to make our own decisions,' he said. 'So we have to delay them and I have to prove myself worthy.' He kissed her hand again. 'The Protostrator will help.'

He felt her nod, her hair caressing his cheek like a zephyr. 'He looks like you.'

It had been said before and sometimes it pleased him. The Protostrator was a golden hero of Byzantium, a slayer of giants and dragons. But Marchese Longo was noble and kind and wise beyond measure. Sometimes he wanted to be like them both. He turned to her. 'We have to find a reason for delay. I want to marry you.'

She nodded again. Her chin fell to her breast so that he could see her eyelashes but not her eyes. She said: 'Three popes. The time is coming when a council will be called to replace them with just one.'

'What has that to do with us?' he asked.

She shrugged slightly, her hair catching light from the windows above. 'I don't know, but it might. I am niece to a man who might become pope.' She looked up at him. 'What the Malatestas choose to do will be important.' She paused and took his hand again. 'I may be part of it.'

Giovanni knew that the very subject was being discussed downstairs. 'Should we rejoin them?' he asked.

She nodded and rose, still holding his hand. They left the room and joined Isabella outside. Cleope stopped to kiss her lightly on the forehead. 'Thank you.'

The Malatestas finally agreed to bring their pope to the church council to be held in Constance, but it took two weeks to persuade them. Distracted by the negotiation, the Malatesta dei Sonnetti didn't notice that his daughter spent her time riding with Giovanni, and, some way behind, Isabella.

They rode on the long beach outside the city walls where the sand was soft beneath their horses' hooves and some measure of breeze came in from the sea. They'd rest next to a summer house, built by a former Malatesta among the grassy dunes. There they'd talk while Isabella sewed.

The days were blessed with a sun that rose over the sea and stayed unblemished until it went down behind the mountains to the west. They were days of white: white sand, white surf, white fishing boats all in a row. And every day Cleope dressed in white lawn and bent low on her white palfrey as she galloped in front of Giovanni, her hair thrown out behind her like salt.

125

What did they talk about? Her life had been less eventful than his but he found joy in its every moment. Most of all, he loved her curiosity.

'We live in beautiful times,' she said once. 'This Rinascimento has come to Rimini and suddenly my father and uncles want to broaden everyone's minds. They find me tutors who teach Aristotle and Cicero.' She paused. 'My poor mother had to learn St Augustine of Hippo.'

She was lying on her back outside the summer house, her head in Isabella's lap. Luke was on his front, looking through the dunes at the fishing boats scattered across a sea laced with tiny surf. He'd been trying to count their sails.

He said: 'I have been taught by Plethon.'

She looked at him, her eyes wide. 'Plethon? My father admires him. What is he like?'

Giovanni considered this. In truth, he'd spent more time over the past year with Luke than Plethon. But it was Plethon she admired. 'He's quite short, quite fat and wears a toga. Always.'

She laughed. 'I meant his *mind*, Giovanni. What's that like?'

'Dangerous,' he said, rolling on to his back. 'He thinks he's Plato but he's more dangerous than Plato. He doesn't believe in God and he wants Mistra to return to the laws of Sparta.'

'Where women were quite free, I've heard,' she said, running sand through her fingers. 'Perhaps it's not such a bad idea. For all this Rinascimento, I don't feel very free. I will be married to someone old and important to my family.' She looked up at her nurse. 'Isn't that right, Isabella?'

'Very probably,' said the woman, not missing a stitch. 'We should return.'

126

Luke was waiting as Giovanni entered the room they shared. He was lying on the bed, his hands behind his head. 'Where have you been?' he asked.

'Riding on the beach with Cleope. Don't worry, the nurse was there.'

'I don't worry. How are you getting on?'

Giovanni lay down next to his father on the bed. 'We love each other.'

Luke smiled. 'I know that already. Well, I have news. The negotiations are complete.'

Giovanni sat up. 'So we must leave?'

'Yes, we must leave. I must go to Edirne. The Ottomans' war may be over. Suleyman has agreed to some sort of truce and Mehmed wants me there to make sure it happens.'

Giovanni didn't look much pleased by the news.

'Don't you want to know what I've agreed with the Malatestas?'

The boy recovered himself. 'Of course.'

'Well, first there's been the grant to Gregory of certain lands from the papal estates if Cossa becomes sole pope. Then there's the papal debt. The Malatestas want a share in it.'

'Alongside the Magoris and Medici Banks?'

'Yes. They want to become rich after all. Oh, and there's another thing. They want Plethon to come to Rimini after Constance to teach. I said you'd go and persuade him.'

'And could I come back with him?'

'Possibly.'

CHAPTER TWELVE

EDIRNE, SPRING 1411

Luke and Giovanni took ship from Rimini and arrived back at Patras a week later to find the Varangian Company waiting for them. Giovanni took the road south to Mistra with two of them for escort, while Luke led the rest north to Edirne. On the way, Matthew described what had happened.

'Zoe seems to have brokered the agreement with Bedreddin,' he said. 'Suleyman is to take comfortable retirement in Constantinople. He knows he's lost the war.'

'And Manuel has agreed?'

'Mehmed has written to the Emperor. If Suleyman's surrender makes him sultan, there's no more threat to Byzantium. He'll be a good ally.'

'And who are we to meet now?'

'Musa and Bedreddin at a village outside Edirne. Suleyman's general Evrenos Bey is to bring Suleyman. With Zoe.'

Zoe.

He'd last seen Zoe Mamonas nine years ago on a bridge on the road to Constantinople. She'd been Tamerlane's creature then, seductress of the most dangerous man on earth. She'd tamed him with her lips, her body; but they'd been no match for the grief he'd felt for an heir who'd died before his time. So she'd disappeared into the ranks of the Mongols and Tamerlane had let her go, knowing, perhaps, that some people were just meant to survive.

It was early and the day's energy was yet to ignite. They had just crossed a river by a bridge that had maidenhair sprung between its stones and mist on the water below. The road ahead was bordered by hedgerows noisy with bees while lizards scuttled between the horses' feet. The landscape was all grass and poppy and, in the distance, cistus burst like surf over a sea of leaf. The air was filled with the smell of garlic and thyme and Luke should have been happy to be alive on such a day. The plan to set Musa against Suleyman had gone better than he could have ever expected.

He turned in his saddle to look at the men behind. Even on horseback, the Varangian Company had the swagger of men accustomed to winning battles. They had fought Suleyman and then Venice and they'd won. They laughed as they rode, knowing that they'd soon be on their way to new employment in Italy.

Matthew was watching Luke's smile. 'We've not lost a single man,' he said. 'Not one.'

Luke nodded. 'And not a single battle either, I've heard. Mehmed will be delighted. You've won the war for him.'

'What about Musa? Hasn't it been his war as well?'

Luke pondered this. It had certainly been Musa's war but Mehmed would be the victor. The meeting they were going to would confirm it. Mehmed would be the next sultan, which meant peace for the Empire. At least for now.

He thought of Murad's words: *No wall will save you once I come to rule.*

129

But the Hexamilion Wall would be finished well before that, and they'd have a navy. The Magoris Bank was awash with money that Cosimo had taken to Rome to put into the soundest investment in the world: the papacy.

And there had been more good news to greet him at Corinth: a letter at last from China. Nikolas was mending fast and he and Shulen had re-established trade with the Ming. Chen Cheng and Admiral Zheng had returned to China and the mandarin Min Qing had been arrested. Soon there would be a ship laden with gold on its way.

So why do I feel uneasy?

A week later, they arrived at a village as the first heat of the day began to prick at Luke's collar. He'd changed into his protostrator dress but his dragon sword lay in his lap. He looked down at the eyes, the open mouth, the scaled neck. Siward's sword. Just in case.

The Varangian Company had been joined by Yakub and a hundred of his gazis, who were to escort Suleyman to Constantinople. Yakub rode on one side of Luke, Matthew the other.

Luke looked around him. The village was full of people who'd come out to stare. They were riding up a single street and there was a little square at the end with a well and a chestnut tree above it. A small mosque stood on one side; made of wood, its minaret was a single trunk of oak with a platform at the top. A ladder leant against it. Two men on horseback were waiting for them.

Musa and Bedreddin.

Luke had last seen Musa on the field of Nicopolis. That was fifteen years ago but he'd changed little: the unformed face, the flabby lips, the angry eyes that stared out between an aventail of golden mail. Beside him stood Bedreddin.

Luke came to a halt, Yakub beside him. Their little army drew up on opposite sides of the square, the gazis in front of the mosque.

Yakub made no greeting. His loyalty was to Mehmed, not Musa, and he considered Bedreddin a dangerous revolutionary. He said: 'We have brought the guard as agreed.' He looked around him. 'Where is Evrenos Bey?'

Musa pointed. 'Coming. That's him there.'

Luke and Yakub turned to see a man riding towards them in a cloud of dust. Dogs were running and barking by his side. He drew up, his horse turning on the rein. He was dressed as an Ottoman general and had tall plumes erupting from his helmet. Luke had heard much about this man, who'd been born Christian but converted to Islam. They said that Ankara was the only battle he'd ever lost and, after it, he'd been responsible for getting Suleyman and the army over to Thrace. He was a man of honour.

Evrenos Bey bowed stiffly to Musa, ignored Bedreddin and nodded to Luke. He studied Yakub for a while before nodding again. Yakub had been the reason Bayezid had lost Ankara. It had been the gazi's change of side that had turned the battle. He looked back to Musa. 'Suleyman is on his way. She is with him.'

It had all gone to plan. Suleyman had been persuaded to leave Edirne. Musa's army was at its walls and Suleyman's own ready to surrender. He would go into gilded exile in Constantinople and could smoke opium until he died. It was over.

Evrenos Bey spoke to Musa. 'It is as we agreed? Suleyman goes and Mehmed becomes sultan?'

Musa shifted in his saddle, waving away a fly. 'As we agreed, general. My brother becomes sultan. You have my word.'

Evrenos Bey looked at Luke. 'And your emperor has agreed to this?'

Luke nodded. 'Manuel will be at the city gates to receive Suleyman.'

The general grunted. He'd been loyal to a prince who'd become someone no longer worthy of loyalty. He hated what he did but his empire needed another brother to lead it. He looked again at Musa.

'What will you do now?' he asked.

The Prince shrugged. 'As my brother commands.'

Evrenos Bey studied him for several moments. He glanced at Yakub, then Luke. 'Very well. I will cross to Anatolia to tell Mehmed how it is.'

He bowed and rode away and the party watched him go in silence. Evrenos Bey was that rarest of creatures: a man of fervent faith yet cold judgement. He and Zoe had persuaded Suleyman together, helping him up to the highest tower in the palace to see the army outside the walls for himself. Evrenos Bey had pointed out the regiments that had already defected. Now Zoe was bringing Suleyman to the village.

Luke watched the street through the brackets of Eskalon's ears. Some of Musa's Kapikulu were pushing villagers inside their homes; Suleyman would not want his humiliation to be seen by any living thing. Soon the street was quiet.

Silence.

Luke narrowed his eyes to see. The sun was hot now and there were no clouds to relieve its glare. A dog strolled to the middle of the street and looked around without hurry. It stared at them and yawned and lay down. Flies came and it rolled over. Luke tightened his grip on his sword. It was wet.

There was the sound of hooves, the jangle of harness. Then dust. The dog got up. Into the street rode a troop of sipahi cavalry, pennants on their lances, armour flashing in the sunlight. They rode in tight formation, knee to knee, so that it was hard to see what was behind them. They came into the square at the gallop and fanned out to left and right in perfect order. At their end, two figures came on together.

The pair rode up and stopped.

Suleyman looked as if he'd just risen. He wore a tunic with half its buttons undone and his long hair was in disarray. His face was pallid, his beard uncombed, and there were deep shadows beneath his bloodshot eyes.

Luke was staring at Zoe. She'd hardly changed. He saw the same predatory beauty, the hair black as panther-pelt, the pride that made her lift her head to the perfect angle to see men as they should be seen. She looked back at him, something unreadable in her eyes.

'You are a banker, I hear.'

He dipped his head. 'It is a modest affair beside your family's, but we have to start somewhere.'

'The Medici are hardly "somewhere". They tell me you share the Pope's banking with them. That was clever.'

Musa coughed and they looked over to him. He was gazing at Suleyman. 'What have you become, brother?' he asked. 'Caligula? Is your horse to be made vizier?'

Zoe's hand went to Suleyman's arm. She looked at Musa. 'Lord, is it necessary?'

She needn't have worried. It seemed that it would take a lot to provoke Suleyman. He sat slumped in his saddle, staring down at his hands. He might not even have heard.

133

But Musa continued: 'It has not been hard to defeat you, brother. Your generals despise you and your men hate you.' He paused. 'They want a Sword of Islam to lead them at last.'

Yakub said: 'Who is to be Mehmed, your brother. He is wise.'

'And I'm not?' Musa had reddened. 'Am I not wise?'

Yakub paused before answering. 'In some things, yes. In others, less so.'

Musa put his hand on his sword. He was glaring at Yakub. His voice dropped to a whisper. 'You forget yourself, emir.'

Bedreddin raised his hand. 'It is agreed that Mehmed is to be sultan. We have fought only for him.'

Zoe turned back to Luke. 'Prince Suleyman wishes to leave for Constantinople without delay. Where is his escort?'

'My gazis will escort him,' replied Yakub.

'You do not bring your Varangians?' Zoe spoke only to Luke.

Luke shook his head. 'They go to Italy.'

Luke should have felt relieved as he rode towards the coast, Matthew beside him. Suleyman had been defeated and Constantinople spared. Mehmed would be a good friend to the Empire and the trade route to China would be in friendly hands. So why did he feel uneasy?

He wished he'd been able to supply the Varangians for Suleyman's escort, to go with them himself. But Cosimo had been categoric: the company was needed in Italy. The new Pope was making enemies and Braccio needed help.

Matthew was asking him a question. He had to repeat it. 'I was wondering what is to happen in Italy?'

Luke rallied his thoughts. 'You'll be fighting for Pope John, under the command of Braccio da Montone. He's good.'

'And the pay? The men will want to know.'

'You'll be paid by Florence and they're generous. Fifteen florins a lance, and your food at cost.'

Matthew whistled through his teeth. 'It's magnificent.'

'Yes, but there'll be extra expenses now. We'll need to employ a surgeon, barber, blacksmith and *collaterali* to oversee everything. They don't come cheap.'

'What about plunder?'

'Everything portable in enemy territory. The captain takes a quarter-share.'

They rode on in silence, Matthew doing some multiplication. Nikolas would not be the only Varangian to grow rich. He said: 'I don't understand why we must do banking as well. Soldiering and trade will give us the money we need.'

Luke turned. 'What's so bad about banking?'

'Well, for a start it diverts you from Mistra where you should be.' Matthew leant in towards his friend. 'And it means we're supporting a reptile like Cossa, which can't be right.'

Luke considered this. Was he diverted from Mistra? Or was he, perhaps, escaping from it? Did he even need to be here? Matthew could easily have done what he was doing now.

The unease stayed with him. It clung to him despite the sunshine and companionship of a man he loved. He thought suddenly about Musa. He was agreeing to all this too easily. Luke stopped his horse suddenly. 'We must go back.'

Matthew reined in ahead of him. 'Back? Back where?'

'To Suleyman. Something's wrong.'

Matthew frowned. 'He'll be halfway to Constantinople by now.'

But Luke was already turning his horse. 'It doesn't matter. We have to go back.'

They rode as fast as they were able to ride. They returned to the village to find it empty of soldiers. They galloped through, ignoring the dogs and the surprised looks of people who thought they'd seen the last of giants for the day. The sun beat down and their horses panted with the effort of carrying them. Luke wanted to go faster. 'I'm going on ahead,' he shouted over his shoulder.

Luke kicked and his horse leapt forward. He whispered into the animal's ear the words he knew would work best. They joined a road that was wide and straight and empty of travellers. He felt the rush of wind against his cheek. Without the worry of what might lie ahead, he could have felt joy.

He looked behind him and saw nothing on the road. He was far ahead of the others and putting more distance between them with every mile. He bent low over his horse's neck and loosened the reins. It would do what he'd asked of it, would find its own perfect rhythm to give it the speed that he'd said he wanted. Its ears lay flat against a head that rose and fell with the motion of its hooves.

They were coming to a defile, wooded on both sides. There were birds circling above. Big birds. Black birds.

He kicked again.

There were shapes on the road ahead. Bodies, lots of them. Some of the birds stood beside them, their heads bent. They took to the sky as Luke approached, wings flapping, things in their beaks. Luke felt sick.

He rode up and leapt to the ground. Around him was Suleyman's escort. The gazis lay at awkward angles, some with limbs broken by the fall. The arrows were buried deep, which meant that they'd been fired at close range. Luke knelt next to the gazi nearest to him. The man had his eyes open, surprised, a shaft in his throat. Luke heard a shout and looked up. A man was walking towards him. He rose and put his hand up to the sun.

Yakub. Thank God.

'What happened?' he asked. He knew what had happened.

'It was planned,' said Yakub, his voice cracked. He had dirt on his head and dried blood on his cheek. He stopped and looked around him at the bodies. 'Musa's men ambushed us,' he said, wiping blood from his lips. 'They couldn't miss.'

'Where's Suleyman?'

'Taken away.' He spat. 'He'll be put to the bowstring.'

Luke nodded. 'And Zoe?'

Yakub bent down to tighten a bandage on his leg. 'She left with Musa. She must have made herself part of the bargain.'

'But why did they let you live?'

Yakub straightened. 'To take a message back to Mehmed,' he said quietly. 'Musa has declared himself sultan. He is going to march on Constantinople.'

PART TWO

ENEMY AT THE GATES

CHAPTER THIRTEEN

CONSTANTINOPLE, SPRING 1413

Plethon stood next to the engineer Benedo Barbi in the audience hall of the Blachernae Palace where, once, emperors had elevated themselves on thrones and mechanical lions roared. Barbi was wishing they still did.

The two men had arrived at Constantinople that morning; Plethon from Mistra and Barbi from the new Hexamilion Wall being built at the Isthmus of Corinth. They'd both sailed from Monemvasia.

The palace stood on one of the city's seven hills with views over the siege works. Musa's army had been there for two years now and had made attempt after attempt to take the walls. But none had succeeded because the walls were the greatest in the world. And Musa had no cannon.

But now things had got worse for Constantinople. The plague had come.

Plethon heard the doors open behind them. He turned to see Emperor Manuel enter with his empress on his arm. He watched Helena Dragaš detach herself and come up to them, thanking each in turn. Both of them had, in their different ways, helped save Constantinople in recent years.

141

'I'm sorry to bring you here,' she said. 'The plague hadn't struck when we asked you to come.'

Plethon saw the deep lines etched beneath her eyes. This was an empress who hadn't slept for some time. She gestured to chairs. 'Let's sit. The palace is too big and we walk a mile from room to room.' She turned to Barbi. 'Perhaps you can invent something to carry us?'

The engineer smiled. The last time he'd visited the city, he'd been carried in through the Turkish blockade in a submarine of his own design. This time, there was no blockade. Musa's power was on land and ships were able to arrive and leave at will. One had brought the plague.

'Do the Turks know?' asked Plethon, smoothing his toga to his knees.

Manuel shook his head. 'They're too busy praying to notice that the men have gone from our walls,' he said. 'This army is different from the last. It's full of fanatics like Bedreddin: Bektashi dervishes whipping the bashibozouks into a frenzy of faith. Suleyman needed cannon to break our walls. Musa's army can now climb in over the bodies of martyrs, with no one to stop them.' He shook his head. 'How did he die?'

'Suleyman? Killed by Musa himself. The bowstring, I heard. Luke should have brought him to Constantinople himself.'

'And Venice?' asked Manuel. 'We hoped Negroponte might dissuade them from any designs on Mistra, but we hear there's been an incident.'

There had. The week before, a Venetian merchantman had reported being stopped and boarded by a Byzantine galley out of Monemvasia. The Doge had protested in the strongest terms.

'It never happened,' said Plethon. 'None of our few galleys was anywhere near there.'

Manuel nodded. 'But such lies start wars. Which is what Venice seems to want.'

'Which is what she'll continue to want until Musa is defeated,' said the philosopher. 'They worry he'll take Mistra.'

'And the wall? How does Luke's wall progress?' asked the Empress. 'We hear it's impressive already.'

Plethon sipped wine. 'Impressive but half-built. But we're working day and night.'

'You?' Helena Dragaš had raised an eyebrow, smiling.

'Well . . .'

The doors opened and a servant came in carrying a tray with wine on it. Helena Dragaš intercepted him and served the men herself.

'All of which', she said as she poured into Plethon's cup, wiping a drip from its rim and straightening, 'would matter less if we didn't have the plague here in Constantinople. People are dying by the hundred and men won't go out to the walls when their families are in danger.'

'And those that can are fleeing the city,' said the Emperor. 'Every day, more ships carry the rich away to Mistra.'

'Why don't you stop them?' asked Plethon. He thought of the building site that was Mistra and the Magoris Bank's thriving deposits.

'Because they'll leave anyway. The rich always find a way.' He shrugged. 'Anyway, the poor deserve better leaders. Let them go.'

'And Luke?' asked Barbi. 'Should you not recall him too?'

Manuel shook his head. He drank wine and studied the side of his cup. So much in the palace wasn't gold these days. 'Luke is better off where he is: in Belgrade trying to put together a new alliance. He is meeting the Kings of Serbia and Wallachia.'

Plethon nodded. He said: 'We need something more immediate.'

They sat in silence pondering their options. It all looked very bleak. Then Barbi rose and walked over to the window. He stood there looking out for a time before speaking.

'I have an idea,' he said.

In Venice, the night was warm and Pavlos Mamonas was sitting alone in the office above his fondaco on the island of Murano, preparing to write a letter. There was a light breeze coming in from the lagoon and he'd opened the window over his desk to receive it. Through it he could see the moon looking down over its silver causeway and, above it, a constellation of stars. He tried to remember its name.

Apart from the moon and stars, there were no lights out there, just the occasional cry of waterfowl or warning shout from a lighter. They should be carrying lanterns at their bows, he thought, but the mist rising from the water was shielding all but sound. He heard the bell of Santa Maria e San Donato across the island. It chimed eleven times, each hour joining the next, echoing across the infinite melancholy of this soggy lagoon.

Pavlos Mamonas's gaze settled on the glass in the mullioned window. He seemed to make fortunes as easily as others lost them. He'd bought this factory in Murano and now the world wanted glass for their windows rather than horn, and spectacles to help them see it. And his bank was now the biggest in Venice.

Why then, with the world at his slippered feet, was he writing this letter?

He looked around the room. The wall behind him was covered by a map of the world, given to him by monks of the San Michele monastery nearby. The monks were famous for their maps. The Portuguese caravels were said to carry them as they inched their way down Africa. He hoped so, for he had money invested in them too. The map was lit by candles beneath and had little flags on every country that took his factory's glass. The flags threw tiny shadows.

His eyes settled on England, where he'd never been. That island had mists too, they said. Mists and giants who became Varangians. He frowned, lifting the pen to rest its feather against his brow.

Luke Magoris.

Somehow, it all came down to Luke Magoris. Everything bad that had happened to him over these past twenty years came down to Luke Magoris. Damian's death, Zoe's blame, his own wretched, miserable solitude. It all came down to one man, who was now Protostrator of Mistra.

He turned back to the window, dipped the pen in ink and began to write. The letter was to Zoe and it would be his last. He'd written to his daughter countless times over the years and received not a single reply. He didn't know if she'd even read them. He hoped she'd read this one. He reread its final line.

The Serenissima has pardoned you at last. You are free to return and run our empire.

He paused to let the ink dry. She'd no longer be obliged to seek sanctuary with that viper Musa. He smiled.

He sealed the letter and put it into a tray from where it would be collected the next morning. He rose and put on the doublet that hung over his chair. He picked up a candle, walked slowly to the door and descended the staircase to the factory below.

All was quiet. The big room was dark and full of indistinct shapes, the only light coming from the shuttered furnaces that never went out. That's why we're here, he thought: we moved from Venice to this island to prevent fires, yet with a craft so valuable that no glass-maker could leave the Serenissima to work abroad. The glow fell on tools leaning against the walls, the *borselle* – pliers – the *canna da soffio* for blowing the glass, the clippers for cutting it. The air smelt of potash and saltwort and something else that caught in his throat. He found himself sweating.

He passed piles of quartz pebbles, taken from the lagoon, that would be ground into a fine sand and put with soda ash from the Levant. He passed shelves with glassware on them, their colours vague. There were vases that were ruby red, black obsidianus bowls, enamelled glass pewters. He stopped to look at a jug, lifting it and turning it in the soft light. Aquamarine. What was the compound? Was it copper and cobalt? He frowned and put the jug back.

It doesn't matter now.

He came to a shelf with small glass jars in a row, each one labelled. Here were the compounds. He looked along them until he found the one he wanted, the one that removed the bubbles in the glass. The one that would remove him.

Arsenic.

A week later, Zoe was lying in a tent being massaged by a eunuch who seemed to be making her bruises worse. On the table beside her was an unopened letter that had arrived from Venice by courier. It was from her father. She was on her front and the smell of healing lotions was all around her.

Outside the tent were fifty thousand unwashed soldiers preparing for evening prayers. They'd be spreading their rugs out on the ground for the *maghrib* as far as the eye could see, taking their cue from a man kneeling on a podium to their front.

Bedreddin, the Sufi mystic. Bedreddin, the friend of the

dispossessed. Bedreddin, who exhorted his followers to share their land and withhold their taxes. What did he say?

All things must be shared except the lips of the Beloved.

What nonsense. Jesus had said the same before popes needed palaces.

But Bedreddin's influence over Musa was real. She just wished he'd use it to bring the Prince to a gentler part of Islam. Their last coupling had been as bad as the others. He was cruel as only a hater of women could be; and he was little more than a boy. She'd tried to teach him but he'd hated her for trying. Now she had the bruises and he the shame.

She had converted to Islam at his command, making the *shahadah* in that very tent, closing her eyes and affirming that there is only one God and Muhammad His last and final messenger. Bedreddin, watching her, had not believed it. But it had been his condition for allowing Musa to defile himself with her body. Now she saw the world outside through a veil and felt loathing for a creed that denied sun to her face.

She waved away the eunuch and rose from the bed. The evening was warm and, looking down at her body, she could see a light film of perspiration above the bruises. In the light of the torches, her skin was the colour of honey, made darker where he'd hurt her. She was nearly forty but her breasts were firm and her face uncensored by lines. She might have been Musa's mother if she weren't his lover. Perhaps that was why he hurt her.

She looked towards the letter. Another from her father. Would she even bother to read it? Later. It might contain news she wanted to hear.

The prayers outside had begun, a deep murmur of sound that rose up from the earth like a choir from the underworld. Five times a day she heard it, and every time was worse. She crossed to the tent door and pulled back the flap. The sun was creeping down the walls of Constantinople, turning ochre to black. There was the glint of armour as it reached the outer walls. Not many.

She'd guessed that something was wrong inside the city. She'd seen the spearheads on the walls get fewer by the day, seen the ships sail south into the Propontis flying the flag of quarantine. It could mean only one thing.

Plague.

She'd not mentioned her suspicions to anyone. She hardly cared any more who won this war. It didn't seem likely to be Mehmed. She'd heard he was stuck in Anatolia with no ships to ferry him across to Europe. No, let Musa's army finally break the walls that night as was planned. Let them enter a plague-stricken city. It would send Bedreddin's fanatics to Allah's bosom all the quicker. She hoped the Sufi fraud would catch a nasty strain himself.

She turned and went back into the tent, dressed and veiled herself, and walked back to the door. Looking out, she could see the podium with Musa and Bedreddin on it, side by side in prayer. There were flags all around it, huge things that caught the breeze coming in from the Propontis. Osman had had the dream of a crescent moon stretched from pole to pole across the earth. Now it was on his flags beside a five-pointed star: one for each Pillar of Islam.

Looking towards Constantinople, she could see the dark scar of the trenches running from sea to sea, empty of men now the attack was to begin. She'd seen this ground mutilated by siege works for twenty years. She'd seen mines dug, palisades erected, engines dragged forward again and again. But this siege was stranger and more disordered than the others, its army full of wild men from Anatolia, armed but not paid, who'd come to spread jihad and earn what they could from plunder. They were fearless in the attack and merciless when they got there. God help the people of Constantinople tonight; they'd be better off with the plague.

She heard a dull thud, then another. They came from the walls of the city. They were sounds she recognised: catapults being released. She looked up. The sky was dotted with tiny black shapes that rose high, high into the night. Then they seemed to hover. Other shapes opened above them as they fell towards this army at prayer. She narrowed her eyes to see better. The sky was full of little boxes floating down to them beneath parachutes. She gazed up in wonder, shaking her head slowly. Whatever they were, the soldiers went on praying, their faces to the ground. Suddenly she knew what was in them. She smiled.

Very clever.

Down they came, down to meet a landscape packed with men shoulder to shoulder; men so lost in their communion with Allah that they'd not see them until it was too late. On, on they came, swaying a little in the breeze, perfectly silent in their descent.

The first one landed. Fascinated, Zoe saw a man turn, his eyes wide with horror as the box fell open and a dozen rats exploded across the backs of the faithful. Another landed, then another. Men were sitting up now, some standing. Some were shouting. There was a scream. The boxes were landing every moment and the rats were everywhere, running, biting, bringing their fleas wherever they went.

Prayer turned to panic. Men were standing everywhere now, beating their clothes, pushing their neighbours away. Plague had come from heaven to infect them. Musa and Bedreddin were standing on their podium. A box had landed beside the Prince and he was trying to stamp on an animal. Bedreddin was shouting, holding the Koran aloft, jabbing it with his finger.

Zoe stood at the door of her tent and saw it all. She smiled. Then she began to laugh, softly at first, then louder. It was genius, pure genius, and so, so fitting. She might get the plague. She didn't care.

She turned and walked over to the letter.

CHAPTER FOURTEEN

VENICE, SUMMER 1413

A month later, Zoe came to Venice.

The letter she'd received outside Constantinople contained the last testament of her father and a pardon, signed by the Doge. She'd read the testament briefly without shedding a tear, then read the pardon with pure joy. She'd left Musa's army by the first horse she found, turning only once to smile at an army chased by rats.

She took ship to the southern tip of Italy and travelled up its coastline, savouring the sweetness of freedom and summer. The first of the harvest was being gathered in the fields and the air was full of husks that caught in her throat and hair. At Bari she stopped to buy a hat, a maid called Veronica and good horses for them both. She considered hiring guards as well but bought a crossbow instead.

When at last they reached Venice, she went straight to the Doge's palace to make her reverences. He was busy, so she returned the next day. He was busy again.

So, since her pardon seemed to exist in the shadows between the acknowledged and less so, she decided to seek out the people who thrived in those shadows: the city's courtesans. If

151

she wasn't welcome at Venice's palaces, she'd find her entertainment elsewhere. The advantage, of course, was that the cortigiane oneste knew everything that went on in Venice and, indeed, all of Italy.

On a warm evening, she took a gondola from the Mamonas palace to the waterside home of Alessandra Viega, Venice's greatest courtesan. The gondola had the black Mamonas castle on its side and a rich awning at its stern where Zoe reclined amidst cushioned silk and scent, her maid opposite her and a lutenist by her side. The awning's sides were raised for she wanted to be seen.

The courtesan's house was near the Rialto and more theatre than home. Its hall was a riot of frescoed gods and goddesses in playful coition amidst the clouds, and the stairs up to the boudoir were garlanded at their rails. Veronica sat on a chair at their bottom while Zoe went up.

Alessandra rose as she entered. The courtesan was in her thirties with good teeth and skin and a beauty softened by the plumpness of age and gentle living. She was said to have three patrons, one of whom was a Grimani. She wanted for very little.

As Zoe entered, Alessandra embraced her. 'An honour,' she said.

Zoe was only fleetingly bemused. Of course. She'd tamed a Mongol emperor and two Ottoman princes and, to Alessandra Viega, she was an artist.

They sat side by side on the couch and took wine from a boy Tartar of striking looks. Alessandra held his hand as he poured.

'So the Doge won't see you,' she said, lying back against cushions. 'Steno is a cautious man.'

'Am I that dangerous?' asked Zoe, also leaning back. 'I'm pardoned for Tamerlane, after all.'

Alessandra Viega gave a little shrug. 'You nearly brought him to Constantinople's walls. People remember.'

Zoe looked into her wine. 'Can you help me?'

The courtesan smiled. 'Well, that depends on whether you come to Venice as competitor or banker. You are beautiful.'

'I am nearly forty,' said Zoe, 'and tired of men. I am in Venice to take over my father's bank.'

Alessandra leant forward and put her glass down on a little table to their front. 'Good, because there are too many courtesans in Venice already. Did you know we number one in ten of the women?'

'But most are the *cortigiane di lume*. There are few like you.'

Alessandra nodded. 'But many aspire. The life of an educated woman of Venice is a dull one. As a *cortigiana onesta* you have the ear of powerful men.'

'Which is why I'm here,' said Zoe. 'To learn how things are run. Perhaps then I can persuade the Doge to see me.'

So Alessandra told her. They sat long into the night talking and sipping wine and Zoe learnt first that Venice was still in mourning for its Negroponte fleet.

'The captain was Carlo Malatesta of Rimini,' Alessandra told her. 'He was nearly drowned.'

'And do they know who did it?'

The courtesan shook her head. 'Either the Turks or the Greeks.'

Zoe snorted. 'It was the Varangians. The Turks would never have managed such a thing.'

Zoe learnt that Venice was undecided as to whom to support in the war between Bayezid's sons. She was inclined to remain neutral, quite liking the spectacle of the Ottomans destroying each other. But she was worried about where Musa might go next.

'And Venice should be,' said Zoe. 'I left a siege in disarray. Musa may turn on Mistra now.'

As to the papacy, Venice backed Pope Gregory in Rimini but wanted, above all, a single pontiff who'd renew her vital monopoly of trade with Alexandria. But the Doge was concerned about who might emerge victorious from the impending council at Constance. Baldassare Cossa seemed to have developed links to Genoese Chios.

'The Magoris Bank has interests on Chios, doesn't it?' asked Alessandra. 'And Chios is Genoese.' She paused. 'This Pope spends more than any before him. The Medici and Magoris Banks are getting a good return. Venice is jealous, and she certainly doesn't want Mistra to get rich enough to defend itself.'

Finally, as the dawn poked fingertips through the shutters and the first cries of the lightermen rose from the canal outside, they drank chocolate and talked about influence. Alessandra Viega, who had the ear of most men of influence inside the republic and many without, had seen the need for Zoe to exert hers.

'For influence, you need information,' she said, pouring the last of the chocolate for them both. 'For information you need spies. Courtesans are the best spies and the best are in Venice. I will tell you which ones to put on your payroll.'

She drank, put down the cup and rose. She stretched. 'Now we should go to bed. But one last thing I will tell you before you go. The members of the Grand Council are rich, but most are also in debt, including the Doge. You should look through your ledgers.

So the next morning, Zoe went to her bank and looked through her ledgers to learn which of the Grand Council were in debt to her. She met all of the courtesans on Alessandra's list and agreed terms for their services. Then she had an idea.

She started to call in those debts, first from the nobles who'd scorned to receive her. She sacked most of her bank's staff and exchanged them for men known for their ruthlessness. When one of the oldest of Venice's families refused to either pay or receive her, she appropriated their palace. Then she liquidated her bank's holdings in alum and other commodities and in a month had built enough money to fill her bank's vaults.

Then she sent a message to the Doge.

A day afterwards, she was approaching the water gate of the Doge's palace in sea that was choppy and empty of craft. It was a day of low cloud and brisk wind and the little sun that broke through to the lagoon came in brief stabs, quickly swept away. The water around the barge was marbled green, cusped with waves, and cool to the fingers of her trailed hand.

She arrived and was shown into the anteroom to the Doge's apartments, a high-ceilinged place with red damask on its walls between narrow windows whose glass gave little impression of the world outside. The doors to the apartments opened and a secretary ushered her in.

Doge Michele Steno was old and ill and looked like someone born into the wrong age. He wore a dressing gown that predated the sumptuary laws and his gouted foot, propped up on a stool, was wrapped in satin above its bandages. He held a stick in his hand but made no attempt to get up. He waved it instead. 'Zoe Mamonas, forgive me for not rising. It is painful.' He beckoned. 'The return of a prodigal daughter is a moment to be savoured. Come here to be kissed.'

Zoe stepped forward and bent herself. The Doge lingered a little too long in the embrace, old habits dying hard. 'La

Serenissima has missed you, Zoe,' he murmured. 'Your beauty suits our melancholy.'

'We are neither of us young.'

The Doge smiled. 'No, indeed. And age brings tolerance. You are forgiven your adventure with Tamerlane.'

'For which I should feel a daughter's gratitude,' she said, straightening. 'What church has new frescoes?'

Michele Steno frowned a little, leaning forward. 'Tush. You speak of a good man greatly missed. You had heard that we had made him a Knight of San Marco?'

Zoe nodded. 'I had heard.'

There was a small silence. The Doge had yet to abandon her hand.

Zoe stepped back, letting go. 'May I sit?'

As she did so, she looked around. They were in the Scudo Room and it was full of insinuation. On its walls were maps of the three continents of the world and the message that Venice, somehow, joined them all. There was a winged lion with two feet on land, two in the sea; there were galleys everywhere pushed by little winds, lion pennants streaming; there were women at the four corners of the earth, lying in muscular majesty surrounded by the fruits of Asia and Africa, every inch of them the courtesan. Above the fireplace was the Steno coat of arms.

The Doge lifted and then set down his bandaged leg, grimacing. It looked the weight of a young bullock. 'Did you see what happened at Constantinople?' he asked. 'Rats flown out in sortie. Ingenious.' He paused. 'Unfortunately, they didn't do their work. Musa's army is repaired.'

Zoe remained silent. The Doge would tell her as much as he wanted to.

'The extraordinary Protostrator of Mistra, meanwhile,' he continued, 'is in Serbia, knitting together an alliance of Christian princes to join Mehmed when he crosses to Europe. But Mehmed has no ships. Perhaps we should help him.'

Zoe fixed her gaze, calm and speculative, upon the Doge. 'You know perfectly well you can't help him,' she said. 'You already have a treaty with Musa.'

The room went very quiet. A seagull barked outside and a bell chimed from a distant church. The Doge moved his leg again to find comfort.

'A treaty?' he asked.

'Signed beneath the walls of Constantinople.'

The colour rose in Steno's cheeks. 'You may be mistaken.'

'I was Musa's concubine,' Zoe said quietly. 'I know what treaties he made.'

The look Steno now gave Zoe was less fond and had no trace of lust in it.

Zoe smiled. 'The treaty spoke of Venice supplying Musa with galleys to prevent Mehmed's crossing. Surely you remember?'

The Doge looked at his swollen foot. 'If such a clause existed, it might be ignored.'

'As you have ignored me since I arrived in this city. I have been twice to present myself to you.'

The Doge began his excuses but Zoe interrupted. 'So I have used my time wisely. I have reviewed my bank's business and called in some debts. You will have heard that the Participazio family lost their palace?'

The Doge had heard. Suddenly he knew where the conversation was going. He said: 'You are about to remind me that I owe you a lot of money.'

Zoe looked shocked. 'Lord, please!' She paused. 'I merely

wondered why the Malatestas were moving substantial funds from their account. They bank with me too.'

Steno, in spite of himself, was beginning to like Zoe. Not only was she beautiful in the most Venetian of ways but she was harder than the Arsenale's most seasoned wood. He said: 'They are to share in the papal debt. It is part of the agreement they've made to support this Church council and bring their pope.'

'Ah, I thought so.' Zoe smiled. 'This same Protostrator of Mistra's doing, I dare say. But why stop at them? Wouldn't you yourself like a share of the safest investment in Christendom?'

The Doge stared at her. He was a military man, unused to finance, but he had debts.

'I think', continued Zoe, 'your condition for supporting this council at Constance – which by the way will make this same Protostrator of Mistra very rich indeed – should be that Venetian banks also participate in the Curia's debt, and . . .' She paused and smiled. '. . . of course you with them.'

'But I have no money.'

'Ah, but I do, said Zoe. 'May I suggest we intercept Magoris on his way back from Serbia and invite him to Venice?'

The Doge put a finger to his lips and looked at her keenly. 'You have a plan?'

'Yes, I have a plan,' she said, 'a plan that might deliver Mistra to us.'

Intercepted by Zoe's messenger, Luke arrived in Venice to find that the Doge had insisted on him staying in his palace and had arranged entertainment. That evening, he ate with the *signori* beneath pictures of past doges while a choir sang *chansons* to an ottavino and viols. The food was fish and molluscs, since it was a fast day, all from the lagoon. The wine was spiced differently for each dish and so plentiful that several of the signori fell asleep.

Afterwards, a courtesan arrived to sing bawdy songs to the rhythm of banged forks and was joined by others. Then the ottavino quickened its tempo and the dancing began.

Luke was watching it when the Doge approached. He turned. 'Am I to know why you have summoned me to Venice? Your letter was vague.'

'You have been in Belgrade making an alliance against Musa,' Steno said. 'Venice would like to help. Also, there is the matter of the Church council to be held in Constance next year.'

A Venetian knight swept past them joined to a courtesan. Her bosom, at the point of escape, was scented without discretion. Steno breathed in.

'Fiametta,' sighed the Doge. 'Her poetry is as good as her lovemaking.'

Luke frowned. He wanted to go to bed quite soon.

The Doge continued. 'The Grand Council is undecided on both fronts,' he said. 'Perhaps there is something you could do to help them in their decision. Many of them are bankers. Like you.'

Luke glanced at the Doge. 'Your meaning?'

Steno shifted his bandaged foot. 'We might sit. I am old.'

They moved to a bench. They watched the dancing for a while and were served wine.

'You have the Curia's debt,' Steno said, slowly stretching his leg out before him. He drained his glass and rested it on his knee at an angle, watching it. 'You and the Medici. The debt is safe and the returns good. Our bankers would be interested in sharing it.'

Luke nodded slowly. 'And what might the Grand Council decide in return?'

'Well,' said Steno. 'For a start it could send a fleet into the

159

Dardanelles. I hear there's an army there anxious to cross over to Europe.'

Six weeks later, Mehmed crossed the straits at Scutari with five thousand men. His ferries were galleys from the Venetian navy.

Once in Europe, the army marched quickly, crossing the Maritza River and reaching Kosovo within a fortnight. As they went, disgruntled *uc begleri* and their retainers joined them, as did sipahi knights from the borderlands. But the army that reached the Morava River was still only a quarter the size of Musa's.

Within a week, it had been joined by the Serb and Wallachian armies, as well as men from Hungary and Bosnia. The combined host crossed the Cerna Gora mountains and was joined by the Byzantine General Leontaris with the Thessaloniki garrison. It marched north along the River Karasu until it reached the village of Çamurlu at the foot of Mount Vitosa. The army that camped there now numbered half that of Musa's.

The month was July.

CHAPTER FIFTEEN

ÇAMURLU, BULGARIA, SUMMER 1413

It was mid-morning and Luke felt himself part of his saddle. The sun was fierce, cooking the Serbian knights in their armour and making the handguns too hot to handle. The ground was limp from the heat, cowed beneath insects too heavy to feed. Across was a landscape of scorched, sweeping hills crested by woods from which birds erupted in sudden bursts. Thin columns of smoke rose into the air and stayed, and the sound of chopping trees arrived on no wind. Luke's brow was a waterfall and the kerchief given him by Anna a sponge. He was sitting on a hill overlooking Musa's army and with him were Matthew and Arcadius.

'That is a big army.' Arcadius broke the silence that had been there for some time.

'Big but clumsy,' said Matthew. 'And likely to act before it thinks, I'd guess.'

Luke turned in his saddle. A hundred paces behind stood Mehmed in mail and turbaned helmet; beside him Prince Stefan of Serbia in white Milanese armour: blond and chivalrous. Yakub's pony stood apart to avoid the comparison of height. He wore a lamellar cuirass and baggy trousers tucked into knee-high boots.

Mehmed's army looked bigger arranged for battle. At its centre were Serb, Bosnian and Hungarian foot soldiers, armed with bows and a few handguns. On either wing were the cavalry: to the left, the gazi tribes of Anatolia; to the right, the Wallachian Tartars. The Serbian knights stood in reserve.

They had just heard the unusual sound of twenty-five thousand bottoms hitting the ground. After three hours of standing, Prince Stefan had ordered the army to sit and its sigh of relief had been the only wind of the morning. Within the army, only the water-carriers moved, darting like lizards with their gourds, lip to lip. Behind them, pages walked the destriers up and down, up and down, while knights sat and dreamt of winter jousts. There was no sound but the snort and jangle of horse and the curses of men visited by flies.

Worst, thought Luke, was the smell. Nervous men had nervous bowels and the ranks were littered with excrement. Suddenly he needed to move. He said: 'I'm going to join Mehmed. I'll meet you in the wood.'

He arrived to find Prince Stefan standing in his stirrups and asking a question. 'Wallachia knows what to do?'

Yakub slapped a fly to his neck. 'Mircea knows. We just have to hope his Tartars understand.'

Luke looked over to the army's wing. The Wallachian army was a strange mix of nations. It had eight thousand Mongols, Bulgars, Magyars and Pechenegs in its ranks, wild men whose ancestors had ridden down the five-thousand-mile highway of grass that ran between taiga and desert into the very heart of Europe. They were born in the saddle and could fire thirty arrows a minute from their small, deadly bows.

'Well, it's simple enough,' said Mehmed. 'He has to hold our wing. We know what Musa will do. He'll throw the bashibozouks at our centre as a screen for the janissaries to advance. Then he'll use his akincis against our cavalry to stop them interfering.'

Stefan was nodding. 'We just have to hold the janissaries long enough for the akincis to be driven back. Then Mircea and Yakub can ride in from the flanks and my knights can counter-attack from behind.'

Luke knew the plan and it made sense. Mehmed might have the smaller army, but he had good cavalry. And there were bombards and ribaudekins filled with shrapnel hidden among the front ranks of the Serbian infantry. He looked across at Musa's force. He'd watched it since dawn, seen the unhurried movements of an army certain of victory, heard the muezzins call it to prayer, and watched fifty thousand men prostrate themselves to Allah. He'd seen them eat breakfast and send work parties off to the woods to cut arrows, hearing the chop, chop of wood. And all the while, the akinci horsemen had fanned out in front, back and forth like an angry sea, challenging Mehmed's army to make the first move. He'd felt his horse's excitement grow beneath him.

Mehmed turned to him. 'Where are your Varangians?'

'Behind us, lord. They're in reserve to go to the aid of any that need it.'

'And you'll be with them?'

'Unless you need me elsewhere. Look.'

Luke was pointing to the front. A drum had begun to beat across the valley and the bashibozouks were moving to the front of Musa's army. Some were waving flags, others swords and spears.

'At last,' said Stefan. He turned to a rider behind. 'Tell the men to stand. We are about to be attacked.'

Luke knew where he'd find the Varangian Company. There was a little wood on a hill from where the two armies could be seen without being seen. He rode at an easy canter until he reached the trees and saw the company amongst them, Matthew at their front. There were two hundred of them now, with pages to hold the horses. He drew up next to his friend. 'They're about to attack. Are you ready?'

Matthew gestured to his rear. 'Have you seen men more ready?'

Luke looked behind him. The Varangians were busy with their weapons, doing the things men do when they're waiting for battle to begin. Some were counting their arrows, others tightening their girths. He studied his friend. He wore the armour of an Italian knight and the helmet that sat before him on the saddle had a rearing dragon for its crest. He said: 'I hear you have a surgeon from the East.'

'My idea,' said Arcadius. 'The Arabs saved my life in Bokhara. Our Church won't even allow corpses to be cut open.'

Luke turned to face forward again. 'Well, let's hope he's not busy today.'

There was a trumpet blast to their front that echoed down the valley. Then one almighty cry.

'*Allah akbar!*'

The army across the valley had become a tide. Thousands upon thousands of men had flung themselves into the charge behind green banners covered in script. The forces of jihad had been unleashed and they looked unstoppable.

'Come on.'

They rode to the front of the wood to get a better look. The space between the armies had been half a mile; now it was less. The bashibozouks were running as fast as men can run

164

to reach their enemy, waving swords, spears and shields and screaming the screams of the faithful. They were men drunk on faith, men for whom martyrdom was a better outcome than staying alive.

The first salvo of arrows left the Hungarian bows and soared into the air as a mist. Their sound was of wind through saplings: the wind of death. They fell and men fell before them, but still the bashibozouks came on. More arrows went into the sky and more men went down, their cries lost to the cry to Allah.

Now the bashibozouks were a hundred paces from the front line and the Serbian bombards and ribaudekins had them in their range. There was a bang, then another, and smoke rose. Turks were hurled backwards, lifted into the air with their entrails following. Each explosion brought a dozen men down and those behind tripped on the dead and fell in their blood.

Luke had thought it would slow them. It did, but only for a moment. The bashibozouks paused to pick up weapons, then came on. The Christians were a sling-shot away and soon they'd be sending them to the hell they deserved.

'*Allah akbar!*'

One shout above the others and Luke saw a different advance beginning behind the bashibozouks. These were men who strode forward in unbroken ranks, Bektashi dervishes dancing before them. They wore tall white hats that swayed as they marched. They had the look of men who knew they were invincible. At their front was a giant, his arms rising and falling to the sound of music. Beside him marched two men who swung a cauldron between them.

The janissaries.

Luke looked beyond. There was a *mehterhane* band behind, playing music to the beat of kettle drums. There were trumpets and pipes and the sound of carnival. The louder it played, the more the Bektashis danced.

Now the bashibozouks had fallen on the Serbs, slashing and thrusting and clawing their way into their ranks like men demented, hurling their hate into the faces before them. The Serbian ranks wavered, concertinaed, fell back in some places. Then the men behind pushed forward and the line held.

Luke looked on and put his hand on the dragon by his side. They could hold the bashibozouks. Once the fury of their first rush had been checked, the wild men of the steppe were no match for the Hungarian men-at arms. But the janissaries coming up behind were a different enemy altogether. Luke watched them march forward in their ranks, men of the Devshirme, mail hauberks flashing in the sun and tall red boots raising dust around them. There were *azap* archers behind, their white *borks* bent back as they aimed over the heads in front.

The akincis were fanning out by the side of the advancing janissaries, sending cloud after cloud of arrows into the gazi horsemen on the Serbs' left, keeping them where they wanted them – keeping them away.

'Why don't the akincis attack the Wallachians?' asked Arcadius. 'They're leaving the janissaries' flank wide open.'

It seemed inexplicable. There was open ground between Mircea's Tartars and the janissaries: ground over which to charge. Yet the Wallachians hadn't moved.

'It might be a trap,' said Matthew. 'Perhaps the Turks have something hidden.'

There was a trumpet blast and the kettle drum quickened its tempo; then a shout and the Yeniçeri Ağasi leading the janissaries began waving his arms again. The men behind him shouted as one: '*Allah kerim!*'

God is generous.

Then the cauldron was lifted and they broke into a trot and began to wheel to the left, towards where the Wallachians stood, waiting on their horses. Matthew shook his head in disbelief.

'What are they *doing*?'

It was against every rule of warfare: infantry advancing on cavalry. It was madness. But the Wallachians still hadn't moved. Not a soldier among them had even raised his bow. Luke stared at the figure of Mircea, motionless on his horse, surrounded by riders with great wings on their backs.

There were more shouts from the janissaries. A rider had appeared behind, between them and the band, thrusting a spear with six horsetails to the sky again and again as he rode. He wore golden mail like Mehmed's.

Musa.

He galloped up and down behind the ranks of the janissaries, waving and pointing the spear, shouting: '*Allah kerim!*'

The men holding the *kazan* banged its sides with sticks and swung it from side to side as they marched. Those behind pressed on, quickening their pace, running to meet the Tartars.

But they were not to meet them.

Horrified, Luke watched the Wallachian army turn around. He watched it begin to march away. It was done with calm and order; not a rout but a retreat.

He'd seen the Wallachians do this before. At Nicopolis, he'd seen Mircea march his men away when he knew the battle was lost.

Then it came to him. It was all too calm, too organised. This had been planned long before the battle. This was betrayal. Mircea was deliberately leaving the right flank of Mehmed's

167

army unprotected. It was a catastrophe. He turned to Matthew. 'Are the men's bows nocked?'

His friend nodded.

'How many sheafs to a bowman?'

'Ten.'

Luke added. Twenty-four arrows to the sheaf, 240 per man. It was not enough. He gathered his horse's reins. 'Follow me.'

'Where are we going?'

'To stop the janissaries,' Luke shouted over his shoulder.

Luke cantered out of the wood. There was not much time before this battle was lost. Every moment counted. He kicked and his horse started down the hill as if a fire had been lit behind it. Two hundred men followed at the gallop. Two hundred against ten thousand.

The janissaries were coming up fast. Luke rose in the saddle to judge the distance. He had to be exact. He raised his hand, pulling his horse to a halt. He leapt from its back. 'Line them up here.'

Matthew drew up, his horse turning on the rein. Peter of Norfolk had dismounted and was already directing the men into line, archers in front, men-at-arms behind, pages holding the horses in the rear. The men spread themselves out, five paces between, covering the line of the advancing janissaries. Their bows were in their hands, huge things of Spanish yew. An arrow was on every string.

'Peter,' yelled Luke. 'Three hundred paces and fire. Understood?'

Peter raised his sword. He looked left and right down the line and brought his hand to his mouth. 'It's Crécy all over again, lads! Maximum range, and they can't touch us with their little bows!'

The janissaries had slowed a little. They'd watched giants on horses appear from nowhere and form up to their front with bigger bows than any they'd seen. They'd meant to wheel round on to the exposed flank of the enemy's centre but to do so now would mean exposing their own to this new weapon.

The Yeniçeri Ağasi had his back to the Varangians and was shouting, marshalling his men. The band had stopped playing and the Bektashi dervishes were no longer dancing. Musa had ridden out to their front and was yelling at them, pointing to their enemy. Then he thrust his spear into the ground and rode over to a man with a flag and seized it. It was the *bayrak*: red with a single white crescent at its centre. It was the flag of martyrs and the janissaries cheered to see their leader hold it aloft. They re-formed and came on. The band began again and the dervishes danced.

Luke looked at Peter.

The archer shook his head. 'Not yet.'

The janissaries had regained their swagger. They picked up the time of the band and looked invincible again. The English Varangians drew their bowstrings to the jaw.

'*Now!*'

Peter lowered his sword and a hundred arrows soared into the air, each a cloth-yard long and pointed with iron. There were few deadlier missiles in the world and they fell upon the leading janissary ranks like hail. Men fell by the dozen.

The Yeniçeri Ağasi shouted and the men behind him stopped and parted, and the azap archers ran up to the front line and released their own volley. But the composite bows hadn't the range of the longbows and the arrows fell harmlessly to the ground.

Another hundred arrows left the Varangians' bows, then another. The men-at-arms were feeding them with new shafts as soon as the last had taken to the air. The air rang with the whoosh of wind through feathers.

The janissaries could do little but advance and die as they'd been trained to do; and their discipline meant that not a man faltered. The Aga, ten paces in front, remained unhurt and urged them on. The Bektashis danced and danced around him, making whirlpools of faith to suck in the rain of death. Meanwhile, the men behind them died by the score.

The Varangians had spent half their arrows and it wouldn't be long before they ran out. Peter gave the shout and the men-at-arms moved back to the horses while the pages ran forward to collect as many of the azaps' arrows as they could carry. Soon the Turks were falling from their own shafts.

The janissaries came on, stepping over the men fallen in front, leaving them for the water-carriers that followed. The distance between them and the Varangians was closing fast and the pages returned to the horses while the men-at-arms drew their swords and came forward. The bowmen sent a last volley into the ranks before them and stepped back.

Luke had drawn the dragon-sword and stood between Matthew and Arcadius in the front line. The Turks were thirty paces away and were forming themselves into a wedge to make the final rush, their aga at their front. Luke could hear Musa but could not see him.

'*Allah akbar!*'

The janissaries charged. They launched themselves forward with God on their lips and no thought of mercy in their minds. Within seconds they were in mortal combat with the men-at-arms: sword to sword, mace to mace. The Varangians were outnumbered forty to one and it would only be a matter of time before their arms tired. The janissaries were the best of soldiers, men who could never marry because their family was their *orta*; men who lived and died for their comrades. But the line that held them was a Varangian line. And it wouldn't break.

Luke had felled his second janissary when he heard the shout. He glanced to his left and saw Mehmed there. The Prince was grinning. 'I've brought reinforcements.'

There were sipahi knights among the Varangians now, well-armoured men who knew how to fight. They slashed and parried with their curved swords, spitting in the faces of the men in front of them, men they despised for being slaves.

Luke let his sword work its magic. The dragon seemed to come alive and his blade was a blizzard of lethal movement, finding every gap in his enemies' armour to cut and stab. Men fell before him and the dragon dripped with their gore.

Beside him, Mehmed had just killed a man with a blow from his mace. But the arm that raised it again was tiring. Luke saw that a new, bigger enemy had stepped up to challenge him. The Yeniçeri Ağa.

The janissary Aga: a man of Varangian dimensions who towered over Mehmed. Like his men, he was beardless but the moustaches beneath his bork were as fat and curved as his weapon. He wore silver mail and his hauberk bore the Dhu'l Faqar, the double-bladed sword of Ali. Next to him were the men with the cauldron.

The Aga struck first and Mehmed danced back on his heels and parried the sword with his own. With a roar, the Aga swung again and this time Mehmed threw himself to the side so that the giant lost his balance and fell backwards on to the ground. Mehmed was immediately in front of him, his sword at his throat. 'You would kill your sultan?'

Luke and Matthew sprang forward to fend off any janissaries.

'Would you kill *me*?' Mehmed breathed again. 'Bayezid's son?'

Luke and Matthew had been joined by Arcadius. The janissaries before them had drawn back, watching what was happening. Luke glanced back to see the Aga try to recover his mace. Mehmed put his knee to the arm and the giant grunted in pain.

'You fight beside Christians,' said the Aga.

'And you for a usurper. Think on it.'

Mehmed rose to his feet, his sword level with the Aga's nose. He stepped backwards. 'Think on it,' he repeated, lowering his sword. 'Get up.'

Luke saw the Yeniçeri Ağa rise slowly, one arm nursing the other. His hat had fallen from his head and he stooped to pick it up. He collected his sword and his mace. Word of what had happened was passing from man to man along the line and enemies parted from one another, their weapons pointed at each other's hearts. The Aga was staring at Mehmed, indecision in every muscle of his body.

There was a yell and Luke looked down the gap to see a lone horseman forcing his way through, striking to left and right with the flat of his sword.

Musa.

He came up to the Aga and his horse reared slightly. He leapt from the saddle, sword drawn, and ran up to the Aga. He pointed his sword at Mehmed and shouted.

The Yeniçeri Ağa didn't move.

Musa slapped him hard across the face.

The sound was like gunshot and its shockwave hit both armies. A terrible thing had been done. The Yeniçeri Ağa had his hand to his cheek and was shaking his head slowly, staring at his leader in disbelief. Then he walked over to the men holding the huge cauldron and nodded to them. They lowered it to the ground. The Aga looked again at Musa, then at Mehmed. He bent down and seized the cauldron in both of his huge hands and, lifting it up, flung it, upturned, on to the ground.

Luke knew what this meant. The upturned cauldron: the sign of janissary revolt.

Musa knew it too. He turned to the Aga and hurled insults, raising his sword, perhaps to attack. The two cauldron-bearers drew their blades and stepped forward to protect their leader.

There was noise all around them and Luke looked up to see the two armies move slowly together: not to fight but to form an arena. These two should fight each other. Brother would fight brother. Whoever won would be sultan. It would be the will of Allah.

Slowly, Mehmed removed his helmet and threw it to one side. Then he pulled his aventail down to his shoulders. He wiped his brow with his mailed arm, his eyes never leaving Musa's.

Musa attacked. With a roar, he ran forward, his sword raised above him in both hands. The blade fell and Mehmed blocked it with his own. But he was not as strong as his brother and the force of the blow brought his hilt to his brow. Deliberately, he stepped back and Musa lost his balance and plunged forward to the ground, landing on his elbows. Mehmed danced to one side.

Musa scrambled to his feet and they parted again, each breathing hard. Mehmed's black hair coated his skull and the eyes beneath watched every move of the other man: judging, judging. His brother was angry and he was rash.

Musa charged again, this time with his sword thrust forward like a spear. Mehmed reacted too late and the blade tore into his arm as he sidestepped. Musa half turned and drove his elbow into his brother's midriff, winding him and sending him staggering back.

Mehmed was clutching his sword arm, blood running through his fingers. There were strips of golden mail hanging on either side of his hand.

'You are wounded, brother,' said Musa. 'Allah favours me because I do His word, while you consort with Christians.' He gestured both ways with his head, breathing hard. 'My army knows that.'

Luke thought of something. He shouted: 'Are the Wallachians not Christian? How did you persuade the voivode, Musa?'

Musa couldn't help himself. 'By marrying his daughter,' he shouted. 'Mircea knew who'd win this battle.'

Luke saw the janissaries around Musa look at each other. They'd just heard their leader announce he'd married a Christian. And he'd slapped their aga.

But Musa was oblivious to the changing mood around him. With another roar, he sprang forward with his sword raised. He brought it down so hard that he broke Mehmed's blade. The older brother staggered back and lost his balance. He fell to the ground.

Musa raised his sword again. Before him, lying unhelmeted and defenceless, was the only thing between him and the throne.

There was the sound of a bowstring released and Prince Musa suddenly straightened up. An arrow-tip had appeared between his breasts and a look of infinite surprise was on his face. He pitched forward and fell to the earth, dead.

Behind him, with a longbow in his hand, stood the Yeniçeri Ağa. Beside him stood Peter of Norfolk.

*

174

It was as night was falling that Luke found himself walking with Prince Mehmed over the battlefield. Around them were bodies, thousands of them piled on top of each other in the entanglement of death: some leaping as if they'd been stopped mid-dance. The air smelt of blood and fear and birds rose into the air as they approached, some with their beaks full.

The victor of Çamurlu seemed angry.

'He should not have killed him,' Mehmed said. 'The Aga behaved rashly. The fight was brother to brother.'

Luke understood, but he said: 'Highness, just be thankful that you've won.'

Mehmed stopped and put his hand on Luke's shoulder, looking up at him. His anger had gone. 'It is all thanks to you. You put together the alliance, you found the ships and you saved the battle.' He stopped at the body of a janissary, a sipahi lying beneath him. The two were almost kissing. A crow rose abruptly from a hidden space between them. He knelt and closed the eyes of both men, then looked up. 'What should be your reward, Luke Magoris?'

'Constantinople is relieved; Mistra is relieved. It is enough.'

'But is not Mistra threatened by Venice too?'

'It was threatened because Venice was worried that Suleyman or Musa might get there first. They feared corsairs plundering their main trade route. Now, with you as sultan, they'll fear it no longer.'

Mehmed nodded slowly, his hand to his beard. 'But you still fear for the future. I heard you beat Murad.'

Luke frowned and Mehmed raised his hand. 'Please. Bedreddin was too long with him.' He looked up into eyes red with fatigue. 'Luke, I fear you will need to build your wall, but at least you can now take your time.'

He embraced Luke, and then drew back.

'But know this: I owe you my throne and probably my life. I will repay the debt. I will be looking for the time when I can do so.'

CHAPTER SIXTEEN

RIMINI, SUMMER 1413

Giovanni and Plethon arrived in Rimini to find a city in celebration, news of Mehmed's great victory at Çamurlu having arrived the day before. They entered through walls rippling with banners and topped by soldiers with flowers on their helmets. Petals fell like snow around them and the air was scented with summer.

They dismounted and led their horses through the noisy streets, accepting kisses and wine from strangers, until they came to the palace of Malatesta dei Sonnetti. In the square outside it, a bonfire had been lit with an effigy at its centre.

'Is that Musa?' Plethon had stopped and was standing with his hand on the small of his back, rocking backwards and forwards as he did after long rides.

Giovanni considered the husk before them, engulfed with flames except for the turban at its top. 'I suppose so.' His horse started and he patted its neck and whispered into its ear. The square was filled with people dancing and banging drums. They made their way through the crowd and walked under the palace gate. Servants arrived to take their horses to the stables.

A voice came from above. 'My brother is not here to welcome you. He has no manners.'

Carlo Malatesta was coming down the stairs. He was dressed for occasion in long red silk and slippers. His hat was a red box and he held a gold-tipped baton in his hand, which he tapped on the balustrade as if a military band might be following. He landed and bowed low to Plethon, eyeing the toga as he did so. 'Your fame comes before you,' he said, straightening, 'preparing the way.'

Plethon bowed back. 'Ah, and I had thought the celebrations to do with Mehmed's victory.'

Malatesta glanced at Giovanni but made no greeting. With a shock, Giovanni saw one side of his face rippled with burns.

Carlo Malatesta took Plethon's arm, turning his back on Giovanni. 'I hope you plan to stay long. Plato is unknown in Rimini.' Giovanni climbed the steps behind them, watching Plethon's hands twist and untwist behind his back, watching Carlo's big arm on his shoulders. 'I'd like you to teach my nephews and nieces while you're here. Their education means much to me.'

They arrived on the balcony where a servant waited with a tray, only two cups on it. Carlo Malatesta presented one to Plethon and lifted the other.

'To Plato,' he said.

Despite his welcome, the next three months were the happiest of Giovanni's life. He lived under the same roof as Cleope; breathed the same air; ate the same food. He spent the mornings sharing Plethon's lessons with her, hearing the same words, touching the same books. The biggest shadow that encroached on his joy, as summer turned to autumn, was the thought of ever leaving.

They never talked of it, but then they never talked alone as

178

they had before. The nurse Isabella was sick and her replacement watchful and stern. Their conversations were shared by others and it was only in their looks, furtive and quickly transferred, that they spoke.

Plethon preferred the castle's gardens for lessons. They were really more orchard than garden, with little fruit groves clustered to provide shade. Giovanni, Cleope and her cousins would sit at Plethon's feet – much, he hoped, as Plato's students had sat at his – and talk of ideas ancient and new and the connections between.

'We should talk of love,' Plethon announced one morning as he sat on a stone bench beneath peaches. 'Platonic love.' He plucked a peach and brushed its downy skin with his thumb. 'Not every love can find its fulfilment in this world, but *all* love can help us in our ascent towards the sublime.'

Giovanni had a question. 'But is Platonic love possible between man and woman without the sublime interfering?'

Plethon bit into the peach and smiled. 'Certainly. But it misses the point.'

'And is it permissible in a marriage?' asked Cleope. 'I mean, *beyond* a marriage?'

'Assuredly,' said Plethon. 'In fact, it is to be encouraged.' He looked around him. 'Most of your marriages will be arranged: it is the curse of your class. A Platonic love may be your salvation.'

Later, in the evening, Giovanni was walking alone in the garden, pondering Plethon's words. The air was still and bats flitted between the fruit trees like anxious mourners. He'd spent the afternoon riding on the beach and thinking about Cleope. It seemed to him easy for a middle-aged man to talk of Platonic love, but Giovanni was sixteen and his love for Cleope was urgent and physical. When he imagined them together, it was in embrace not conversation. Above all, he needed to be alone with her, even if just for an instant.

He found Plethon reading on the same bench he'd taught from.

'What are you reading?' Giovanni asked, sitting down beside him.

Plethon closed the book on his knee. 'Catullus. I'm reviewing it.'

'Reviewing it? Why?'

'Because I want to give it to you. It is the poetry of love.'

Giovanni took the book and opened it. He read a page, then another. 'Some of it is quite strong,' he said, looking up at Plethon, surprised.

'Indeed, which is why I was reviewing it. But it'll do.' He paused. 'It's the perfect antidote for Platonic love.' He glanced at Giovanni. 'Which I doubt sounds very appealing to you at present.'

Giovanni didn't answer. He'd not told Plethon of his love for Cleope but knew it was more than apparent. He read another page, then closed the book. 'If you were to give Cleope her lessons separately, you could choose where to give them, couldn't you?'

'Quite possibly,' said Plethon. 'Where do you think she'd learn best?'

'Well, the beach is quiet. I ride on it in the afternoons. There is a summer house there.'

'I know of it.' Plethon hummed for a while. Then he stopped and turned to Giovanni. 'You know she may be obliged to marry soon, don't you?' He hitched up his toga at the shoulder and regarded him for a while. Then he put his hand on his arm and spoke quietly. 'You should heed my words about Platonic love, Giovanni. It's not perfect, but it may be all you can aspire to. One day.'

A week after Plethon had spoken to him of Platonic love, Giovanni rode on the beach with Catullus on his saddle and wings on his horse. Plethon had introduced him to a poetry whose music still played in his ear.

He approached the pavilion where Plethon now taught Cleope in the afternoons. He saw a figure sitting on the verandah. It looked up as he approached.

Cleope.

Giovanni brought his horse to a stop. He looked around. There was no sign of anyone else.

Cleope rose and walked down the pavilion steps. She stopped and shielded her eyes to look up at him. 'Isabella has returned to me. She's inside, talking to Plethon.' She saw the book. 'What have you brought?'

Giovanni dismounted with Catullus and took her hand. Her hair was gathered above her neck and had flowers in it. She wore the same dress of white lawn beneath which her feet were bare, sand between her toes. He glanced down at the book in his hand. It was covered in thick vellum that seemed to absorb the sunlight. The title was in Latin.

'Catullus,' he said. 'It's the poetry of love. Some of it is rude.'

She laughed. 'Good! Then I will learn from it. Can I see?' She took the book and opened it, sitting down in the sand as she did so. He saw a flower fall from her hair. He sat beside her and watched as she turned the pages.

She read aloud:

'Give me a thousand kisses, then a hundred,
Then another thousand, then a second hundred.
Then when we've made many thousands,
We'll muddle them so as not to know . . .'

She looked up at him. 'It's beautiful.'

Giovanni nodded. 'Yes, it is. You can have it. Plethon gave it to me and I give it to you.'

She closed the book and put it down beside her. She put her palm against his cheek, then beside his eyes, moving his hair to one side, staring at him. 'I have never seen eyes like yours,' she murmured, leaning forward and kissing his cheek, then his mouth. She drew back. 'I have news.'

Her voice had changed so that he knew the news was not good. He prepared himself, breathing in.

'I am to be wed,' she said. She was smiling but the smile was thin. 'To a d'Este from Ferrara. It seems that money has intervened.' She'd brought both palms up to his cheeks to keep his eyes on hers so that he'd know she was serious. He saw tears in the eyes that looked up into his. 'I've come to say goodbye, Giovanni.'

Giovanni was trying to shake his head.

'There's more,' she said, still holding his face. 'You, Plethon . . . you're no longer welcome in Rimini. My uncle Carlo suspects something. He doesn't like you, Giovanni. You must go.'

The door of the hut opened and Isabella appeared. She was carrying a bag in one hand and Cleope's slippers in the other. Her face was red from the heat and wisps of white hair had escaped from her bonnet.

Plethon appeared beside her. He said: 'Cleope's right, Giovanni; we have to leave.'

182

The nurse said: 'And we must go too, lady. We'll be missed.'

Cleope bent forward and kissed Giovanni on the forehead. Then she rose, bringing him with her. Giovanni hadn't spoken. He stood without moving, hearing the sea against the shore and the echo of words he'd not wanted to hear. He tried to think of a way to confound what she'd just told him. He looked at the book, still in the sand. He picked it up and swept sand from its cover with his palm. He gave it to her.

'I will see you again,' he said. 'I'll find the way to do it and until then, you'll have this to read.'

She brought the book to her lips. 'And I will read it. Always.'

Plethon walked up to them and placed a hand on each of their shoulders. 'There is always Constance,' he said quietly. He looked at Cleope. 'Perhaps your father might let you come to Constance.'

CHAPTER SEVENTEEN

YANGTZE VALLEY, AUTUMN 1413

Shulen and Nikolas rode on either side of Chen Cheng on a road lined with poplars whose autumn leaves coppered the blue above. On one side of them flowed the mighty Yangtze River, half a mile wide, its brown waters moving faster than they could gallop. On the other stretched fields of ruined rice.

'Where are all the men, Chen Cheng?' asked Shulen.

The Confucian was staring at the fields, a fly whisk in his hand and a thin frown on his brow. He was wearing a high-collared jerkin and a sunhat that put most of his face into shadow. 'Taken to work on the Emperor's projects,' he said. 'Building roads, bridges, things we need.'

Shulen remembered countries like this on the way to Samarcand. 'Like Tamerlane.'

Chen Cheng shook his head with force, his hand to his hat. 'Not like Tamerlane. They're not slaves.'

'The men can choose to stay?' asked Nikolas. 'I don't think so.' He pointed to the nearest field where the women were too few, and the rice, overblown and decaying, floated unharvested on its surface.

Chen Cheng's frown had deepened hourly since leaving

184

Nanjing and the impending famine had grown too obvious to deny. They'd left later than planned because Chen Cheng had been right: despite Min Qing's torture to the eighth degree, the mandarins still did everything in their power to delay the treasure fleet. Nikolas and Shulen had passed the days checking and rechecking their orders for mastic and horses.

At last they'd been told they could travel to the port of Tanggu where the fleet was gathering and where they'd collect the gold to pay for it all. It would come from the imperial treasury since no gold could leave China without the Emperor's permission. They were to journey slowly down the Yangtze Valley with Chen Cheng whom the Emperor had asked to gauge the people's mood and explain to his own class why his mission deserved their support. A report was to be given to him personally when they arrived at Tanggu.

Nikolas's hand swept the fields to their right. 'Do *they* understand this Emperor's mission?' He turned to the Confucian. 'What exactly is this mission, Chen Cheng?'

'A rebirth of classical Han culture,' said the Confucian, 'like your Rinascimento in Italy. We've had a hundred years of Mongol rule and it is time for China to rediscover its greatness. But it's expensive and the people are hurting.'

And, as the days passed, they saw the hurt. The whole male population of China seemed to have been mobilised for the imperial project. On the third day they met mandarin gentry carried in their sedan chairs beneath sunshades, wearing the cap and girdle of their rank, with servants out in front, raising banners proclaiming their achievements. Chen Cheng stopped. He shook his head.

'The banners say they're setting up new Confucian schools in each prefecture, where the students will learn Zhu-Xi's four

185

texts by heart, preparing them for the exam. They're getting ready for a future without this Emperor.'

'What exam?' Shulen asked.

Chen Cheng waved flies from his horse's mane. 'The *jinshi* was established eight hundred years ago by the Sui Dynasty. It takes four days and the candidates sit in a cubicle open on one side to stop cheating. At night, the desk becomes a bed, though no one sleeps. It is the most difficult exam in the world but those who pass it will rule and be rich. They will become the next mandarins.'

They rode on in silence, coming to a hamlet where only the old and young watched them from doorways, bellies distended and fear in their eyes. A stone qilin sat on its hind legs next to the village well; a young boy perched cross-legged on its head. Chen Cheng dismounted and knelt before it for a long time and the child looked down in silence.

On the fourth day, they saw hills rising in the distance with forests of bamboo climbing their sides, and maple ablaze above. The riverbank was lined with weeping willows whose trailing branches swept the muddy shallows above alligators and turtles with pig-snouts. Golden eagles circled high in the sky and swallows rode the air like paper darts. They came to a pier that reached over the mudflats. At its end was a giant wheel, vertical and turning, with cogs and smaller wheels joined to it, then a low building.

Chen Cheng stopped his horse. 'Rice-grinding mill,' he said, pointing. 'Powered by the Yangtze.'

'With no rice to grind,' said Nikolas quietly. He shifted in his saddle. 'What use is the diadan's genius if the people are starving, Chen Cheng?'

The Confucian turned. 'Because machines like this, and the

186

roads and bridges that connect them, will feed the people of the future. You wouldn't be here now were it not for Chinese knowledge, Nikolas. Shulen didn't set your bones.'

It was true, but then Nikolas preferred to forget the extraordinary contraption that had held him to mend. He was still in pain, but he was alive and could ride. He looked back at the fields. 'So what will you tell the Emperor?'

'I will confirm what Zhu Chou has already told him.'

Nikolas felt despair arrive and stay. He missed her. 'Zhu Chou?'

Chen Cheng dipped his head. 'She is more intelligent than most of his ministers and the Emperor favours her above all concubines. She has read the diadan and advises him where to apply its knowledge. And she is the only one who dares tell him when it goes wrong.' He smiled. 'You chose the wrong woman to break your heart, Nikolas. After Admiral Zheng, Zhu Chou is perhaps the most powerful person in the Middle Kingdom, though few know it.' He sat upright, then rose in his stirrups. 'I see more mandarins to convert ahead.' He kicked his horse forward.

Shulen brought her horse close to Nikolas's. There were men with banners who'd reached them and stopped to stare at their mounts, both Eskalon's offspring. Shulen ignored them and turned to Nikolas. 'You must forget Zhu Chou. She'll never leave the harem.'

'I know. But it's hard.' He looked at her. 'Isn't it?'

Shulen took his hand and they rode in silence for a while. 'Yes, it's hard,' she said. 'But then you have two loves. Perhaps it's easier.'

'The second being Luke?' He glanced at her. 'I suppose it's why we're both here.' He began to cough, softly at first, then in great, wheezing bursts. He let go of her hand and brought it to his chest, leaning over his horse's neck.

Shulen took hold of his rein and brought them both to a stop. 'This journey has come too soon,' she said.

Nikolas shook his head, his hand raised. At last he could speak. 'I had a horse land on me and things got a little crushed, that's all.' He paused. 'I'm a Varangian.'

Shulen tilted her head to one side. 'Varangian pride.'

Nikolas took a deep breath and smiled. 'I suppose our brotherhood was based on a sort of pride. Luke the leader, Matthew the strongest, Arcadius the fat one.' He paused. 'Wasn't I supposed to be the funny one?'

Shulen took his hand again. 'No, the clever one. It's why he sent you to China.'

'To practise the sedentary business of trading.' He turned to her, a trace of sadness in his eye, she thought. 'In which case a little injury doesn't really matter.' He coughed again. 'Matthew wouldn't have come. He'd have seen it as a betrayal of our Varangian oath.'

'He'd have been wrong.'

Nikolas was silent for a while and Shulen wondered if he agreed. Probably not, she thought.

'Were we supposed to fall in love, do you think?' she asked. 'You and I?'

Nikolas smiled. 'Well, he got that bit wrong, if we were.' He looked at her, serious again. 'I mean . . .'

'I know what you mean. It would have happened during your repair, if it were to happen at all. And then there's Zhu Chou, of course. She might have minded.' She looked up at the willows where a breeze was stirring their branches. 'But I *do* love you, all of you. I am the sister in your brotherhood.'

Nikolas nodded. 'Yes, you are.'

'And you have no idea how important that was . . . *is* to me,' she said quietly. 'I grew up on the steppe, alone. Then I found Luke. Then all of you, his family.' She leant forward. 'It's why I came here with you, Nikolas. If I couldn't go west to be with him, then at least I could be with someone who loves him.'

Two weeks later, they took to the Yangtze in a boat powered by giant paddles. Day by day, the river grew wider and busier and the air they breathed became salted and made them cry. At last they arrived at Tanggu to find the treasure fleet waiting. They paddled into the bay, passing forts wreathed in the smoke of saluting cannon, to find an armada of more than fifty leviathan ships riding at anchor, pennants streaming from their masts. At every prow, dragon eyes glared out; at every stern, their bodies lay coiled and ready to strike, golden scales catching the evening sun and turning the bay into a furnace afloat. Around them were hundreds of smaller warships, merchant ships and supply vessels. There were more than four hundred craft in that bay and the population aboard them would be greater than any city the fleet would visit on its voyage.

Chen Cheng pointed towards the shore where kites were afloat on the breeze. Most were the shape of animals and had long strings. They were of every colour imaginable. 'The Festival of Qingming when we honour our ancestors and decorate their tombs. It marks the start of the ploughing season. People dance, sing and are happy.' He paused. 'Perhaps a good time to meet the Emperor.'

That night, Shulen lay awake and saw fireworks from her cabin window. She remembered meeting another emperor in

Samarcand to whom she'd given glasses to see. Could this one be as terrifying?

The next morning, she and Nikolas were instructed in etiquette. They were not to look at the Son of Heaven, keeping their eyes downcast while in his presence. When summoned forward, they were to kowtow with three kneelings and nine knockings of the head. They were to remain kneeling since they were commoners. Only those who'd passed the imperial exam were permitted to sit.

Now, dressed in her ankle-length *chang*, Shulen waited for the most powerful man on earth to arrive. On her head was a soft cap, also in red, and her hair was gathered into two pigtails. Beside her stood Nikolas dressed as a mandarin. In front were Admiral Zheng, Chen Cheng and the Minister of Rites.

There was a fanfare from the bank. Along the coastal road came a procession surrounding a curtained carriage pulled by eunuchs in livery. It was led by horns and drums and cymbals with dancers in dragon headdresses alongside, shooting fire from their mouths. In front were men sweeping the road with long brushes and others shaking willow branches to left and right. Behind the carriage came courtiers in a hundred different hats, then the royal guard. There were banners everywhere.

Nikolas asked: 'Why the willows?'

'To ward off the evil ancestors of others. During Qingming, they are all around us.'

A man appeared at the top of the gangplank, running. He wore a black tunic that had two cranes on its front and carried a rolled carpet. He kowtowed to the admiral and minister and then, with one fluid movement, unrolled the carpet to where they stood. Four more men ran on to the ship carrying tall

190

bamboo screens which they placed on either side of the carpet. This Emperor was not to be seen as he came aboard.

Shulen raised herself on tiptoe to look over the side of the ship. She could just see the top of a curtained sedan chair being carried slowly up the gangplank. It had willow branches attached to its roof. 'Why are they all running?'

'Shhh. Lower yourself,' whispered Chen, taking her arm. 'Everyone must run in the Emperor's presence and never look at him.'

Four more men trotted on to the deck. They were stout and wore long garments and hats with buttons of different colours. Their brows were wet but their features composed. They kept their hands in their sleeves as they ran.

Chen Cheng explained. 'The buttons are important,' he said. 'They will pass through nine different shades as their wearers move through the ranks. These four are ministers.'

The men came to a standstill, two on either side of the carpet between the top of the ramp and the screen. They kept their eyes lowered.

Then the sedan chair came into view, stable despite the climb. Its bearers placed the chair gently down on the deck as men arrived behind with cymbals.

The ministers in front of her obscured Shulen's view of the Yongle Emperor as he emerged from his transport. She heard the crash of cymbals and the sound of horns but she didn't see him. She looked between the strange hats before her and saw a flash of yellow pass.

Then the Minister of Rites turned. He bowed from the neck and addressed them. 'You are to go to the admiral's cabin and await the Emperor.'

Admiral Zheng's cabin was the width of the ship and most of the fleet could be seen through its rear windows. Because of the ship's height, the view was mostly of masts and pennants. Every colour in art and nature was there and blowing in the wind. All except one.

'Nothing is yellow,' Shulen whispered to Nikolas, who stood beside her. She was looking through the window. 'Not a single pennant.'

'Yellow is the Emperor's colour,' said Chen Cheng, 'only his. There will be a yellow pennant above this ship while he is on board.'

They heard footsteps on the deck outside. The door opened and Admiral Zheng appeared with someone behind him. Immediately, they fell to their knees and brought their foreheads to the floor. They heard the door close and the tread of a big man in slippers. They heard him cross the floor to a chair.

'You can sit up and look at me.'

The voice was deeper than any that Shulen had heard before, yet there was music in it. She sat back on her heels and saw a man, dressed from head to toe in yellow silk, who filled his chair without waste. The face was large and jowly and held a small nose and eyes; the beard was long and thin. The man looked neither pleased nor displeased, merely composed, as if all Confucian harmony resided in his ample body. Admiral Zheng stood by his side and was, as usual, smiling.

'The four of us are alone and will not be disturbed,' said the Emperor, arranging his sleeves. 'So there is no need for etiquette.' He glanced up at the admiral. 'And when you've hidden in the gutters of Nanjing with a man, it's hard not to look at him.'

Shulen remembered what Chen had told her of the Yongle

Emperor. When his father, the Hongwu Emperor, had died and given the throne to a grandson, he had risen in revolt with Zheng at his side. The two had spent a year on the run before raising the army that would bring him to power. It was said that they were like brothers.

The Emperor smoothed the silk over his thighs. 'You see the fleet outside, ready to sail. You are expecting gold to come aboard this ship to buy more of your horses and the substance that keeps my harem so fragrant.' He brought his hands together in his lap. 'It will not be coming.'

Shulen saw Nikolas recoil slightly as if he'd been hit.

The Emperor sat for a while, huge and impassive. 'You have seen my empire over these past years.' He looked at Shulen. 'Is it content, would you say?'

She knew that Zhu Chou would have told him that it wasn't. She thought about all that she'd seen on their journey up the Yangtze Valley. She thought of the famine to come.

'Your people are not united in believing in your vision, majesty,' she said carefully. 'They feel the weight of your taxes and the labour imposed on them without understanding their benefit.'

'It is true and you know why. The scholar gentry do not explain my dream to them. They defy me.' The Emperor paused. 'What would you advise me to do?'

Shulen's heart was racing. She'd told the most powerful man on earth that his people didn't love him and now he was asking her advice. She thought of what Chen Cheng had told them.

'What does Zhu Chou advise?' she asked.

The Emperor's eyebrows lifted a fraction. 'Zhu Chou? She tells me to slow down, not to try and do everything at once.'

'Perhaps she is right.'

The Emperor nodded. 'Perhaps. But I have so little time.' He paused. 'It is different in China. It is the will of one man, not city elders, that makes things happen. And how long will I live?'

Shulen remained silent, thinking that it hadn't been a question in need of an answer. She hoped Chen Cheng might say something. Zheng did. 'The people need a sign of heaven's favour, majesty,' he said quietly.

The Emperor nodded. 'Yes they do.' He rose slowly and walked to the window. He stood there for some time, looking over the fleet. He turned to Shulen and said: 'Do you know of the qilin?'

Shulen remembered what Chen Cheng had told her. The qilin had appeared before Confucius's mother to tell her that her son would be a 'king without a throne'. It was the Angel Gabriel in the body of a musk deer, horse, giraffe, or however the ripples of time had reshaped its reflection. It was said to appear only in the reign of divinely favoured rulers.

'Tamerlane had one,' continued the Emperor, before she could answer. 'Does Ulugh Beg have it still, do you know?'

'I saw one in Samarcand,' she said.

The Emperor dipped his big head and walked back to the chair. The hat he wore had a flat top and tassels hung from its ends, bouncing as he sat. 'We would ask you to bring it to us.' He stared at her for some time, perhaps expecting some reaction. 'Then you may have your gold.'

Shulen heard Nikolas beside her draw breath. She put her hand on his arm but he couldn't restrain himself.

'Majesty, there are ships in this fleet that have been fitted to carry horses.'

The Emperor turned slowly to him, no trace of composure lost. 'The trade for horses, and everything else, will have to wait for the next fleet. We need a qilin first.' He leant forward fractionally, still looking at Nikolas. 'If you were to meet with success, you would find us more generous with the gold than we would have been.'

Shulen was thinking. She could sail with the fleet to Calicut at the bottom of India, then go up to Samarcand via Delhi. But it would all take time.

'If I were to find it, majesty,' she asked, 'how would I get it to you most quickly?'

Admiral Zheng answered. 'Your ship will wait at Calicut. I will command it. Quarters for the qilin are already prepared on board.'

Shulen nodded. She wondered if giraffes slept standing up, like Tamerlane's elephants. She asked: 'What do I offer Ulugh Beg in return?'

The question seemed direct but then the etiquette of the Ming Court had been left outside the cabin.

'The *Almagest*,' said Zheng. 'Ptolemy's study of the stars. We have it.'

Shulen nodded. 'And that will be enough?'

'To astronomers, it is the philosopher's stone,' said the Emperor. 'It will be enough.'

Shulen glanced up at the Yongle Emperor. The inscrutable eyes were matched by a sliver of a smile. She began to see how important the qilin was for China if it kept this man on the throne.

'If it is still there, majesty,' she said, 'I will find it.'

'Good,' replied the Emperor, rising from his chair. He began to walk to the door but stopped. He looked around, his finger to his lips. 'One more thing,' he said. 'You will take someone with you.' He looked at Nikolas. 'It is a gift for you to make up for the gold.'

195

He clapped his hands once and the door opened.

Standing there was Zhu Chou.

A month later, Nikolas was watching five concubines playing cards on the stern deck of Admiral Zheng's flagship. Zhu Chou was not among them. Next to him stood Amiral Zheng and Shulen. Since leaving Tanggu the fleet had travelled fast, sailing before the monsoon winds beneath tight sails and streaming pennants, red to please the dragon that lived in the clouds. Zhu Chou was somewhere aboard but as hidden as the dragon.

His gaze turned to a group of astronomers standing at the ship's rail. The evening sun was hovering above the western horizon, turning the Yellow Sea into the Emperor's silk, and the Pole Star was dead astern. The astronomers were leaning over the ship's side, measuring its altitude with sextants and astrolabes that flashed in their hands as they moved. One of them called the time from a giant hourglass while another passed on the news to the helmsman. Their voices came and went beneath the sails.

He looked behind. Zheng's flagship was well ahead of a fleet that stretched out in a giant arrowhead covering all parts of the wine-dark sea. Supply ships, troop ships and *fuchuan* warships fanned out behind while messenger boats buzzed between. Serpents' eyes glared from prows as they rose and dipped in the swell and great bronze mirrors blazed from sides to scare evil spirits away. This was a fleet that would frighten the sea monsters into letting them pass.

Nikolas was thinking of Zhu Chou. A concubine laughed and slapped a card to the deck. He turned and looked up at the Pole Star.

'It doesn't move; everything moves around it,' said Zheng. 'Like the Emperor.' The rail creaked as he leant his big frame against the teak. He had a rolled map in one hand, which he used to point with. 'We circle the Son of Heaven as the stars circle Polaris. Those closest are brightest, as they should be.'

An officer walked over from the group of astrologers. He passed the admiral a piece of paper. Zheng read it and nodded. Nikolas put his hands to his ears.

BONG.

The gong boomed out across the sea, the deck shook and the concubines shrieked. A moment later, Nikolas saw messenger.pigeons take to the sky in a fluster of wings. Those going west were silhouetted by the last of the sun. He asked: 'Are we changing course?'

'No,' said Zheng, unrolling his map, 'we are stopping for the night.'

The fleet's diet was mainly fish and Nikolas and Shulen dined on it that night with Admiral Zheng. The ships had trained sea otters in their forward bulkheads that worked in pairs, herding fish into nets hung from the sides. Earlier, they'd watched them as grain ships moved from one vessel to the next, dispensing wheat, millet and rice, followed by fruit ships with lemons and pomelos.

They were sitting in the admiral's cabin, waiting for their fish to be served. The admiral's map was unrolled before them, its corners secured by candlesticks. Zheng was pointing at it. 'In five days we will get to Malacca. We'll stay there a month, then the fleet will split up. We will go on to Calicut in the Hindu kingdom of Kerala where the Zamorins rule. That is where you'll disembark.'

'And go to Samarcand,' said Shulen, 'where we hope to find a qilin still alive.'

Zheng's face suddenly had the moon in it, tilted in merriment, his eyes two stars above his smile. Talk of the qilin always provoked a smile in the admiral, as if its existence was a joke they shared. His finger, big as a boy's arm, travelled across the oceans. 'Yes, and we'll go on to Basra to trade silk with the Persians.'

Shulen and Nikolas were to take the qilin from Samarcand to Basra at the top of the Persian Gulf. A wagon with tall sides was aboard for the purpose. Then they'd return to China with the fleet to collect their gold.

The fish arrived on blue china, a steaming island of ribbed pink with rice banked as a reef around it. The rice was many-coloured; the smell of spices filled the cabin.

Nikolas thought of Zhu Chou. It had been her smell rather than her person that he'd encountered throughout the voyage; the rich jasmine scent that he'd first smelt in the library. Whenever he'd entered his cabin, her scent had been there. But not her.

He asked: 'I have been meaning to ask, admiral: why are the concubines' feet not bound?'

Zheng waved aside the steam. 'The women come from the floating brothels of Canton. They are of the Tanka tribe and refuse the lotus feet.'

Nikolas remembered Zhu Chou shuffling into the cabin where they now sat. Were her feet bound? Perhaps Zheng could see into his mind, for he said: 'Zhu Chou does not bind her feet either. She was a gift from the King of Korea where they prefer their women's feet unbound.'

Nikolas said: 'We've not seen her on the voyage yet.'

Zheng looked surprised. 'She only awaits your call, Nikolas. She sleeps in the room beside you.'

Shulen looked up from her plate, eyes wide. 'You've not . . .?'

Nikolas looked down, feeling the heat rise inside his face, busying himself with the business of separating meat from bone. He'd had no idea. But then what had he been supposed to do?

Zheng was laughing. 'Nikolas, Nikolas. She's even cut her nails for you!'

Later, sitting on his bed in his cabin, Nikolas was still wondering what to do. He was wearing a silk nightgown and had the doors to his balcony open to every whisper of wind. The sound of the sea came to him in all its versions: the slap of wave on wood, the gasp of it receding, the creak of rigging, the snap of battened sail. Zhu Chou's scent was still in the room.

He'd never been with a concubine. She was more cultured than any woman he'd yet met. It seemed monstrous to open the door to her cabin and summon her to his bed. But desire infused every part of his body and mind. He'd certainly not sleep now that he knew she was so close.

There was a knock on the door from her cabin. He looked at it for a while. It came again. He rose to his feet, smoothing the silk against his thighs.

He walked over to the door and opened it. She was very different from the last time they'd met. Her hair was not gathered and fell beyond her shoulders in a waterfall of ebony. She was wearing a long red tunic buttoned down the front above slippers. Her face was the same shell-white but without powder. The only artifice had been applied to lips, which she'd painted into a vermilion heart.

'You are in full sail,' she said, moving past him into the cabin. 'You may need to consider a reef if we're to outlast the storm.'

Her clever eyes, unpainted, sparkled like the phosphorescence outside. She walked on to the balcony and he followed.

'You had not realised that I needed a summons?' she asked, turning. 'Perhaps women are less formal in Byzantium.'

Nikolas had no idea what to say. Here was a creature he had not thought likely to meet in this world. She knew his language and made it beautiful. But he felt bigger and clumsier than ever before.

She cocked her head to one side. 'Do you speak?'

Nikolas thought he should try. 'I am overwhelmed, lady.'

She took his hand, looking at him now with curiosity. The tease had left her eyes. 'Yes, you are.' She glanced around her. 'What would you like to do? I could tell you a story or play the *pipa*. Or we could lie together.'

'Or we could talk.'

A breeze came in from the sea, sudden and with an edge of cooler air. She shivered.

'We could talk inside,' he said.

Nikolas turned and walked into the cabin. It was almost as big as Zheng's and had a bed the size of a continent at its centre. The bedspread was embroidered with blossom. There were diaphanous veils hung around that moved in the breeze and made the blossom move with them. The light came from gimballed candles on the walls and was soft and subtle.

They sat opposite each other and didn't speak for a while. There was wine on the table that Nikolas poured for them both. He felt the questions crowding his mind, stumbling over each other in their rush to come out. In the end he simply said: 'I want to know about you. Your life.'

She smiled and placed her cup carefully on the table. The ship was so large that it hardly moved in the swell. She looked down at her slippers. 'I was born in Korea, the daughter of an important man. I was brought to the Son of Heaven as a gift when I was thirteen because my country pays tribute to the Middle Kingdom. I have lived in the harem ever since, rising to be *guifei*, a first-ranking concubine. But I am old now, twenty-six, and the Emperor does not come to me. So I asked to accompany you on this expedition.'

It was all said with calm and exactitude. There was no hint of complaint. It was the story of her life, and she addressed it to her feet.

'Why did you ask to come?'

'I could either teach younger concubines or be yours and travel across the world. It was not a difficult choice.'

Nikolas nodded, looking down in his turn. So he was, after all, part of a process of logic, of survival. He glanced back at her to see puzzlement and curiosity in the eyes that were now searching his.

'I am good at what I do,' she said quietly, her eyes staying on his. 'I can make an aphrodisiac that will keep you in sail for hours.'

He frowned. She was playing him as she would the pipa, pressing his strings to test different sounds.

He said: 'Let's talk about the diadan.'

She sat back in her chair and linked her hands to her front. 'It has eleven thousand books and I have read all of them. It contains secrets not known in the West. Whichever countries are given the diadan will gain great advantage.'

'And will you be the one to decide who gets this knowledge? Is that why you're here? Is that why the Emperor sent you?'

Zhu Chou studied him for a while, deciding. Then she rose from the chair and walked over to the door and opened it. She spoke to someone on the other side. She turned. 'Go and lie on the bed.'

He did as she instructed. She went around the cabin, blowing out the candles one by one, then came and lay down beside him, not touching any part of him. She said: 'Watch.'

He heard the sound of machinery, wheels connecting to cogs and cogs to chains. Looking up, he saw that the ceiling of the cabin was drawing apart, opening slowly to the sky. First one, then ten, then a thousand stars appeared in a night clear of cloud and moon. Someone's god had pulled every jewel from the earth and scattered them across the heavens. He heard the snap of a sail.

'Is it not beautiful?' she whispered. He felt a faint wind on his face and heard her soft breathing. Her scent was all around him. Then her hand was in his.

Nikolas couldn't speak, awed by the power of the universe and the woman beside him who wanted it all explained. He felt her turn her head to him on the pillow. 'The Emperor has the stars counted every night. He has persuaded Ulugh Beg to do the same.' He felt the pillow move as she looked back to the night. 'Before, they would have fought.'

And it came to him then. She was talking about a new world, similar to the one Plethon talked of, a world of Confucian harmony created by trade and shared knowledge. It was a world in which frontiers advanced through reason not war, in which people no longer feared the unknown but embraced it. He looked at her and saw that she was looking at him.

'Can you love?' he asked.

'Do you mean, am I capable? I don't know. I've never tried.'

He leant over her and kissed her on her forehead, his lips staying there.

'I want you to try,' he said.

PART THREE

A GAME OF POPES

CHAPTER EIGHTEEN

CONSTANCE, SPRING 1415

The city of Constance, blooming on the banks of the Bodensee.

The season of spring brought anarchy to the shores of the lake. Rhododendron and narcissi sprang up to lay siege to path and mooring. A thick carpet of snowdrop and primrose rose to assault ankles and senses. The lake grew with new rain and fish grew within it, jumping to the flies, turning somersaults and making mayhem. The great Rhine flowed in from the south and left northwards, fattened like its fish.

This was the richest of the imperial cities, made so by its markets and the sober production of linen. It was about to get richer still by holding the greatest council in the history of the Roman Church.

Anarchy might have come to its streets too had it not been for the monks of the Benedictine Abbey of Peterhausen. The city's population had multiplied twenty-fold and the brothers, whose task it was to organise the council, had been forced to impose rules beyond those of their order. Dogs were to be chained, pickpockets too, prices controlled and sheets and tablecloths changed fortnightly. The seven hundred whores, summoned to feed the confessionals, were to be inspected daily and a fire brigade had set up its happy headquarters next to their place of inspection.

Thirty cardinals, three patriarchs, thirty-three archbishops, one hundred abbots, fifty provosts, three hundred doctors of theology, five thousand monks and friars and eighteen thousand priests had arrived last November by foot, horse, carriage and boat. Kings, princes, dukes, electors and ambassadors had turned the city into a parliament of jostling precedence.

Pope John XXIII's retinue of six hundred had travelled over the Alps. They had ridden in big, six-wheeled wagons with curtains and crossed keys on their sides. They had brought a small army to guard them. A second army of mendicant monks had walked behind swinging incense, selling relics, and holding roadside masses with special indulgences to mark the passing of the Vicar of Christ. The Holy Father's new order of nuns, the Sisters of Sacrifice, had ridden close to the pontiff's own carriage for their protection and his comfort. Behind it all were innkeepers who would never have to work again.

John XXIII had brought with him the greatest humanists of the day: Bruni, Vergiero, Rustici and, of course, Poggio Bracciolini; for this was a cultured, if erring, pope. He had ridden into the city at the end of October, entering its gates clad in white vestments and mitre, mounted on a white horse. Four city burghers had carried a golden canopy over his head while two dukes walked by his side, holding his bridle. Behind him had ridden nine cardinals in long mantles with wide red hats. In front had stretched a line of nine white horses, each covered with a rich saddlecloth, carrying the Pope's wardrobe. A single horse, a little bell jingling on its head, led them all with a casket of silver gilt on its back, to which were attached two candlesticks. Inside was the Holy Sacrament.

Pope John XXIII meant to impress from the start.

Luke was glad to have missed the Council's opening and didn't plan to stay long. He and Giovanni had travelled over the Alps in February, bringing more gold to fund Cossa's extravagant display. Matthew, Arcadius and the Varangian Company had been their escort through late snows and early rain, the rutted mountain tracks parting wheels from their axles. They'd passed abandoned roadside shrines strung out like endless Stations of the Cross.

The journey had been mostly silent. Giovanni's mind was far away in Rimini and Luke had received bad news before he'd left. The gold he was expecting from China would not arrive after all.

At the Monastery of St Gallen, they'd met Cosimo and Poggio Bracciolini.

The Apostolic Secretary had been busy preparing for this council. Now, with it under way, he and Cosimo had gone hunting. He was excited.

'Cicero *and* Quintilian, here in this library. Abbot Gundelfingen likes to gossip so I traded venality for vellum. The manuscripts are extraordinary.'

'He let you take them?'

'Well, no, just copy them. But you'll be amazed at what's in them.'

They were standing looking down on Constance and its lake. There was the cathedral on its hill with the Prince-Bishop's palace beside it where Pope John had made his home. Fingers of smoke reached into the sky and the smell of baking was in the air. Outside the walls was another city of tents.

Luke turned to Cosimo. 'How are things at the council?'

'His Holiness may have misjudged things,' he said, 'which is unusual for him.'

'How so?'

'The mood of the council. People think he's gone too far.' He paused. 'They've passed a decree giving primacy of authority to the council over the Pope. And there's a Frenchman. A theologian.'

There was always a Frenchman. 'The cardinal from Cambrai? I'd heard.'

'Pierre d'Ailly. He leads the delegation and has a mandate from his king. He wants all three popes to abdicate.'

Luke shook his head. 'Impossible without a majority of cardinals, and our pope has two to their every one. Have the Malatestas brought their pope?'

'Not yet. Zoe Mamonas is here.'

'Zoe?'

'She arrived with a party of Venetian bankers before Christmas. She's up to something. Rinaldo degli Albizzi arrived and went straight into a meeting with her.'

Luke considered this. He and Cosimo had last seen Albizzi at the dinner on Mount Olympus. Albizzi was Cosimo's chief rival in Florence.

Luke kicked his horse and they joined the road to the city gate. Was he worried? No. Thanks to Medici efficiency, Pope John was pulling in more money than ever. Every week, new relics were found and more indulgences went on sale. Money arrived from Scandinavia, Iceland, from poverty-stricken Scotland. Why would he be worried how much this Pope spent? The Curia's future income was the best security in the world. He glanced at Cosimo. 'What if Cossa is made to abdicate along with the other two?'

'Then the Curia would have to honour his debts,' said Cosimo. 'He would have done what he'd been asked to do.' He waved away a fly. 'We just couldn't guarantee to get the banking of a combined Curia, that's all.'

'There is another problem,' said Poggio. 'You've heard of Jan Hus?'

Luke glanced at him. 'The heretic preacher from Prague? Has he come to Constance?'

Poggio nodded. 'He came and was immediately arrested by His Holiness. It pleased the cardinals but has set the King of Hungary against him. Sigismund promised Jan Hus safe conduct.'

This was not good news. Constance was in Sigismund's lands and that made him moderator of the council. He was a dangerous man to antagonise.

Cosimo said: 'Cossa is the only pope here at present so he's trying to assert his authority.' He paused. 'But he needs Hus to recant.'

'And if Hus doesn't choose to?'

'Then Sigismund of Hungary will be our pope's enemy and that matters because Sigismund is the host of this council. He decides how it's run.'

'So what do we do?'

Cosimo looked at him. 'I want you to go and talk to Hus, see if you can persuade him to recant. I can get you the permission.'

'Me? I'm not even of your Church.'

'All the more reason for you to try. He'll see you as objective.'

Luke frowned. The Bohemian priest had been raging against indulgences and the excesses of Baldassare Cossa. He'd been telling his followers to desert their clergy and commune directly with God. It wasn't very different from what Plethon was saying and perhaps what the clever humanists wanted to say. Luke could see why a city full of princes of the Church might want such a man jailed. But was he Luke's concern? Unfortunately, yes. Cossa had Luke's money.

'I'll go and see him.'

Later in the evening, Luke and Giovanni were making their way over the small bridge that connected the city to the Dominican Island.

The monastery was a severe structure of stone that occupied most of the island, with four towers and high windows that were little more than slits. Beneath the moon, it cast its image across the lake like a stain. At the gate, they were met by a monk who brought them to the abbot's quarters.

The abbot seemed too young for his station. His face beneath the tonsure shone with unsettling zeal, as did his habit, particularly at the knees. There was no word of welcome.

'Why do you want to see the prisoner?' he asked, rising from behind his desk. Luke saw that he was a small man and that his close-shaved chin was blue in the candlelight. 'To talk to him? It will only encourage him in his heresy.'

Luke stared at him. He was a reptile in every respect. Even his voice was a hiss. He said: 'You will take us to see him. Here is your authority.'

'And I will stay with you,' said the reptile, reading the permit. 'My instructions are to record his every word of heresy.'

Heressssy.

They walked through the door and along several passages. They emerged into a courtyard with a chapter house where the French delegation stayed. They entered a round tower and descended narrow steps to its basement. A monk sat on a stool outside a door studded with iron with a small grille at eye level. The monk rose as they came into view. He had keys on a ring at his waist.

212

The abbot took a torch from the wall. 'Open the door.'

The abbot entered first and Luke and Giovanni had to stoop to follow him. Inside, they were met by the stench of disease and excrement. Lying on the stone floor, surrounded by black straw and chained to the wall, was a tall man of bone and loose skin. His long hair and beard were matted with filth and he had scabs all over his face and body. Next to him were a plate and a bowl of dirty water.

Luke was too shocked to speak. He looked around the cell. It was the width and depth of three men lying end-to-end. It had big rings driven high into walls that dripped with slime. On one side was a low grille with water beyond. They were on the edge of the lake. He turned to the abbot. 'Does King Sigismund know you keep him like this?'

The man shook his head. 'We are outside the King's jurisdiction here. We report only to the Holy Father.'

Luke clenched his fists, fighting the urge to raise them. The man lying before them hadn't moved. 'You are supposed to practise God's mercy,' he whispered.

'We are *Domini canes* – Hounds of God,' said the abbot. 'Our order was founded to combat heresy. The Holy Father Innocent IV permitted us the use of torture. We use it wisely.'

Luke felt sick. He approached Jan Hus and knelt before him. In the light of the abbot's torch he could see a face beneath the hair. Some of the scabs were open and pus ran from them. He turned to Giovanni. 'Your kerchief.'

The hesitation was momentary. Giovanni reached inside his doublet and brought out Cleope's kerchief. He gave it to Luke, who dipped it into the water. When he had wiped the pus and dirt from the face, Luke found a middle-aged man with a good, straight nose, prominent chin and thin, ruptured lips above the beard. The eyes were heavy-lidded and the pupils hidden beneath. He heard the very faintest of sounds and realised that the man was softly humming.

Like Plethon.

He turned again to Giovanni. 'Here, help me.'

Together, they lifted Hus into a sitting position. Luke knelt again, Giovanni beside him. He spoke in Latin. 'Can you understand me?'

Jan Hus didn't answer. He stared at his knees stretched out before him and continued to hum.

'He speaks Latin,' said the abbot, in Latin. 'He understands you.'

Luke looked again at the man opposite him. 'King Sigismund will be told of your condition.'

The man spoke. 'He promised me safe passage.'

The abbot laughed. 'No promise made to a heretic is binding,' he said. His high voice echoed off the stone walls. He moved the torch and the light retreated. Luke rose and took it from him. He let its light play over Jan Hus's body. He was dressed in a brown habit speckled with dried blood. The limbs below were emaciated.

Luke asked: 'When did you last eat?'

'Two, three days.' Hus had turned his head towards him. 'I don't remember.'

The monk with the keys was still standing in the doorway. Luke said to him: 'Get this man proper food and water. Now.'

The monk didn't move.

'If you don't leave now,' said Luke, 'I will break both of your arms.'

There was an awkward silence. Then the abbot spoke. 'Go.'

The monk left, locking the cell door behind him.

214

Luke sat down on the floor next to the heretic. 'Can I talk to you?'

Jan Hus nodded slowly. 'Of course.' His eyelids lifted and Luke found himself looking into clear blue pools; there was humour deep within them. Jan Hus attempted a smile, with care, for his lips were cracked. 'You are here to persuade me to recant,' he said softly. His eyes moved to the abbot. 'They have used torture. You will use kindness. Your way is worse.'

Luke closed his eyes for a moment. It was painful to look at the man before him. 'There is a contradiction here,' he said quietly. He spoke low but knew that the abbot heard every word. 'If this Church is an aberration, what meaning does your recantation have?' He paused. 'They've used the same argument on you: you're a heretic, so no promise to you is binding. If they don't represent your God, isn't your recantation equally invalid?'

Jan Hus smiled. There was blood on his lips. 'What is your name?'

'Luke Magoris.'

'Ah, I have heard of you,' said Jan Hus. 'You are Protostrator of Mistra. They say you saved an empire.' He shook his head slowly. 'But you cannot save me.'

Luke rested his hand on the rough fabric of Jan Hus's sleeve. 'You can let me try,' he said gently.

Hus shook his head again. 'Your argument has been tried. Many times.' He wiped blood from his lips. 'There is logic to it, but how can anyone believe in my word if I don't stand by it?' He glanced across at Giovanni. 'Who are you?'

Giovanni was sitting now. His hands were clasped and there were tears at the rims of his eyes. He brushed them away.

'I am Giovanni, son of Marchese Longo, and page to the Protostrator.'

'Do you know what I believe, Giovanni? I will tell you, so that you will know why they kill me.'

Luke was shaking his head. 'They won't kill you,' he whispered. Suddenly this man's existence was more important to him than any gold. Here was a man brave enough to say what had to be said: that the Roman Church was rotten to the core.

'Of course they'll kill me. They have to.' He smiled again. 'I made my will before I came, Luke Magoris.'

'But –'

'Don't waste your breath. Let me waste mine. If I am to die, it has more value. I am forty-six years old and have had a good life. I do not fear death, I welcome it. The Pope before this one excommunicated me but I think I have God's ear.'

Luke heard an intake of breath behind him. He raised his hand. 'Go on.'

'The Church has become a canker, a parasite,' said Jan Hus. 'It colludes with kings to keep the poor in their place so that they can be ignorant and frightened and robbed. And our Mother Church does worse: she denies them proper communion with their God: the one solace they might have in their wretchedness.'

Jan Hus paused to draw a rattling breath through his lungs. Luke suddenly realised how ill this man was. He'd been three months in this wet, stinking place and its evil had infected every part of his body.

'And this Pope?' Hus went on, shifting himself up the wall and glancing at the abbot. 'Baldassare Cossa is the worst yet. He exchanges salvation for gold to pay for wars he should not be fighting. The Lord told us to love our enemies, not slaughter them.'

The abbot could bear it no more. He moved closer to his prisoner and the hiss became a shout. 'You damn yourself further

216

with every word you speak! You will burn in hell for what you've said against God's Vicar on earth!'

Jan Hus smiled at the abbot. 'What happened to your order, Father?' he asked softly. 'Your founder Dominic was a man who eschewed worldly goods.'

The abbot was breathing hard.

'Was it the Cathars?' continued the heretic. 'Was it what you did to those poor Frenchmen that so poisoned your order? Massacring people just because they wanted to find a new way to their God?'

Luke heard the abbot's breathing quicken.

But Jan Hus hadn't finished. 'Don't you see', he continued, his voice lower, tired, 'that our Church has been captured? Don't you see how these evil, greedy men have perverted God's word to suit their ambitions? We are both prisoners, Father Abbot.'

The abbot had had enough. He stepped forward and slapped the heretic. The blow was so hard that Jan Hus fell back against the stone, hitting his head. In an instant, the abbot himself was on the floor and Giovanni was standing above him, nursing his clenched first. Luke took his arm.

'I know,' said Giovanni. 'A mistake.'

Luke looked down at the man. He wasn't moving and had blood around his head. 'No. I was about to do the same.' He turned to Jan Hus. 'We must get you out of here.'

The heretic shook his head. 'How? Do you have wings?'

Luke had dropped to a knee and was searching the abbot's habit. There were no keys. He heard footsteps outside the cell. Someone was coming down the tower's steps.

He turned to Giovanni. 'The monk. He's got the keys. Quick.'

They moved in front of the fallen abbot, shielding him from view from the door. But Jan Hus was trying to shuffle past them, his chains scraping the stone behind him. He looked at them and his voice was firm. 'No. That is not the way.'

The door opened and the monk stood there with a plate of food in one hand and a candle in the other. He'd left the keys in the door. He looked in amazement at the heretic who had attempted to rise but got only as far as his knees.

Jan Hus had joined his hands in supplication. 'Heaven forgive me, Father. I have knocked your abbot into unconsciousness.'

Luke entered the papal apartments still angry. He had left Giovanni to make his own way back to the inn and strode up to the Prince–Bishop's palace as if marching to war. He would talk to this Pope whose squalid office he was helping pay for.

Inside, Cossa was waiting with his hands folded in front of him. He was smiling. 'Do you have my gold?'

Luke ignored the question. 'Do you know how they keep him?'

Cossa looked surprised first, then frowned. He went over to a table and picked up a glass half-filled with wine. 'Hus is a heretic, Magoris. He is lucky to be alive.'

'Sigismund gave his word.'

Cossa turned. 'But I didn't.' He drank and wiped his lips. 'Anyway, no oath made to a heretic is binding. I've told Sigismund that.'

'Hus is a good man, a man of God,' said Luke. He found that his fists were clenched. 'He simply wants your Church to speak to its people.'

'He is a heretic,' repeated Cossa, 'one who disobeys my edicts. To the point: will he recant?'

Luke suddenly felt very tired. It had been the longest of days and the ride had been hard. He sat in a chair. He wanted wine but wouldn't take it from this man. He closed his eyes, putting fingertips to his eyelids, shaking his head slowly. 'No, he won't recant. Of course he won't recant; he is a man of unusual principle.' He breathed deeply. The smell of the dungeon was still on him. 'Sigismund is not a man to make your enemy, Cossa,' he said quietly. 'He has influence at this council.'

'As do I,' said Cossa. 'I am pope.' He paused. 'I know what I'm doing.'

Luke looked up. 'Do you?' He paused and leant forward. 'Then release Hus before it's too late.'

Cossa drank again and put the glass back on the table. 'And show weakness when I want the Church to unite behind me? I don't think so.'

There was a long silence while the two men looked at each other. Luke had wanted to leave this council the minute he'd delivered the gold but Hus had changed things. He thought of the starved man in his dungeon and of Giovanni's face when he'd seen him. He'd have to stay, at least to talk to Sigismund who might have the authority to release him.

'Do you have my gold?' Cossa asked again.

Luke stared at him. Whatever the benefit to Mistra, he could no longer support this man, could no longer breathe the same air as him. He rose to leave.

'No,' he said.

Zoe found Carlo Malatesta waiting for her at the inn. She'd arranged a room at the back where they might talk alone. It had a table and two chairs, one of which was built into the wall. There was a table between with a jug and goblets on it. She knew how to recognise him.

'It's a burn,' he said as she stared.

She saw that he took no trouble to disguise it as others might. The scar disfigured half his face but his collar was low and his beard trimmed around it. He put his hat down on the table and sat.

Zoe was dressed as if for mourning. All was Byzantine and black: a long tunic that fell from neck to ankle in discreet embroidery. Only when it caught the light was the pattern apparent. She watched Carlo's gaze rake her body and felt contempt. His eyes came back to hers and she saw the violence in them.

'The Varangians have much to answer for,' she said quietly, sitting opposite him and moving the jug nearer him.

Malatesta poured beer. She saw that his hands were scarred. 'If it was them.'

'Oh, it was them,' she said. 'Musa had an alliance with Venice. He learnt of Venice's plan to attack Monemvasia and told the Varangians. I was Musa's concubine.'

Malatesta watched her as he drank. 'Are you sure of it?'

Zoe leant back against the panelling. It had been the seat of gamblers and there were numbers etched above her on the wood. 'Can you think of any reason why I would lie to you?'

Carlo Malatesta looked down into his beer. He had begun to tap the goblet against the table, both hands encircling it. She saw that his fury was barely controlled. All of the world had heard about Negroponte. Venice had been humiliated, along with her *generalissimo*. Here was a man who wanted revenge.

'You asked for a meeting,' he said.

'Yes,' said Zoe. 'I am the Malatestas' banker. Or was.' She paused. 'Your family has moved all its money into the Magoris Bank.'

Malatesta frowned. 'Whatever Magoris has done, his bank

has the papal debt,' he said. 'It is a good place for our money to be.'

'Not if Cossa is no longer pope.'

Malatesta shook his head. 'The Curia would honour the debt of any pope that resigned his office, though none have ever done so.'

'If he resigned, yes. But what if he were deposed?'

The goblet's tempo quickened. 'It would never happen. It has never happened.'

'Wouldn't it? What are Church councils for, if not to change things? And this one is the biggest so far.'

Malatesta stared at her, his mouth working beneath his beard as if tasting something new. 'What do you know?'

'I know what the courtesans of Venice know, and they are the best-informed people in Europe. Many of them are here. I know that Sigismund makes the rules for this council and that he wants to be Holy Roman Emperor. I know that the Electors of Germany won't elect him unless an example is made of Cossa.' She paused. 'I think this council might become quite exciting soon. Where is your pope?'

Malatesta now had his chin in his hand, his beard parted by his knuckles. 'Gregory is in Rimini. He will come when Avignon comes, not before.'

Zoe nodded. 'I hear that Benedict may not come at all,' she said. 'Sigismund has spoken with the French King. I expect he may want to speak to you about Gregory as well. He may make you a better offer than the Medici's.'

Malatesta's frown was universal: in his brow, his lips, the set of his broad shoulders. He was used to stupid mercenaries, not clever bankers; not clever *women* bankers. 'What about my money?'

'I should ask for it back. I hear Magoris has brought more gold to Constance for Cossa. He may be pleased to unburden some.'

Malatesta was nodding slowly. Zoe thought it time to change the subject. 'I'm told you've brought Cleope to Constance, but without her father.'

'For her education,' he said.

'Magoris's page Giovanni Longo spent time at Rimini while you were recovering at Baden. Was there an attachment, do you think?'

She'd guessed his suspicions and they were there in his eyes. Nothing about this man was complicated.

'You should know that they've met,' Zoe continued. 'Briefly, in the square, with others present. But they talked.' She paused, seeing the question. 'The courtesans told me.'

She rose and looked at the man still sitting with his beer. 'I should watch her if I were you,' she said.

CHAPTER NINETEEN

CONSTANCE, SPRING 1415

It was early morning and Luke was standing in an upper room of King Sigismund's palace in Constance. He had asked to meet the King of Hungary straight after leaving Cossa, sending a note up to the palace. Now he was looking out of the window watching ducks flying in raucous formation with the sun on their backs and vermilion on their wings. The lake they had risen from was still shrouded in mist; trees without foundations hovered above its banks. Far out, two fishermen talked across their nets, dismembered from the waist. Luke's eyes travelled in over the city walls to streets beginning to fill, to innkeepers sweeping their porches while their wives sat and counted the takings of the night. A wagon was being unloaded behind two horses that nuzzled each other's noses. Monks shovelled manure into sacks while bakers deployed portable ovens to tempt out their first customers. He watched people gathering to walk up to the cathedral.

The door opened and Sigismund strode into the room. He was tall, heavily bearded and dressed in plain robes: more monk than king. 'You knocked out the abbot,' he said. 'Or your page did. Was it wise?'

223

Luke bowed from the waist. He'd not met the King before. 'It got Hus fed, highness. They were starving him.'

The King had stopped in front of him. 'Your page will apologise to the abbot.'

'He's already done so,' said Luke. 'And gave him ice for his head.'

Sigismund was studying him closely. He'd heard much about Luke Magoris, once Varangian, now banker to the Pope. They said he was a good man, but was he persuasive? 'I am assuming you didn't manage to make him recant?'

Luke shook his head. 'He'll not betray his followers.'

'And you went to see your pope afterwards to persuade him to release him.' He paused. 'Now you come to me.'

'Your highness guaranteed him safe passage.'

Sigismund was looking at him with curiosity. 'I would expect you to argue Cossa's case now, to justify his stand. You do not.'

Luke remained silent. No question had been put to him.

The King shrugged. 'Well, Hus's release is no longer my priority. In fact, it may better suit me to keep him imprisoned just for now. He is a distraction.' Sigismund turned and walked over to a desk. He looked at some papers, then up at Luke. 'The council's second session opens this morning and I must prepare. Will you be attending?'

Would he? He'd never meant to, but should he now? Something important was happening in Constance that he knew mattered. He could leave or he could bear witness. 'I will attend, majesty.' He bowed and walked to the door.

Outside was an anteroom with two people standing in it: Carlo Malatesta and an elderly cardinal. They were dressed in their finest clothes and Carlo had his hat beneath his arm. Luke saw the condottiere's ravaged face and met his eye for an instant. He saw hate without horizon within a single eyeball and looked away. He thought of Negroponte and he thought of Giovanni. Carlo Malatesta had been back in Rimini when Giovanni had been there last. Could he suspect something?

Luke looked everywhere for Giovanni, wanting to warn him. He was not in the cathedral when Luke arrived to celebrate the opening of the council's second session.

Now the mass was drawing to a close and the session was about to begin. Luke looked up at the vaulted ceiling, its image vague behind incense. Thick bolts of sunlight cleaved through the smoke and it seemed that heaven might conceivably be looking down on Constance.

There was the sound of shuffling and he looked down to see cardinals forming a ring of red around Pope John XXIII, who was blessing the congregation with raised hand while sacristans held open his mantle. The hosannas rang out and the incense rose.

He looked back to the altar. The choir and lesser clergy were filing out, their heads down. The cardinals remained and monks appeared from the side chapels with chairs for them. Four men brought in a throne, which they placed in front of the altar.

Pope John was moving towards the throne.

'Holy Father.' Sigismund had risen from the front row.

The Pope stopped and looked at him, surprised. Sigismund walked up the three steps to the altar, his boots loud on the marble. He whispered in the papal ear and then sat on the throne.

Another chair was brought in and placed in front of Sigismund at the bottom of the steps. The Pope looked at it, then at Sigismund, then at the circle of cardinals. With the

225

smallest of shrugs, he walked over and sat. There was complete silence.

King Sigismund turned to the cardinals and nodded. With one movement, they also sat. Then he nodded to the congregation. It sat too. No word had been said beyond Sigismund's whisper. The council's second session had begun and much had already changed. Luke looked around him.

Much of the congregation of city burghers, merchants and their wives had been replaced by theologians and clerks. The sea of coloured silk and damask had swept out and a tide of sober black, worn and patched, washed in. Secretaries carrying lecterns with scrolls tucked under their arms now stood silently on either side of the church, pens aloft. Poggio had placed his own behind the Pope's throne and now caught Luke's eye. His face was solemn.

The cardinals sat in a ruby necklace around King Sigismund's throne. Most of them were Italians, appointed by the man who sat below the King. They cast anxious glances at their patron.

Finally, when all was ready, the King raised his hand and two more chairs were brought in and placed together at the bottom of the altar steps, across from the Pope. Luke saw a small frown pass across Cossa's brow.

Sigismund rose and looked about him, opening his arms in greeting. 'Holy Father, Majesties, Lords Spiritual and Temporal, brothers and sisters in Christ, I bid you all welcome!'

His words boomed through the cathedral and lingered above the congregation long after he had spoken. Six hundred heads sat motionless upon their shoulders. The King waited a while and then spoke again. 'We have gathered in this church to try to end this shameful schism that has so disgraced our Church for too many years. We ask God to grant us the wisdom to return a single pope to the throne of St Peter!'

The only movement in the cathedral was the languid swirl of incense high above the altar and the sun's play upon it. Someone coughed far away and Luke's fingers found moisture on his palms.

Sigismund continued: 'There are men more learned than I amongst this congregation who have argued the merits of each of these popes and the means to make them one. I myself have spent many hours in prayer seeking guidance from my God.' Sigismund paused. 'In his infinite goodness, He has shown me a path.'

Luke felt his heartbeat quicken. A path?

Silence among the congregation, every breath suspended. The only sound the scratch, scratch of quill on parchment.

'They must all go.'

Luke looked at Cossa. He hadn't moved. His face had drained of colour and he blinked once, twice.

King Sigismund spoke again, raising his arms to his audience. 'But it is not for me to decide this, it is for you. The council has decreed that its judgement will sit above everyone else's, even a pope's. The council will put its views to these cardinals' – here he gestured behind him – 'and they will cast their vote. Their majority view will hold on this matter.'

Pope John's shoulders seemed to fall slightly. He had the most cardinals, after all.

'But two rules I wish to introduce, rules which the learned Monsignor Pierre d'Ailly from Paris has told me are within my jurisdiction as moderator of this council.'

King Sigismund stayed silent for a while. He had put a finger to his lips as if bidding silence in others. He glanced at the clerks who watched him, pens poised. He looked down at the Pope, who was whispering into Poggio's ear. Sigismund waited for him to finish.

'First,' he said, the finger now a numeral, 'I propose to yield presidency of this session to two men I have chosen.' He turned and gestured to an elderly cardinal who sat at the end of the semi-circle. He was the same man Luke had seen in Sigismund's anteroom. 'The cardinal for Ragusa will be one.'

The cardinal for Ragusa rose slowly. He walked past the King and down the steps and sat in one of the chairs.

'The other', said Sigismund, looking at the front seats of the congregation, 'will be my friend and wise counsellor, Carlo Malatesta, Prince of Rimini.'

Noise came to the cathedral, whisper spreading from row to row like a swarm. This was extraordinary. Carlo Malatesta had risen and walked over to the second chair to take his seat. He turned and embraced the man next to him.

Luke looked back at Pope John. Poggio was again at his ear, making little gestures with his hands. Cossa seemed distracted. The whispers were rising and the King raised his hand for silence.

'Prince Carlo Malatesta.'

Carlo got to his feet, turned and bowed to Sigismund. He was dressed not as a condottiere but as a stateman: rich, powerful and wise. His long gown was as black as a doctor of divinity's, but finely woven. His sword and dagger were absent. He waited for silence, then spoke. 'The King of Hungary has talked of two rules,' he said. 'The first is the appointment of myself and my lord cardinal of Ragusa. The second . . .'

Now the condottiere turned around and faced the cardinals. His hand swept across them, gathering them to his call. 'The second relates to the method of voting. Up until now, it has been the custom for the cardinals to vote individually, each man's vote counting as one.' He turned back to the audience. 'But this does not reflect the reality of how the three popes draw their support.' He paused. 'Their support comes from kings and the countries they rule.'

Luke fixed his gaze on the Prince of Rimini. Carlo Malatesta was enjoying himself. His eyes were bright above his scar and he was opening and closing his hands as if preparing for battle. 'So this will change,' he said. 'From now, the voting will be done in blocs, one vote for every nation. The Italian city states will vote for Italy. It is fairer.'

The cathedral exploded. Suddenly it was full of shouts, not whispers. Pope John's advantage of cardinals had disappeared at a stroke. Luke looked at Cossa. He was trying to rise but Poggio had his hand on his shoulder. He was shaking his head, his mitre askew.

Carlo Malatesta raised his voice. 'There is more!' He produced a scroll from beneath his robe and waved it in the air. 'I have a bull from Pope Gregory in Rimini,' he cried. 'It permits me to place his resignation from the throne of St Peter before the council. We have the same from Benedict of Avignon.'

Now the uproar was universal. Men were rising everywhere to shout their approval or otherwise. Scrolls were being shaken in the air next to fists. Monks were running down the aisle, begging people to resume their seats. Luke saw soldiers with halberds appear from the side chapels.

Carlo Malatesta was pacing up and down as if looking for someone to fight. He raised both his hands for silence but none came.

The cardinal from Ragusa had got to his feet. He'd done so by stages for he was old and arthritic. As he rose, he patted Carlo on the arm with a scroll he held in his hand. He raised it for quiet and the congregation gradually grew silent. It took some time and the cardinal spent it slowly opening the scroll.

'Baldassare Cossa,' he said at last, turning to the Pope. He paused, waiting for the last murmur to subside, for the two words to be understood for what they meant. 'Baldassare Cossa. You are hereby accused of certain charges that have brought ignominy to our Holy Mother Church.' He paused. 'Among these are the charges of incest, heresy and murder.' He looked up at the cathedral congregation, then back at the cardinals, who were sitting still as granite. 'It will be the duty of this council to assess these charges and, if they are deemed to be fair, to decide if they warrant not only your deposition from the throne of St Peter.'

Two hours later, Luke arrived at the papal apartments to find Cosimo de' Medici and Poggio but no pope. He'd left the cathedral soon after watching Cossa walk with what dignity he could muster through the silent, staring crowd to the big doors at its end. He'd found the Varangians in the square outside and they'd split up to search the city for Giovanni. They'd not found him.

The apartments were a mess. Everywhere there were signs of haste: clothes strewn across the floor, an empty jewel box on its side. The papal mitre sat alone on a table. The air smelt of lavender.

'He's fled,' said Cosimo as Luke entered. He had a letter in his hand. 'He left this for us. He leaves the mitre in part-recompense for the sums he owes.'

'Where has he gone?' asked Luke, taking the letter and reading it.

'He doesn't say. Perhaps to Braccio?'

Luke considered this. Cossa had been persuaded to leave his condottiere behind and it was a long way to Montone. 'No, he'll have gone north. Not all the German princes like Jan Hus.' He looked at Poggio. 'Will they depose him in his absence?'

Poggio brought his hands together. 'They'd prefer to find him and bring him back.'

'To depose him?'

The secretary shrugged. 'And possibly pretend he never existed. If Cossa is deemed never to have been pope then his debts will not be seen as belonging to the Church.'

Luke felt sick. It was beyond his worst imaginings. He looked at the mitre. 'Will this help?'

Cosimo shook his head. 'It might cover a fraction,' he said. 'But everything comes down to time. If the Curia won't honour his debts, we can still pay them off from revenues provided we keep the banking. We just need time.'

'Which', said Luke, 'is what we may not have. It depends on the Venetian banks.' He thought of Zoe. 'I fear Venice will be impatient.'

There were footsteps on the stairs outside and the door opened. Arcadius was there, panting, his hand to his stomach. 'You must come quickly,' he said. 'We've found Giovanni.'

As Luke left the palace, Zoe was entering a discreet inn by the back door. She came into a room without windows. Two men rose from the table as she entered. Both were Florentines.

'The Pope has fled,' she said, sitting down. She patted her hood to her shoulders. 'He was seen leaving the palace in disguise.'

Albizzi, sitting, said: 'You speak for Venice?'

Zoe nodded. 'I speak for Venice's banks and, you may conclude, the Doge.'

Rinaldo degli Albizzi spread his hands on the table. It was a worn piece of oak that had been reshaped by words carved into its surface, the doodlings of generations of drinkers. He leant back in his chair. 'Then let us review where we are. Pope John has been charged with crimes incompatible with the papacy. He has chosen to flee, which means his cardinals will desert him. When he is brought back and deposed, the Roman Curia will be given the excuse to default on his debts, debts that are held by the Medici and Magoris Banks and some Venetian banks as well.'

The other Florentine was of the Spini banking family, another rival of the Medici. He said: 'Please remind us of the conditionalities of the Venetian debt, Donna Zoe.'

'Well,' said Zoe, 'the conditionality *was*, of course, the future income of the Curia. But our banks were specific when they took share of the loan: a secondary charge over Medici and Magoris assets should that income ever cease. Venice's banks are likely to require immediate repayment.'

'And if repayment cannot be made?'

'Then seizure of assets,' said Zoe. 'Although we expect that to be uneccessary with the Medici.'

'And', said Albizzi, 'you'll have to go to Mistra to seize the Magoris Bank's assets.'

'Quite possibly,' she said without expression. 'That will depend on the Doge.'

Spini leant forward. 'As for the popes, we have two resigned and one about to be deposed. Where does that leave us?'

Zoe turned to him. 'Venice, and others, will push for a successor who'll remove the banking from the Medici. This will be your chance.'

'But why would the Mamonas Bank not take the Curia's banking for itself?'

232

Zoe looked from one to the other of the men, seeing the greed in their eyes. 'Because we have lent money to a man who has been deposed from the papacy. We are seen to share some of his sin. The Curia cannot give us the banking.'

As Luke sped through the streets, Arcadius told him what had happened. 'Giovanni was at an inn, upstairs with Cleope Malatesta. Then Carlo arrived with some men and Cleope's nurse wouldn't let them pass. We heard her shrieking – it's what brought us out. Matthew told me to get you.'

Running down the hill from the palace they could hear the sounds of fighting ahead. Then they saw the inn. Varangians and Malatesta henchmen were face to face with swords. Below them was a body.

Luke pushed them aside. Matthew was lying on the cobbles with a hand clamped below his heart. Blood was pumping through his fingers. He looked up and saw Luke. His face was ashen.

'He missed,' he said.

Luke looked down at the wound, gently moving aside his friend's hand. 'He did. You'll live.' He looked around. 'What happened?'

Peter of Norfolk spoke. 'They were trying to get in and we were stopping them. Then a window opened above and Giovanni shouted to us to stop fighting, to let Carlo Malatesta in. Matthew looked up and Carlo stabbed him.'

Luke got to his feet and went through the inn door and ran up the stairs, taking two at a time, Arcadius hard behind. One turn, two turns, the banisters shaking. There were screams coming from above, women's screams.

The bedroom door was open and he could see ankles:

uncovered, prostrate. He bounded up the last flight and entered the room.

Carlo Malatesta was standing above the body of Giovanni, breathing hard, a dagger in his hand. It had blood on it.

Cleope was standing in a corner of the room, her maid's arms around her, covering her nakedness, holding her back. The girl's hair was disordered and her face splashed with tears.

Luke knelt by his son, lifted his head and saw a face covered in bruises. He looked down at his body. There was a gash in his side, close to the heart. Arcadius turned and took a sheet from the bed, ripping it, He knelt beside Luke.

'Here, use this.' He was already using it to stem the flow of blood. 'Let me.'

Luke moved to one side, his eyes never leaving Giovanni's face. His son's eyes were closed, the eyelids flickering. There was a bruise at his temple and another at his jaw. His mouth was set with pain.

Luke looked up at Carlo Malatesta. 'If you have killed him,' he said, 'I will kill you.'

CHAPTER TWENTY

CALICUT, SPRING 1415

Admiral Zheng's treasure fleet put into Calicut ahead of the monsoon rains. It had taken more than a year for it to reach India and not a ship had been lost on the way. Much of the time had been spent at the port of Malacca, which guarded the straits through which the treasure fleets must pass to reach the west. King Parameswara was the new ruler there and Admiral Zheng wished to make an ally of him.

Shulen, Nikolas and Zhu Chou had passed the time in different ways. Shulen had ventured into the jungle to find plants for medicine, learning the local Malay language to do so. Nikolas and Zhu Chou had explored the diadan together. All of them had preferred the comfort aboard to the mosquitoes ashore and they'd whiled away the monsoon listening to the drumming of rain on teak.

Now Shulen was on deck, looking at a city that seemed home to every nation. There were as many minarets as Hindu domes above its walls and the harbour bristled with the masts of Arab dhows. It was undoubtedly rich, since gold flashed through the smoke that rose from pyres cluttering the beach in front.

She glanced back at the three hundred junks that filled the

horizon. 'Is the Zamorin ready for so many of us, do you think?' she asked.

Admiral Zheng was gazing through a tube that he used to magnify the view, another wonder of the diadan. 'There are many Chinese in the city already.' He pushed the tube back into his belt. 'And the Zamorin will be pleased to see us. Our army will help him win his war. He fights with the city of Cochin further down the coast.'

'Why don't the Hindus themselves trade instead of fighting?'

'Because', replied Zheng, 'they believe that the ocean is the resting place of God. If they disturb it, they will lose caste.' He smiled the same way he did when talking of the qilin. 'They seem to do well enough through others' trade. Chen Cheng thinks Calicut the richest city in the world.'

Shulen looked back to the shore where a sudden wind had parted the smoke. Next to the temples were huge factories and warehouses for the spices, silk, porcelain and everything else bartered from this Malabar coast. Luke had been right to look east for the gold to save Mistra.

Except we don't have it.

She'd written to him before she'd left, explaining what had happened, why she was coming west to find a jornufa that she thought might be still in Samarcand. She hoped a reply would be waiting for her there.

They dropped anchor in the port as a late sun honeyed the sea and made fireworks of the leaping fish. She, Nikolas and Zhu Chou went ashore, taking an hour to cross the bazaar, bartering as they went with Indian merchants who counted on their toes as well as their fingers. The Chinese quarter lay on a hill to the north-west and Zhu Chou led them there. They entered the visitors' compound and were shown to rooms.

236

Later, Admiral Zheng joined them for dinner. They ate on a verandah, the city lights strewn below and, beyond, the black swell of a limitless sea. The hum of the city's voice came up to them with the smell of its cooking and a million stars mirrored the fires of man. Zhu Chou had brought with her papers from the diadan and, when they'd eaten, she spread out a map.

'The world,' she said, smoothing it with her palms, 'both what is known and unknown.'

Nikolas lifted a candle and moved it across the surface. He stopped and pointed. 'That is *terra incognita*. They think there is a continent between China and Europe.'

'Which I will find,' said Admiral Zheng, 'if it's there.'

The distance was immense. 'Can your ships sail so far from land?' asked Nikolas.

The admiral opened his big hand and put two fingers on the map, turning them twice as if they were dividers. 'Who knows? We can only try. Perhaps others will do it before us.'

Nikolas moved the candle south. 'Africa,' he said. He came to empty space and travelled west. 'What's this?'

He was hovering over something that caught the light. It was the picture of a black king sitting on a throne holding a nugget of gold. 'Ah, that,' said Zhu Chou, smiling. 'That is the Emperor of Mali with his gold.' She brought her finger down to the image and traced a line up to Alexandria, then Venice. 'And this is the route by which it comes into Europe.'

Zhu Chou moved her finger to the bottom of India. 'But to our route. We are here and we are to go here, then here.' She pointed to Delhi, then Samarcand. 'When we've found the qilin, we'll bring it here.' Her finger moved across the map to the top of the Persian Gulf. 'Basra, where Admiral Zheng will meet us.'

237

The admiral nodded. 'And, when we begin to trade with the West, Basra will be where our sea route ends and the land route will begin. No longer will Alexandria be the only way into Europe.'

'Which is why', said Nikolas, 'we must get the qilin back to the Emperor. Mehmed has won his war and Luke can open the land route at last. In Samarcand, we'll talk to Ulugh Beg.'

They left Calicut after a week and rode up through India with a small army of Ming scholars, scribes and soldiers, as well as the transport to carry a qilin. They arrived at Delhi where Khizr Khan now ruled and saw how a great city resurrects itself from annihilation. Like other parts of Tamerlane's empire, Delhi had declared itself independent soon after his death. The long shadow of terror that had stretched from Samarcand to Constantinople was shortening by the year.

In Delhi, Shulen hardly saw Nikolas and Zhu Chou. She heard they'd asked Khizr Khan if they could meet the city's learned men, then disappeared with them to cities further south that Tamerlane hadn't reached. They'd taken with them scholars, translators and the instruments needed for measuring and recording. They'd returned with books full of numbers and drawings, with seeds and samples of plants and people who'd join the great diadan enterprise.

One evening, she found them bent over some papers in their bedroom. She passed a boy working a ceiling fan with his toe and discovered them kneeling on the marble floor, their heads almost touching. The papers were full of drawings, their corners lifting as she came in. She sat down on the bed. 'What have you there?'

Nikolas looked up. He was wearing glasses, the first time

Shulen had seen him do so. He took them off and rubbed his eyes. 'It's a chain pump for irrigating rice fields. We need to adapt it for other crops.'

'For the Indians?'

Nikolas nodded. He put on his glasses, looked down again and turned a page. She asked: 'Is it in the diadan?'

'Yes,' he said, yawning, 'and it will solve a problem for Khizr Khan whose kingdom has too many mouths to feed, even after Tamerlane's best efforts.'

Shulen moved from the bed and came to kneel beside him. She looked down at the drawing and others of locks and sluices and conduit channels. She asked: 'And what will you get in return?'

Zhu Chou looked across at her. 'Tribute,' she said.

'Gold?'

'No, knowledge. There are things the Indians know that we don't. We'll collect them for the diadan, then move on.'

Shulen glanced at Nikolas, noticing that he'd taken Zhu Chou's hand as she'd spoken. He looked up.

'Shulen, there are things here that you wouldn't believe possible, things that could make a man rich, and dangerous.' He paused. 'We must make sure they fall into the right hands.'

They left Delhi a month later, their horses splashing through monsoon rivers on the road north. They crossed mountains and left the rains behind, their clothes strung up to dry between soldiers' lances. They came to Kesh and spent a night at Tamerlane's palace there. Some said it was the biggest building on earth, with so many rooms that Tamerlane could never have visited each in his time remaining.

Then they came to Samarcand, city of Ulugh Beg.

Almost as soon as she'd arrived, Shulen left to find her qilin. Nikolas and Zhu Chou, meanwhile, presented Ulugh Beg with Ptolemy's *Almagest* and stayed to talk about trade.

Shulen took only her mother, Khan-zada, with her, and together they entered the Garden of Earthly Delights on the outskirts of the city where she'd last seen Tamerlane's giraffe. It was evening and the towers and domes of Samarcand were a shimmer of aquamarine and gold in the distance. They were talking about the past.

Shulen looked around the garden. 'It's not what it was.' She held her mother's hand in hers, using the other to loosen the collar of her tunic. The sun's heat was still strong and the trees they were passing offered no shade. The garden had become a vast area of weed and grass, grazed to its roots, with skeletal trees on their sides. They were approaching a pool with mud around it where an old elephant was lying half-submerged, a mahout on its neck.

Khan-zada stopped. She pointed towards a slope rising gently from the other side of the pool. A wooden platform sat at its summit, waist-high, with a broken rail around it. There was fine carving still on its sides. 'Do you remember that?'

Shulen stared at her. She hadn't seen her mother for eight years but she'd hardly changed. When she smiled, the lines bracketing her mouth were the only ones on her face.

'I remember Tamerlane sitting there, almost blind,' Khan-zada continued. 'I remember the ambassadors from China being lifted to him by their armpits.' She paused. 'And I remember you giving him the gift of sight: glasses to see through.'

They were both silent then, thinking of an old man who'd probably loved them both in his madness. Now the garden where he'd set his tent had its own sort of madness. Shulen, still holding her mother's hand, asked: 'What has it been like these last years, without him?'

'It's like a great wind has been sucked back into the earth.'

'Thank God Ulugh Beg is not like his grandfather.' Shulen turned towards the pool. The elephant was standing now, the mahout next to it in the water, washing its sides with a long brush. She called.

'You know him?' asked Khan-zada.

'I gave him blankets against the cold once,' she replied. 'Outside Damascus. He'll know where the qilin is.'

The mahout left his elephant and came towards them. He was wearing nothing but a loincloth that clung to his legs and groin. He was small and wiry and had grey stubble around his smile. He knelt before Shulen.

'Ravindi,' she said, 'get up. Where are your friends?'

The man rose and pressed Shulen's hand, kissing it. He said: 'Majesty, most mahouts die when their animals die; it usually happens that way. There are five of us left here, the rest inside the city.'

'We look for the jornufa,' said Khan-zada. 'Has it survived?'

'The jornufa?' The man shook his head. 'The jornufa died of cold last winter. They built a house for it with fire beneath the floor and space in the walls for the heat to rise. But the house fell down.'

No qilin.

Shulen felt the sadness of the garden steal over her like its weed. Tamerlane's buildings, built in such a hurry that they had no foundations, were falling down one by one, like his empire. This one had taken the giraffe with it.

Khan-zada reached into her sleeve and took out a small bag of coins that she gave to the mahout. She led Shulen to a tree

241

and they sat. Khan-zada brought out a rolled parchment from her sleeve. 'This letter arrived for you. From Luke, I think.'

Shulen opened it. It was from Luke. It told her what had happened at Constance and what since.

'He's in trouble,' she said, resting the letter in her lap.

'What sort of trouble?'

'Money. He's set up a bank that lent money to a pope who's been disgraced and they can't get it back. The Venetians had some involvement in the debt and are threatening Mistra to recover it.' She paused. 'He needs gold.' She looked down at the letter, reread it, then looked up at her mother. 'And there's Bedreddin. He was exiled to Anatolia when Mehmed became sultan. Now he's risen against Mehmed and men are flocking to his banner. He may cross to Europe at any time and threaten Mistra too.'

'And what has Luke done?'

'He's built a wall.' She smiled as she spoke, looking away to hide it. 'He also says that Bayezid had a jornufa in Edirne.' She paused. 'He'll meet me there.'

Khan-zada was looking at her carefully. 'Will you go?'

Shulen gazed out into the garden. It was a place of memories, most of them connected to him. She felt him there more than Tamerlane. Then she looked back at her mother.

'I think I must, don't you?'

CHAPTER TWENTY-ONE

HEXAMILION WALL, CORINTH, AUTUMN 1415

The Hexamilion Wall was nearly finished. Luke had used the gold he had brought back from Constance to hire more stonemasons and labourers. Under Arcadius's supervision, they had worked through the hot summer months to build six miles of wall from sea to sea, with towers every fifty yards and a fortress in the middle. It would be the teeth in the mouth of the Peloponnese, but it would be useless without a navy.

Luke was thinking this as he stood on the wall looking out over the Gulf of Corinth. He would finish the wall but there would be no money over for anything else. Six warships sat unfinished in the shipyards of Kiparissi and the iron furnaces at Voutamas lay cold.

It was mid-morning and the sea was a brittle blue beneath sky that seemed all sun. Behind him the plain of Corinth stretched out to mountains almost lost to the haze. The earth was red and dry in fields exhausted by summer. Mistra longed for rain.

Beside him sat Arcadius and Matthew. They were all stripped to the waist and Matthew's scar was almost invisible against his sunburnt skin. They'd been working all week on the wall and were passing a wine skin between them.

'Four choices is too many,' said Luke from a frown.

'Well,' said Matthew, 'let's examine them. The right place for you to be will become obvious.' He paused. 'First we have this wall which should be finished in a month. Bedreddin is assembling an army of fanatics but doesn't have the ships to cross to Europe. If he manages to get here, he'll fight Mehmed first, then Constantinople. If he comes to Mistra, I can manage without you.' He glanced to his right. 'With Arcadius, of course.'

Luke tried to interject, but Matthew raised his hand. 'Wait, or I'll lose my train of thought. Next, we have the Baden springs in Germany where Fiorenza has taken Giovanni to repair. We know he'll live now, so you'd only get in the way.'

Luke stayed silent. His son was recovering in the care of the woman who'd borne him. He thought about him every moment of the day.

'Then we have Venice, where Cosimo says you must go to plead with the very people who are holding us to ransom. But begging is beneath the Protostrator's dignity and better left to the Italians.'

Matthew pointed north. 'Finally, we have Edirne. Shulen's letter is very clear: the gold from China is dependent on finding this jornufa. She hasn't found it in Samarcand, so Edirne must be the right place to go.'

But Matthew hadn't mentioned the most important factor of all: Anna. Since Luke's return from Constance, she'd been withdrawn and angry in equal measure. They had not lain together for six months. She had minded his absences but now she minded something else more.

Giovanni.

He missed his elder son, and it showed.

Then there was Shulen. How would Anna react to him meeting her again? He would find out soon enough. She was bringing Hilarion to see the wall.

He rose. 'Let me think about it. I'll join you later.'

Luke walked some way to another stone and sat. He opened Shulen's letter and reread it. She would be at Edirne within the week. Matthew was right: he should go there. He'd be back soon enough and Anna would have to understand. Cosimo could meet the Venetians on his own.

He looked up at the wall. It ran into the distance, its towers still ribbed by scaffold, the ground raw beside it. It was a patchwork of coloured stone gathered from the ruins of this ancient landscape for one last effort to hold back the barbarian. He wondered if the glory of former civilisations still clung to those stones. A breeze came in from the sea and he tasted salt on his tongue.

He heard a shout and looked up. Hilarion was approaching, Anna behind him. He put the letter away and rose. He waved.

Hilarion was twelve now and growing fast. He had long hair, redder than fox-fur, falling to broad shoulders above a body starting to form the angles of adulthood. His arms were covered in fine orange down above a chaos of freckles. His face was freckled too and held eyes of startling green. He was becoming more like his mother every day.

'Three miles this way' – Hilarion was running with his arms stretched open – 'and three miles that. The isthmus is fortified as it was in the days of Ancient Greece.'

'Ha!' laughed Luke, embracing his son. 'So you do listen to Plethon! Did he tell you when it was last built?'

'A thousand years ago by Theodosius after Alaric the Goth attacked Greece.'

245

Luke held his son away and smiled. 'Hilarion, I never tell you enough how proud you make me.'

'What were you reading?' Anna was coming up to them. She looked hot and tired. 'What was that letter?'

Luke glanced at Hilarion. 'It was from Shulen. She wants me to meet her in Edirne. I'll explain later.'

Anna was already shaking her head. 'But you're needed here – we have Bedreddin at our gates!' She was staring at him. 'You're protostrator, for God's sake.'

'Anna, please.'

But she had already turned and was walking away. Luke watched her go. He turned to his son. 'Let me show you the wall.'

They climbed to the ramparts and walked along them, passing masons dressing the last of the stones and soldiers sitting in their shade, taking their ease. They came to a tower where archers were firing arrows into a target far away, their forearms shaking with the effort of drawing strings to their chins.

Hilarion asked: 'Where are the Varangians?'

Luke passed an arrow to one of the bowmen. 'Further down the wall. They're teaching the Albanians how to fire the longbow.'

Hilarion looked out to sea. Blue water stretched to the horizon, empty of anything bigger than a fishing boat. The sun was hot and Luke's arm heavy on his shoulder but there was nowhere he would rather be. His mind was as peaceful and uncluttered as it had ever been. The fits came less often now and, when they did, were less violent. Every month, Fiorenza sent nasty liquid from Chios and it seemed to be working. Soon, perhaps, he might be rid of them forever. He had only one worry: why were his parents arguing?

They descended the steps of the tower until they reached the ground. They found a well and sat on its edge.

Luke turned to Hilarion. 'Do you like the wall?'

'Yes. Will it work?'

Luke nodded. 'When we've built the ships. Anyway, it's as big as we could make it with the materials available.'

'How did you pay for it?'

'Ah, now that is the right question. I used the money I was meant to give to the Pope. I'm glad I did.'

'The Pope who fled?'

'The Pope who fled, was caught and brought back.'

'What happened to him?'

'He was charged with terrible things and stripped of the papacy. It was right.'

Hilarion frowned. He found a stick and began prodding the ground. 'So why did you support him?'

Luke had asked himself that question so many, many times but somehow, coming from the lips of his son, it was much harder to answer.

'It was a mistake.' He glanced at Hilarion, who was still poking the earth. 'But not all men of God are like that. I met one at Constance who would have changed the Church.'

'Would have? Is he dead?'

Luke thought about the last time he had seen Jan Hus. It had been in the main square of Constance where Hus was tied to a stake with wood piled high around him. A man with a torch had been waiting to one side while the heretic cried for God's mercy in the pain to come. He remembered the princes of Christendom, laity and clergy, sitting on a balcony drinking wine, the German Electors not among them. He remembered a crowd that jeered as a good man screamed in agony.

He closed his eyes, hearing Hus's screams as the flames rose, seeing the melting of his body, his face. At least the soldiers had allowed his followers to add wood to the fire and it was soon over. He was glad Giovanni had not been there to see it.

He opened his eyes to find Hilarion staring at him, the stick poised in his hand. 'Do you hate the Pope now, Father?'

Luke managed a smile. 'There is no pope, Hilarion. The council grinds on and still they can't decide whom to make pope next.'

Hilarion nodded slowly, absorbing these strange facts. He turned to Luke. 'Will Venice attack us or Bedreddin, do you think?'

'Who knows? We seem to have plenty of enemies. Let's hope they don't all come at once.'

Luke took the skin from his waist and they both drank. The sun was high and the stones hot beneath them. They sat in silence for a while, each thinking his own thoughts.

Hilarion made his into a question. 'Why must you go to Edirne?'

Luke looked down at the skin. 'Because the Ming Emperor is not sending gold until he gets a qilin.'

'A what?'

'A qilin. It's the same as a giraffe and seems to be sacred to the Chinese. The Emperor asked Shulen to get him one and she went to Samarcand to see if Tamerlane's was still alive. It wasn't, so she's on her way to Edirne to see if Bayezid's is alive. She wants to meet me there.'

Hilarion frowned. Shulen was the person her parents seemed to argue most about. 'And if it's not in Edirne?'

Luke drank more water, squeezing the last drops from the skin into his hand and running it through his hair. 'Then I suppose she'll need to find it from somewhere else.'

It was six hundred miles from Corinth to Edirne but the road up the coast was good and much of it back in Byzantine hands following the peace with Mehmed. Luke rode fast, stopping only to sleep. He changed horses once in Thessaloniki.

As he approached Mehmed's capital from the south, the going got slower. The road was clogged with soldiers marching in the opposite direction, hurrying towards the straits between Asia and Europe should Bedreddin find the ships to cross them.

It was evening when Luke arrived at the palace. The muezzin's call to prayer had just ended and one side of his tower shimmered in the late-autumn sun. He found Mehmed in the throne room looking at maps. They embraced warmly as old battle-comrades do.

'I am putting an army into the fortress at Gallipoli,' Mehmed said, leading Luke over to a table. 'From there it can watch the straits.'

The table had a map on it with little blocks of wood for the armies. There seemed to be many more on the Asian side of the straits.

'How many men does Bedreddin have?' asked Luke, leaning over the map.

'Sixty thousand at least.'

'And you?'

Mehmed sat and picked up one of the blocks still at Edirne. 'The problem isn't numbers, it's loyalty. There are many in my army who sympathise with Bedreddin.' He paused. 'Murad is one.'

'So what have you done?'

'I've kept the less reliable troops here in Edirne and put my son under house arrest. He'd like nothing better than to go and join Bedreddin.'

Luke pondered this. So Murad's fanaticism was unchanged. It wasn't surprising with his old tutor so close.

'Bedreddin could go to Egypt,' Mehmed continued. 'The Mamluks might give him ships. They'd like to see the Ottomans fight each other.' He paused and looked up at Luke. 'That could be a problem for you.'

'Why?'

'Because the Mamluks might like Bedreddin to take Mistra before Constantinople, then give it to them. It's better for their trade route to Venice.'

Luke hadn't considered this. He'd have to think about it later. He asked: 'Have Nikolas and the others arrived?'

Mehmed straightened. 'Yes, and they've told me why you've come. I must tell you what I told them: the giraffe or jornufa or qilin, or whatever you're calling it, is no more. Apparently it died soon after Bayezid.'

Luke's surprise was not to feel disappointment. After all, no qilin meant no gold. But it might mean something else.

Mehmed walked round to Luke's side of the table and stood before him. 'I know why you want your jornufa,' he said quietly. 'I wish I could help you, if only for the debt I still owe for Çamurlu. But every penny in my treasury is needed to beat Bedreddin.'

Luke nodded. 'Of course.' He put his hand to his heart and bowed from the waist. 'I should go to my friends.'

Luke had not seen Nikolas or Shulen since Samarcand eight years earlier and the palace corridors seemed endless. At last he was shown into the room where they were. It had couches set around a table with jugs and glasses on it.

'Nikolas.'

His Varangian friend was first into the embrace. Luke stepped back, holding him at arm's length, looking him up and down. 'Can you walk?'

'I can run, ride horses and weather storms,' said Nikolas, 'of which we had many on the way. I'm mended.'

'No, I meant in that dress.' Luke was shaking his head. 'What are you wearing?'

'It's what the Chinese wear,' said Shulen.

He turned and saw her as he had never seen her before. She was dressed in a blue silk dress that covered her body like skin. Her hair was tied into two pigtails that fell to her waist. But her oval face held the same opaque beauty that it had in Samarcand, the same slim, animal grace that had so bewitched Tamerlane. She approached and kissed Luke on each cheek, rising on tiptoe to do so. She said: 'Here is proof.'

She gestured to Zhu Chou, who came forward and knelt in one graceful movement, keeping her head bowed. Her dress was of crimson and had gold qilins on it, perhaps to remind her of her quest. 'I am Zhu Chou,' she said, raising her white face to Luke's. 'I have heard much about you.'

'And I you,' said Luke, bringing her to her feet and glancing at Nikolas. 'There are many things to thank you for.'

Luke's eyes passed back to Shulen and stayed there for a while. She was being more formal than the occasion required. He turned to Nikolas and embraced him again, then drew him to one side. They walked over to the window.

Luke studied his friend. He was thinner, greyer, and there was something in his eyes that was older than the eight years they had been apart. 'I've missed you,' he said. 'The brotherhood has missed you.'

'And I you.'

'Have you changed?'

Nikolas smiled. 'I'm less funny than I thought I was, but possibly cleverer. I'm still working at it.'

'Do you speak Chinese?'

'And write it. I've had long enough to practise. How are the others?'

Luke smiled now. 'Matthew is all that an akolouthos should be. He wins his battles and grows rich on the spoils. Arcadius has rebuilt the Hexamilion Wall at the isthmus. It's nearly finished.'

Nikolas nodded. 'And just in time, I hear, if it's Bedreddin.' He paused. 'But what if it's Venice? They've got ships to go round it.'

Luke glanced beyond them where the others were talking. 'That's why we need gold, why we must find this qilin.'

Nikolas studied Luke for a while, seeing how the ambiguities of power had changed the set of his face. 'Have we given up on Constantinople?' he asked softly.

'No,' replied Luke. 'Of course not. But Mistra may now be our priority.' He looked hard at Nikolas. 'After all, it's our home.'

Shulen walked up to them and put a hand on both their arms. 'Are we to talk politics all night? Venice will still be there in the morning.'

Luke laughed. He walked over to the couches. 'I don't know where we begin. Does it matter? We won't sleep tonight anyway. Let's sit.'

They sat, each to a couch, and Luke looked around the room. It was a curious mix of Byzantine and Ottoman. Corinthian columns with empty plinths stood before walls afloat with calligraphy. The script looked newly placed and Luke wondered if Suleyman's pictures lay beneath. He picked up a jug and poured. 'Perhaps we should talk first about what to do about this qilin,' he said, handing a glass to Shulen, 'before we drink too much. Where next?'

'Africa,' said Shulen. Her eyes met Luke's, then moved quickly away. 'Egypt is where both qilins came from. They were gifts from the Mamluk Sultan.'

'And their transport?'

Zhu Chou sat on the edge of her couch, perched like a little bird. She said: 'We will send a message to Admiral Zheng to meet us somewhere in the Red Sea.'

Luke nodded. 'Do you have maps?'

Zhu Chou had brought the map of the world they had seen in Calicut. She moved the jugs and spread it out across the table, using the glasses to hold it down.

Luke stared at it for a long time in silence and Shulen watched him trace the journey they had made to Samarcand together, his finger crossing mountains and deserts. He stopped over a line of little camels and brought his eyes to hers. 'It doesn't seem so far, does it?' He went back to the map and pointed to Africa where the king with the gold nugget sat enthroned amidst desert dunes. 'Mali, the basis of Venetian wealth,' he murmured. 'That's where there's gold, lots of gold.' He looked at Zhu Chou. 'Are these maps part of the diadan?'

The concubine dipped her head, a short, quick movement.

Luke returned to the map. 'There are new lands to find. How exciting.'

'The diadan has more than maps,' said Nikolas. 'Look at these.'

He bent to a pile of papers beneath the table and brought one up, laying it out on top. It showed the same designs for irrigation pumps, sluices and conduit channels they'd used in Delhi. There was Chinese script beneath.

'What does it say?' asked Luke.

Zhu Chou translated, pressing her neat fingers to each character as it passed. Luke listened with his head to one side. Occasionally he shook it in wonder.

'Extraordinary,' he said at last. He thought for a while. 'Do you have the engineers to build them?'

'No longer. We sent them back to Calicut from Samarcand.'

Luke turned to Nikolas. 'Then you should send for Benedo Barbi. He might be useful on your journey.'

'*Your* journey? Aren't you coming with us?'

Shulen said: 'Of course not. He's needed in Mistra if it's about to be invaded. We can manage on our own.'

Luke glanced at her. She was looking down at the map, her eyes wide as if something new had appeared on it. There was colour in her cheeks. Was she waiting for him to say something? He turned to Zhu Chou instead. 'Have you brought something for Plethon the philosopher? A Nestorian codex?'

'Yes,' she said. 'But it is only to be read by him.'

'We saw it,' said Nikolas. 'Chen Cheng took us to the diadan and showed it to us. It's written in Hebrew. Chen Cheng knows what it says but he wouldn't tell us.'

Luke nodded. He went back to the map. 'Zhu Chou, we should plan where the admiral is to meet you.' His finger went to the Horn of Africa and rested on a port with Chinese script next to it. 'Where is this?'

'Berbera,' said Zhu Chou. 'In Abyssinia.'

Luke looked at Nikolas. 'Abyssinia's Christian, isn't it?'

They did talk all night and Luke was tired when he mounted his horse at dawn. He had the long ride to Mistra ahead of him but he would do it slower than before, grudging the distance that connected him to where he really wanted to be.

It was in the low hills south of Edirne that he stopped. He'd been thinking of Shulen, how certain she'd been that he should not come with them to Egypt; trying out more comforting reasons for her certainty than the obvious one.

He had stopped because another image had come suddenly to his mind. It was the map of Africa that Zhu Chou had shown him. He saw the Nile, the Red Sea with little dhows on it; he saw the Horn below. What was that port?

Berbera.

Berbera. Part of the kingdom of Abyssinia, a Christian kingdom where the Ark of the Covenant was supposed to be. His mind travelled west, across the vast emptiness of Africa, to the King with the gold nugget. Mali, where the gold is.

He sat staring out at the landscape, not seeing any part of it. He pulled his rein to turn.

Perhaps.

He completed the turn and kicked the horse into a canter. He was heading back to Edirne.

Cosimo de' Medici was standing at the prow of a lighter, peering into mist that hung over the Venetian lagoon. Behind him, somewhere, were the mudflats, tidal shallows and salt marshes that made these waters some of the most dangerous in the world. A heron rose suddenly to his right and disappeared into the swirl.

'You've seen that one?' He'd turned to the man at the helm, pointing to where the bird came from. Cosimo didn't like boats even in fair weather. He shouted: *'Ahoy!'*

He waited for the echo to subside, head thrust forward, hand to his ear. They were coming into St Mark's Basin and the mist was thinning quickly beneath a soft, liquid sun that wrapped land and water into a shifting brew. A great galley emerged suddenly to their right, sea splashing its topsides and cascading from its oars. Creatures of gold, ridden by sirens, crowded its prow and stern, water dripping from their blank and hollow eyes.

Then they were through the mist.

Venice.

The fair and ferocious Republic of Venice, in all its crenellated majesty, was laid out before them beneath clear sunshine. Older than Florence, richer than Florence, stranger than Florence, Venice was eastern splendour afloat in a lagoon, as treacherous as the waters on which it sat. No Florentine, especially a Medici, could look at Venice without envy. And some fear.

They came to the sea gate of the Doge's palace and Cosimo disembarked. Everywhere around him, on bollard and plinth and gate, was the winged lion, one foot forward in its march of conquest. The Doge was waiting for him beneath an umbrella.

This one was different from the man who'd welcomed Zoe Mamonas back into the scented bosom of La Serenissima. This one was Tommaso Mocenigo, commander of the Venetian fleet at Nicopolis and the man who had helped turn the Genoese out of Choggia. This was a bellicose doge who had already ordered the Arsenale to build a dozen new war galleys, one of which Cosimo had seen in the lagoon.

'You enjoyed the spectacle?' he asked.

'I nearly collided with it. Was it there for me?'

The Doge laughed. 'Its presence was coincidence. But you'll have seen its cannon.'

'And thought about the walls of Monemvasia, yes,' said Cosimo. 'The message was clear.'

Mocenigo gestured to the gate. 'Let us go in.'

He was a tall man of advanced years who strode rather than walked and bowed from the neck as though he was pecking seed. His long hair, tucked beneath his tiara, was as white as Whitsun cloud. He was all nose, chin and condescension as heavy as his robes.

They entered a room whose walls were covered in plans of forts and citadels stretched over the Venetian Empire. Like the great galley, the room was a warning. It was also cold.

The Doge gestured towards two chairs beside a fire, each with a side table. The door opened and the smell of cinnamon and cloves came into the room.

'Hot wine from Monemvasia,' he said, sitting and lifting the glass to his nose. He breathed in. 'Stronger than its walls, and more fragrant than its streets, I'd hazard. Drink.'

They drank, contemplating each other over the golden rims of Murano glass. Tommaso Mocenigo drained his in one swallow, a finger pressing cinnamon to its side. He raised a napkin from the table and dabbed at his beard.

'They tell me that you are made Priore of the Republic,' he said. 'Will they keep you such with this new debt?' He held out his arm for more wine. 'We call the submerging of our city in spring the *acqua alta*. It seems that Florence will have its own sinking.'

'There is no pope yet and, until there is, we still have the Curia's banking. Within three years we will repay the debt.'

'And why should we give you three years?' asked the Doge. 'The banks in Venice are impatient.'

Cosimo blew over his wine, then pretended to sip it. 'The debt is in florins,' he said.

'Which means?'

'It will be repaid in florins. Which we mint.'

Cosimo watched the Doge absorb the information. His face, already beaten by wind and rain, assumed a darker crimson. He said: 'You wouldn't dare.'

'Wouldn't we?' asked Cosimo. 'To save our Republic and stop Venice taking over the world's money supply? I think we would.'

'You would compromise your own currency?'

'Not compromise. Revalue. It would help our trade.'

The Doge studied the man next to him for several moments. He began to twist a heavy ring on his finger and Cosimo wondered if he missed the simpler battles at sea. Mocenigo said: 'There are two debts: yours and Mistra's. We might agree three years for Florence.' He paused. 'But not for Mistra.'

Cosimo spread his hands on his knees and smiled. 'We do not desert our friends so easily, magnificence. Three years for Florence, three years for Mistra. It's both, or we devalue.'

The Doge's mind was working hard beneath the furrowed movement of his brow. 'The Mamonas Bank shares much of the debt. They have been insistent.'

Cosimo shook his head. 'The Mamonases are enemies of Mistra. They lost their estates there when they sided with Bayezid. They want to recover them.'

The Doge's frown relaxed a little. 'What about the Malatestas? We hear they shifted their debt from the Magoris Bank to the Mamonas just before the Pope was deposed.'

'And thereby aligned themselves with Venice.' Cosimo paused. 'In Constance, Carlo Malatesta stabbed the Protostrator's page. You keep pleasant friends.'

Mocenigo frowned and looked at his knees. 'We had heard. How is the boy?'

'He is recovering in Baden,' said Cosimo. 'He has been lucky.'

CHAPTER TWENTY-TWO

BADEN, WINTER 1415

The dagger with which Carlo Malatesta had stabbed Giovanni had been little short of a sword. Its blade had entered his abdomen, severed all organs in its way, and induced a haemorrhage that had come close to taking his life.

He had been taken straight to the Benedictines at Peterhausen, who had scoured their garden for herbs to lessen the pain and summoned a surgeon from Basel to treat the wound. The abbot had given Giovanni the Last Rites before the surgery began.

By the time that his mother arrived at Constance, Giovanni was considered more likely to live than die, but it was close. Much would depend on his will to live and Fiorenza had doubts on this subject. He had said only one word to her as she had entered his bedroom.

Cleope.

Poggio had come to visit often; he had been asked to by Luke before he had left. With his pope disgraced and imprisoned, the secretary had time to spare and he had befriended Fiorenza whom he thought as wise as she was beautiful. It was his idea that the three of them should go to Baden.

And so they had.

On a clear summer's day of no wind, they had put Giovanni into a boat and taken him downriver to Schaffhausen and then on to the Rhine Falls where he rode in a wagon above five feather mattresses. They had travelled at the slowest of walks, stopping to guide the horses round anything that might startle them.

They had come to Baden in the evening and booked into an inn. Fiorenza slept in an attic high up in the eaves. She heard laughter in her sleep, then woke to it.

She sat up in bed. The sun was shining through open windows, straight into her eyes. She rose, went to the window and looked out.

Below was a street thronged with men and women who were almost naked. The men were wearing short leather aprons that left their buttocks exposed; the women loose linen shifts that fell to their knees. Some had flowers in their hair and some were holding hands. There was song and a little dancing.

Fiorenza stared and stared, wondering at first if she was still dreaming. She heard a shout from below. Poggio was standing by the side of the street, fully dressed. He was waving up at her.

'Come down! Giovanni has had a draught and is asleep.'

Fiorenza looked down at herself. She was wearing her nightgown. She saw flowers in a vase by the bed and put them in her hair and went barefoot down to the street.

Poggio laughed when he saw her. 'Lady, you've understood this place better than I!'

They joined the crowd and walked down to a series of steaming pools with low galleries at their sides. The water was full of people bathing or floating on their backs or talking. There was a long lattice dividing the pools, women and children on one side, men on the other. It had small windows through which people could speak. She asked: 'Poggio, what have you brought me to?'

'Either paradise or madhouse, lady. Will you go in?'

Fiorenza glanced around her, lifted the hem of her gown and tiptoed into the water, waving aside the steam with her hands. Soon she was submerged to her shoulders, her buttercup hair spread around her like rays from a Madonna. She turned to Poggio, still at the side. He had his arm outstretched, pointing to a hundred heads bobbing like dumplings in the steam.

'My guess', he said, 'is that these are, or soon will be, admirers of Jan Hus.'

'Is that why we're here? But how does Jan Hus affect us?'

Poggio crouched and dipped his hand in the water, bringing up pebbles that shone in the sun. 'Not us so much as Giovanni,' he said quietly, looking up. 'I think Hus may be a large part of his sickness.'

So autumn had turned into winter and Giovanni did get better. His wound gradually healed, the ruptured skin came together, and only a livid scar remained to remind him of an unequal fight. When he finally took to the baths, he would have found himself admired by women and men alike, had he noticed.

Giovanni was not noticing very much. As the days grew shorter, Poggio left to visit monasteries nearby and Fiorenza walked with Giovanni in the forests around Baden, thick with oak and birch. They walked on carpets sprung with leaves and listened to the crack of wood all around them. She would talk and he would listen. And when they stopped talking, Giovanni thought about Cleope. And her uncle.

The year turned and spring arrived and still Giovanni brooded. One day, Poggio returned and saw how things were and thought the time right for some distraction.

'I'll take him to the Cistercians at Wettingen,' he said one morning to Fiorenza. 'It's a mile to the south and I've got to know the abbot. They have a good scriptorium there. He can learn to copy; it will distract him.'

So, on a day of watery sun, the two men walked the mile to the monastery down an avenue girded by golden beech. On the road, they talked.

Giovanni asked: 'Why did you bring us to Baden, Poggio? Was it only the spa?'

Poggio was kicking stones before him. 'Not only, although it's done you good.' He glanced at his companion. 'At least in body.'

Giovanni thought for a while. Then he said: 'This happened to Luke once; he told me. It was when he was with Tamerlane, sickened by the destruction.'

Poggio took his arm. 'He saw no goodness in the world. Is that what you feel?'

Giovanni wasn't sure what he felt exactly, beyond misery.

'You are sickened by our Church,' Poggio continued. 'Which is one reason I've brought you to Baden. People here live without fear.' He paused. 'There are more alternatives than Jan Hus, or were before this Church was founded. Have you heard of Epicurus?'

Giovanni had been taught by Plethon. 'He believed the pursuit of pleasure to be the highest good.'

Poggio nodded. 'A world free from fear and superstition. A world like Baden, free from fear of popes.'

'But we were responsible for Cossa, weren't we? You, me, Luke, Plethon . . . all of us.'

Poggio said: 'Yes, but perhaps we were working to a higher purpose.'

Giovanni thought about this. Was Mistra worth it all? Were Poggio's and Plethon's ideals worth anything when they were so tarnished by expediency? He said: 'I'm not even Greek.'

They were silent then, both considering this last sentence. Was it another lie? They heard sounds on the road before them, singing. There were soldiers approaching, four of them with bandaged wounds. They stopped.

'Is Baden ahead, sir?' asked one with his arm in a sling.

Poggio nodded. 'You've been in battle?'

'We've been fighting for the eight cantons,' said the man. 'Now we go south, after some mending at Baden.'

'Where to in the south?' asked Giovanni.

The soldier shrugged. 'Wherever we're sent. We'll fight for Perugia.'

'Who is to be your general?'

'Prince Malatesta. The one they call Carlo.'

Giovanni stared at him. 'And your enemy?'

'Braccio da Montone.'

Poggio and Giovanni said goodbye to the men and walked on without speaking, reaching the monastery as the first flecks of rain hit their cloaks. It seemed more castle than place of prayer. It had a wall with turreted towers at four corners. The wall had sharpened stakes driven into its top.

'I don't like monasteries,' said Poggio as they approached, pulling his cloak to his shoulders. 'They are refuse pits for those unfit for the world: the dim-witted, weak or paralytic children of those wanting to forget them.'

At the monastery gates, they were met by the abbot who took them straight to the scriptorium. They came into a large room where thirty desks, partitioned, were arranged in lines, each with a monk seated behind it, huddled over a manuscript. Lead weights on strings hung over the sides of the desks.

'My pupil' – Poggio gestured to Giovanni – 'would like to join you for a month. To learn how to copy.' He paused. 'I will pay, of course.'

Fiorenza and Poggio were having breakfast at the inn when the abbot arrived with a letter for Fiorenza.

'He left during the night,' said the abbot. 'He must have climbed the wall.'

Fiorenza had not invited the abbot to sit. She was too busy reading the letter. She folded it and looked up. For a while, she was silent in thought. Then she turned to Poggio. 'He has gone to join Braccio.'

A month later, Giovanni reached the hamlet of Sant'Egidio where the road from Perugia to Assisi crosses the Tiber. He was exhausted and hungry.

Outside Baden he had exchanged his doublet for an old horse that had limped its way over the Alps down into the devastated land of Umbria. On the way, he had stopped at Bologna and spent what little money he had buying the gossip of taverns. The city had been alive with rumour and speculation. Braccio had invaded Umbria and laid claim to Perugia, which had made the mistake of exiling his family some time before. Perugia had hired Carlo Malatesta to defend it, which meant that two of the greatest condottieri of the day were finally to do battle. People laid bets as to the outcome and the only conversation was whether the *Braccesca* school would prevail over the *Sforzesca*. Carlo Malatesta was an admirer of Sforza.

It was now summer on the plains of Umbria and the sun

sucked the heat out of the ruined earth and boiled the sweat out of anything that moved on its surface. Giovanni soon regretted selling his hat.

He had other regrets. Hardly a moment passed when he didn't blame himself for taking Cleope to the inn that night, for exposing her to such violence. The scene had played over and over in his mind: the shouting outside, the opening of the window, Carlo's boots on the stairs, the words.

The words.

You are a bastard whelp that whores above its station.

And the dagger had gone in so deep. He'd never known such pain.

He passed through Sant'Egidio without meeting a soul. Every door was shut and locked, everyone's daughter somewhere else. Only the church was open and a priest stood on its steps, still in his vestments.

'Braccio's army? They're camped outside the village,' said the man, pointing. 'They've just heard mass here. The battle must be soon.'

Giovanni hurried on. He came to the camp and found it in motion. He entered without challenge, passed an armourer carrying swords and pioneers filling wagons with bundles of fascines. Men were forming up in their squadrons, their *caporali* checking their equipment. A friar was hearing a knight's confession outside his tent.

Giovanni looked around. A flag with a black goat on it should be flying above a tent somewhere but there was no wind. He wanted to avoid Braccio da Montone but find his recruiter. He saw two provosts putting a man into stocks.

He left his horse and approached them. 'Are you in need of men?'

265

One of the men straightened up, looking him up and down. 'Maybe.' He pointed to a tent where a man sat outside at a table. He was writing in a ledger. 'Over there.'

Giovanni walked over with his horse. 'Sir, I am trained in the sword and lance and have a horse,' he said. 'I can fight.'

The man looked up at him, then at his horse. 'Where are your arms?'

'Lost. Stolen.' He glanced towards the armourer's tent. 'Can I borrow some?'

The man looked down again. 'Go away.'

Giovanni heard a curse nearby. He saw the knight, now confessed, being dressed in his armour by a squire wearing two colours of hose. The squire was young: some minor nobleman's son who'd escaped the Church or Law. He walked over to them. 'Sir, I want to fight in this army.'

The knight grimaced as a strap was tightened. His armour was already too hot to touch. He glanced at Giovanni. 'Can you handle horses?'

Giovanni nodded. 'I have grown up with them.'

The knight studied him for a while, seeing his height, his breeding beneath the dirty smock. There were questions to ask later. 'You can hold my second stallion.' He turned back to the squire. 'Give him arms.'

The squire finished his work and led Giovanni through the camp. They passed a surgeon's tent with a fat man outside in an apron arranging saws on a table. There were leather straps on the table's sides. Giovanni looked away, something moving deep in his stomach. This would be his first battle.

The squadrons were formed up in their lances now. There were Italian men-at-arms, English bowmen in buff leather jerkins still with the cross of St George stitched on them, bundles of arrows at their belts. There were Hungarian *schiopettieri* with handguns and sticks, crossbowmen from Genoa. Some of the lances had two men holding long pikes between them to fend off the cavalry. In front of them were boys with drums and pipes.

They came to wagons being filled with jars of water by men stripped to the waist with wet shoulders that glistened in the sun. One wagon, bigger than the others, was festooned with the flags of Perugia and had a raised platform in the middle.

'Braccio's *carroccio*,' explained the squire. 'It's where he'll direct the battle from.'

'But where's his flag?' asked Giovanni.

The boy laughed. 'He thinks he is already Lord of Perugia, so his carroccio carries the city's flags.'

There was a trumpet blast and they turned to see Braccio emerge from a tent. He wore long spurs for the peaked saddle and they clicked on the wood as he climbed on to the wagon. He wore black armour and a beret with a pumpkin top. He was carrying a baton.

The caporali marched their men over to the carroccio. They fell silent and Braccio spoke. 'This battle', he shouted, turning his head so that all men could hear, 'will be fought on water.'

There was silence in the ranks. A few men looked at each other, not understanding.

'I don't mean we'll climb into boats,' he said. 'I mean we'll have water and they won't. Look.' He gestured to the wagons still being loaded with jars. 'The battle will be long and it will be hot. I ask of you only one thing: have patience and drink water, as much as you can.' He paused. 'Malatesta thinks me impetuous. He's seen my scars.' He looked around again and lifted a finger towards heaven. 'Today, my children, I will have patience: God's patience.'

His speech ended, Braccio climbed down from the carroccio. The men cheered and the drums and pipes started up. They were to march out to battle. The two great condottieri were to fight at last. Giovanni went to be armed.

Carlo Malatesta had chosen a good position between the Tiber and some hills, fronted by a deep drainage ditch, now dry. He'd arranged his five thousand men in a wide semi-circle of two lines of dismounted men-at-arms supported by cavalry and mounted archers. To the right of the line were his bombards, perhaps ten of them.

Giovanni was standing on a little hill at the rear of Braccio's army holding the knight's second charger by the reins. Next to him stood Braccio's carroccio with its tabarded trumpeters blowing out his orders and Braccio himself too busy to notice anything but the battle in front.

For seven hours Giovanni watched a perfect display of the Braccesca school of fighting: small groups of heavy cavalry charging different parts of Perugia's line, jumping the ditch and probing for the weaknesses, then retiring to rest and drink water while archers advanced to pour arrows into the enemy's ranks. All the time, Malatesta's army stood under a July sun, unable to move, unable to drink.

The squire with the multi-coloured hose explained: 'Braccio's looking for the city's militia,' he said. 'They're poorly trained and will buckle under a charge. Meanwhile they all die of thirst!'

The knight came back twice to change horses. When he returned, his squire would remove his armour and give him water. But he was still cooking under this merciless sun. Giovanni looked out towards Malatesta's army. What must they be suffering?

Too much, it seemed. For now, in between the charges, the Perugian men-at-arms were beginning to drift off to the river in ones and twos. Braccio was watching them go. At last, he issued orders for the pikemen to prepare themselves to advance. They drew up and the fascines were taken from the wagons and distributed among them.

On the other side of the hill, Malatesta's army was beginning to disintegrate. The captains were riding up and down the riverbank, beating men with the flats of their swords, shouting at them to get back into their ranks. It wasn't working. More men were coming to drink.

Braccio had left his carroccio, mounted his charger and gone down to the massed ranks of pikemen. He was riding back and forth in front of their line, standing in his stirrups and waving his baton, pointing towards the enemy with great flourishes. A trumpet sounded and the pikemen began to advance.

Giovanni was shielding his eyes to see properly. The sun was lower but still shone straight into his eyes. He looked for Carlo Malatesta's carroccio. It wasn't there. He remembered Cleope telling him something.

He sometimes keeps to his tent in battle.

He searched the enemy army for tents. There were some behind the bombards, one large one amidst several smaller. He couldn't see the flag above it. He looked back to the enemy's ranks. Men were coming back from the river but not enough. There were gaps, particularly in one area.

'The militia.' The squire was pointing. 'Braccio was right: no discipline.'

The phalanxes were advancing on that part of the line and Giovanni could see the Perugian cavalry moving up to support it. The pikemen reached the ditch, threw in the fascines and crossed it. Then, with twenty paces between the armies, they charged.

For a while Perugia's militia held their line. But there were too many gaps in it and not even the cavalry behind could fill them all. Braccio's pikemen doggedly pushed them back so that the whole Perugian line concertinaed and buckled. Giovanni glanced at the carroccio. It was empty.

Now.

He yanked the stallion's rein and led him over to the wagon. He took a fistful of Perugian flags and pulled them free from the wood. He mounted the horse and broke into a trot. He heard the squire shouting behind him, then another voice, louder. He turned for the hills by the side of the armies.

Giovanni leant low over the animal's neck and said the words Luke had taught him and the horse lifted its head and lengthened its stride.

He reached the foot of the hills. They were thickly wooded: cover for Giovanni to do what he must do. He dismounted, pulled a long, straight branch from a tree and knotted one of the flags to it. The other flag he tied around his neck so that it fell from his shoulders like a tabard. It might fool them.

He mounted again and wove his way through the trees until he reached the edge of the wood. He could see the battle raging outside. Malatesta's men were being driven back by the phalanxes, which now had heavy cavalry support on either side. The battle was reaching its climax. Giovanni looked beyond the fighting. Where were the tents?

He couldn't see them from where he was standing. He emerged from the trees at the gallop. The air was full of shouts and screams and the bangs and smoke of handguns. This was battle and it was a terrifying chaos.

He rode around the back of Malatesta's army, holding the flag aloft on its stick. The tents were in front of him now, but he needed something else. He saw crossbowmen running to join the fighting. He stopped and dismounted to let them pass.

When the last man ran in front of him, Giovanni tripped him. The man fell and Giovanni kicked him hard in the head. A moment later, he was back on his horse with a crossbow in his hand. He arrived at the tents, dismounted and said to the nearest guard: 'The Captain-General's tent? I have a message from the signori of Perugia.'

The guard was looking at the flag, the branch, the torn flag across Giovanni's front with disbelief. He was frowning slightly.

Giovanni walked up to the man. 'We are losing this battle. I must deliver it.'

At that moment the flap of the tent opened and Carlo Malatesta strode out, buckling his sword belt. Behind him came two of his captains.

Giovanni swung the crossbow so that it was aimed at the condottiere's heart. 'Drop the sword and return to the tent.'

Malatesta stared at him. He let the sword belt fall to the ground. He turned to his captains. 'Leave me.'

The two men looked at him, then Giovanni, then him again. They had their hands on their sword hilts and didn't move.

'Go.'

The men moved slowly away.

Giovanni didn't take his eyes off Malatesta or his finger off the trigger. He gestured with the crossbow. 'Go into the tent.'

Malatesta lifted the flap and entered, Giovanni following. There was a young page inside, polishing a helmet.

'Tell him to stand outside and not let anyone come in. The

first that does will get you a bolt through the heart. Tell him to leave the helmet.'

The page did as he was told. They were alone in a tent with a table, four chairs and an unmade cot. There were the remains of a meal on the table: two wooden plates and a bowl with fish heads in it. Next to the bowl sat the condottiere's helmet and, beside it, a jug of water. The air was stifling and smelt of fish.

'Sit.'

Malatesta sat, adjusting his cuirass for comfort. In his armour, he looked too big for the chair, too big for the tent. He said: 'I am your prisoner and unarmed. You will permit me to take off my armour?'

Giovanni didn't answer. From outside came the clash of steel and screams of pain. They were getting closer. He shook his head.

Malatesta frowned. 'The tent is hot.' A rosary of sweat had appeared at the top of his brow and some beads had detached themselves. The burn was becoming livid on his cheek. 'I am hot.'

'Put on the helmet.'

Malatesta glanced at the helmet, heavy and plumed, its visor pointing skywards, like the fish heads beside it.

'Why?'

'To make you hotter.'

Malatesta put his head to one side. 'You seek revenge by cooking me? There is a dagger beside the cot and my page can bring another. We could do this fairly.'

Fairly.

'Put on the helmet.'

The condottiere looked at him for a while; then he reached over to the table and picked up the helmet. He put it on. His face, framed by the metal, was all beard and eyes. A dog barked outside.

'If the dog enters,' said Giovanni, 'you die.'

Malatesta turned his head. 'Keep hold of the dog!'

The page outside said: 'Lord, the militia have broken.'

Malatesta cursed quietly. He shifted in his seat and Giovanni moved the weapon slightly. With no opening, the tent was a furnace. The sun was making the canvas piebald above them.

'How long do we do this for?' asked the condottiere, his face a film of sweat. He coughed. 'Until I die of heat?'

'Until the battle's won,' replied Giovanni.

They studied each other in silence. Ten paces and thirty years separated them. And an ocean of hate.

'How did you know where to find me in Constance?' asked Giovanni.

The condottiere shrugged. 'Who knows? You have enemies.' He coughed again and wiped sweat from his face with his mailed palm. 'I had reason enough to be angry.'

'Reason enough to murder?'

Malatesta tried to laugh. 'If I'd wanted to kill you, I would have.'

'You were drunk. You missed.'

The minutes passed. The sweat was now running from Malatesta's face and dripping to the ground. He blinked his eyes, shaking his head, putting his thumb and finger to the bridge of his nose. He was breathing quickly. The noise outside was of triumph and agony. The battle was reaching its end.

'This is madness,' said Malatesta. 'You are torturing me.' He put his fingers between the cuirass and his neck. Giovanni watched him pull the metal away and swallow, then glance at the water jug. An arm stretched out.

273

'No.'

Suddenly the condottiere was angry. 'You want money?'

Giovanni's finger tightened on the trigger. Ten paces. The armour would be as paper. Malatesta's insides would pattern the tent walls.

Malatesta spoke quickly. 'I am Prince of Rimini. She is my niece. It was always impossible.'

Giovanni nodded. 'You called me *bastard*.'

Malatesta searched his memory. Had he? Was that what this was all about? 'It is a general term,' he said, taking sweat from the bridge of his nose and flicking it to the floor. 'It signifies nothing.'

The fighting outside was very close now. A trumpet called the retreat, another the pursuit. Soon, it would be over.

'*You are a bastard whelp that whores above its station.* That's what you said.' Giovanni paused. 'It seems a particular term, not general at all.'

Malatesta glanced towards the door of the tent. It appeared unlikely that he'd be allowed to leave it alive. 'I will talk to her father on your behalf,' he said.

Giovanni was shaking his head. 'I think it's too late for that.'

Outside the tent there were shouts. Braccio da Montone was approaching. They could hear the roll of his spurs on the hard earth. The tent flap opened. Braccio stood there and looked from one to the other of the two men inside. He was fully armoured but had exchanged his helmet for the pumpkin beret. His face was red and washed with sweat. His hair clung to his forehead like a claw.

For a moment he seemed amazed. Then he laughed, filling the tent with the sound. He sat and shook his head in wonder. 'Who are you?'

'I am Giovanni Giustiniani Longo.'

'Well, Giovanni,' said Braccio, wiping tears from his eyes with the back of his hand, 'you've got yourself a valuable prisoner.'

PART FOUR

LOVE'S RANSOM

CHAPTER TWENTY-THREE

ALEXANDRIA, SUMMER 1416

Luke sailed into Alexandria under a Florentine flag, approaching a forest of masts and rigging before which two Venetian galleys rode at anchor, pennants flying like birds of paradise. As they passed the stubby remnant of the lighthouse on its island of Pharos, Shulen remembered something. 'The Kalyan Minaret,' she said. 'Do you remember?'

Luke remembered; so did Nikolas. It had been the lighthouse that had guided them into Bokhara from the desert on their way to Tamerlane. It had saved Arcadius's life.

They were all in some awe. Alexandria was the biggest port in the world, joining the trades of east and west. They were entering one of its two great harbours and before them were more boats than they could count.

'They say more ships dock here than in Genoa, Venice and Ancona combined,' said Nikolas. 'Imagine.'

The city beyond the masts was a second forest of minarets. Low smoke smudged the sky above and swallows came and went from it like cinders. The air smelt of fish and filth and Zhu Chou had gone below to escape it. For the first time in days, Luke felt some small joy at the sight before them.

Having rejoined the others in Edirne, he had travelled with them to Constantinople where they had spent Christmas at the Emperor Manuel's court. The new year had been full of storms and it wasn't until the late spring that they had taken ship for Alexandria. He had spent much of the time going over the diadan maps again and again with Zhu Chou, especially those relating to Africa. The rest he had been worrying about how Anna had reacted to their Christmas apart. And to the letter he had sent her.

Just Cairo, he'd written. *I'll just go with them to Cairo to meet the Mamluk Sultan. I have an idea that might bring us the gold we need to save Mistra.*

How would she have received the news? He knew well enough. He had gone with Shulen to pursue an idea he wouldn't commit to paper. It had happened before.

He looked at the two Venetian galleys, then scanned the sea front for the walls of their *bailate*. He wondered how quickly the news of his arrival would reach the Rialto and whether the ducat might fall. Trade through Alexandria was Venice's monopoly, granted by the Mamluk Sultan and agreed by the Pope. It provided the Republic's largest revenues by far.

They came ashore and took a house overlooking the compound of the bailate, a place of silk and porphyry. They found themselves escorted whenever they went out into the city and, after a week, they were still there. There seemed to be some difficulty in transplanting them to Cairo where the Sultan held his court.

'Clearly Venice doesn't like us here,' said Luke as the four of them sat around dinner one evening. 'They're doing everything in their power to stop us meeting the Sultan.'

Nikolas nodded. 'And you need to be back at Mistra, I know. When will you have to leave?'

'Not until we've seen the Sultan,' replied Luke. 'We've not only got to persuade him to give us the animal, but let you take it south to Berbera. Abyssinia is a Christian country; he may not choose to allow it.'

Shulen was watching him carefully. 'You've been away from Mistra for a long time. It must look like desertion.'

Luke looked into those dark, intelligent eyes that absorbed so much and gave away so little. She'd not spoken to him much since they'd met in Edirne. He said: 'Plethon can manage things until I return.'

Two weeks later came the news that they were to be allowed to travel to Cairo.

In the street outside, they found horses and a Mamluk body-guard, all mail, plume and lance. They rode out of the city and covered the hundred miles to Cairo in just three days. They travelled through the lush Nile Valley beneath a liquid sun and birds of every size and deity. There were pink flamingos, pelicans, storks, cranes and bald-headed ibis foraging amidst the mudflats, their black-stick legs painted brown. They passed herds of horses, running free over the unplanted fields. Luke saw them and thought of Eskalon in his stud and of the message that he'd sent from Alexandria.

They entered the city, riding through Saladin's walls as the sun was setting. It was Friday and the narrow streets were clogged with people making their way to the mosques, dressed in clean *galabayas* and carrying their mats. Blind muezzins called to them from a hundred minarets, their voices clear in the evening air. The shops in the Khan El-Khalili bazaar were shut and boarded, the caravanserais' gates closed. Out of the madrassahs came lines of boys, hand in hand, carrying amber prayer beads and wearing small white hats on their heads. They arrived at a central square where the Al-Azhar Mosque stood, its arches clogged with people waiting to enter. Some were already setting out their mats in the square while the snake charmers, storytellers and fruit-sellers packed up their wares to leave.

They came to open ground overlooked by the citadel, which was built into the city walls on a promontory of the Muqattam Hills. Two aqueducts strode out from it to gather water from some distant well. There was a racetrack with marble columns for the horses to race between and, to one side, a wall with palm trees above and a large house behind. They entered a courtyard with fountains circled by a garden in hibernation. They dismounted and were shown into rooms heavy with comfort. Here, they were told, they would stay until the Sultan summoned them.

Luke looked around him. The floors were of patterned marble with thick carpets on them, the walls hung with tapestries. There were tall windows with velvet curtains and a round table with miniature pyramids and a sphinx on it. Fat cushions were arranged around a fire at one end of the room.

Shulen went over to warm her hands; Zhu Chou joined her. Nikolas walked to the table. 'There's a letter here. Shall I read it?'

He read in silence while Luke looked out of the window. He looked up. 'They've arrived and are on their way. They'll be here tomorrow.'

They had to wait a further two weeks to see the Sultan, who was away hunting ostrich in the south. They spent the days indoors playing games: chess, draughts, and one they'd invented that used the miniature pyramids and sphinx. They ate well to music, went to bed early and slept deeply on scented sheets, Nikolas and Zhu Chou in one room, Luke and Shulen in two others.

At least Luke could sleep now. Among other things, the letter he had received had told him of the three-year truce that Cosimo had arranged with Venice. He had been given time to find the gold.

But then there was Shulen. Since his return to Edirne, she had been cool and purposeful and disinclined to talk much beyond their project. She made clear that she would come to Cairo, collect the qilin, and then return with it to China.

One morning, they awoke to sunshine, a summons and fine clothes laid out for them. They were to go to the citadel where the Sultan would meet them. They were taken up through the streets until they came to the *tibaq* – the barracks –where young Mamluk slaves were turned into soldiers by eunuchs with long sticks. It was Friday again and the students were emerging from the Nasir Mosque with their mats and shoes in their hands.

At the Hall of Justice, they were met by chamberlains who showed them through anterooms to the *iwan* of the citadel, which was full of turbaned amirs arranged according to rank. One wall was lined with soldiers, the other arched and open to the square outside. There were tall leather buckets with sugared water in them and cups on strings. At the far end was a canopied pulpit reached by steep stairs. It was empty.

There was a blast of trumpets and Luke looked into the square. Two files of stirrup-holders had fanned across it, flanking others who carried the Sultan's saddlecloth, which they waved from side to side. Then came a band of drums and double-reed clar-inets and behind rode a pair of horsemen dressed in yellow tunics. Golden ropes tied them to the royal horse in case it should shy or stumble. The Sultan rode with a parasol above him. Halberdiers, all in yellow, surrounded him.

Luke pointed. 'There they are.'

Two of Eskalon's children stood beside grooms at the other end of the square. Luke had had them shipped over from the stud at Mistra because the Mamluks were besotted with horses and their mix of Berber and Andalusian blood would be prized. Even from that distance, they looked magnificent. One of the grooms nodded to them. Luke smiled.

Benedo Barbi.

The Sultan was approaching the hall now, preceded by the *alamdar* who carried the royal banner and the chief chamberlain carrying his staff of office. As he entered, every man in the hall looked down at the ground. The Sultan was all black today, the colours of the caliphate, and wore a small turban on his head with its ends dangling between his shoulders. He walked over to the pulpit and began to climb, holding up his skirts. He reached the top, turned and sat. The chamberlain banged his staff on the ground and looked at Luke.

Luke knew what to do. He fell to his knees and kissed the carpet that led to the throne. He rose and did the same two more times before arriving before the pulpit. He knelt. He heard the sound of hooves on stone behind him, then a neigh. The gifts had been led forward. A man came to stand beside Luke.

'You may rise,' said the man. 'I am the *mushir*, through whom the Sultan will speak to you. You will never address him directly.'

Luke got to his feet. 'May I present my companions to His Majesty?'

The mushir said: 'The Sultan already knows who you all are. He is more interested in your gifts.'

Luke turned to them. Two young horses, a stallion and mare, stood behind him, Barbi between them. Luke said to the mushir: 'They are two years old and broken in. They are the children of the horse that took me to Tamerlane. His Majesty will not ride finer animals.'

The mushir spoke to the pulpit and received a long reply. He signalled and the horses were led away, Barbi with them. He said: 'The Sultan wonders why you have allowed horses to be imported into his kingdom. You are aware of our arrangement with the Venetians?'

'I did not come to Egypt to trade horses,' said Luke, 'but to give them. My friend Ibn Khaldun, heaven preserve his soul, told me of the value placed on such a gift by the Mamluks.'

The mushir nodded. 'The Kadi was my friend. You were with him at Damascus, I'm told.'

This was hopeful. 'We worked together to secure the release of certain of your men before the city was razed by Tamerlane, yes.'

The mushir spoke to the pulpit again and the voice from above waited a while before replying. There was more conversation between the two. At length the mushir turned to Luke. 'The Sultan considers you foolish to have requested an audience. The Venetians have informed him that you owe them a great deal of money and are fleeing your debts. They have asked for you to be handed over to them.'

In spite of himself, Luke glanced up at the pulpit. The Sultan was leaning over the rail, studying him from behind a fly-whisk. He gestured. 'Come closer.'

Luke rose and walked to the bottom of the pulpit's steps. He began to climb.

'Stop!' the mushir cried but the Sultan beckoned him on.

Luke continued until he stood two steps below the throne. The Sultan put up his hand. 'No further.'

Luke looked at the man above him. Sultan Sayf ad-Din was about his age and had large eyes set within a face no more Arab than the rest of the Mamluks. He spoke in Greek.

'Unless you have something better to give me, I will hand you over to the Venetians. They are waiting outside.'

Luke studied him for a while. He said: 'If the horses are not to your taste, then they'll be given to King Yeshaq. We go to him next.'

A frown came and went from the Sultan's brow. 'And why do you presume that I'll let you go to Abyssinia?'

'Self-interest, majesty. I have a woman from China in my party. We travel to meet a Chinese fleet at Berbera which, I believe, Yeshaq now rules.'

Sayf ad-Din produced the thinnest of smiles. He rose. 'I think we should talk,' he said. 'But not here. Come with me.'

The Sultan walked past Luke down the steps. The four of them followed him back through the anterooms until they arrived at a room without windows. When they were seated, the Sultan looked at each of them in turn, spending some time studying Zhu Chou. At last he turned to Luke.

'Now, tell me why you are really here.'

'We seek a qilin, what you call a jornufa or giraffe,' said Luke. 'Two came from here as gifts to Bayezid and Tamerlane. We hoped you might have others.'

The Sultan looked surprised. 'That is why you've come?'

Luke glanced at Zhu Chou. 'The Ming regard the jornufa as sacred,' he said. 'Their emperor has need of one.'

The Sultan nodded. 'I see. Well, they are not native to this land. They come from the south. As you said, you'll need to go to Abyssinia.'

Luke said: 'Which we cannot do unless you allow us to.'

The Sultan studied Luke with his head tilted back, his beard raised, Luke's size perhaps demanding the added distance. He asked: 'Did you know that the Medici have lost the Curia's banking?'

Nikolas reacted as Luke managed not to. He said: 'What?'

The Sultan nodded. 'The council at Constance has decided that they are too contaminated by their former association. The Spini of Florence have it now. This is not news you want to hear.'

It was not, and Sayd ad-Din, thoroughly advised by the Venetian *bailo*, knew it. Without the Curia's income, the Medici Bank's debt to Venice suddenly looked very precarious. As did the Magoris'. But they still had the three-year truce.

'So,' continued the Sultan, 'you would seem in a weak position. I am interested to understand why I shouldn't give you to the Venetians.'

The news was bad but Luke's face remained as composed as when he'd entered the room. 'May I tell you first what I know of you Mamluks?' he asked. 'There is purpose to it.'

The Sultan nodded.

'You are a warrior caste from various lands who were once Egypt's slaves but are now its rulers. Under your dynasty, Egypt has become as rich as it was under the Ptolemies. You are tolerated by your subjects because you are successful and your success has much to do with your monopoly of trade from the East into Europe, a monopoly you share with Venice.' He paused. 'But things have changed. You lost Syria to Tamerlane and, perhaps worse, the Portuguese have taken Ceuta.'

The Sultan frowned. 'I know this but why is it important to me?' For the first time he looked uneasy.

Luke continued: 'Ceuta is the first Portuguese foothold on the west coast of Africa. So far they've not gone beyond Cape Bojador but now we can expect them to travel further south every year.' He reached into a pocket and produced a copy of the map he'd seen in Edirne, opening it on the table. He pointed to Egypt. 'All the trade from Africa has come up to Alexandria these past decades because the Marinids of Morocco have been in chaos. This has included most of the world's gold from Mali.' He paused. 'But when the Portuguese control the west coast, where will the gold go then?'

Luke left the question hanging in the air, but only for a moment. 'And what when they have rounded the bottom of Africa and gone on to the spice lands of the East? What of Cairo then?'

The Sultan was watching Luke carefully, his subtle eyes occasionally darting to Zhu Chou. He said: 'That is what we're waiting for you to tell us, Luke Magoris.'

Luke looked at the fire. The scent of different woods, mainly pine, was in the room and he breathed in. 'Then Egypt and the Mamluks will begin their decline,' he said quietly. 'You will become irrelevant and the Venetians will move on.'

The words were brutal because the conclusion was brutal. The Sultan placed his hands on the table, palms down. 'So we must open a new trade route,' he said, 'one that gets to the East quicker than the Portuguese can.' He looked at Zhu Chou. 'One that uses Chinese ships out of Berbera?'

'Yes,' said Luke. 'Which is why you must send envoys with us to Abyssinia.'

'Why with you?'

Nikolas decided to speak. Luke had done well but it was not he that would be going on to Abyssinia. 'Because of us.' He gestured to himself and Shulen. 'We have made trade agreements with the Ming.'

Now the Sultan sat very still, watching the fire. The frown had reappeared on his brow. At last he sighed and looked back to Zhu Chou. 'We are different from you Chinese. Muhammad was a merchant and trade lies at the heart of Islam. We Mamluks live or die by it.' He turned to Luke. 'Tell me what you suggest.'

'That we take a mission to Yeshaq to agree a new trade route.'

Nikolas stared at Luke.

We?

'And what do I tell the Venetians?' asked the Sultan.

Luke shrugged. 'That I go in search of Prester John or the Ark of the Covenant? Both are said to be there.'

The Sultan thought for a while. 'They won't believe it but I'll try. After all, Prester John is said to rule Abyssinia.' He rose and gathered the folds of his gown. 'What else do you want?'

Luke sat back in his chair. 'I would like to meet men of the law, men recognised for their probity. I wish to make my will.'

CHAPTER TWENTY-FOUR

MONTONE, UMBRIA, SUMMER 1416

The condottiere Braccio da Montone's castle at Montone was a bully of a building. It stood astride high ground with its hands on its hips, its squat towers planted in the rich Umbrian earth, challenging all comers. Its walls were thick, its garrison plentiful and cannon stuck out of the top firing windows like tongues. It was, thought Giovanni, a provocation made in stone.

The castle had always flown the flag of Perugia but now did so with conviction. After a lifetime of trying, Braccio had finally taken the city, as he had all of Umbria and much of the Romagna.

Giovanni was sitting with Braccio at the top of a tower looking over the countryside. It was evening, and they were expecting to be joined soon by Carlo Malatesta.

'La terra dei santi,' said Braccio, gesturing to the landscape around them. Their table and chairs were raised on a platform to see over the battlements. 'So many saints from one region. I wonder what I need to do for the next pope to count me among their number.'

Giovanni laughed. 'You could start by giving it all back: Umbria, Romagna, Bologna,' he said. 'And my prisoner.'

'Which I would gladly do,' said Braccio, picking grapes from a plate and biting one off, 'if you'd let me. I suppose you think it's shrewd; his ransom goes up every week.'

Giovanni didn't reply. They'd discussed it so many times before and he was enjoying the view. This was the green heart of Italy, a landscape as gentle as its saints. It was a country in miniature: cypress-topped hills with ranks of vineyards shuffling up their sides and peaceful olive groves at their feet. At this time of year, the fields were awash with yellow ox-eye daisies, poppies and milkwort; the paths between strewn with wild tulip and orchid; the glades full of peonies interwoven with asphodel: blood-red and saint-white.

'In Cascia, not far from here,' said Braccio, 'they have a new saint I like the sound of: St Rita, patron of lost causes. It's said she put up with a drunken husband who she couldn't reform. One wonders why she bothered.'

Giovanni looked at the condottiere. Braccio was as blustering as his full-blown lips and cherried cheeks suggested. But there was no side to him. Or perhaps he was all side, Giovanni could never make up his mind. He said: 'You refer, yet again, to my affection for Cleope Malatesta. It is not a lost cause.'

'Yes it is. She'll marry a prince, not a merchant's son.' Braccio belched and waved the smell away. 'You haven't seen her for a year and her uncle, our guest, will kill you one day.'

Giovanni remained silent.

'You should take the money,' Braccio continued. 'Why make more enemies?'

Giovanni was watching a hawk circling above the fields below, waiting for it to dive. Its wings were motionless against a blue sky empty of other birds. He looked back at the older man. 'There is a reason. Am I to trust you on this?'

Braccio shrugged. 'You may as well. The most trustworthy man is the one most in need. Luke has lost all my money and I need him to get it back.'

Giovanni leant forward. 'I want you to talk to Carlo.'

He couldn't explain further. The door on to the tower opened and a guard appeared in the Montone livery. Behind him came Carlo Malatesta. He was wearing a long housecoat of silk lined with ermine. He had put on weight since Giovanni had last seen him. Braccio rose.

'Highness.' He bowed lower than was necessary. 'Welcome to my tower. You catch me trying to persuade Giovanni to release you.'

Carlo stepped up on to the platform and poured wine for himself. He glanced at Giovanni. 'I should be pleased he's let me out of my armour. What's my ransom up to now?'

Giovanni said: 'A hundred thousand florins.'

Carlo drank and looked out over the countryside, wiping his beard. He whistled softly. 'I'm flattered. But don't be too greedy.' He sat and took some grapes. 'You should listen to Braccio. He and I have both been in this game a long time.'

Braccio said: 'We expect another envoy soon.'

Carlo nodded. 'My brother Pandolfo, I expect.' He leant back in his chair and stretched out his legs, closing his eyes to the sun. 'You should think of the bigger picture, Longo. The Medici have no pope, a big hole in their pocket and no means of mending it. Meanwhile Venice or Bedreddin are about to take Mistra.' He opened his eyes and turned his head. 'Your side has lost.'

Giovanni sipped his wine. It was all true. Bedreddin's army would invade Rumelia if it got ships and some said that Murad would desert his father and join him.

And where was Luke? Wherever he was, he must be there

for a good reason. His letter had said that he was in Cairo and would leave soon for the south, but not where he was going.

In fact, Luke had left Cairo some weeks before. He had left with Shulen, Nikolas, Zhu Chou, Benedo Barbi and a man called al-Tabingha, who was the Sultan's envoy. They had travelled down the Nile into the Nubian kingdom of Alodia. At its capital Wayula, they rested a week.

The engineer Benedo Barbi had been drawn to Africa partly to help Luke, a man he had loved since first meeting him in Chios twenty years ago, and partly by news of the diadan. In Cairo, once the audience with the Sultan was over, he had come straight to their quarters.

'Where is it?'

Luke had barely embraced him and Nikolas was waiting to do so. Barbi was, after all, almost part of the Varangian brotherhood.

Luke had laughed. 'The diadan can wait. First we want to hear how you sent the rats over the walls of Constantinople.'

'I used parachutes, but imperfect ones. The diadan may have better ones.' He'd looked around and seen Zhu Chou. 'I'm sorry. My manners. Have you got it?'

The engineer had had to wait until Wayula to properly explore the diadan. Zhu Chou had shown him what she had brought with her and none had contained a parachute. So he spent the week learning instead about the science of irrigation and other things that might be useful in a land of deserts.

At Wayula, they had hired camels. They hired a lot of them because the Sultan had been generous with their escort: a hundred Mamluk knights had accompanied them as well as cooks, tent-carriers, interpreters, and everything else they might need to make their mission a success.

Then they had set off east across the desert towards Abyssinia. The going was slow because the roads were poor. This was still a Christian kingdom of many kings who seemed too busy fighting each other to rule. No one asked the purpose of their journey.

Now, Luke rode up to join al-Tabingha at the front of the caravan. They were both dressed as Bedouins in blue hooded thoubs and sandals. Luke lowered his mask to talk. 'Where are we?' he asked, lifting himself to ease the pressure on his buttocks, his palm flat on the saddle. He was not used to riding camels and they didn't listen when he whispered.

Al-Tabingha pointed with his whip to the road in front. 'We crossed into Abyssinia five days ago. Tonight we will reach Axum, Yeshaq's capital. It is a sacred city.'

Luke had heard this already. 'They say it holds the Ark of the Covenant. How did it get there?'

Al-Tabingha waved the whip across his face against the flies. He was a tall, thin man of middle years whose skin was loose and angled by bone. His face was all skull and beard, his eyes sunk deep within craters. He said: 'King Yeshaq claims descent from King Solomon. You have heard of Makeda, the Queen of Sheba?'

'I have heard that she came from here. She travelled to Jerusalem to learn from Solomon's wisdom.'

Al-Tabingha nodded. 'And had a very personal tuition. They say she bore him a son, Menelik, who returned to Jerusalem to meet his father and smuggled the Ark back to Abyssinia. They have it here in a church.'

'And you believe that?'

The Mamluk glanced at him. 'Of course. Why would they lie?'

Luke thought about relics. They said that there were enough splinters of the True Cross to build a village.

294

They rode on, al-Tabingha watching Luke with some curiosity. The Mamluk was a difficult man to like: taciturn, suspicious and usually silent. But he was one of the Sultan's closest advisers and could speak for him to Yeshaq. They were approaching some buildings by the side of the road: low, crude houses of baked mud with uneven windows. Dogs rushed at them from doorways and shy, naked children looked up through their fingers. Some ran beside them. Al-Tabingha shooed them away with his whip.

'We are there,' he said.

They ambled their way into the outskirts of Axum, through dust slanting through the evening sun. They looked across a city of white, flat-topped houses with many, many churches in between, and obelisks of astonishing height. Even in the waning light, it all made Luke's eyes ache. There was noise all around from street stalls and women who left them to walk at their ankles, holding up their wares and shouting. They were dressed in bright colours – blue, orange, indigo – with ornaments that flashed in their hair. At wellheads they stopped to watch the rest of the caravan pass, nudging each other, whispering behind their hands, admiring the tall men from the north who had come to see their king.

They came to a central square surrounded by tall stelae with a big, domed church on one side. Outside the church doors were men, women and children standing in a queue who turned to watch them. Al-Tabingha pointed at the church. 'That is where the Ark is held,' he said, 'although it's always covered so the pilgrims don't see anything.'

On the other side of the square were tall gates with guards dressed as Roman soldiers outside: long black men with fine features and tall plumes. When they saw the caravan, they opened the gates on to a wide avenue with gardens on either side. The drive was lined with palm trees leading up to a palace. Grooms appeared to take their camels. Luke brought his to the kneel and dismounted.

Shulen came to stand on one side of him, Nikolas and Zhu Chou the other, Barbi behind. They were all silent for a while. Then, shaking her head and smiling, Shulen said: 'Well, that was easy.'

They were looking beyond the palm trees to the necks and heads of three jornufas who were eating from the tops of trees.

CHAPTER TWENTY-FIVE

MONTONE, UMBRIA, SUMMER 1416

Braccio da Montone looked out from his tower and watched a long line of mules winding its way up to his castle gate. At their head was a curtained carriage with the Malatesta chequers on its side. On either side rode two hundred of his best soldiers, their new armour polished into mirrors, their hauberks emblazoned with the Perugia city arms.

It was early and, above knee level, the morning was clear. Lower down, mist moved like the ghosts of snakes. The hills of Umbria were tonsured, bobbing like monks queuing for matins, their wooded sides vague through the haze. Braccio watched the mules emerge one by one, their heads nodding to their step, their snorts filling the air like gunshots. He turned to Carlo Malatesta. 'So many mules.'

'So much treasure. One hundred thousand are a lot of florins. I hope you're right about this.'

'I'm right. The boy trusts me.'

'One of the few.'

Braccio laughed. 'They should trust us condottieri more. We always keep our word when a lot of money's involved.'

'When a lot of commission is involved. Twenty per cent is robbery.'

Braccio looked hurt. 'Is it not fair? I'm guarding your gold from bandits.'

'But they're *your* bandits,' said Carlo, moving to watch the carriage disappear beneath the gate.

Braccio shrugged. It was a difficult thing to deny. He said: 'You could be a free man tonight.'

They both walked over to the other side of the tower from where they could see the courtyard. The carriage had stopped in front of steps leading up to the castle doors. Smaller steps were brought and a foot appeared, slippered and pointing. Cleope emerged in a white dress as if to her wedding.

Braccio whistled softly. 'Now *that* is beauty. No wonder he likes her.'

Carlo looked at him sharply. 'And no wonder he cannot have her. She was made for better things than that urchin. She's soon to be niece to a pope.'

Braccio asked: 'There is news from Constance?'

Carlo nodded. 'They all want Colonna to be pope. They're just waiting for the end of the council to make it official.'

They looked back to the courtyard. They watched Cleope take a servant's hand and descend to earth. Braccio's wife, round and welcoming, was bouncing down to greet her. Cleope's father, dressed in black, emerged next from the carriage. He held his hat in his hand and looked around. The courtyard was filling with donkeys.

'You don't forget, do you?' said Braccio. 'It's more than a year since you caught them.'

Carlo Malatesta turned to him. He said quietly: 'I will never forget or forgive what he's done to my family. Never.'

*

298

The meeting was held in a room dressed in scarlet. Cleope might have thought it held some message but it was, in fact, Braccio's favourite colour. There were scarlet tapestries, scarlet curtains and a carpet woven in different shades of the colour. The five of them sat in tall chairs, facing each other. Giovanni sat beside Braccio; Cleope between her father and Carlo.

Since entering, Cleope had not once looked at Giovanni. She'd smiled at Braccio and embraced Carlo but turned her back to Giovanni's greeting. Now she looked directly ahead with her arms folded in her lap. The red made her whiteness ethereal.

Malatesta dei Sonnetti addressed himself to Giovanni. He was grave. 'You have said that you will only consider our latest offer of ransom if it is brought to you by my daughter.' He glanced at Cleope, who hadn't moved a hair. 'Well, she's here, reluctantly, and she's brought a hundred thousand florins. Are you satisfied?'

Giovanni stared at Cleope. They'd lain together and he'd murmured Catullus in her ear. He'd kissed her eyes while she slept. Now, she wasn't looking at him. He said: 'I might be if my lady would allow herself to acknowledge me.'

Braccio shook his head: 'Not in the agreement. She just had to come.'

Giovanni frowned. 'But she's not here. She is somewhere else where she can't hear me.'

Cleope turned to him. There were tiny spots of colour in each cheek. 'I can hear you as I hear a tap dripping. Say what you have to say, take our gold and then permit us to leave. We are listening.'

Giovanni didn't, of course, have anything to say. He'd just wanted to see her and there she was: first cold, now warmed by anger and, if possible, even lovelier than in Florence six years ago. 'May we not speak alone?'

Malatesta dei Sonnetti snorted. 'Of course not! You will never be alone with my daughter again.'

Giovanni frowned. 'Then I may not agree to the ransom.'

Braccio shook his head. He said softly: 'I am fond of you, boy, but not that fond. Your lord has lost me all of my money and here I have the chance to make some of it back. I'm not inclined to sympathise with any second thoughts you may be having at this point.'

Giovanni hadn't stopped staring at Cleope and now she held his gaze. Everything in her face expressed contempt.

'What do you want?' she asked quietly.

He shook his head slowly. His shoulders slumped.

'Nothing. I want nothing.'

In Abyssinia, Luke was awaiting an audience with King Yeshaq.

The day before, he had arrived at Yeshaq's palace and found it a curious mix of stone and wood, one laid on top of the other, with tall windows looking out on to lawns. A man in a tunic of impeccable white had come down the steps, greeted them in Latin and then shown them to rooms where they were to eat and sleep. Al-Tabingha and the other Mamluks had been taken somewhere else.

That evening, they feasted on partridge roasted in *kalita* butter with bowls of rice and maize and stiff breads. Afterwards, they had taken cushions out on to the lawn and lain on them looking up at the stars. Luke had drunk a beer of fermented goat's milk and, for a while, watched the stars dancing.

He shook his head and yawned. 'I wonder how many jornufas there are in this park?'

Barbi, who'd also drunk beer, hiccoughed. 'Enough to please an emperor. We can go home.'

Shulen lay next to the engineer. She rolled on to her side. 'Hold your breath and count to ten. Slowly.' She glanced at Luke. 'Are you going to tell us why you've come with us?'

Nikolas shared another cushion with Zhu Chou. His head rested on her lap and he looked up at the stars. 'It must be important to keep him from Mistra. And if it's important, he won't tell us.' He paused. 'At least, not until we've spoken to King Yeshaq.' He lifted his head. 'Is that correct?'

Luke thought for a while, straightening the stars before answering. He said: 'I can tell you some of why we're here, most of which you already know.' He paused. 'As of last December Venice agreed a three-year truce for us to repay their debt. Now that the Medici will lose the Curia's banking, the gold has to come from somewhere other than papal revenues. We may assume that we have our qilin, which can be exchanged in China for gold.' He turned to Nikolas. 'But will it be enough, and will it be in time?'

Nikolas shrugged. 'We'll take at least a month to get to the coast.' He looked at the woman above him, who had her fingers in his hair. 'Zhu Chou, how long then to sail back to China?'

The concubine was sitting with her back as straight as a spear. 'That may not be the issue. I've told you of the mandarin class. They will be given the task of assembling the gold and they will not be in a hurry. It could take years to come.'

Benedo Barbi asked: 'But will Venice *really* be allowed to take Mistra for her debt?'

'Why not? Who will stop her?'

Shulen turned to Luke. 'So what was the point in you coming to Abyssinia?'

Luke held her eye for some moments. She knew it was the question he asked himself every night before he slept. In Mistra, a baffled populace must be asking each other that question every day. They must be asking Anna too. And Hilarion.

'There *is* a point to coming here,' he said quietly. 'I told you that Chen Cheng suggested a new trade route to our mutual advantage, one that required the treasure fleets to come into the Persian Gulf, then connect to Constantinople through Mongol and Ottoman lands.'

Nikolas nodded. 'Which is now possible with Ulugh Beg and Mehmed on their thrones.'

'Yes,' said Luke. 'But after them? Will Murad be as amenable? Or will we even get to Murad with Bedreddin at large?'

Shulen asked: 'So what is your alternative?'

'The treasure fleets put into Berbera on the coast of Africa and the goods go overland up to Alexandria.'

'But what about the Venetian monopoly?' asked Barbi.

Luke sat back in his chair. 'Why shouldn't Venice agree to share the monopoly with us? Monemvasia is much closer to Alexandria, after all. We allow them access to the China trade in exchange for Mistra's independence.'

Shulen nodded slowly. 'But there's still the issue of the gold. It doesn't sound as if it will arrive from China in time. Do you have a plan?'

Luke looked at each of them in turn. He said: 'Yes, I have a plan. I've not told it to you yet and I don't even know if it's possible. We'll see what happens tomorrow.'

The following morning, Luke rose early to the sound of peacocks on the lawn outside. He went to the window and watched them strut up to each other and change from commoner into courtier, barking their pleasure in the alchemy. The sun had just risen, turning the grass into rippled silver so that the birds seemed to walk on water. He thought suddenly of the Ark.

He dressed and left the palace, nodding to guards who made no attempt to stop him. He walked down the long avenue, the early sun playing hide and seek between the trees, until he came to the gates. They parted as he approached, the Roman guards smiling to him as they bent to pull them open. Abyssinia seemed unthreatened by enemies.

The Church of St Mary stood on the other side of open ground and was surrounded by borders of vivid flowers planted in red earth. Its doors were open and there were no queues waiting to enter. A woman was sweeping its steps, hooped earrings of gold glinting from beneath her veil. He watched her stoop to pick up a flower; she raised it to her nose, then tucked it behind the veil. He walked across to her.

'Can I go in?' he asked, gesturing.

She looked up at him with curiosity, pulling back her veil to see better. She was young, her beauty already cracked by the sun, but she had a grace that was far older. She smiled and waved him past.

Inside, the church was quite small and its unadorned brick-work was stark in sunlight that came through the high windows. In the middle stood something large and rectangular, covered by a cloth of green silk hemmed with tiny jewels. A sizeable crucifix hung from the ceiling above, on which was painted a black Jesus who looked down through eyes slanted by pity. There were worn wooden kneelers and a rail surrounding the object.

Luke felt someone behind him and looked round.

'The Ark of the Covenant,' Shulen said quietly. 'But empty.'

Luke studied her. She was dressed as he'd seen her the night before and he wondered if she'd slept. She walked over to the rail and knelt and Luke came and knelt beside her. 'So they say.'

'So where are Moses' tablets?'

Luke shrugged. 'Who knows? Probably somewhere beneath Jerusalem.'

Shulen's voice fell to a whisper. 'And the Ark only has power when the tablets are returned to it. What a pity – we could take it too.'

He smiled. 'You're well informed.'

'The diadan,' she said. 'Zhu Chou told me last night when we went to bed.' She paused and looked straight ahead. 'Shall we pray for gold?' Her hands were joined in front of her. 'Am I right to assume you believe you can somehow extract some from this King?'

Luke looked at her as she stared ahead. They had hardly talked alone since Edirne but they were talking now. 'Perhaps,' he said. 'Or perhaps from somewhere else. But it won't affect you. You'll take the qilin east to Berbera, if we get one.'

She turned to him. 'I'll go where I please, Luke.'

He frowned. 'Of course. I meant – '

'You meant that your gold is dependent on me returning to China as quickly as possible, gold that will benefit a place I have no connection with whatsoever.'

He turned to her. 'But I never asked you to go to China, Shulen. You wanted to.'

'And I'm pleased I went. I have seen extraordinary things – the diadan, for instance. It can change the world.'

Luke nodded. 'It can. Provided it's given to the right people.'

Shulen smiled. 'Like you.' She rose and walked over to the door of the church. 'The Ming Emperor is a wise ruler, a great ruler, perhaps the greatest so far.' She paused. 'His vision for the world is worth following. It's what I follow now.'

Luke, still kneeling, watched her leave. He sat back on his heels and thought for a long time about what he'd just learnt, feeling an emptiness steal over him that filled the church. Then he rose and left.

He crossed the open ground to the gates, which were still open. He saw Shulen ahead of him walking up towards the palace. He saw a man standing on the grass watching her.

Al-Tabingha.

Al-Tabingha did not join their audience with the King. It was held in a room full of people with gold bands on their arms and skins decorated in henna. The women's hair was full of ornaments that sent a murmur over their heads as they moved. A carpet, lined with Roman soldiers, ran down the middle to a gigantic gold throne, raised on a dais, with a small man sitting in it. From a distance, he looked like a child.

'King Yeshaq, I suppose,' said Luke from the corner of his mouth. 'I'm not sure of the procedure. Al-Tabingha didn't tell us.'

Nikolas said: 'Let's use the kowtow. Three of us are good at that by now. Luke and Barbi, you'll just have to watch what Zhu Chou does.'

They walked down the carpet, Luke leading them. When they were ten paces from the dais, he stopped and ushered Zhu Chou and Shulen to the front. All five of them dropped to their knees and performed the kowtow. There was a ripple of laughter around them.

'Probably wrong,' whispered Luke. 'Let's stand up.'

They did so and found themselves looking at a man far from

305

childish. King Yeshaq had a face as brown and mottled as a coconut, out of which sprang hairs and a hooked nose that almost covered his lips. His eyes were roofed with heavy lids and arched by a forest of eyebrow whose branches joined above his nose. He was bigger than he'd looked from the doors, but not much.

Luke stared at him.

Prester John.

He was the stuff of fable: the Christian king in the heart of Africa, the descendant of Solomon whose people had been Christian since Roman times. He was said to be limitlessly rich, had armies beyond counting and owned the Ark of the Covenant. It was said that some day he would use it all to turn the tide of Islam.

And here he was: small, hairy and unremarkable.

The King spoke in Latin: 'Which of you is leader?'

Luke walked to the front and bowed. 'I am Luke Magoris, Protostrator to the Despot of Mistra in the Empire of Byzantium.'

The King scratched himself. 'And your companions? Not their names, what they do.'

Luke glanced behind him. Zhu Chou's turquoise dress was perhaps the brightest colour in the hall. 'These two are merchants. The blue lady is from China. The other is an engineer.'

The forests parted and the eyes turned to Zhu Chou. 'Might she have something to do with the big ships seen in our waters off Berbera?'

Luke's heart lifted. Admiral Zheng had arrived. He would be there, waiting for the qilin.

'It is why we are here,' said Luke.

The King sat forward on his throne, putting a hand to his crown. There were gold bangles on his wrists that jangled as

306

he moved. 'There is a big market in Berbera. Many ships come from India, but none have come from China for years. Why are they there now?'

'To trade with you,' said Luke. 'The Emperor of China wishes to trade with you.'

'To trade what?' asked the King.

'Silk, porcelain, weapons . . . things you desire.'

'Weapons? What sort of weapons?'

'Weapons that fire balls of stone for half a mile, that can shoot thirty spears faster than you can blink.'

Yeshaq was stroking his beard against his chin with his finger, leaving wisps of hair waving like grass. He asked: 'What does he want in return?'

Luke's hands were clasped to his front. Now he opened them. 'To start with, a simple token of your friendship, majesty. A jornufa. They are plentiful in your kingdom but rare in his.'

The King considered this. 'He just wants a giraffe?'

'For now, yes. But in the future: gold.'

'What makes you think I have gold in my kingdom?'

'You have some,' said Luke, 'but not enough. You will need to reopen the trade route with the Empire of Mali. Their gold now only goes north to Alexandria.'

The King frowned and the forests reunited. His eyelids closed a little in thought. He was watching Luke with some curiosity, his head moving slowly from side to side. 'How do you know all this?'

Luke thought about the nights at sea, poring over the diadan with Zhu Chou. He said instead: 'The historian Ibn Khaldun. He told me once.'

The King nodded. 'Ah, Ibn Khaldun.' He leant back in his throne. 'He came here. Tell me what else he told you.'

Luke glanced behind him. Behind his four friends were hundreds of courtiers turned in his direction. Did they speak Latin too?

Yeshaq understood. 'I will dismiss them,' he said. He shouted something over Luke's head, then nodded. 'They will leave now.'

It took ten minutes for the hall to clear. It was a noisy process of shuffle and grumble because Latin was understood among many of Yeshaq's courtiers and they too wanted to hear what else Ibn Khaldun had told Luke. At last the doors closed.

Yeshaq rose from the throne and walked to the edge of the dais. He gestured. 'Sit.' He stepped down from the platform and sat himself on its edge. The rest of them sat on the carpet looking up at him, Zhu Chou balanced on her knees. The King turned to Luke. 'Now, what else did Ibn Khaldun tell you?'

Luke reached into his pocket and produced the same map as he had shown the Mamluk Sultan. He unfolded it and straightened it on the carpet. He pointed. 'Here is your kingdom of Abyssinia, here is Alexandria, and over here is the Mandinka Empire of Mali with its king of that time, Mansa Musa, holding a golden nugget.'

King Yeshaq got down from the dais and knelt on the carpet opposite Luke, looking down at the map. He leant forward and Shulen wondered if he needed spectacles as Tamerlane had done. He said: 'It is right for him to be holding gold. The Empire of Mali is the richest in the world. It is said their women have their hair plaited with gold and their dogs have gold collars around their necks.' He paused to attack a fly on his shoulder. 'A hundred years ago their emperor, Mansa Musa, went on pilgrimage to Mecca with sixty thousand retainers. He took so much gold with him to Cairo that it caused the price to collapse for twelve years.'

Luke nodded. 'All this I've learnt, majesty. Mali produces more than half of the world's gold and trades it from near Timbuktu. It is called the silent trade because the Wangara tribe, who mine the gold, want to keep the place where they do it secret.' He pointed at the map again. 'Most of the gold goes into Europe from Alexandria and the Mamluks have grown rich by it. Now the Chinese want some of it to come to them from Berbera. And they will pay more.'

Yeshaq had produced a fan from his sleeve and was waving it in front of his face, the hairs moving in its breeze. 'But why will Mali trade with us?' he asked.

'Because, majesty,' said Luke, 'the Chinese have better things to trade. The Emperor of Mali knows that the Portuguese are coming further down the coast every year trying to find the source of their gold. They will need weapons to repel them.'

'But Mali only trades with Muslims.'

'They need salt and yours is the best in the world. You call it "white gold" and sell it in blocks which you hack from the salt flats in the north. You used to trade it pound for pound for their gold.'

Yeshaq nodded. 'Because it preserves their food. But now they've found their own supply in Bilma.'

Luke played his card. 'Which they've just lost to the Songhai.' He glanced at the King, who was frowning. 'The Mamluk al-Tabingha told me this.'

Yeshaq was silent after this, nodding slowly. His eyelids were so low that he could have been asleep. At last he said: 'How do you propose to reopen this trade route? Timbuktu is six months from here. The journey is hard.'

'I will make it myself, majesty. With your help.'

Luke heard movement behind him. This was new to his companions.

309

'You would go alone?'

Luke dipped his head. 'I will ask only one of my companions to make the journey with me: the engineer. I would ask you for guides and an escort.'

'What else will you need?'

'Salt, cowrie shells,' replied Luke. 'I will buy the gold and bring it back to Berbera. The Chinese will keep a ship there to transport it.'

'So you will keep the gold?'

'The first of it, yes. It will be my price for opening the trade route.'

It was dawn at Montone and the birds were raucous in their reveille, erupting from the trees like children from Friday prayers: all chatter. There was heavy dew on the grass and the first blinding rays of sun were sewing cobwebs blade to blade. The horse's breath came and stayed in an air of no breeze.

Giovanni was standing just inside a little wood holding two horses, both saddled. He was cloaked against the morning chill and wore a cloth to his face like a mask. He was watching a small door in the castle's wall.

He'd spent the last hour watching it and, to pass the time, wondering about Luke. He must be as hated by the rich in Mistra as he was by Murad in Edirne. Not only had he lost everyone's money, he'd made an enemy of Venice which, if its debt was not repaid in time, would attack Mistra. And Bedreddin might do it sooner. Thank God, at least he'd built the wall. But there was one question above all others.

Where have you gone?

It seemed Luke had deserted Mistra. He: the Protostrator to a despot who'd barely learnt to rule. It seemed unforgivable.

Giovanni shut his eyes and shook his head. So many questions. And so little time.

He heard a whistle and opened his eyes. Standing before the castle's door was Braccio da Montone. Someone cloaked and hooded was by his side. Braccio waved and walked towards him across the dew, the other by his side. Then they'd arrived and Giovanni could hardly breathe.

Cleope came up to him and pulled down her hood. 'I am here.'

She was dressed as a boy. She wore a loose doublet over thick cotton hose with leather stitched to the insides. Her cloak was patched and frayed at its edges. She held a saddlebag in one hand and a skin of water in the other. She was prepared for a journey.

Giovanni felt giddy with joy, relief, wonder that the plan had worked. 'Was it easy?'

She smiled up at him, brushing hair from her eyes. 'It is easy to escape what you cannot tolerate.'

He bent over to kiss her and Braccio put his hands on their shoulders. 'Later. You must ride.'

Giovanni nodded. He gave Cleope her reins. They mounted and he brought his horse over to Braccio. He looked down.

'Thank you,' he said. 'I won't forget this.'

Braccio grunted and patted Giovanni's horse. He checked his girth, then Cleope's. He asked: 'Where will you go?'

Giovanni was already turning his horse. 'To Mistra,' he said. 'If they'll have us.'

CHAPTER TWENTY-SIX

ITALY, SUMMER 1416

Advised by Braccio, Giovanni and Cleope took the road east from Montone towards the mountains and Ancona on the coast.

The Malatestas had taken the flight of Cleope as badly as it is possible to take news. Once back in Rimini, they had sent out armed search parties in every direction, their instructions to retrieve Cleope and kill Giovanni, whether he resisted or not.

Anticipating this, the lovers soon made themselves less obtrusive. They sold their horses, cut their hair and changed into clothes that would not raise questions amongst the journeymen, tinkers, knife-sharpeners and split-lipped vagabonds who travelled the road. They were to be dyers, both male, one of them apprenticed. They slept in barns with owls, in shepherds' huts with weakling lambs, in woods where trees cradled the moon between their branches. They awoke to dew and the onrush of sap in creaking limbs. They were never happier to be alive.

At the coast, they took the long road south to Brindisi where they planned to take ship to Monemvasia. The waters to their left were a Venetian sea and the ships that hurried past were galleys flying the Lion of St Mark. They pressed on towards the Kingdom of Naples where they'd be safer.

As they walked, they talked of the wonder of a nurse called Isabella.

'Luke persuaded her to take ill after Constance,' said Giovanni. 'She took the baths at Lucca and he met her there. That's how you knew what to do.'

They'd just passed a donkey carrying a Jew in a conical hat with his pregnant wife behind. Cleope had exchanged a bracelet for food, which they now ate.

Between mouthfuls, she talked. 'It was hard. To show contempt for one you love for so long. That was hard.'

Giovanni took her hand and smiled at her. 'But you did and we are here.'

Cleope looked out to sea. There were ships of every size seemingly motionless upon its crystal surface, tiny wakes behind them. 'Which is where exactly? The sea doesn't change.'

'We are about to reach the Kingdom of Naples, where Queen Joanna rules.'

'And Naples is no friend to Rome or Rimini. Will they dare to look for us there?'

'You have a father and two uncles looking for us. They'll look everywhere.'

Cleope sighed. 'And another uncle who will soon be pope, I'm told. I thought him a good man once but perhaps he'll be no better than any other.' She laughed. 'I'm sounding like you.'

Giovanni considered this. She was not like him, except in the issue of their love. She still believed in her popes, her saints, her miracles. She thought Jan Hus a heretic and Cossa an aberration. They had argued it in barns, haystacks and stables, each baffled by the other's certainties.

'Who is pope is not the point,' he said. 'How can you admire a creed that makes curiosity a mortal sin?' He swept the loaf he

313

was holding across the landscape. 'How can anyone deny this wonderful world for another?'

'So this mortal world is enough for you?'

He looked at her then, at her near-white hair, her face framed by the sparkling blue of the sea: a Madonna surrounded by stars, but no suitors in sight except him.

'If you are in it, yes,' he said softly. 'But then you're not mortal.'

She laughed. There were butterflies on the road before them, sylphs of colour that chased in pairs. They were proof of some God. 'We can disagree about my Church,' she said, 'but not about my God. He shows Himself everywhere.'

'In Cossa?'

'All right, no; but what about Luke?' She glanced at Giovanni. 'Is that not a good man? Is that not a man to love?'

Giovanni thought about it. His love for Luke was different from his love for Cleope. Different and more complicated.

She was watching him. 'I saw how he looked at you that night.'

They hadn't talked of the night at Constance since it had happened. Giovanni wasn't sure he wanted to now. She watched his dimples disappear.

'He has your goodness, and you his.'

He shook his head, knowing what she meant. 'Luke Magoris is not my father,' he said quietly. 'Marchese Longo is my father.'

Cleope drew close, pressing his arm to her bosom as they walked. 'Then why did my uncle say what he did, Giovanni?'

'Because we look alike. It was a guess.'

She shook her head then. 'I don't think so.'

Giovanni stopped and turned to her. 'But, Cleope, don't you see? If I'm a bastard, I'm even further from marrying you.'

'And you're so close now? Giovanni, we have banished our-selves from the world. Even if no d'Este wants me now, they still won't let us marry. We don't even know if Mistra will take us in.'

He looked at her for a long while. He'd put flowers in her hair earlier, splitting their stems with his teeth to join one to the next. The chain was crooked and he straightened it. He said softly: 'Cleope, I don't want to be a bastard.'

'But don't you want to know *who* you are? I do.'

'You really care who my father is?'

She put her arms around his neck and rose on tiptoes to kiss him. For a moment she watched the sunlight play through his torn hair. 'Certainly I care, and don't care. You can be the son of God or the Devil and I will still love you.' She paused and put her head to one side. 'I already know. I just want to know that you know.'

Giovanni looked down and saw how serious she was, how much it mattered to her that nothing should be secret between them. They were alone on a road, chased by uncles and but-terflies, with few certainties in their lives. It was important to embrace those they had.

'I know,' he said.

They came to Brindisi one evening as the sun was setting behind them, turning its deer-head harbour into a bonfire of masts and rigging. Giovanni stood on a hill above and wondered if Negro-ponte had looked like this after their fireship had struck. There was a breeze that came in from the sea and smelt of Mistra. 'Most of those will be Venetian,' he said, pointing to the ships in the harbour.

Cleope was gathered to his side like an olive basket, his arm the solid strap. He looked down at her head. In the six weeks since they'd left Ancona, her hair had grown whiter both on her head and arms, her skin browner by tiny degrees. She looked up at him. 'So how will we find a ship to take us to Monemvasia?'

Giovanni didn't answer at first because he didn't know. What if every ship's captain had been told to look for them? 'We'll look for a Byzantine ship,' he said at last. 'Then we'll use Luke's name.'

They walked down to the city gates and entered past guards wearing the triple-banded arms of Anjou-Durazzo that proclaimed lordship of Jerusalem and Hungary as well as Naples. They kept their heads hooded and shuffled in with the crowd returning from the fields, Giovanni's height obscured by rakes and threshing fans. They weren't stopped.

Inside the city, the streets were narrow and noisy with people and animals. They pushed their way through the crowd towards the port, avoiding anyone dressed in black, anyone with a sword. They kept their heads low and held hands in the dark space below the jostle. Every now and then Giovanni looked up to see if a Palaiologos eagle flew amidst the pennants in the harbour. He saw something else.

'Soldiers,' he said, ducking to her level, 'lots of them. They seem to be ringing the harbour. We'll not get past them.'

She looked up at him, two anxious eyes wide in the darkness. 'They could be here for many reasons, couldn't they?'

Giovanni would have preferred to turn back but the human tide was strong and they were being pushed closer to the soldiers. To turn now would create a spectacle. 'Keep your hood up,' he whispered. 'We're dyers, remember?'

She squeezed his hand and remembered her name.

Piero from Ancona. Dyer apprentice to the journeyman Marco.

She lifted her hand and saw the stains they'd applied to their fingers the night before. She heard Giovanni speaking above her. The people around her smelt of armpits and breath and she longed to be away from them. Her hood smelt of fish. Someone dug his elbow into her neck. She heard curses. She saw spittle next to her foot.

More talking above. Something was wrong. They weren't being allowed past. She pulled Giovanni's arm. 'Let's go back.'

But it was too late. The soldiers had seen them and wanted them to go somewhere else. Two mailed hands were holding Giovanni's arms, pulling him away. She gripped his wrist and followed.

They were brought out of the crowd to the quayside behind the soldiers. It had fewer people on it, just those who'd been allowed through to join ships or say goodbye. The air was fresher and Cleope felt some relief.

She asked: 'What are they doing?'

'They've gone to get someone.'

It took some time before the person was found and, by that time, Giovanni was sitting on a bollard with Cleope at his feet, her hood pulled so far forward that no part of her face was visible. A man was coming down the quayside towards them. He was tall, well built and dressed in a magnificent doublet embroidered with gold fleur-de-lys, with pearls for buttons. As he drew closer, Giovanni saw that he was middle-aged and had a paunch that stretched the fabric at his front. He was smiling.

'Welcome to the Kingdom of Naples!' The man's arms were outstretched in greeting. He stopped in front of them. 'But you should have told us you were coming!'

Giovanni rose, leaving Cleope with her face to the ground. He found the man was almost as tall as he. He tried to look puzzled. 'Lord?'

'Ah, my name. Sergianni Caracciolo, adviser and friend to Her Majesty Queen Joanna of Naples.' He gave a little bow. 'We've been looking for you.'

Giovanni summoned a frown. 'Lord, we . . .'

But Sergianni was laughing. 'Please, no more.' He looked down. 'You must be Cleope Malatesta. I have seen your painting. I should like to see your face.' He stretched out his hand for her to rise.

Cleope looked up and then rose. She pulled back the hood.

'Your hair!' exclaimed Sergianni, his hand to his mouth. 'What have you done?'

'It was necessary, lord,' she said.

'What a desecration! Your father will be upset.' He looked at Giovanni. 'But not as upset as he was at your escape. They say he had to be pulled off Braccio da Montone.'

Giovanni said: 'Braccio had nothing to do with it.'

The man put his finger to his lips. 'No, of course not.' He glanced at Cleope. 'And I imagine that the lady came against her will? You must have forced her every inch down the coast.'

Giovanni looked around him. They were circled by soldiers, each with a crossbow. He said: 'We thought Naples an enemy of Rimini and the papacy.'

Sergianni smiled. 'Who knows who are enemies and who friends, Giovanni Longo? Italy is a complicated place these days.'

'And what will you do with us?'

'With you? Why, save you, of course.' He gestured behind him and lowered his voice. 'Every Venetian in this harbour is waiting to arrest you. You have ten thousand ducats on your head. We're here to save you from them.'

Giovanni looked at the ships behind Sergianni. Most had men

leaning over their sides, watching what was going on. He turned back to Sergianni. 'So where will you take us?'

'We will escort you by road further south to Otranto before any ship in this harbour is allowed to set sail. There you will be taken to Monemvasia. They won't catch you.'

It was everything they needed and more. But why was Naples helping them? Giovanni asked the question.

'The Queen is a romantic,' said Sergianni.

The journey from Otranto to Monemvasia was uneventful. They sailed in a round ship full of *fiordìlatte* cheese before a mild westerly that lifted the smell and made their cabin a place of stale milk. The captain was Genoese and treated Giovanni as a wayward son, winking his way through every conversation. They spent much of the week climbing the mast to avoid him and watch for dolphins.

They sailed into Monemvasia as the sun was setting over the Goulas and the sky furrowed by long orange clouds. There was little wind and, above the slap of the waves, they heard the murmur of evening greeting from the city walls and the screech of cats beyond. Tiny columns of smoke rose from the houses and the smell of cooking wafted over the water to them. Dolphins played at their bows and Giovanni held Cleope's hand and wished they never had to arrive.

They watched it all in silence, each asking the same question: would they be welcomed?

They were; at least in Monemvasia. The Protostrator had grown up there and anyone fleeing the Roman Church was beyond scrutiny. News of their arrival had preceded them and the quayside was crowded by those who wanted sight of the famous Italian beauty.

As they came ashore, a man Giovanni knew stepped forward.

'Arcadius,' he said, embracing him. 'How did you know I was coming?'

'Naples sent a message and I was here.' He held Giovanni's face between his hands. 'I'm glad I was.'

'Can we stay?'

Arcadius looked down at Cleope and smiled. 'Ah, the reports are true.' He took her hand and looked back at Giovanni. 'You are a lucky man.'

'But can we stay?'

'Here? Of course. Luke's palace is prepared.' He glanced at Cleope. 'As to whether you can stay in the despotate, that will depend on others. Come.'

He led them through the narrow streets, showered with flowers thrown by people who laughed and reached out to touch Cleope's hair. The fugitive lovers found themselves loved.

They climbed the steps to Luke's palace which Giovanni knew well. It was late summer and the Goulas was still full of flowers, its orchards sprinkled with tiny dots of colour that made patterns in the breeze. They spent a week there gazing out to the horizon and talking of a future every bit as indistinct. They watched ships gather in the roads and wondered how many carried angry demands from Italy. They heard nothing from the capital.

At last the summons came. They were to travel to Mistra to meet the Despot and his advisers. They were to go at once and Arcadius would go with them.

Arcadius arranged mounts from the Mamonas stud and they rode off on a day of bluster that made the horses skittish beneath them. They left early and reached the castle at Geraki by noon. Below the castle walls, they found a stone with writing on it. Giovanni dismounted.

'Alexis Laskaris,' he read, brushing away the dust and leaning forward. 'Anna's brother. He died here twenty years ago, shot by crossbow from those walls.' He looked up at Cleope. 'He would've been my uncle. In a way.'

They reached Mistra early in the evening, met at the gate by guards with the Palaiologos eagle on their hauberks who escorted them up the steep streets to the palace. Arcadius left to find Matthew while Giovanni and Cleope were shown straight into the throne room where Theodore, Anna and Plethon sat on one side of a long table. The room was high and cool and its floor was dappled with evening sunlight from tall windows. The sounds of the city were faint.

Giovanni and Cleope sat down side by side on single chairs placed opposite the table. The scene was a court hearing.

Theodore had risen to greet them. He looked nervous and kept his hands on the table, perhaps to stop them shaking. He had the Palaiologos grace but was thin and pale and given to sudden illness. He was also devout and bookish and seemingly indifferent to women. 'You are returned,' he said to Giovanni, 'but without our protostrator. We miss him.'

His eyes passed to Cleope and stayed there. Then he bowed. 'And you are Cleope Malatesta.' He paused. 'Your beauty is all that they said it was.'

Giovanni glanced at Plethon, who had also risen and was staring at Theodore in amazement. Neither of them had heard him express such warmth to a woman before.

Anna, still seated, chose to come straight to the point. She addressed Giovanni. 'By bringing Cleope here, you have put this city in even more danger than it was. It was wrong of you to come.'

Theodore sat, still staring at Cleope with curiosity. Then he turned to Giovanni. 'Why didn't you go to Chios? After all, that is your home.'

Giovanni looked from one to the other. 'I felt I could help here,' he said simply. 'They're not going to invade Chios.'

Plethon put his hand on Thedore's arm, leaning in. 'We can't turn them away, majesty.'

Theodore looked uncomfortable. 'No . . . no, of course not.'

Anna said quietly: 'But they might choose to leave of their own accord.'

Giovanni examined her. She wasn't meeting his eyes. He saw in her an anger that had grown in his absence. He knew that, as he sat there, he reminded her of a man he looked like. He said: 'I had thought Cosimo bought three years before any attack came from Venice. Surely, the bigger problem is Bedreddin? Whether we are here or not will make little difference to him.'

'Not if Murad joins him,' said Anna. 'He hates every part of Mistra. My husband beat him.'

'But how will Murad join Bedreddin?'

Plethon answered. 'We're told that there are those at Mehmed's court who don't like the peace with Byzantium. They look to Murad to lead them, however young he is. They may enable him to escape Edirne and go to Bedreddin.'

Giovanni nodded slowly. He looked back at Anna and saw how tired she was. Her eyes were ringed with darkness and her skin was pale and creased. 'Then perhaps the fact that Luke's not here might be enough to turn them towards Constantinople.'

Anna looked at him without emotion of any kind. 'And you believe that is the reason my husband has deserted this city? Because he doesn't want to provoke Murad? You must believe him very virtuous.'

It was what Giovanni had wanted to believe. There was no other explanation he could think of. 'I think it was one reason, yes.'

Anna stared at him. There was new colour in her cheeks. 'Where is he anyway?' she asked. 'Presumably still with the shaman's daughter?'

'In Africa,' replied Giovanni. 'I know no more than you.'

'His place is here. What good is Africa?' She rose and went to the window, her hands entwined and moving. Something was rising within her. She turned. 'How has it come to this? Plethon, how has it *come* to this?'

Plethon gave a little shrug. 'Zoe, probably. She wants her estates in Mistra back, perhaps Mistra itself. She is leading the Venetian bankers' demand for repayment.' He looked at the Despot. 'But the truth is that we wouldn't have our wall without Luke. We would be defenceless against Bedreddin.'

Anna gave a snort. 'Who wouldn't attack us if Murad hadn't been beaten.'

Giovanni said: 'But Luke was protecting Hilarion. He –'

Anna turned, the full force of her anger no longer surprised. 'No. *You* were supposed to be protecting Hilarion, *you*! But you chose to abandon him instead.'

The Despot rose suddenly. He wanted to go back to his books. 'I will leave you to talk further,' he said. He looked at Cleope and produced a half-smile. 'Giovanni and Cleope can stay in Mistra but for how long you will decide between you. Let me know your decision.'

Theodore turned and hurried out, accompanied by four pages and two dogs. The four of them were alone. Anna stayed at the window, gazing out at nothing.

Plethon was the first to break the silence. He turned to Cleope

323

and said quietly: 'You must think us ungracious. In Luke's absence, I welcome you to Mistra.'

Cleope nodded. She thought it wise to remain silent. Giovanni waited a while before asking: 'Have you heard from the Malatestas?'

Plethon nodded. 'They want Cleope back.' He turned to her. 'They'll be concerned that you'll be subjected to ungodly teaching in Mistra. My syllabus has changed from Rimini.'

Cleope smiled. 'No more Catullus?'

Plethon remained serious. 'Poggio has worked a miracle in Germany. He struck gold in Fulda.'

'Fulda?' asked Giovanni. 'What's Fulda?'

'It's a monastery. They had the Lucretius.'

Giovanni exchanged glances with Cleope. He had no idea what Plethon was talking about.

'Lucretius was a Roman thinker. He wrote a long poem called *De Rerum Natura* —*On the Nature of Things*. It may be the most important thing ever written. We thought it lost but Poggio's found it at Fulda Monastery in Germany.'

Cleope was leaning forward in her chair, suddenly curious. 'What is the poem about?'

'How the universe works, nothing less.' Plethon had his hands pressed together as he did when excited. 'It's based on the teaching of Epicurus.'

Giovanni remembered what Poggio had told him about Epicurus. 'And now you're teaching it at your school?'

'Not just to my school, to everyone in Mistra. It provides a basis for this kingdom's new polity: one based on logic and service to a perfect state.' Plethon was nodding now. 'With Luke's wall, it's how we'll save Mistra.'

Anna turned from the window and walked to the end of

the table, putting her fists down with emphasis. There were tears in her eyes. 'Save Mistra, Plethon?' she said. 'We have fifty thousand Turks waiting to cross and join with whatever Murad can muster. If they don't destroy us, then we have the greatest sea power in the world waiting to take over.' She was speaking with her head thrust forward, her copper hair hitched behind her ears. There were veins in her neck. 'Do you *really* believe that a wall and a handful of Varangians will save us? Even with your Greek myths ringing in their ears?'

Plethon had placed his hands wide and flat on the table, as if holding it to the floor. 'What else do we do?' he asked quietly.

'We don't antagonise our enemy!' she cried. 'We don't teach heresy to our young and we don't harbour our enemy's enemies!'

Plethon frowned. 'But Giovanni is one of us, Anna. Whatever happened at the fair with Murad doesn't change that.'

'He is *not* one of us!' she hissed through gritted teeth. 'He's not even Greek.'

Giovanni rose from his chair, amazed at his own calm. 'I am as Greek as you,' he said. 'More so, in fact. You know that.'

At that moment everything seemed to stop. Everyone was frozen, their breath held. The only movement came from six eyes, widened now, that suddenly fixed themselves on Giovanni. Something had been said.

Giovanni was looking from Plethon to Anna. 'Why are you staring at me? Did you think I didn't *know*?' He laughed. 'I was page to a man who could *only* be my father!'

Anna opened her mouth to speak. Her face was drained of colour. She glanced at Cleope.

Giovanni said: 'Cleope knows. Like everyone else, she'd guessed.' He paused and took Cleope's hand. 'But the difference

325

was that she saw how unfair it was to continue the lie. So, from now on, we won't. At least to you.'

Cleope was looking at him as if something had been won. She kissed the hand in hers and held it to her cheek.

Plethon rose and went over to Anna, who was now staring down at the table, her shoulders hunched. She looked exhausted. He stood behind her and put his hands on her arms. 'It was inevitable,' he said softly.

Anna did nothing for some time. Then she nodded. Plethon began to lead her from the room: slowly and with care. Cleope rose and came to Anna's other side, taking her arm. Plethon opened the door and spoke to someone outside. Then he spoke to Cleope. He waited for them both to leave, then closed the door and turned to Giovanni.

'Yes,' he said quietly. 'You are Luke's son and Siward's descendant. Now there is something I must show you.'

A party of four set off from Mistra when it was dark, leaving the city by the main gate where they collected horses. It consisted of Plethon, Giovanni, Matthew and Arcadius. The two Varangians had arrived quickly after Plethon's summons and now carried tools on their saddles.

They turned west, following a path that ran before the city wall, to woods that climbed beside it. There, they rose until the path veered off to the left and wound around the back of the hill on which the city stood. There was a deep gorge here and, had they spoken, they would have heard themselves echoed through the trees. But Plethon had forbidden all sound and they rode in silence, the only noise the soft pad of their horses' hooves.

Giovanni looked up at a moon that was almost full. He looked over towards the peak of Mount Taygetos, its snow glowing in the half-light. Plethon had told him that the Melingi were still up there somewhere, living in their caves.

The night was not cold but he felt cold, and a little frightened. Plethon had just spoken words that would change his life forever.

Of course he knew what he was being taken to. The Varangian treasure had been the favourite story of his childhood, told again and again by the man he thought his father: how Siward and three other Varangians had brought the treasure to Mistra from Constantinople two hundred years ago, escaping by boat as the city burned; how their descendants had stayed in Mistra to guard it ever since. Now he was one of them, son to a man who'd fled Mistra to arrive at Chios where Marchese and Fiorentina had taken him in, given him education and wealth. And love.

He liked the legend, especially the part that said that it might one day save the Empire of the Byzantines. He had once imagined a vast hoard of gold guarded by a dragon in the middle of Mount Taygetos. But, later, Marchese had talked of diamonds and balas rubies so huge that each held the value of a city. Then he'd come to Mistra and asked Plethon who had shrugged and said that it was all probably myth. Now he was taking him to it.

They were coming to a clearing where the trees stopped and formed a circle. In the middle stood a tiny chapel with a tower and no bell in it. The building was smothered in weeds and broken stones lay in the grass around it.

Giovanni drew up his horse next to Plethon's. 'A church?'

'A former church,' replied Plethon quietly. 'We stand on deconsecrated ground. We put out the story that the Devil had been seen dancing on the roof of the chapel. Nobody comes near it now.'

They dismounted and tethered their horses to trees. The two Varangians brought torches from their saddles and lit them. Then they took tools and a key. Matthew went to the door and turned. He said: 'You two wait here and keep watch. When we've dug it up, we'll call you.'

Giovanni and Plethon found stones to sit on from where they could watch the forest. They heard the sound of digging from within, then the sound of metal on metal.

'They're bringing it up,' said Plethon. 'Not long now.'

Giovanni looked up. The trees were mountains, black and silent, their summits stark against a sky of stars and no wind. He shivered and held his arms to his chest. He heard humming beside him and tried to think of something besides what was happening in the chapel behind.

'I should return to Chios,' he said.

The humming stopped. 'Really? Why?'

'I should talk to Marchese Longo.' Giovanni glanced at Plethon. 'Shouldn't I?'

Plethon rose and came over to him. He sat on the same stone and put his arm around Giovanni's shoulders. 'I have known Marchese Longo for a very long time,' he said softly. 'He is a man of great goodness and greater wisdom. He knows many, many things.' He paused and looked at Giovanni, his eyes catching the moonlight. 'But there are some things he may choose not to know.'

Giovanni stared at him. 'I love them both,' he said. 'Equally.'

Plethon nodded. 'Yes, you do.' He brought his hands to his knees and looked down at them. 'And that love might persuade you to keep what you know secret.' He paused. 'We talked of different kinds of love at Rimini. You have two fathers whom you love equally, but may learn to love differently.'

328

The door to the church creaked open and Matthew's head appeared. He was sweating. 'It's up,' he said. 'Arcadius and I will keep guard now.'

Giovanni got to his feet and helped Plethon to his. He noticed that they both had clammy hands. He felt drumming in his chest and more at his temples. Holding Plethon's arm, he entered the chapel.

Inside was a pile of earth and a casket beside it. The casket was made of wood so ancient it was impossible to know from which tree it came. It had iron hoops around it, all broken. A metal bar leant against the wall.

Giovanni suddenly felt even colder than he had before and knew Plethon did too for he'd pulled his cloak tight to his shoulders. Plethon walked to the casket and knelt. He held out his hand. 'Give me the bar.'

Giovanni passed it to him. Plethon pushed it between a hoop and the casket edge where the wood was strongest. He pressed down and the hoop parted. He did the same with the others. Giovanni held the torch above him.

Plethon leant forward and used his fingers to prise up the casket's lid, moving from one end to the other. When it was free, Giovanni helped him lift it off. A cloud of dust rose and drifted away.

Inside was the skeleton of a man about five and a half feet in height. At its feet was an ancient piece of linen, holed and frayed. The hands had been crossed at the pelvis and, resting on them, was a ring that looked as though it was made of gold. It had an inscription on it. Giovanni studied what was beneath him for a long time. The only sound in the chapel was that of breathing. At last he spoke.

'Who is it?'

'It is the body of Jesus Christ.'

Plethon had whispered the words but they filled the chapel as if they'd been shouted.

The body of Jesus Christ.

Giovanni didn't understand at first. The words held no meaning. They formed a sentence but it didn't make sense. He felt cold yet there was sweat at his brow. He put a hand on Plethon's arm to steady himself.

The body of Jesus Christ.

An image flashed into his mind: a church on Genoese Chios, *Christian* Chios. He saw himself as a boy kneeling between Marchese and Fiorenza. He saw what the little boy saw, *always* saw: the image of the risen Christ, angels bearing him up to heaven where his Father sat to welcome him, arms open. He closed his eyes and his hand tightened on Plethon's arm. Here was a philosopher's flesh and blood; it was real.

'I know,' said Plethon quietly. 'It's a shock. Luke had much the same reaction.'

Giovanni found his voice. 'So the Muslims were right all along,' he whispered. 'He was only a prophet.'

'Yes.'

Giovanni took a deep breath and let his hand fall to his side. He felt numb. 'How do you know it is him?'

Plethon sat back on his heels, wiping dust from his hands. 'First there is the skeleton,' he said. 'The bones are all broken where they should be: the wrists, the feet, the side where He was speared; the five Holy Wounds.' He pointed at each, then at the skull lying on its side. 'The head is pitted with small holes where the Crown of Thorns was placed.' His hand travelled down the skeleton. 'There is dislocation at the shoulders and chest bones consistent with crucifixion.'

Giovanni was shaking his head slowly. 'Whose is the ring?'

'It is the ring of Joseph of Arimathaea,' replied Plethon. 'He was the man who buried Jesus. His name is inscribed on it.'

Giovanni turned to him. 'But is it enough? Many have borne the stigmata. Didn't San Francesco from Assisi have them?'

'True. But then there's the history. The casket was dug up when the Emperor Constantine rebuilt Jerusalem. It was brought to Constantinople by his mother, Helena, who thought it the body of Barabbas. It was left for a hundred years, then reopened by the Patriarch Nestorius. He reported his findings to the Emperor Theodosius who found it convenient not to believe them. Nestorius was expelled and carried his evidence east to China.' He paused. 'It may be there now.'

Giovanni stared at the skeleton below him. Slowly, the implications of what he was seeing were finding space in his brain. 'If this is Jesus Christ,' he said, 'then the Church has no foundation.' His voice was low. 'St Peter was appointed by Jesus as God, so the Pope has no authority. It must all end.'

Plethon nodded again. 'It will be as St Paul wrote: "If Christ has not been raised, our preaching is useless and so is your faith."'

Giovanni let out a long breath. The numbness was leaving him and his mind was clearing. He looked up. 'What will you do with it?'

'I may use it to persuade the Pope to save Byzantium. After all, the legend tells us that is its purpose.' The philosopher reached up and slowly closed the lid of the casket. Then he rose, using Giovanni's shoulder for support. He dusted the earth from his toga.

Giovanni remained kneeling. He looked up. 'Do Matthew and Arcadius know what it is?'

Plethon shook his head. 'No one knows but Anna, Luke and me. Now you.'

'But why me? Why do I need to know?'

Plethon glanced down at the casket. Then he brought his hand back to Giovanni's shoulder and looked at him. 'Because you are Luke's heir, Giovanni: his eldest son. You are the descendant of Siward, the first English Varangian, and you are sworn to protect this treasure. One day, you may have to decide to use it.'

PART FIVE

AFRICAN GOLD

CHAPTER TWENTY-SEVEN

VENICE, SPRING 1417

Zoe Mamonas closed a curtain of the *Bucintoro* to shut out the sun and the leer of the oarsman to her front. It was the Feast of the Ascension and every Venetian was either afloat or crowding the quaysides of San Marco, Giudecca and San Giorgio Maggiore to watch the Festa della Sensa. The Doge's barge was rowed by Venice's young nobility and one of them was insolent.

It was not that she found the oaf's attention offensive; it just irritated her. For too long, she had used her beauty to ride the tide of fortune, becoming Suleyman's, then Tamerlane's, then Musa's whore. Now, thanks to a dead father's talent for trade and banking, she had the wealth and power to do as she pleased. And it didn't please her to flirt with a man half her age.

She looked through the awning to her side and saw the water obscured by every kind of vessel: great galleys, merchantmen, skiffs, all of them laden with people cheering the man who stood at the *Bucintoro*'s bow: Doge Tommaso Mocenigo, hero of Choggia. At any moment, he would throw a ring into the water and reaffirm the Serenissima's unending marriage to the sea.

She smiled and lay back on the cushions. She was paying for

much of the celebrations this year: the regilding of the *Bucintoro*, new uniforms for the rowers, the feast that would follow in the Doge's palace. She even paid for the free wine that would make the city's canals bob with drunken revellers that night. It was worth it. She wanted a grateful doge.

She heard a cheer, then a shout, and felt the pull of three hundred oars. There were footsteps outside and the curtain opened. The Doge's tiara appeared, then his face. He looked aged but happy.

He said: 'You can come out now. The ceremony's over and we are to pass the Arsenale. They're launching a new galley.'

Zoe rose. The Arsenale was spouting new galleys every week now. This Doge had taken his republic to the pinnacle of its power and wanted it to stay there and, quite possibly, invade Mistra should a debt not be repaid.

But why wait for that?

The Doge held the curtain aside as Zoe emerged into the sunlight. She glanced at the oarsman now working his oar. He was handsome enough in his uniform, but the face was callow. She found experience more attractive these days. The Doge, for instance. Now there was a face you could iron.

She looked across the water to the Riva degli Schiavoni, to the palaces that lined its front, their ostentation the trumpet-blast of this city's wealth. Constantinople was like this once, she thought. Until Venice had plundered her wealth and brought it here.

Zoe looked towards where the Doge was pointing. A path through the boats had been cleared to the great gates of the Arsenale where she could see a galley emerging. The ship was without mast and was being pulled by lighters. There were cannon on its rembata and something between them.

'A siphon for Greek fire,' said the Doge. 'We think we have the formula right at last.'

They approached the Arsenale and then turned towards the Grand Canal, the great snake of Venice whose maw was fed by the world's trade. There were more palaces at its sides, each with its gate, its jetty, its fondaco above. These were temples to work as much as pleasure, warehouses for the riches of the East to be sold to the West. There were people on every balcony, huge emblems draped beneath them, each with its lion. Zoe had now been entertained in most.

Tommaso Mocenigo stretched out his arms. 'We are immaculate, a city without comparison, Zoe. Was Constantinople ever this magnificent, I wonder?'

Zoe moved to stand next to him at the rail. 'It was once more splendid even than this,' she said.

'But what is it now?'

'A city of fields and ruins. Whatever Venice didn't take has moved to Mistra.'

The Doge nodded. 'But now everything in Mistra is forfeit to Venice. If we choose to take it.'

Zoe spent a while studying the face of a man of honour; so rare in Venice. She'd have to be careful. 'May you not choose to do so?' she asked.

'I would prefer not to. Mistra is a Christian kingdom.'

'But what if Bedreddin takes it instead?'

The Doge turned. 'He hasn't any boats to cross with.'

'He may find them. And Murad may join him. He has support in Mehmed's army.'

The Doge considered this. He raised himself to wave at the crowds, his back straight as a sword. 'So you think Bedreddin will steal Mistra from us?'

'I'm sure he will. He knows our intentions.'

The Doge frowned. 'But I have given my word to the Medici. They have until Christmas next year to repay the debt.' He waved again to the shore. 'And the debt is in florins. He says he'll devalue them.'

'He's bluffing, lord,' said Zoe. 'Would Florence undermine its own currency to save an ally? I don't think so.' She paused. 'And have you ever said you'll attack Florence?'

Mocenigo examined this. She was right: he hadn't. But there was something else, something important to this man. He said: 'The Doge cannot break his word.'

Zoe looked back towards Venice. She saw a city that had broken her word whenever she had seen advantage in doing so, growing rich in consequence. This Doge would have to be led to a place where he saw such advantage. She said: 'The Doge can break his word where heresy threatens a Christian kingdom. King Sigismund did it at Constance with Jan Hus.'

Mocenigo stopped waving and looked at her. 'Heresy? Where is there heresy?'

'The philosopher Plethon preaches it in Mistra every day.'

'What does he preach?'

Zoe spread her hands on the rail. Its polished gold shone through her fingers like fire. 'You've heard of Poggio Bracciolini's famous discovery? He's found a manuscript in Germany written by the Roman Lucretius. It denies our Christian God.'

The Doge had heard something of this but not thought it worthy of worry.

Zoe continued: 'Plethon is using it to return Mistra to its ancient past. He recommends the worship of pagan gods.'

Mocenigo shook his head. 'But Mistra belongs to the Eastern Church.'

338

'Mistra also has many who adhere to our Church. There are Franks there still.'

The Doge was stroking his long beard, his other hand suspended in gesture. The *Bucintoro* was now making its gilded, stately progress towards the Rialto and the beating heart of this lethal city of commerce. Zoe wanted them to get there, to see its bridge open its arms to gather Tommaso Mocenigo into its courtesan bosom. She waited until it came into view before she spoke again.

'When we have our new Colonna pope, he can call a crusade against Mistra,' she said at last. 'You have great influence with him and Plethon's teaching is reason enough.'

The Doge shook his head, the movement slow, uncertain. 'He'll not proclaim a crusade against fellow Christians,' he said.

Zoe was quick. 'No? He'll need our money to fight the Hussites. Do they not also claim to be Christians?'

Tommaso Mocenigo, hero of Choggia and man of principle, finally saw where advantage lay. His barge was slipping past the fondachi that clustered around the Rialto. He had floated down the main artery of this city he loved to its vital organ. He was a soldier but he understood Venice's purpose. He nodded. 'We should talk to Colonna.'

Zoe's heart lifted. She looked out over the skiffs and gondolas all around them, the palaces and churches beyond, and allowed herself to feel some satisfaction. She had tamed this man by intellect alone, and not one part of her body had played its part.

She changed the subject. 'He plays a dangerous game, this protostrator, leaving his city at its time of greatest peril. What was he thinking of?'

They were approaching the bridge now and the crowds on either side of it were shouting their joy. The Doge acknowledged them and Zoe waited for the moment to pass.

'We know that Magoris is in Africa,' she continued. 'Al-Tabingha has told us that he's travelled south to Abyssinia with the Sultan's blessing. Why is he going there?'

Mocenigo hadn't considered the matter. 'Who knows? To flee his creditors?'

Zoe shook her head. 'Luke Magoris doesn't flee anyone, lord. No, there has to be some bigger purpose.'

The barge was sweeping round the great bend of the canal now, where only fondachi fronted the water. The Doge turned from the rail. 'And what purpose do you find in the Protostrator's travels, Zoe?'

Zoe heard music from the water in front of them. She put her hand on the jewelled sleeve of the man beside her, understanding the value of suspense. 'It can wait. Let's see what's ahead.'

They walked down the central gangway of the barge, high above the rowers on either side, until they reached the platform at the bow. It was from here that the Doge had pledged himself to his bride; from here he had thrown her his ring. Before them was a riot of small boats blocking their passage. There were musicians in some with viols and lutes and ribbons tied to their instruments. There were men standing at their bows, one hand on their hearts, the other holding a ring aloft. They were singing. The other boats were full of painted women of all ages, dressed in fabulous silks with jewels in their hair. They were fanning themselves and laughing.

The Doge sighed. 'The young don't appreciate tradition,' he said without much seriousness. 'They mock us.'

Zoe was waving to the women, many of whom were waving back, one whore to another. The most intelligent were, after all, still on her payroll. She said: 'The courtesans *are* your tradition, lord. Without them, these men would be fighting, not singing. After all, your wives and sisters wear black and spend their lives on their knees.'

She saw the Doge wave at one beauty alone in a gondola, reclining against heavy cushions. One of her breasts was bare and she wore a tiara on her head not unlike the Doge's. She blew Mocenigo a kiss.

'You're right,' he said, turning. He smiled. 'You wanted to tell me of Magoris's purpose.'

'Ah yes. I suppose you have heard of the Varangian treasure?'

'The one said to be hidden somewhere in Mistra? I had thought it myth.'

Zoe shook her head. 'I have seen it. Not what it is, but the casket that holds it.'

Mocenigo looked surprised. 'Is it very large? Could there be enough gold to repay us?'

'No. The treasure isn't gold or jewels, but something else. Something more valuable.' She paused. 'The legend has it that it will come to Byzantium's aid at the Empire's moment of greatest peril.'

The Doge nodded slowly. 'Do you know what this treasure might be?'

Zoe turned to him. 'What is supposed to reside in Abyssinia?'

Mocenigo thought for a moment. Then his eyes widened. 'The Ark?'

Zoe nodded. 'The Ark of the Covenant: the golden chest containing the two stone tablets on which the Ten Commandments are inscribed. It was carried in front of the Israelites and caused them to win all their battles. It demolished the walls of Jericho for them.'

The Doge's brow was furrowed in disbelief. He looked for

341

the tease in Zoe's face and found none. 'How do you deduce this?'

'Because it makes sense. We've always believed the tablets lost after the Romans destroyed Jerusalem, and we've believed Abyssinia's Ark to be an empty chest. The Byzantines could easily have found the tablets when they held Jerusalem and brought them to Constantinople when it fell to the Muslims. Then they sent them to Mistra when Constantinople was sacked two hundred years ago. Magoris now wants to reunite them with the Ark. Al-Tabingha's report said that he took unusual interest in the church at Axum where the Ark is said to be kept.' She paused to let her reasoning settle in the martial mind. Then she said quietly: 'The Varangians were tasked to protect the treasure, which is why it's called what it is. Magoris is chief among the Varangians.' Zoe looked out at the canal, waving at the Loredan barge that had rowed close. 'There's also the ship.'

'The ship?'

'Al-Tabingha tells us there is a ship waiting at the port of Berbera. It must be waiting for something.'

Tommaso Mocenigo pondered this logic and found it bizarre but sound. But why would this Protostrator of Mistra want the Ark so badly he was prepared to desert his people at their darkest hour to fetch it? He asked the question.

Zoe shrugged. 'There could be many reasons,' she said. 'He may think it will make his army invincible in battle, as it did the Jews. Or he may see it as a way of uniting his people to the cause of saving Mistra, as relics are said to do at Constantinople.' She shook her head. 'I don't think either of those likely.'

The Doge's barge was making its way through the courtesans now, and its way was slow. Many of the oarsmen had left their stations to make assignations, returning to their benches with

342

flowers in their hair and wine on their breath. Zoe waited for the diversion to pass. She wanted the Doge's full attention. Eventually, she had it.

'There is a further explanation. What if Magoris plans to offer it to the next Pope?' She paused. 'What if he were to offer it publicly, and from Mistra? The Pope would have to be grateful for such a fabulous gift.'

The Doge saw where Zoe was leading him. 'Indeed,' he said. 'And he would hardly sanction an attack on the city that had made it.'

'Exactly. Which is why, lord, you must find Magoris and his Ark before he makes use of it. He will be sailing up the Red Sea to Cairo, then Alexandria. He must not be permitted to leave there.'

Tommaso Mocenigo looked in some wonder at the woman at his side. He had been made widower by the plague and had enjoyed the subtle services of the city's best courtesans ever since. But here was a woman to rule with. He took Zoe's hand and kissed it. 'Tonight,' he said, 'you will sit beside me at the feast. We will talk more of this then.'

343

CHAPTER TWENTY-EIGHT

AFRICA, SPRING 1417

Luke left Axum in the spring, having celebrated a Christian Christmas at King Yeshaq's court. He left at the head of a caravan of two thousand camels and mules that carried salt and cowrie shells, lifting dust as far as the eye could see. The salt had arrived from Abyssinia's north in giant blocks, hard as granite, which were strapped to the camels' sides in wooden boxes that would take gold on the way back. The shells came in hessian sacks that rattled as they moved.

The caravan would travel twenty miles a day and take six months to cross the continent. It would do it in two stages. The first would take them as far as a great lake where they'd rest for two weeks. The second would take them to Bilma, then across the desert to Timbuktu.

King Yeshaq had provided a small Roman army for escort. The men wore armour, whatever the heat or danger, and had bright plumes in their helmets. When they camped for the night, they sang round their fires and their deep, rich voices sent their music up to join the stars.

Benedo Barbi and Shulen had also come: the first invited by Luke, the second by herself. Also in the caravan was al-Tabingha, who said that his sultan had instructed him to stay with Luke for his protection. Luke didn't trust the Mamluk but the man claimed to have made the journey before. Luke allowed him to come on one condition: that the rest of the Mamluks return to Cairo. Nikolas and Zhu Chou, meanwhile, would take the jornufa east to Berbera with an Abyssinian escort.

They followed an ancient trading route west through land that divided desert from forest. It was a hard land of scrub and rock and wasted trees, a hinterland between two extremes. The people who lived there were wanderers, as tall and thin as the spears they carried. They moved their flocks slowly with the seasons, exhausting the ground they travelled over, plundering it of what little food it could muster. They saw nothing strange in the vast caravan going west.

It was a country of no kings and no laws and tribes that recognised no frontiers – easy prey for the Tuareg who came south to gather slaves. These were dark men of the desert who mastered their horses with quick, abrupt movements and spoke through *alashas* to ward off evil. Quite often they would just stand at the roadside and watch the caravan pass, counting the animals one by one, calculating the risk through eyes as blue as the sky above them.

One morning the caravan arrived at a village to see Tuareg rounding up men, women and children, beating and shackling them together. Luke drew his sword.

'No,' Shulen said. 'We don't want to make enemies.'

'But we've an army behind us!'

Shulen was holding his arm. 'And cowrie shells too, beaches of them. We'll buy the slaves.'

They did, and feasted on goat that night. The next morning the villagers joined the caravan, for to stay was to invite the

Tuareg to return. Luke saw al-Tabingha watching them gathering their herds.

'He doesn't like to see slaves freed, does he?' said Shulen. Luke hadn't heard her approach. 'Do you trust him?'

Luke shook his head. 'Did you know he's been sending couriers to Cairo?'

Shulen knew. She asked: 'Have you used them to write to Mistra?'

Luke glanced at her. There was no tease in her face, no anything. 'They have taken my letters, yes, and al-Tabingha will have opened them. I have chosen my news with care.'

Shulen smiled. 'Such as that concerning Axum's Ark. That was clever.'

Luke was pleased by the compliment. Since leaving Axum, Shulen had concerned herself with the business of the caravan: feeding the soldiers and caring for their sick. When he'd approached her to talk alone, she'd moved to join others. When he'd offered a walk beneath the stars, she'd been tired.

'Does he know where we're going?' she asked. 'Aren't you worried he'll be telling the Sultan?'

'How? All of his couriers have returned to Cairo.'

Shulen saw the plan: cast out the net of mistruth, then leave it there. But there was something she still didn't understand. 'If we take the gold back to Berbera, we will have opened a future trade route that bypasses Egypt. Why will the Sultan allow that?'

'Because', replied Luke, 'the Sultan knows that not all of it will go east; some will still go into Europe from Alexandria. And the loss of the revenues from gold will more than be made up by the Chinese goods coming to him from Berbera.' He turned to mount. 'Besides,' he said, 'the Sultan's real concern is Portugal. He can see the day when there may not be any trade routes

346

across the desert, just those from the coast. He's looking to the future.'

Luke hauled himself up on to his camel and brought it to its feet with his stick. He pulled its neck round and trotted to the front of the caravan. Shulen mounted and joined him, bringing Benedo Barbi with her.

They rode on in silence and the day turned to night and the night into day. The days became weeks and the weeks, months. And the land never changed.

They knew they were coming to the lake because of the birds. Great swarms of duck and cranes flew over them in raucous formation, squawking their joy to be soon touching water. The land around them turned green, then wet. The people became fatter and the villages bigger. Soon they came to marsh and swamp where the houses stood on stilts. They hired a guide to keep them on firm ground.

When at last they saw the lake, they wondered if they'd reached the sea instead. Its infinite blue stretched out to the horizon where it somewhere joined the sky. In its shallows were hippopotami with white birds on their backs and crocodiles watching them from the reeds. Further out were boats and fishermen on poles with spears in their hands. Further still were islands that floated, some with houses on them. It was landscape as much alive as what they'd passed earlier had been dead.

They stayed two weeks there, sleeping and eating fish and guarding their animals from the crocodiles. One night they lost a soldier to them: a man who had fallen asleep on guard duty. His armour hadn't saved him from the crocodile's teeth and his screams had echoed around the camp. In the morning, not even his plume could be found.

On leaving, they took the northern road to Bilma, circling

the lake and stopping finally to fill every skin to the brim. The country became harsher and the only living things they met were snakes that darted out from rocks. Sudden storms would arise from the north, blowing with a violence that lasted for days. They would sit, hunched on their camels, their cloaks covering their nodding heads and pray for them to end. The storms would vanish as quickly as they had come, leaving them numb and parched. The water got low.

Two weeks later they reached Bilma, the oasis town protected from the desert by its Kaouar Cliffs, with its great saltpans outside. Some said it was the hottest place on earth. It was from there that Mali had always got most of its salt and now it was in the hands of its enemies: the Songhai.

And the Songhai were not pleased to see two thousand camels and mules laden with Abyssinian salt arrive on their way to Timbuktu. It would undermine their own promising negotiations with the Koy.

So they stayed there only a night and Luke deployed Yeshaq's army, all in its armour, to watch over their salt. He himself stayed awake with Barbi, the handgun they had brought trained on the governor's palace.

The trouble stayed away until morning. Luke and Barbi were raising their camels at the head of the caravan when they heard shouts from behind, one of them Shulen's. They dismounted and ran back to where she was.

There were two men kneeling in the sand with their heads down, naked. Above them were Songhai soldiers, their swords drawn. Trying to place herself between them was Shulen. A crowd of Songhai and Yeshaq's men were gathering to watch. Luke and Barbi pushed their way to the front.

'They're executing them,' said Shulen.

'Why?' asked Luke. He turned to one of the Songhai. 'Which of you is leader?'

One of the men with his sword drawn said: 'It is the governor's order. The slaves are from Timbuktu. It will send a message.'

'What message? That they should not take their salt from Abyssinia?' Luke had Yeshaq's men around him now and they outnumbered the Songhai five to one. He raised the slaves to their feet by the elbow. Both were tall men of extraordinary grace. Their wrists were bound and he ordered the ropes cut. Then he turned to Barbi. 'Go and get one of the bags of cowrie shells.'

When it arrived, Luke had Barbi put it on the ground and open it. A mountain of shimmering white appeared, taking its time to settle inside the hessian. 'You are to give your governor this. It is in exchange for these men and is ten times their worth. Now, take it and go.'

The Songhai looked at each other, then at the cowries. They sheathed their swords and one of them closed the sack and swung it on to his back. Then they left.

Ten minutes later, the caravan left too, with two more added to its slaves. It took an hour before the last camel wobbled its knock-kneed way out of the oasis, passing a man who stayed to watch it disappear behind the dunes. He was the Songhai governor of Bilma and he was smiling.

The country around them was changing more quickly now, the desert creeping closer by the day. It stole up on them in the arid air and the death that they passed. There were skeletons everywhere, picked clean long ago, with sand now for skin. It grew hotter and the leather of their saddles burnt to the touch. Their faces were hardening into beaten copper, their eyes narrowing beneath bleached eyebrows, their hair stiffening into straw. The soldiers at last shed their armour, then most of their clothes. They rode naked sometimes, sitting atop their camels like black gods, defying the sun.

As the days became weeks and the desert became empty of all life, they began to travel by night, gathering what sleep they could in the heat of the day. They rode between dunes that rose like waves to the moon and flowed out to the horizon as an endless sea. The soldiers sang from their saddles now. Barbi said that they sang to keep the stars in the sky, fearing they would fall if they stopped. Sometimes a star would fall and the soldiers would sing louder.

Luke was lying back on his camel when Shulen came up beside him, bringing her animal close enough to talk.

'Were you asleep?' she asked.

Luke sat up. 'No. I was thinking of another journey we'd made in a desert, you and I. It was worse than this.'

Shulen remembered. 'Much worse. We were lost and Arcadius was dying.'

He looked at her and saw how her face had thinned over the journey, bringing forth its angles, making her eyes into dark pools. He watched the casual grace with which she moved with the camel, saw how much she was part of this lean and savage country. She'd grown up on land like this and been shaped by it. There was nothing superfluous to her, or it. How different she was from Anna, whose beauty was as rich as the Vale of Sparta, whose hair was as red as its earth.

'Then you saved us,' she said. 'With a compass. Did you know they've had them in China for centuries?'

Luke was not surprised. Everything seemed to have been invented in China long ago. He said: 'We've hardly spoken of your time there.'

350

Shulen's camel barked and she leant forward to stroke its neck. 'Not a great deal happened. I learnt Chinese and watched Nikolas nearly die, then fall in love. It is a strange and wonderful place. And it has a great emperor who wants to bring its wonder to the world.' She paused. 'If he's allowed to.'

'Who will stop him?'

Shulen looked up at the moon and remembered it poised over the treasure fleet, turning the sea and a thousand sails into silver. 'He has enemies who are waiting for him to fail. That's why the qilin is so important.'

Luke thought about this. 'And you found it for him. Why didn't you go back with it?'

Shulen was silent for some time, her body rocking to the gentle rhythm of the animal below her. Then she said: 'You think I wanted to come to Timbuktu for you. I didn't.'

Luke turned to her. 'I thought you came to use your healing. For me and everyone else.'

'You were wrong. I came because it will take more than a qilin to keep this Emperor on his throne. He needs gold as much as you do. Opening the trade route between Timbuktu and Berbera will give him it. When we've brought your gold there, I'll return to China.'

Luke felt despair creep over him like a shadow. She'd said it all with the same precision that she'd deployed everywhere on this expedition. It left no room for doubt. He asked: 'And who'll bring back the gold we're owed for the qilin?'

She shrugged. 'Nikolas? I don't know if he plans to stay with Zhu Chou.' She paused. 'What will you do with so much gold, Luke? Will you need it all to pay back Venice?'

'I'll need it for Mistra,' he said. 'First to pay back its citizens, then to build things.'

'Build what?'

'Ports, roads, ships . . . many things.'

She was nodding. 'To save Mistra by making it into a trading power even greater than Venice. That's why you sent us to China.'

Luke said quietly: 'You chose to go, Shulen.'

Shulen changed the subject. 'How does Anna like being wife to the Protostrator?' she asked.

'She was the daughter of one, so she's had practice,' replied Luke carefully. 'We've quarrelled.'

'What about?'

'About Giovanni. She thinks I love him more than Hilarion.'

'And do you? After all, they're both your sons.'

He glanced at her, trying to remember when he'd told her. He didn't think he had.

She said: 'I knew it from the first time I saw him on that bridge.' She looked at him a while, hoping, perhaps, for some further explanation. Then she shrugged and turned her camel away.

A week later, Luke's headaches began. Like the storms, they came out of nowhere and hit with equal violence. However still he tried to keep his head, they assaulted him in waves of pain that took longer and longer to pass. They were the purest kind of agony.

He told no one, hoping they were just a product of the heat. But then the pain moved to his throat. His breath got hotter and he craved water every moment of the day. The oases were further apart now and water scarce. He forced himself not to drink more than his share.

Unable to sleep by day, he spent the nights in a kind of delirium, watching the stars turn somersaults to the music of the soldiers. He dreamed of hippopotami eaten by crocodiles, only waking to the onslaught of another headache. He realised that he'd stopped eating.

He grew weaker by the day, strapping himself to his camel to stop himself from falling. He didn't find it hard to avoid Shulen and Benedo Barbi. They were all too tired to speak now. Even the soldiers had stopped singing.

He fell to the back of the caravan and was the last to notice that the land around them was changing again, becoming greener. He barely noticed when they entered forest and heard the chatter of monkeys in the trees above them. When the caravan stopped one day, he went on, passing the animals and soldiers in a trance. He reached the front and his camel stopped beside Shulen's. They were overlooking a vast river but he didn't know it.

Shulen turned to him and saw. 'You are sick,' she said. 'Very sick.'

CHAPTER TWENTY-NINE

TIMBUKTU, AUTUMN 1417

Luke came to Timbuktu by boat, cradled there by Shulen and the gentle currents of the Joliba River. The rainy season was imminent and the river's waters low. The boatmen poled between the carcasses of dead animals, passing sombre fishermen crouched on sandbanks with nets spread at their feet. They approached a city hidden behind uneven walls of mud and pointed towers where birds perched like weather vanes. A single spire rose from within like a mast, pricked by sticks, a sickle moon at its peak.

Timbuktu: city of the desert, of Allah, a giant sandcastle at the edge of the Sahara, its strange beauty never constant, its eccentric lines tempered by the river's annual flooding. Luke didn't see its walls but he sensed its hot charcoal air on his face, smelt its markets and the rank scent of decay that meant the rains would come soon. He felt flies on him and then felt them brushed away by someone he knew.

They brought the boat to the jetty as gently as the currents would allow and Luke was carried ashore by Yeshaq's soldiers, Shulen by his side, Barbi and al-Tabingha leading. They walked past men firing bricks and women beating out their washing on stones. They came to vast timber gates studded with gold. Al-Tabingha knocked, then spoke, and the gates opened.

In his fever, Luke opened his eyes and saw the gates part. He heard Shulen's quiet call to the slaves they had saved from the Tuareg and Songhai to come forward to say goodbye to the man who had freed them, for they might not see him again. They came past him one by one, all grave. The last was one of those who had come from Bilma and he was tall and beautiful. He bent to kiss Luke's forehead and his tears stayed on it after he'd left.

Luke entered the city and passed buildings of every size and shape that sometimes hid the sun, and sometimes didn't. He felt some faint gratitude for the shade. He glimpsed green gardens through ornate doorways, saw strange pyramids and crooked towers. People passed him in silence, near and far, all dressed in dazzling white with small caps on their heads. They might have been sleepwalkers, had they not talked.

They entered a courtyard with marble between lawns and columns topped by fragile stucco-work. Between them, men moved in the shadows, slowly, some of them watching him. He entered a dark room where sunlight broke through louvred shutters and was lifted on to a bed softer than anything he'd known. He felt himself weightless.

The last thing he saw was Shulen dipping a sponge into water.

She sat with him every day and every night, calm and watching. She slept in her chair and woke to find Barbi offering her food. Sometimes doctors would join her, their robes whiter than egrets. They began by murmuring between themselves but soon took instruction from her. She produced plants she'd brought from the Malay jungle and made pastes and lotions and medicines to drink. Some she burnt in little crucibles. Luke's bed became her shrine.

The rains came and the river outside burst its banks, bringing lilies to the gates of Timbuktu, and Luke sweated and shivered and slept and talked. He spoke sometimes in Greek, sometimes in Latin or Italian. He spoke of things she knew, and much she'd guessed. Occasionally he sang, which she'd never heard him do. His voice was deep and good enough to keep the stars aloft and sometimes she'd join him, holding his hand and watching his lips as they moved.

At one point, she'd thought he might die. He'd passed through an attack that had convulsed all parts of his body and she'd called for help to keep him on the bed. Then he'd lain quite still and let out a long sigh that seemed like an ending. That was when her calm had finally broken. She had climbed on to the bed and covered his mouth with hers, pushing back the breath that mustn't leave his body, that might be his last.

Then, as the year turned, Luke began to recover. Shulen watched every moment of it, bringing the sponge to a brow fluted by a determination found somewhere deep within. He'd stopped talking in any language and never sang, mustering every part of his unconscious mind to the business of expelling the sickness. He slept for days, his breathing slowing to an unhurried rhythm. Then he woke.

Shulen was alone with him when he did so, the bowl still in her lap. He opened his eyes and saw beams of cedar crossed by sunlight above. He felt cool sheets against his skin and smelt herbs in the air. He turned to her and saw eyes sunk deep into shadows. 'You are tired,' he said.

'I am happy. You lived.'

He blinked twice. His eyes were cannon balls, his head full

of their smoke. She became two Shulens, then one. He asked: 'How long have I been sick?'

She shrugged. 'I lost count of the days. A long time.'

'And you were here always?'

She didn't answer but looked down at the bowl. There were tears somewhere in the water.

He smiled. 'You were here. That's why you're tired. You can sleep now.'

'I don't want to sleep. I want to talk. You've done it all these past weeks.'

Luke frowned, his blue eyes fixed on hers. 'What did I say?'

'Things I knew; others I didn't.' She paused. 'Fiorenza, for one.'

He waited for her to continue.

She put the bowl on the table beside her. She poured water into a cup and gave it to him. 'I should really apologise,' she said. 'I'd thought it a callous adventure. Unworthy of you.'

Laughter came from the street outside and she looked towards the window, then back. 'I know now that Giovanni was forced upon you.'

Luke drank the water and found it delicious. He said quietly: 'Perhaps. But there's no son I'd rather have.' He put the cup down and found her hand. 'So, am I forgiven?'

She rose, taking her hand with her. 'It's not a matter for forgiveness.'

It took a week for Luke to leave his bed and two more to venture outside the house. He spent the time eating, sleeping and worrying about the time they'd lost through his sickness. It was less than a year before the truce with Venice ran out. And where was al-Tabingha?

357

He spoke only with Shulen. Benedo Barbi had been busy since knowing that Luke would recover. Luke had brought him from Axum with pages from the diadan that might make a difference to the people of Timbuktu. Most important was controlling the annual flooding, making use of the precious water to irrigate a wider area for longer in the year. So the engineer built channels and gates and sluices and used mathematics to calculate the flow rate of dykes. He built machines that would dredge and others that used the water's power to work grinding mills. And he built the chain pumps that Shulen had seen in Delhi. Then he taught them how to grow rice.

Long ago, Ibn Khaldun had written of Africa's famines, how too much desert and too little rain led to them. Luke had seen rice planted in the Po Valley of northern Italy and knew that its yield was several times that of wheat. He'd brought Benedo Barbi to Timbuktu to bring bring rice to its people. And so it was happening. Rice had been planted in the water meadows that now surrounded the city and would stay as such through Barbi's engineering.

The summons had come from the Timbuktu-Koy, governor of the city. It was issued with courtesy but made plain that Luke should attend the audience before going elsewhere in the city, or outside it. So he, Shulen and Barbi bathed, combed their hair, and put on new robes they had been given. Luke's hung from his bones like a shroud.

They stepped out into a street of sand and people dressed in white, if they were dressed at all. Some walked as naked as the day they were born.

'We're used to it,' said Barbi, nodding at a clothed man who passed, perhaps a farmer. 'Their beauty makes it acceptable.'

Their beauty was without question. The people of Timbuktu

were tall and flawless. Even the old had a grace and symmetry that astonished Luke.

'I go naked at their baths,' said Shulen. 'You should come.'

It was said without invitation. Luke glanced at her. 'Are they for both sexes?'

'Of course, or you wouldn't be welcome. Barbi comes now. He likes to read there.'

Luke was surprised. He'd imagined Barbi the last to surrender his clothes. 'What do you read?'

Barbi was nodding at more passers-by. He seemed popular in Timbuktu. 'Everything. The baths are libraries and places where people meet to talk.' He looked at Luke and smiled. 'We have arrived at ancient Athens, old friend.'

And the more Luke saw, the more it seemed they had. Timbuktu was filled with fine buildings with elaborate façades and high walls heaped with creepers and flowers. The mosques were large, their pyramid domes covered in gold and their mud walls ornate at their tops. They passed universities and schools and baths. And its people, shaded by trees in every street, seemed happy and gentle, talking in low voices and laughing as they walked. There was much touching between them.

They came to the palace of the Timbuktu-Koy, a three-storeyed building with tall pinnacles and gates that opened on to courtyards and gardens. They were met by men who bowed and put hands to their hearts. They were shown into a room of blue majolica tiles and a fountain that produced no water. A man was standing with his head to one side watching it. He turned to them, bowed and spoke to Barbi.

'We had thought to ask you to mend it,' he said, smiling. 'But you have been busy.' The man spoke in Latin. He was tall and middle-aged and had prayer beads between his fingers.

Barbi went over to the fountain, lifted his robe and climbed in. He examined the spouts. 'They're blocked, that's all. Does nobody clean them?'

The Koy laughed and gave Barbi his arm to climb out. 'It is a matter for concern that this city is filled with scholars and jurists who don't know how to clean fountains. Or dig canals. We are indebted to you, Signor Barbi.'

Luke watched it all with satisfaction. The Koy turned to Shulen and greeted her as one he knew. Then his quiet eyes came to rest on Luke. 'You have been very ill. The doctors tell us that you owe your life to this lady.'

Luke dipped his head, then glanced at Shulen, seeing her frown. 'Without question.'

'In fact we've learnt much medicine from her, as we have science from Signor Barbi. What might we learn from you?'

It was not a question Luke had expected. He summoned the answer quickly. 'Trade, eminence. Trade and survival.'

'Survival? What could be more important?' He gestured to some couches. 'Shall we sit to discuss survival?'

They sat and Luke watched the Koy as he ordered refreshment, his every movement an act of grace.

When they had palm wine, he said: 'The Mamluk al-Tabingha has met with us.'

Luke had not seen the Mamluk since before his illness. Nor had the others. They'd often speculated as to where he'd gone.

'He has been here before, did you know that?' The question was to Luke.

Luke nodded and sipped his wine.

'He speaks for the Sultan,' continued the Koy, 'but sometimes, we think, he speaks also for Venice. Had you considered that?'

'I had suspected so,' replied Luke. 'Their bribes are generous.' He sipped again. 'Why did you think to tell me this?'

The Koy studied Luke for a while, as he might one of Barbi's inventions, his head slightly angled. He said: 'Because he argues your case with caution.'

Luke began to understand the Mamluk's unsociability these past months. 'May I ask what he says?'

'He tells me that you've met with his sultan and King Yeshaq and persuaded them both that a new trade route needs to be opened up to China, one that begins here with gold and ends in Berbera as well as Alexandria. He suggests that we might consider abandoning our distaste for doing trade with the infidel to achieve this. And he points to the danger of the Portuguese encroachment down our coast with their new lateen-rigged caravels.' He paused. 'We suppose this is what you meant by survival.'

Luke thought about what he'd heard. It sounded as though al-Tabingha had said more or less what he'd intended to say himself. So where was the caution?

The Koy continued: 'But he also talks of Allah and the wickedness of Christian usury. He says you are a banker.'

Luke put down his wine. 'I am, eminence, and with a debt to Venice. He has, I am sure, told you that too.'

The Koy nodded. 'He says you will be without money or country within a year. He worries that his sultan has placed his trust in such a man.'

There was silence in the room while the three of them absorbed this revelation. Finally Luke said: 'What does the Mamluk suggest?'

The Koy gave the smallest of shrugs, too fluid to be given the name. He said: 'The problem appears to be the gold. We understand that, were we to permit you to trade for it, it would become yours as payment for opening up the larger trade.'

Luke waited for him to continue.

'So the gold does not go to China, it goes to pay your debts. Does the Ming Emperor know this?'

Silence. The Ming Emperor of course knew nothing of the gold. But then he was only expecting a qilin.

'I think not,' said the Koy. 'Might he not be upset that no gold had been brought back to China?'

Luke had no idea. He'd never met the Ming Emperor. He asked again: 'So what does the Mamluk suggest?'

'He argues for keeping you in Timbuktu and allowing him to take the gold back to Berbera. A third will go east to the Ming, a third to King Yeshaq, and he'll take a third back to the Sultan. With him doing the trade, no Muslim law is broken. And the trade route is opened.'

'But how would it be paid for? The salt is mine.'

'The Sultan's credit is good. We would be paid later.'

Shulen said: 'And us? Would the engineer and I stay or leave under this plan?'

The Koy turned his easy grace to her, his mouth lifting to a smile. 'You would be free to stay or go, Shulen, whatever your preference.'

Luke saw the completeness of al-Tabingha's destruction. He wondered what of it, if any, had been planned with the Sultan. Not much, he guessed.

The Koy had more to say. 'But all this is not for me to decide. I am governor of this city, nothing more. Something as important as this needs careful thought. And' – he turned his smile to Luke – 'as you say, survival may be at stake. The world is changing fast and the sea takes over from the land. The ancient trade routes of Africa and Asia are threatened, as are the many cities that depend on them, like ours.' He paused. 'I leave for Kangaba tomorrow. It is to hold the Gbara, the great assembly where the Twelve Doors of Mali come together to talk and consult the holy books. It will decide this thing.'

CHAPTER THIRTY

TIMBUKTU, SPRING 1418

Luke didn't sleep at all the night of his audience with the Timbuktu-Koy. It wasn't the muezzin's call, or the heat or the sound
of the Koy's army assembling for the march to Kangaba, that
kept him awake. It wasn't even the unusual sound of water birds
so near to the city. Thanks to Barbi, the January floods were with
them still, locked into the fields around, growing rice.

It was the counting of the months. Nine months remained
before Cosimo's truce with Venice ran its course: nine months to
get gold from Mali and take it back to Mistra. It had never been
likely but now seemed almost impossible. Even if the Gbara
found in his favour, it would take weeks to reach its decision.

And was there any chance that it would find in his favour?
Luke had admired the Timbuktu-Koy and knew him grateful for
all that Barbi had done. But his gratitude would not extend to
risking his empire's future. The Koy had talked with al-Tabingha
and concluded that, in this new trade with China, Venice might
be a more dependable partner than the man who owed it money.

The only thing of value left for him to bargain with was
the salt. There were still two thousand animals parked in the
pastures of the *abaradiou* outside the city walls where the *azalai*

caravans always rested before leaving in May. And with the Songhai holding Bilma, the Empire of Mali needed it more than ever. But might the Koy take it anyway?

Luke turned these matters over in his mind as he lay and listened to the distant shouts of the Koy's army subside, like the city, into sleep. Had it all been a reckless gamble? Despair crept over him and clung.

No. He looked up at the cedar beams and remembered waking from his fever and seeing sunlight on them, then Shulen: two reasons to be glad that he was still alive. What had she said?

You lived. I am happy.

He heard sound from the courtyard outside: someone moving. He rose and covered his lower half. He went to the door and opened it.

She was there, sitting on the steps down to the flowerbeds that gave scent to their house, her legs stretched out into the moonlight, her top half in shadow. That part of her he could see was naked.

He watched her for a while, then felt ashamed. He made a noise and saw her look up. She rose and went back into the shadows. When she came back, she was wearing a sheet, wound to below her shoulders.

He walked out and along a cloister marbled by moonlight from stucco above. Everything was pale, everything calm, as if the garden beside him was lost to worship of the night. It had become the landscape of dream.

He found her sitting again on the steps, her legs hugged now, her chin to her knees. He sat down beside her, their shoulders touching. For a long while, they didn't speak but sat looking up at the night, immersing themselves in the silence of a city at the end of the world.

At last she said: 'Do you remember sitting like this beneath Alamut?' Her voice was almost a whisper. 'We talked of Monemvasia while assassins came down the mountain behind us.'

Luke remembered. 'They drugged us.'

'And I watched you for an hour before you woke. Did you know that?'

He had known; he'd been told of it the next morning by the woman who'd turned into her mother: Khan-zada.

He felt her shoulder against his. They were no more than two tiny islands of flesh merging, but it was enough. Every sense in his being rushed up to meet her there, to draw her in.

He said: 'As you have watched over me these past months. The Koy is right. I owe you my life.'

She looked at him then, turning her face so that the moon divided it: half day, half night. He couldn't see her eyes but knew they watched him with caution. Much had changed since they had come to Africa, much hadn't. But her shoulder hadn't moved.

'How long will he keep you here, do you think?' she asked. 'That is, if the Gbara turns you down.'

'Nine months, I imagine. Al-Tabingha's instructions from Venice will have been precise on the matter.'

Shulen had tilted her head so that her hair now touched his shoulder. It felt finer than any cloth he'd ever known. He could hear her breathing, quicker perhaps. He said: 'But you can go.'

'That will be my decision, not yours,' she said quietly. 'I may choose to stay.'

He closed his eyes, his own breath suspended. He smelt her all around him now, the strange mix of musk and herb that he'd known from their first meeting on the steppe. He felt a rush of longing.

'Shulen . . .'

'Wait.' She'd moved forward, listening, her finger to her lips. 'We are not alone.'

He felt it too and looked out into the garden. There was a shadow moving between the flowerbeds, coming towards them, too tall for Barbi. Luke rose.

'Who are you?'

The shadow stopped, then came into the moonlight. It was one of the slaves from Bilma. He wore black.

Luke had never discovered his name, but Shulen had when he'd taught her his language on the long tide to Timbuktu. She spoke to him. 'N'gara, why are you here?'

The man dropped to his knees in front of them. 'Forgive me, lady. I have frightened you.'

She took his hand and brought him to sit beside her on the stone. She said: 'I thought you had gone to your people.'

The man looked down at her from a height greater even than Luke's. His skin glowed in the moonlight. 'I went and I came back. I wanted to tell you something.'

Shulen put her hand on his arm. 'What do you want to tell us, N'gara?'

'That the Songhai will attack. Soon.'

'Here? They will attack Timbuktu?'

N'gara dipped his head. His eyes passed to Luke. 'They will attack because the Timbuktu-Koy has left with his army. They will take the salt.'

Luke leant forward. N'gara's language was much the same as that of the slaves they'd bought from the Tuareg and he'd understood most of what had been said. 'How do you know this?'

The man looked around him.

'We are alone,' said Shulen. 'Only Barbi's here and he sleeps.'

'The Mamluk talked to the Songhai at Bilma,' N'gara said. 'He arranged it. He told them to wait until the Koy left with his army for the Gbara. It happens at the same time every year.'

Luke pondered this. He remembered that he'd not seen al-Tabingha at Bilma. 'When will they come?'

'Soon. They will wait for the Timbuktu-Koy to be on his journey, then they will attack.'

Luke said: 'We must get word to him.'

N'gara shook his head. 'The Timbuktu-Koy has already gone. He has taken the river.'

'Then his army. We must tell them not to leave.'

'They have left too.' N'gara motioned with his hands. 'And they will not come back if you tell them to, not without the Timbuktu-Koy's word.'

Luke rose. He looked at Shulen. 'Well, we must get word to the Koy. Can we send someone downriver? A messenger?'

Shulen remained seated. She was a child next to N'gara. She looked up and said: 'I think we should wake Barbi, don't you?'

They woke Barbi who, they discovered, was not alone. A beauty of the household was lying next to him and seemed unsurprised to see them.

Luke threw the engineer his robe. 'The Songhai are about to attack. I'm going to get Yeshaq's soldiers. I want you to think about how we can defend this city.'

Leaving Shulen to explain, Luke ran from the house to the gates of the city. It was nearly dawn and the vast African night was surrendering its stars, one by one, to the heat of a new day. He found Yeshaq's men in the abaradiou, still in their tents, their armour propped outside. There didn't appear to be any guards keeping watch.

He woke their leader and told him to bring his men inside the city with the salt. It would take time, for the salt slabs were stacked inside a warehouse and would have to be loaded onto the animals again. Then he sent men into the trees to watch the desert to the north.

By noon, the salt was inside the city and Yeshaq's soldiers on its walls. Luke stood among them, searching the horizon beyond the paddy fields for any sign of an army. There was none.

As the muezzin called the faithful to evening prayers, he was joined on the walls by Shulen, Barbi and N'gara. The engineer's face was streaked with dirt and sweat.

'Still no sign of them,' said Luke. He turned to Barbi. 'What have you managed?'

Barbi leant over the walls. It was not a great distance to the ground. 'They're not tall or strong, these,' he said, straightening up and patting the rampart. 'Made of mud, mostly. Any determined enemy will be over them in an hour.' He glanced along the wall to where Yeshaq's men stood guard. 'And I don't rate these men as fighters, whatever their armour. They sing too well.'

'Well, they're all we have,' Luke said with some sharpness. 'The Koy's taken everyone else to Kangaba.'

Barbi nodded, running his hand through his hair as he did when thinking. 'So we need to think of what else we have, or can make. I've started on some catapults.'

This was more encouraging. Luke asked: 'To throw what?'

'Greek grenades, if I can find the stuff to make them. Or stones if not.'

'Do we even have much stone in this city?' asked Shulen. 'It all seems to be mud and wood.'

'Well, we could shower them with cowrie shells,' said Barbi. 'We've plenty of those. Perhaps we can buy them off?'

Luke heard something. Then he was pointing. 'Look.'

They looked and saw the far desert suddenly crenellated. Thousands of horsemen had emerged in a line that stretched to both ends of the horizon. Luke swore. 'How many is that?'

N'gara came to stand next to him. 'The Songhai will have gathered all their tribes. Many thousands.'

'So, too late for catapults. We'll just have to defend these walls.'

Barbi didn't seem very upset. He said: 'There's something else, but I'm going to hate myself for doing it.'

Luke stared at him. 'What, for God's sake?'

'We flood the land. Open my dykes, sluices, locks, all of them. We turn my mills and chains around to drive the water out.' He paused and looked dolefully across the fields. 'That should do it.'

Luke had grasped him by the shoulders. He leant forward and kissed him on the lips. 'Barbi, you are a genius. Have I ever said it?'

Barbi stepped back. 'Yes. But differently.' He wiped his lips with his hand. 'We don't have much time.'

'So who does it?'

'The farmers. I've already told them. But we need a screen.'

'Of course.' Luke was nodding. 'Why?'

'So the Songhai don't see what we're doing. Otherwise they'll charge.'

'And you've thought of how to make it, I hope?'

Barbi sighed, remembering, perhaps, a canister he'd once strapped to Luke's back. 'We've got bundles of wet reeds above the dykes ready to light. We should begin.'

They ran along the walls, down steps and out of the city gates. The farmers were waiting. They were well known to Barbi and

370

it took a single word to send them on their way, the fastest towards the furthest dykes.

Luke and Shulen ran with them, criss-crossing the fields by the causeways between, jumping the ditches, arriving at the dykes too hot to talk. They helped light the reeds, blowing on them to thicken the smoke. As it rose, they cast anxious eyes towards the horizon where the Songhai still hadn't moved. Closer to, they were even more formidable. Luke could see Tuareg in their ranks.

Luke glanced back towards the fields. There were men clustered around the sluices, dams and locks, hitting them with axes. Some were breaking and water was pouring into the fields. Luke could see the rice plants being swept away. Shulen was running towards him. 'Quick!' he shouted. 'We must get back before the water gets too high. Is everything lit?'

Shulen glanced behind her. 'It seems so. But there's not enough smoke.'

There wasn't. Luke heard shouts from the desert. The Songhai had started to advance. The whole line of horsemen was moving down from the ridge in a slow avalanche of sand. They were no more than half a mile away.

Luke and Shulen ran back down the causeways, some submerged by now. The closer they got to the city, the harder it got. They came to a junction where farmers were still trying to open a dam. One of them was Barbi.

'Well made, you see,' he said, detaching himself and wiping his brow. 'It won't break.' He looked over to the Songhai, who were closer now. He turned to the farmers and said something. They left the dam and started back towards the city.

'We should get back ourselves,' said Luke. 'They're nearly here.'

Shulen pointed: 'We may be too late. Look.'

The Songhai had reached the fields and met the tide of water and rice plants coming their way. It was strengthening every minute but wasn't enough to stop them. Their horses splashed through the tide and came on.

Luke said: 'Barbi, we've got to go.'

The engineer held up his hand. 'Not yet.' He paused. 'Now.'

A series of explosions across the fields threw dirt high into the air. Horses reared and fell, the Songhai with them. There were cries of alarm and anger, screams of frightened horses.

'Chinese gunpowder', said Barbi, nodding, 'is certainly better than ours.' He turned, grinning. 'And she taught me how to make fuses that actually work. We must go.'

They began to splash their way towards the city. The shouts of the Songhai weren't getting any closer. Luke glanced behind as he ran. The attackers were a mass of confusion. Some were swimming, some calming their horses to mount. Many were trying to come on through water that was now up to their horses' withers and rising quickly. He heard a cry in front of him. Shulen had slipped and fallen into deep water and the current was sweeping her away. He jumped in up to his waist and caught her as she passed. He pulled her to him, held her. 'All right?'

She nodded, wiping the water from her eyes and nose and the hair from her face. 'Thank you.'

He lifted her up to what had been the bank, then scrambled up beside her. 'Hold on to me from now on.'

They stumbled on through the water until they reached the city walls where ladders had been dropped. Barbi was waiting at the bottom of one.

Shulen climbed and Barbi followed her up, then Luke. At the

top, they pulled up the ladder and sat to catch their breath. Their clothes were torn and sodden and Shulen's hair was full of rice seeds.

Luke rose to look over the ramparts. The Songhai were in retreat now, running on foot or horseback to keep ahead of the flood, trying to get back to the ridge.

Luke turned to Barbi. 'You did all this yesterday?'

The engineer shook his head. 'I did all this a month ago. The fuses ran through channels we'd already made.'

Shulen took his arm. She'd been never fonder of Barbi than when they had found him adulterous that morning. Now she loved him. 'It was all in the diadan, I suppose?'

Barbi nodded. 'Like everything else.' He paused. 'We'll sell the idea to the Flemings.'

Luke frowned: 'If we ever get back to them. How long will the water stay?'

The engineer shrugged. 'Two, three days at most. It's just given us some time.'

'To build catapults?' Luke shook his head. 'No, we need the Koy to come back.'

As Barbi had prophesied, two days later the water began to subside and the Songhai returned. There seemed to be even more of them this time. They sat on their horses and waited.

Luke had sent a messenger downriver with the promise that he'd get his weight in salt if he caught up with the Koy. The man had found him within a day. He had then been put ashore with a note, sealed by the Timbuktu-Koy, to take to the army ordering it to turn around.

The following day, the Koy caught up with his generals and told them to prepare to do battle with the Songhai who, he believed, were already inside Timbuktu's walls. It seemed unlikely that they'd be able to retake the city and the Koy had resigned himself to an honourable death.

So his relief on seeing the city still held was profound. And the army, who had not been looking forward to scaling its walls, took new heart. They attacked the Songhai with purpose, charging them with the lance beneath banners raised to the will of Allah. Even Yeshaq's soldiers came out of the city to join in. The Songhai held for a while, then wavered, then took to their heels. The only thing that saved them from destruction was the desert.

Much later, Luke, Shulen and Barbi were asleep in their house when the Koy came to visit. They'd expected a summons to the palace but were too tired to wait for it, falling on to their beds like cowrie sacks. Luke was woken by N'gara.

'The Koy is here, sahib. He wishes to speak with you.'

'Here? Where?'

'Outside in the courtyard,' said N'gara. Then, for Luke hadn't moved: 'Waiting for you.'

It appeared to be evening outside which meant that Luke had slept all day. He smelt the garden's scents and felt drugged. 'Have you woken the others?'

N'gara nodded. His head almost touched the cedar beams and, in lesser light, might have been part of them.

Luke stumbled from the bed, robed and went out. He found Shulen and Barbi there already, sitting on benches amidst the flowers. The Timbuktu-Koy was with them.

He rose as Luke approached. 'We were discussing survival,' he said, his hand extended. He took Luke's and guided him to a bench. N'gara stood behind him when he sat. 'You kept your word.'

374

The evening was still. The water birds had gone with the water, feeding far away on orphaned rice. Outside the house's halls, the city wore the silence of exhaustion and relief. The feast would come tomorrow.

The Koy was smiling, his handsome eyes still fixed on Luke. 'N'gara has told me all that has happened, how you saved my city.' His eyes moved over each of them and he turned to take N'gara's hand. 'All of you.'

Luke watched as the Koy kept hold of the hand, then placed it on his shoulder. It was an act of friendship, even respect.

The Timbuktu-Koy said: 'Al-Tabingha apparently arranged it all at Bilma, knowing when I'd have to go to the Gbara. He didn't know that he had a chief of the Wangara among the slaves there.'

Luke stared up at N'gara, who was smiling at him.

The Koy continued: 'Behind me stands a chief of one of the tribes that mine the gold to the south. There are many tribes who practise the silent trade but we call them all the Wangara. N'gara is an important man among them who became a slave by misfortune. Now he will help you.'

Luke's exhaustion had vanished and he was alert. He glanced at Shulen.

'I have no need to go to the Gbara now,' said the Koy, rising. 'You have done more than enough to earn your gold.' He turned. 'And you need to go quickly to get it since your time is running out. N'gara will take you tomorrow.'

CHAPTER THIRTY-ONE

TIMBUKTU, SPRING 1418

It took nearly a day to load the salt on to the boats.

Never had so much been sent upriver to the silent trade and boats were fetched from as far away as Gao to carry it all. A crowd gathered to watch and a market sprang up around it. By mid-morning the riverbank was strung with awnings, the ground heaped with rice and millet and tamarinds, piles of kola nuts, sacks of baobab flour, calabashes of honey and soft cheeses. Goats bleated and chickens flapped and vats of palm oil sizzled. Children shouted and clapped and skipped between the camels and mules bringing the salt down to the waterside. Luke opened a box for them to see, and the grey-white slab that emerged, scribbled over with charms, brought everyone to silence. Gold they were used to. Salt such as this they'd never seen before.

By evening, they were on their way. The men with them were not Yeshaq's soldiers but traders, every one of them known by sight to the Wangara.

'It is how the trade has been kept secret for two thousand years,' explained N'gara as they watched the boats pull away from the jetty. 'The traders understand the rules.'

'And if a stranger took a trader's place?'

'The Wangara would not trade until he'd been killed.'

'So what of us?'

'I have warned them that you are coming. I have vouched for you. I have told them you are a lion among men.'

Luke considered this and quite liked it.

The Lion of Mistra.

'And Shulen?'

N'gara looked solemnly at her. 'Shulen must remain hidden.'

Their own boat would follow the floating caravan. It was more of a raft of tree trunks roped together with a divided cabin above. Luke would sleep in one half, Shulen the other, and they would be comfortable, for beds and mattresses had been provided. N'gara would sleep among the men who would take it in turns to pole the vessel upstream to wherever they were going. Benedo Barbi had stayed behind to mend the dykes.

The journey was slow against the current and it took them seven days to get to the place of the silent trade. On the way, the riverbank became forest. They passed hippopotami among the reeds, snowdrifts of egrets on floating islands and monkeys and parakeets in the trees behind, noisier than the market they had left. They had time to talk late into the night. They learnt how N'gara had come to be a slave.

'The Wangara have many clans, all engaged in the silent trade. We are part of the Empire of Mali but not even the Emperor knows where we mine the gold. Every so often a new emperor will demand to know. Then the trade stops until he relents. Ten years ago, this Emperor made the demand. I, and another clan chief, went to the capital Niani to reason with him. He showered us with gifts and the other chief was wavering, so I killed him. The Emperor was enraged and sent me north to work in the salt mines at Bilma. When the Songhai took it, they made me a slave.'

Shulen asked: 'If the trade is so secret, why not leave us behind? Why don't you do it on our behalf?'

N'gara shook his head. 'It is forbidden for the Wangara to trade with themselves. We trade only with those sent by the Timbuktu-Koy.'

On the seventh day, they came round a bend in the river to find the cargo boats pulled up in a long line along the riverbank with others tied behind. Men were standing in them, passing the boxes, one to another, up to where they were being stacked in piles on the grass. Other men with spears stood in semi-circles on either side, watching for crocodiles.

By evening, the salt was ashore and the traders had made camp, simple shelters of woven palm fronds raised on poles against the snakes. They carried Luke and Shulen's hut up from the raft and set it apart from the rest of the camp, lifting it on to a platform above stilts and putting the beds and mattresses within. Then the traders lit fires, cooked fish and went to sleep, exhausted by the journey. Soon the night was filled with their snoring.

N'gara went hunting with a blowpipe and returned with wildfowl on a string. He cut the meat into pieces and mixed it with herbs unknown to Shulen. Then he steamed it inside bamboo, propped over the fire.

When they had eaten, they sat round the embers and N'gara told them what was to happen the next day. 'There is a piece of raised ground nearby,' he said. 'There will be holes dug in pairs, one for salt, one for gold. Tomorrow morning we will take the first of the salt and leave it there, one slab to a hole, the boxes beside. Then we will retire and light fires to tell the Wangara it is there.'

'And we'll see no one?' asked Luke.

'No one. But they will see us.'

Shulen nodded. 'So what happens after you have lit the fires?'

'If they like the salt, they will place gold in the holes dug for it, then light their own fires. That will tell us that they have agreed to the exchange and we can come forward to collect the gold. It will be done over and over until the trade is complete. There is much salt.'

'More than they've seen before?' asked Shulen.

N'gara nodded. 'Much more. Only their grandfathers will have seen so much salt, and of such quality. They will be generous with their gold because they'll want more.'

They were silent for a while, each of them thinking the same thing, but in different ways. At last, N'gara asked the question. 'What will you do with so much gold, lion? Will they make you a king?'

Luke looked into the embers and at the ash around them and thought of the impermanence of living things. There was no heart to gold; no pulse, no sap. It could endure; and that was its value. He looked up at the Wangara chief. 'No, but it will give me power.'

'To use how?' asked Shulen quietly. 'To make you Lion of Mistra?'

He turned to her. 'No, to give Mistra the power to survive.'

'But won't all this gold just make it more desirable?'

Luke had put a tube of bamboo on to the fire and now watched it become a chimney. 'Not if it's already been spent on armies and ships, the things needed to defend ourselves.'

Shulen shifted the bamboo with her foot and leant forward. She spoke quietly into the fire. 'But that much gold must distort things, Luke. I know little of finance but it seems to me that, here on this riverbank, lies the source of much evil in the world.'

N'gara was nodding. 'You are right. Here lies the spring that waters the greed of the world. Which is why the mystery of its source must be protected by people unaware of its consequences.'

Luke thought about this in silence for a while, remembering the map he'd been shown, the terra incognita between China and Europe someone thought existed. 'Until another source is found,' he said.

Later, when the fire was no more than a glow outside, N'gara sleeping beside it, Luke lay on his bed and thought of what he'd said. He looked up into nothing, for no light came through the palm fronds above, and little air. It was stiflingly hot and the sweat poured from him as if Barbi had opened sluices at every pore.

He couldn't see but he could hear. He wondered if his other senses were heightened by his blindness.

His bed was set against the wall that divided his side from Shulen's and he knew that hers had been set the same way. It meant that she was the width of a palm leaf away from him. He could hear her breathing, imagine the rise and fall of her taut body, filmed, like his, with sweat. He thought of the tiny tremor of the place beneath her breast that sheltered her heart. And he smelt her smell. He turned away.

N'gara had asked if the gold would make him a king. He'd talked instead of power.

He knew that the gold he'd get for the salt would be enough to pay back his debts, to Venice and everyone else, and make Mistra what he wanted it to be. And there would be much left

380

over. He remembered Yeshaq saying that, a hundred years ago, the Mali Emperor Mansa Musa had brought so much gold to Cairo that its price had collapsed for twelve years.

He thought of the Venice Rialto and the Bruges exchange that he'd never seen. He thought of Lisbon. He thought of the whole new beast of international finance that had been given life by the Medicis and others: the beast with two hearts, one in Florence, the other in Venice. The beast whose ferocity was still unknown. Harnessing that beast was power, but could it be harnessed?

He thought back to the evening's conversation. Shulen had asked the more difficult question about the gold. She and N'gara, both creatures of the wilderness, somehow understood the corroding influence of gold: a metal that didn't corrode. They knew that, whatever the trials of the journey so far, the biggest tests were still to come.

Yes, there was her breathing.

'Shulen.'

The breathing stopped. Silence.

'*Shulen.*'

The whisper vast now. But what next? Waiting; his heart pushing aside ribs in its beat. Then the breathing began again. First fast, then slowing. The breathing of the awake.

The next morning they talked, but not about the things Luke had wanted to the night before. They ate millet porridge cooked for them by N'gara and watched mist rise from the river's surface. They could see elephants on the other side, pulling branches from the trees; shaking them free. They were bigger than those they'd known.

'They do not work,' said N'gara as he filled his plate. 'They won't allow men on their backs.'

Luke thought what such elephants might do with the salt. The traders had formed a long line from the river that ended on raised ground that had been cleared between the trees. They were passing up the boxes before the day became too hot.

'We will place twenty at a time for the trade,' said N'gara. 'But we will first stack all of the salt where they can see it. I have warned them of the size of the trade but they will need proof.'

By mid-morning, the salt was in place and the trade could begin. They watched the traders carry the first twenty boxes up the rise and disappear over the other side. Then they came back.

Two fires were lit and the traders returned to the camp where they sat and talked, none of them looking towards the salt.

Luke and Shulen watched it all in silent fascination. They were lying on grass behind a fallen tree and would not be seen from the trading place. N'gara was with the traders, discussing what they'd seen so far. He returned to them and knelt.

He smiled. 'The holes for the gold are deeper than any they've ever seen before. If they are filled this evening, then this will be more gold than even I imagined. We may need more boats. Come.'

They rose and returned to the place behind the hut where they would not be seen and sat around the embers of last night's fire. N'gara said: 'Now, we wait.'

They waited a long time. It was early evening before the Wangara fires were lit, much later than N'gara had expected. Luke had watched the chief's face change as the hours passed, the big brow narrowing to a frown, the jaw setting into silence. He watched him glance often towards the camp from where the message would come that the Wangara wanted to trade. Something was wrong.

But at last it came. A trader came over with the news that smoke had been seen behind the rise. It was time for N'gara to go forward and inspect the gold. He would go alone. He rose. 'Stay here and do not be seen.'

He left, and Luke and Shulen watched in silence as he walked into the camp where a hundred traders looked up at him with anxious eyes.

Shulen asked: 'Why the delay, do you think?'

Luke shrugged. 'It must be the quantity. They'll have counted the salt and what they have in gold to exchange. Perhaps they need to find more.'

They lapsed into silence again, listening to the bullfrogs call from the grass around them, forcing themselves to think of anything but what was happening on that hillside. The evening was creeping in through the forest around them, the animals climbing the trees to see the day off, chattering as they rose. Birds took to the air above in every shade of creation, thin ripples of gold leading them out to the horizon. Night was not far.

The wait for N'gara to return became hard, then intolerable. They didn't speak because there was no subject except the one they couldn't speak of. They sat and listened and watched the traders light their fires and prepare their food and sit down to talk in their low voices, leaning in to each other as they did. When the talking stopped, it could only be for one reason.

'He's returned,' said Luke, rising. 'Now we'll know.'

N'gara's face told them immediately that all was not well. The frown had deepened on a head that hung heavy on his shoulders. He looked at them both, then sat. 'Only one hole was filled,' he said. 'With snakes.'

'Snakes?'

'Poisonous snakes.'

Luke sat down next to him, Shulen on the other side. She asked: 'Has this happened before?'

N'gara stared into what was once a fire. 'Yes. It means they are angry.'

'But you warned them about me,' said Luke.

'These are not my people, sahib. The Wangara decided that with me seeming to act for the buyer, the trade should be done by a clan other than mine.'

'But I thought your people told them I was coming?'

'They did.' N'gara shook his head slowly. 'It is ten years since I was with the Wangara. Things must have changed.' He smoothed his tunic to his knees with his palms. He looked at Luke. 'They wish to see you.'

Shulen shook her head. 'No. Of course not. They'll kill him. We have to leave.'

It was all said quickly and with emphasis. Neither man spoke. She looked from one to the other of the men. 'Of course they'll kill him. He is the stranger.'

N'gara's eyes came up to hers. 'They have not said that. They just wish to see him.'

'But it's been this way for two thousand years, you said so yourself,' said Shulen. 'Why would they make an exception now?' She looked at Luke. 'Why not leave? The trade can happen at another time.'

'Not with me,' said Luke.

'Then with others on your behalf.'

But she knew this couldn't happen. The Wangara would either have to trust him or kill him. He had seen too much.

N'gara rose. 'Whatever you decide, we will not leave tonight. So we should eat. I will light the fire.'

The three of them ate in silence, two of them at least not tasting the food. Shulen tipped most of hers, uneaten, into the fire and the smell of mutton and herbs that rose reminded Luke of the steppe and a time, long ago, when they'd also talked of leaving.

At length N'gara, ever discreet, rose and left. He walked over to the camp to sleep among the traders. He would learn their decision in the morning.

Luke and Shulen sat on opposite sides of the fire and waited for the other to speak. They circled the impending conversation as if it were prey, silently looking for the way into words cornered and more dangerous than any animal. They knew there'd be blood.

At last she said: 'You have already decided.' Her voice was dull with certainty. 'Of course you have.'

Luke looked at her through the thin smoke. He saw her eyes fixed on his, full of fear and anger but no tears. He said: 'I will be with N'gara. He'll not let them kill me.'

'Why not? They're not his clan, he said so. And even if they were, he no longer has their loyalty.' She shook her head. 'If you go, you won't come back. At least be honest.'

Luke rose and came to sit next to her. He took her hand and saw how small it was in his. He watched the firelight play across its veins and the hair above them. He spoke carefully. 'Shulen, how can I not go? I have come to the end of the world to do this. I must do it.'

'And me? Am I not here too?'

'You chose to come, for reasons you've already told me. I didn't come into them.'

She pulled her hand away and brought it to her mouth, as if stopping whatever might come from it. Every word, his and hers, was a weapon that could hurt, had hurt. She moved away, still watching him, waiting for his next.

'I can only explain for myself, Shulen,' he said quietly. 'I am part of a dying empire that has stood for as long as this gold trade. I came to believe that not all of the Empire could be saved and thought I'd found a way to save the bit I love: Mistra.' He paused. 'Instead I delivered it up to Venice.'

Shulen was shaking her head before he'd finished. 'No, no, *no*. Nikolas told me. Venice has always coveted Mistra. You had to sink a fleet at Negroponte, remember? It was always going to happen.' She turned to him, the fire in her eyes. 'You were born a Varangian, Luke, not a god. You were born with luck and a talent for making people love you. Mistra needs you, not your gold.'

Their eyes were fixed to each other like two climbers joined. Neither could slip while the going was this perilous.

She leant forward and took his hand. 'What is this crazed ambition? Where has it come from? Did it arrive with the cloak of protostrator while I was away in Samarcand?' She searched his eyes. 'When did this enormous conceit come upon you, Luke?'

He frowned. *Conceit?* Was it really that?

She continued: 'Where do the people who love you come into this plan to save Mistra? Where do Giovanni, Hilarion, Plethon . . . Anna appear in your plan? What if they care more about you than who rules them?' She paused and nodded slowly, aware of the wounds she'd made. *'That* is your conceit, Luke. Not seeing that.'

He knew then that she was right. But he'd been born to a man who'd talked of destiny and shaped by others who'd thrust it upon him later: Plethon, Fiorenza, Manuel . . . even his two sons. There was no way to leave the path now, for whatever reason. Finally he looked away, letting the fire burn the rope that had joined them.

He spoke quietly, not looking at her. 'I must ask you to do certain things if I don't return. Things you won't want to do.'

She looked at her hands and found them trembling. She waited.

'In our house in Timbuktu, there is a will. It is the one I had drawn up in Cairo. I ask that you to take it to Mistra with my sword, as fast as you are able. But open it first. There are instructions inside.'

She didn't move beyond the trembling. Her body felt somewhere else.

He went on, still looking into the fire. 'The will is simple. The sword goes to Giovanni, my estates to Anna, then Hilarion. The gold goes to the Despot.'

Shulen found her voice from somewhere, hearing it from a distance. 'The gold.' Always the gold.

'Yes. If they kill me, we may still get the gold. Barbi will take it east to Berbera. I have arranged an escort from the Koy to join Yeshaq's soldiers. Al-Tabingha is still out there somewhere.'

She hadn't moved. Her voice, when it came, was calm. 'And what do I say to Anna in Mistra?' she asked.

Luke looked at her then, and found her looking at him. The firelight lit the tears that lined her cheeks.

'That I loved her,' he said quietly. 'That I'm sorry.'

Then she broke. Rocking from side to side, her sobs rising among the breaths, catching them. 'No,' she said. 'I've done all that you've asked: Tamerlane, China . . . not this.'

Luke leant forward to her. 'But, Shulen . . . you are the only one who can. Barbi must make the journey east.'

She fell back on to the ground and hugged her knees to herself, burying her head in them, shutting out the monstrous world, shutting out him. He moved to her but she wouldn't open herself.

He sat beside her misery and listened to it gradually subside, the breaths slowing to a normal rhythm. He said: 'I'm sorry.'

But she didn't reply, just stayed locked in her own embrace. They sat apart like that for a long time. Then he said: 'Shulen, say something to me.'

And she did, her voice muffled by the screen of her limbs. 'Just go. Sleep and leave tomorrow. I don't ever want to see you again.'

Of course Luke didn't sleep. He lay on his bed and tried to think of anything but her.

The door to the cabin was open and the fractioned moon sent only enough light to pool its threshold. The heat was no less, and he pulled a frond from the wall to fan himself. He could hear no sound of her outside. What had she said?

Monstrous conceit.

Was it all just about salvation? *His* salvation? He'd helped get elected a pope so heinous that he had been obliterated from history, leaving only his debt behind: Mistra's debt. Here, on this riverbank, he had the chance for redemption.

She'd said he didn't care about those who loved him: Giovanni, Hilarion, Anna. She'd not mentioned herself. Last night she hadn't answered his call. He lowered the fan and turned on to his side, closing his eyes.

He heard a sound at the doorway and opened them. She was standing, haloed by the pale moon, naked and still.

'Take down the wall.'

He rose and lifted it free with one pull, placing it on the floor of her hut. He pushed the beds together, making them one. He lay down again.

She came and lay beside him on her back, looking up into the darkness. She smelt of the fire.

He sought out her hand and held it. 'I'm sorry,' he said again.

She turned to him and put her finger to his lips. 'No.'

Her hair was spread across his shoulders and he could feel the beat of her heart against his own. He could see the shadow of her head looking down at him, not moving.

'No,' she said again. 'Not now.'

She brought her lips to his. They were softer than he'd imagined and still held the salt of her tears. She brought her palms to his cheeks and held them hard between them so that only their tongues might move. Then her hands moved across the landscape of his face, slowly and with care, exploring every contour, sending every sensation up through her fingers to her brain, to be locked into memory forever.

They were gentle at first, then less so. They both wanted to believe that the time they had left could somehow stretch itself into one eternal night. So they began without hurry but then the desire of years rose and washed over them. And with the torrent came her rage again, so that her hands closed and became fists that beat against his chest and the final cry was as much of anger as love.

I have always loved you.

Afterwards they lay in silence, her body next to his, her hand in his, waiting for the morning and dreading it.

Neither of them slept, but, later, when the first hint of dawn made shape of the doorway, she pretended to. When he rose and put on his clothes and shoes and leant to kiss her forehead, she pretended to.

Only when she heard the murmured greeting to N'gara outside did she open her eyes. And when she went to the door and looked out, he had gone.

It took the traders two days to complete the trade and one to load the boxes of gold into the boats. Then they waited a further day to be sure. Neither Luke nor N'gara had returned.

Shulen hadn't waited, not wanting to hear the news she knew would come. After Luke had left, she had risen and gone down to the raft and found men to take her back to Timbuktu. She'd been calm.

At the city, she returned to the house and found the sword and the will. Then she summoned Barbi from the fields and told him that the man he loved was dead.

Only then did she open the will and read it.

PART SIX

MISTRA AT BAY

CHAPTER THIRTY-TWO

VENICE, SUMMER 1418

The news that Luke Magoris was dead flowed up from Africa like a tide, bringing with it the flotsam of speculation.

It spread quickly through the desert, passing from Timbuktu to Bilma in a week. It took longer for al-Tabingha to get it to Cairo by which time it was also travelling north by a different route.

The speculation concerned how the Protostrator had died. Most agreed that it had happened trying to find gold, and versions from crucifixion to burial with snakes had floated in with the tide, usually with something about hubris aboard. What became known only later was that a fortune in gold was on its way east across the desert to Berbera.

Shulen left Timbuktu a week after she returned from the Wangara. She went under the Koy's guard as far as Taghaza, then by caravan to Sijilmasa, reaching Portuguese Ceuta in the north by June. It was there that she learnt that a new pope had proclaimed a crusade against the Kingdom of Mistra.

It had, after all, been a waste of a journey, a waste of a life. The crusade would sail from Venice soon and the gold would come too late.

The news reached Venice also in June. The part about Luke's death caused the ducat to first rise by a tenth on the Rialto. Then news of the gold began to circulate and it fell by a fifth. If the rumours were true, then as much as a year's supply of gold might be going direct into Persia by way of Basra. Venice feared war and plague and stillbirth, but nothing so much as irrelevance.

On the day that it seeped through the walls of his palace, the Doge sent for Zoe Mamonas.

She arrived by two-oared *barchetta* without flag of any kind, choosing to avoid the anxious crowds thronging the piazza. If she'd been recognised, they'd have wanted news. It was a close day of cloud and discomfort and she wore her banker's black loose and with not much on underneath. She stepped, therefore, with ease from her barge to the Doge's landing and took the staircase two steps at a time, arriving without blush to find Tommaso Mocenigo absorbed by the wall.

'Africa,' he said, pointing at the map there. 'It's going east on two thousand camels and will take six months to reach the coast.'

'Which will make it too late,' said Zoe, taking wine from a tray and joining him. 'The crusade is to sail in two months.'

'But have you thought what damage that much gold arriving in Persia will do to the ducat? And the ducat's fall is the florin's rise and Mistra's debt is in florins. He's been clever.'

Zoe didn't answer. She was not yet used to speaking of Luke in the past tense. The news had reached her the night before during dinner. She'd stopped eating, put down her napkin and risen slowly from the table. She'd thanked her hosts and left, arriving at the Mamonas fondaco as calm as she'd left it, even pausing to send every servant to bed. Only when she'd reached the sanctuary of her bedroom had she thrown herself on to the bed and cried.

She'd cried all night, more than over her brother Damian's death. She had put her face to the pillow and flooded it with her tears, sobbing into one side, then drenching the other. She'd been surprised to cry as she had. She'd known Luke all of her life, loving him for the smaller part, hating him for the rest. Everything she'd done since arriving in Venice had been as much for his destruction as her resurrection. But destruction had never meant death.

The Doge was looking at her strangely. 'You knew him, didn't you?' he said, his head to one side. 'Does his death affect you?'

'No.' She smiled. 'Not at all. What were you saying?'

The Doge studied her for a moment, his old eyes measuring hers and finding nothing but cold purpose in them, nothing new. He said: 'He may be trying, *posthumously*, to render his debt less significant.'

'And he will succeed,' said Zoe, turning from the map.

'So should we attack the caravan?'

'With what? Our galleys don't yet float on sand and we have no army in the desert that I know of.'

The Doge smiled. He liked Zoe more and more. She had more courage than most men he'd fought beside. 'But we have allies.'

'The Mamluks? They want this trade route opened, not ravaged. As should we.'

The Doge considered this. It was true. But that much gold? 'What do you suggest then?'

Zoe drank her wine, her eye on a different map. 'We should talk to the Mamluks, yes, but we should also talk to Mistra. With Magoris dead, the gold becomes the property of whoever he's chosen to leave it to.'

'Such as the nobles who lent him the money?'

'Such as the nobles who hate him but may do less if they're paid back. I think we should speak to them soon.'

Three weeks later, the same tide hit Mistra with even greater force. The news that their protostrator was dead cleaved its people in two: the many who were sad and the few who were angry.

It was a summer evening and the city's stones still held the heat of the day. In the streets, people were emerging from their houses drowsy from afternoon sleep, kicking cats that got in their way. But the philosopher and the woman who sat on a balcony above, holding hands, did not hear the animals' cries.

'How did it happen?' Anna was staring at Plethon from enormous eyes, still dry. 'Why?'

Plethon had heard the versions and dismissed them all. 'Does it matter? He was killed by the people he sought to buy gold from. Why, I don't know.'

'Was he alone?'

Plethon didn't reply. The hand he held was trembling.

'He wasn't alone,' she said quietly. 'She was with him.'

After that they remained silent for a while, Plethon looking at his knees and Anna out over their city from where the first smells of cooking were coming up to them. She thought of how the people would react once they knew.

Plethon said: 'You should know that he succeeded, Anna. There is a caravan with gold on its way.'

She turned to him, something hard in her eyes. 'Succeeded, Plethon?' she whispered. 'Do you really think that?'

'It may persuade Venice not to attack.'

She shook her head. The shock of what she'd heard had shattered much of what she knew, but she knew that. 'It will be too late. They will attack and he won't be here.'

She turned back to a city seemingly unconcerned that the world had just ended. She wanted to stand and shout them out of their ingnorance.

Luke Magoris is dead.

Instead she asked: 'Who else has been told?'

'The Despot only.'

'Not Hilarion, or Giovanni?'

Plethon shook his head. 'No, of course not.' He studied her for a while, gauging the equilibrium between sorrow and anger, wondering if it was at its merging that she was finding this stability.

'I will stay with you,' he said.

'No you won't. You know what this news means. You must go to the Despot and speak to him before others do.'

Plethon nodded slowly. 'And what will you do?'

'I will go and tell Hilarion.'

Plethon was too late to speak to the Despot alone. He arrived at the throne room to find a meeting already in progress around a table that had on it papers franked at their corners by the Lion of St Mark. Theodore looked up as he entered.

'I have told these gentlemen the news,' he said, rising to greet the philosopher. 'It coincides with a letter from Venice.'

Plethon dipped his head to the four nobles as he sat. 'What coincidence.'

None smiled. All were from old Roman families who'd uprooted the wealth of generations to move to Mistra, only to see it disappear. They blamed Luke and Plethon in equal

397

measure: Luke for his ill judgement and desertion; Plethon for the heresy that had turned truce into crusade.

Plethon looked at each of the four, disliking everything about them, but especially their gravitas. Their excitement was barely concealed beneath their frowns. 'So what is Venice offering? Let me guess: forgiveness of your debts.'

'You too, Plethon,' said Michael Vangelis, Theodore's newest minister.

'The difference, of course,' said the philosopher, 'is that I may not choose to be forgiven. Not at the price they're likely to charge. What is it by the way?'

'The terms are generous,' said a man who had once been Constantinople's richest citizen. 'They offer to buy the despotate from the Emperor and forgive all debt. They will allow us to retain our faith, alongside theirs. They will strengthen Mistra's defences.'

Plethon nodded. 'That *is* generous.' He looked around again. 'Why do you think that might be?'

'Well, it's obvious. It will be cheaper for them than using force.'

'I doubt it. What have they said about our protostrator?'

A man called Severus who once had charge of Constantinople's hippodrome said: 'All of Magoris's assets will be forfeit. It is reasonable in the circumstances.'

Plethon shook his head. 'I don't think the people of Mistra will see it that way. That is, those who've spent more than two summers here.'

Severus flushed. 'How dare you, old man? It was we who gave Magoris the money to build the wall and repair the shipyards!'

'Which would seem an extravagance if you're just about to hand them over.'

398

Vangelis was reaching exasperation. 'They were built against the Turk, Plethon!' he said.

'They were built to defend Mistra', said Plethon, still calm, 'against any that might threaten it.' He paused. 'That may not be the Turk at the moment.'

The news that Bedreddin had mysteriously disappeared had arrived not long before that of Luke's death. His army of fanatics was still in Anatolia but apparently leaderless. They still had no boats and were beginning to drift away.

Vangelis asked: 'But what of the future? What of Murad, who'll rule next? If we give ourselves over to Venice, we'll be more able to withstand him when the time comes. You must grant that!'

Plethon began to say something but stopped. He looked down at his hands instead, turning them slowly. 'How long has your family served this Empire, Vangelis?' he asked quietly. He looked at Severus. 'Or yours?'

The two men glanced at each other. Severus said: 'Since the days of Constantine. Over a thousand years.'

Vangelis said: 'Mine not so long.'

'Long enough,' said Plethon. His eyes passed over them all. 'Our Roman Empire has lasted for two thousand years because it has meant something to people, given them an ideal. Your families have shaped it, as it has shaped them. You should be the first to fight for it. Instead you talk of surrender.'

There was silence but not for long. Vangelis sat back in his chair and raised his hands. 'Plethon, this is ridiculous, even for you. Venice has the biggest navy in the world. We have twelve ships.'

'We have gold coming from Africa.'

'If it comes,' said Severus, 'it will be too late. Because your

399

pupils now pray to pagan gods, the Pope has made this a crusade. They're not going to wait.'

So far the Despot had watched the conversation in silence. He'd been Plethon's pupil for fifteen of his twenty-three years but some of his recent teaching was probably heretical – certainly the Emperor thought so. And he knew that his father was desperate for money to repair Constantinople's defences. He asked: 'When does Venice need an answer?'

Vangelis picked up the manuscript and reread it. He looked up. 'They give us a month to decide, majesty, then they will prepare the fleet.'

'And if we agree?'

'Then they propose that the Pope and Doge come to Mistra in September to meet with you and your father the Emperor. They offer the last day of that month for the ceremony.'

Theodore rose. 'So we have time to consider, though not much.' He turned to Plethon. 'Have Giovanni and Hilarion been told? I would be with them.'

Giovanni and Hilarion had been told together, though that hadn't been Anna's intention. She found them practising swordplay in the palace yard. They had stopped as soon as they had seen her face.

'Hilarion.' Her hands were thrust into the sleeves of her tunic, hugging her sides. She was hunched over as if she were sick. 'May we speak?'

Hilarion lowered his sword as the dread rose within him. 'We can talk here, Mother.'

She glanced at Giovanni. 'It has to do with your father.'

'*Our* father,' Hilarion said quietly. 'He's Giovanni's too.'

Giovanni picked up his doublet.

'No,' Hilarion said quickly. 'Please stay.' He turned to his mother. 'Whatever it is, tell us both.'

She sat to tell them, not trusting herself on her feet. She spoke only to Hilarion, as if Giovanni had never stayed. She managed not to cry for most of it, her fingers dug deep into ribs below her tunic. In the end, she fell into Hilarion's arms, sobbing.

Which was how Theodore and Plethon found them: mother and son joined by embrace, brother to brother by hand. Giovanni and Hilarion's love for each other had only strengthened on learning they were brothers. Hilarion's fits, already infrequent, had disappeared. Anna might have even been grateful had she not blamed Giovanni for everything else. She didn't see their hands joined.

She did see the Despot. She rose. 'I will leave you.'

After she'd gone, Plethon sat where she'd sat and Theodore sat beside him, the brothers before them on the ground. It was exactly how they'd all sat when he'd taught them.

'So,' he said gently, leaning forward to the two brothers, looking from one to the other, 'we have a grief so colossal that only reason will temper it. Theodore has a problem that requires reason. So we will apply it.'

Giovanni's eyes were dry. 'Except that I refuse to believe him dead,' he said. 'I won't until I've had proof.'

'And you think what we have is mere rumour?' asked Plethon. His voice was quiet. 'If Shulen were to confirm it, or Benedo Barbi who was with him too, would that be proof enough?'

Giovanni let go of the philosopher's hand, but still held Hilarion's. He turned to his brother. 'Hilarion, do you *feel* him dead? I don't.'

Hilarion frowned. He wanted to feel something beyond desolation. 'I don't know,' he said.

'Well, I know. He's not dead.'

The Despot looked bewildered. He glanced at Plethon. 'So do we assume Luke alive or dead for our deliberations?' he asked, always methodical. 'I'm confused.'

'We must assume what everyone else assumes,' said Plethon gently. 'That the Protostrator died in Africa trying to save his city.' He turned to Giovanni. 'Shulen or Barbi will be on their way to us. We've had no word from them to the contrary.'

Giovanni was shaking his head, his face creased in concentration.

Plethon continued: 'We have a proposal from Venice. If the Emperor sells Mistra to them, they will forgive the nobles their debts. There is only one condition: that the property of the Magoris family is confiscated.'

The two brothers looked at each other. Their hands were still joined.

'It is a clever plan,' Plethon went on, 'because they know it will appeal to our Emperor Manuel and to the new rulers of this kingdom, the nobles. Both will persuade themselves that Mistra is safer in Venetian hands.'

The Despot raised his hand as he'd once done in Plethon's lessons. 'But might they not be right?' He was dressed in long, heavy robes but the arm that emerged from its infinite sleeves was almost hairless. 'They already have forts on our coasts. Will they not want to protect us, Plethon?'

'For as long as it suits them, yes,' replied the philosopher. 'But at some point Venice must fight the Turk. Then it will decide what is expendable, and what not.'

Hilarion had yet to speak, still numb from the shock of the news. He wanted more than anything to feel what Giovanni felt: that his father was still alive.

402

Somewhere.

He thought of his mother. Should he be with her? He glanced towards the gate through which Anna had gone. Cleope was standing there, watching them. Above the white lawn of her dress, there was colour in her cheeks. She'd been running. Giovanni saw her too. He rose.

She walked over to him, her tread as light as a whisper. She held Giovanni's shoulders between her palms and looked up into a face printed with misery; then she took his hands in hers and kissed them, each in turn, before holding them to her cheeks. She said: 'I'm sorry.'

Plethon glanced at the Despot. His eyes had followed Cleope and stayed on her still.

Cleope sat, bringing Giovanni to sit beside her. She placed her palms flat on the ground and turned to Hilarion. She said: 'He loved you beyond measure; never forget that.'

Theodore still watched her. She felt it and looked at him. 'You have an impossible decision,' she said. 'Do you do as your father and the nobles would wish, or do you resist?'

The Despot shook his head. 'You know the answer to that. My duty is to my father the Emperor. His duty is to Constantinople.'

'If it can be saved,' said Giovanni. 'When Mehmed is dead, Murad will besiege it. Mistra can be saved.'

Cleope turned to Plethon. 'Theodore must do his duty, surely.'

Plethon was grave. 'Of course, as it is my duty to point out the consequences of so doing.' He looked at the Despot. 'Luke is loved in this kingdom, especially in Monemvasia.'

'You fear civil war?' asked Theodore.

'It is a possibility.' Plethon put his hands on his knees. 'The nobles are not popular and it is not so long ago that Mistra and Monemvasia fought each other.'

Giovanni said: 'And remember the Varangians. Matthew and Arcadius will not sit by and watch Luke's property seized.'

Plethon shook his head. 'The Varangians will do as their despot commands them,' he said. 'They are oath-bound.'

Cleope was sitting very still, as she did when she knew herself under scrutiny. She reached up and collected a stray hair, tucking it into the band she wore on her head. She looked around and said: 'Well, does Theodore write to his father to warn him of the consequence of selling Mistra to Venice?'

Plethon nodded. 'Yes. But there is one more thing. You.' His eyes had settled on Cleope and they were tired. 'You will be a victim of this surrender – you know that. You will leave Mistra.'

Cleope's eyes settled on Giovanni. 'I know,' she said.

CHAPTER THIRTY-THREE

CAIRO, SUMMER 1418

A month after Mistra had celebrated their protostrator's life with solemn services throughout the despotate, the Sultan of the Mamluks was in his citadel, feeding his cheetah.

He'd been one of those saddened by the news of Luke's death. The horse Luke had given him was the fastest he'd ever ridden and had brought him this cheetah, netted in the hunt two weeks ago.

The Sultan threw meat to the ground, then stooped to stroke the animal's fur, enjoying its furrowed luxury between his fingers. He was in a garden set against the citadel's ramparts and the sunset was a glimpse of heaven. He looked at it, shielding his eyes.

'Tamerlane had a snow leopard, they say. And King Yeshaq, of course, has lions.' He rose and turned to the man with him. 'The cheetah is more subtle, which is what we need to be when it comes to Venice. Tell me again what they say.'

Al-Tabingha had ridden fast from the Venetian bailate in Alexandria and dust from the roads still covered his pantaloons and boots. There was earth on his knees from recent kneeling. 'They want two things, master: Bedreddin's head and the gold travelling east to Berbera removed.'

The Sultan stroked his beard to its point between thumb and forefinger. 'How did they find out that we hold Bedreddin?'

Al-Tabingha knew because he'd told them. He said instead: 'They have agents everywhere, master. Even here at your court.'

'Do they know he came here asking for boats?'

Al-Tabingha dipped his head. 'They are grateful to you for arresting him. Now they'd like him dead.'

The Sultan studied the man in front of him. He knew al-Tabingha was an agent of Venice. It was why he'd sent him south with Luke. 'Well, you can tell them that it doesn't suit me to kill him.'

Al-Tabingha stood perfectly still. The dying sun shone straight into his eyes, making his moustaches orange and his shadow endless. This would not please the bailo.

The Sultan continued: 'Tell them this: Bedreddin will not be killed because, whatever his sins, he is a man of God. Nor will he be released because it suits us for Mistra to become Venetian.'

Al-Tabingha inclined his head again. His hands were clasped to his chest in the manner of a supplicant. He said: 'They wonder why a Greek with Genoese interests was sent to Yeshaq, rather than a Venetian.' He paused. 'Or a Mamluk.'

The Sultan studied him, disliking most things he saw. 'Because no Venetian – or Mamluk for that matter – has the ear of the Ming Emperor. Or am I mistaken?'

Al-Tabingha looked at the ground, no part of him moving.

'Anyway,' said the Sultan, returning once more to the view, 'it makes no difference now. Magoris is dead.' He watched Mamluks racing horses on the maidan below; none as fast as his. 'We are certain of that, aren't we?'

Al-Tabingha nodded. 'I saw his body with my own eyes, master.

I followed him to the place of the silent trade and waited until they had all left. I went up to the trading ground and found him in one of the holes.'

'And you didn't think to remove him?'

'He was covered by poisonous snakes.' Al-Tabingha paused, liking the disgust in the face before him. 'It is their way.'

The Sultan nodded slowly, his hand again to his beard. 'Well, he did us a great service. He reopened the trade with China and allowed us to be at the end of it. The Portuguese can go as far as they want down the coast to bypass us Muslims.' He paused. 'He should be revered for what he has done. Especially by Venice.'

Al-Tabingha didn't revere Luke; he hated him. He'd still not forgotten his humiliation with the Songhai at Timbuktu. He hoped the news of what he'd done there would never reach the man opposite him. He said: 'There is still the matter of the gold, master.'

The Sultan had not known of Luke's plan to trade gold but he didn't blame him for doing it. The reason seemed admirable: he wanted to save his kingdom from Venice. But the amount was worrying. 'Tell me what they say.'

'The gold is travelling east to Berbera with the Genoese engineer, Benedo Barbi, who came here with the horses. From Berbera it is likely to go to Basra and from there to Mistra. The Doge is concerned by the release of so much gold. He remembers what happened when the Malian Emperor Mansa Musa came to Cairo.' He paused. 'He believes it will be in our mutual interests to remove it.'

The Sultan knew very well how dangerous the situation was. Luke's gold, if deployed all at once, might depress prices for years to come.

'And how does he propose that we do it?' he asked. 'We

couldn't attack the caravan when Malian and Abyssinian soldiers were guarding it. It must be nearly at the coast by now.'

Al-Tabingha dipped his head. 'Indeed, master, which is why the Doge proposes we send ships down the Red Sea to Berbera.'

'To attack a Chinese junk? Why would we want to antagonise our new trading partner?'

'They propose we disguise our ships as pirates, master.'

The Sultan pondered this. It seemed an elegant way of removing the gold and filling his treasury at the same time. It might work. 'I will think about it.'

A small breeze came and he lifted his face to it. The sun was low but still fierce, turning the pillars of the aqueducts below into columns of fire. He looked along the city walls that ran from Nile to Nile and thought of the man who had built them. What would Saladin have done? Would he have allied himself with a reptile like Venice? But his Mamluk dynasty, not yet 150 years old, needed trade to survive. He would have to tolerate the Devil and even its repellent servant before him.

He turned back to the man. 'I would ask you to also tell Venice that we continue to look for the Ark of the Covenant.'

He watched al-Tabingha carefully. King Yeshaq's envoys had recently been in Cairo, celebrating their new trading partnership. He had given them one of Luke's horses to take back to their king. They'd been very clear: the Ark had not left Axum. But did al-Tabingha know that? He didn't think so.

The Sultan turned back to the view, indicating by the small wave of a hand that the interview was over. Al-Tabingha left.

For a long while, the Sultan looked out over his two cities, Cairo and Fustat, embraced by their single wall. They crept closer together every year, like shy lovers. There was a line of camels threading its way between them, their shadows flung far

408

out into the distance. He thought of other camels somewhere in the south carrying more gold than had ever been carried by one caravan. The Doge was right: it must never reach Mistra.

He thought about al-Tabingha. Perhaps now was the time to tell him his allegiance to Venice was known. Perhaps now was the time to show him where his loyalties should lie.

He heard a cough behind him and turned. A servant was prostrate on the grass.

'Well?'

'There is an Italian waiting to meet you,' said the man to the ground. If he sounded nervous it was because the Sultan never met with foreigners outside audience hours. 'He said you would wish to speak with him.'

'And his name?'

'His name is Signor Benedo Barbi, majesty. He is Genoese.'

In Monemvasia, it was two hours until sunset and the Goulas was a wall of pitted bronze. At its top, a hundred palaces shimmered between their cypress spears and on the roof of the largest, the Akolouthos of Byzantium watched his two visitors approach up the street below.

The day was still hot and Matthew, dressed in the uniform he used to inspect things, envied one of the men his toga and straw hat. He had spent the day at the shipyards at Kiparissi gauging the fighting strength of the fleet and was tired. His gaze moved to the other end of the plateau where the citadel stood, its garrison now entirely Varangian. Between lay the two giant cisterns of the city. He had inspected them the day before and found them gratifyingly full.

He looked back down at the two men, closer now. He waved. 'Plethon, Arcadius!'

They looked up and he tried to read the message from their faces. Was the news good or bad? It was too far to tell. He looked beyond them at the vast blue of the Mirtoon Sea, its surface ticked by surf. There was wind out there in the sails of ships approaching in the roads. Too many flew the Lion of St Mark these days. And where was the one carrying the cannon he'd ordered from Ragusa a month ago? Had Venice intercepted it?

He moved to the other end of the balcony from where he could see the lower town. The little square was filling with people waiting for Plethon to come to them next, children sitting in the bell tower of the Elkomenos Church, their legs swinging. Their parents would want to know their emperor's decision too: were they to surrender to Venice or fight? Not one of them wanted surrender.

It was the waiting that was hardest. Matthew looked at the mosaic of Neptune beneath his feet. This had once been the Mamonas Palace, the most splendid in Monemvasia. Now it was Luke's, lent to Matthew while his own was being built. Quite soon he'd learn if it was to return to Zoe.

He thought about Luke. He'd known about his best friend for a month now, but his grief was beyond time. Any doubts that Giovanni had expressed had gone with the news that Luke's body had been found in a hole full of snakes. He closed his eyes, remembering the awful ride to Mistra to tell Rachel that her son had gone.

There were footsteps on the staircase below. The door opened and Arcadius appeared, his face pomegranate. He gained the terrace and paused to catch his breath, his hand to his stomach.

'Well?' asked Matthew. 'Do we fight?'

Plethon appeared beside him. 'No, we surrender and Manuel fills his coffers. It can't have been a hard decision.'

Matthew swore and turned back to the view. He gestured to the square below. 'How will you explain that to *them*?'

Plethon had been asking himself the same question. If Luke had been loved by the citizens of Mistra, he was worshipped by those of Monemvasia. After all, he was one of them: born and raised in the little city at the edge of the sea. He had run through their streets once, become the hero who had saved their empire and been made protostrator as a result. He would never have contemplated surrender. He said: 'The Despot wants to know by what authority you removed the Varangians from the Hexamilion Wall.'

A servant had appeared and Matthew ordered water and wine for his guests. He led them over to a marble table in the middle of the terrace. He'd eaten fish with his father there the night before and they'd been mostly silent. He sat.

'By my own authority. The Varangian Company is not paid by Mistra and not needed at the wall now that Bedreddin's gone. When Venice comes, it will be by sea.'

Plethon drank a cup of water, then filled another. The trellis above them, thick with woven vine, was too high to shield them from the evening sun. He wiped his brow with a fold of his toga. 'Well, he told me to ask you, so I have.' He flung the cloth back over his shoulder. 'Now, as to Venice's offer, Theodore has been ordered by his father to accept it. A date has been set at the end of September for the ceremony. The Pope and Doge are coming. So is Manuel.'

Matthew had never really thought his emperor would decide differently but the speed was unexpected. 'They mean to get here before the gold,' he said. 'Why doesn't the Emperor wait for it? If it's in the quantity they say, it may be enough to repay the nobles *and* give Manuel money for his walls.'

'Because', replied Plethon, 'neither the Emperor nor the nobles believe the gold will ever get here. Venice and Egypt are likely to be watching Berbera, Basra, and anywhere else the gold is likely to go. They'll want to take it from us.'

The three of them sat without speaking, twisting their cups in their hands. The waning sunlight drew colour from the glass and cast it across the marble.

Arcadius looked at the other two. 'We can't let them do it,' he said quietly.

Plethon raised his hand. 'Arcadius –'

'No, hear me out, Plethon. What have you been telling us all these years? You've imagined a Peloponnese able to defend itself behind its wall at Corinth. You've imagined a society based on ancient Sparta. It would work.'

'Because *all* of the despotate would benefit from it,' said Plethon. 'Remember that I've also imagined a fair distribution of land among the people of Mistra. It's that the nobles don't like.'

'Which is why they spread rumours of your heresy. They're traitors, nothing less.'

Plethon rubbed his eyes. He was tired from his ride from Mistra, made without stopping. 'What you are proposing will lead to civil war,' he said. 'The poor against the rich. And the rich will have Venice on their side, the greatest power in the Middle Sea.'

Matthew said: 'We'll have my Varangians and every citizen who can carry a sword.' He paused. 'And we'll have Braccio.'

Plethon looked at him. 'Braccio da Montone?'

'He'll take credit.'

The terrace fell silent again. They heard the faint murmur of the crowd waiting for Plethon in the square below. He'd have to leave soon.

412

The philosopher rose, pulling the toga to his shoulder. He looked at them each in turn. 'I'm afraid that our conversation is probably treasonous. The Despot has no choice but to obey his father the Emperor, and you are oath-bound to obey too. He asks you to send your Varangians back to the wall.'

Matthew looked up at the man some saw as the greatest thinker of his age. He just looked old and tired. He didn't envy him his next task. 'What would Luke have done?' he asked quietly.

'He'd have obeyed,' said Plethon, turning. 'But he might have taken his time in doing it.'

In Venice, two weeks later, Zoe Mamonas was considering many of the same questions. She was in her apartment at the top of the Mamonas fondaco, which was small and expensively furnished, as would suit a rich, single banker of forty-three years.

She was lying on a couch, wearing a day-gown of silk and looking out of an open window on to the Grand Canal below. It had just stopped raining and a single shaft of sunlight fell directly on to the steaming roofs of the Rialto, making them shine like washed apples. The canal was as busy as ever, though the traffic had now paused at its edges. A funeral barge was making solemn progress down the middle with a flotilla of mourners behind. Everything about it was black: from the priest who stood at its bow to the rowers that pulled its oars. Only the flag at its stern had colour and Zoe was trying to see whether it was a Bembi, Loredan or Correr who was being rowed to his grave. She'd have to find out: there'd be legacies to invest.

She rose so that she could see the city better. With every week, more of its dark sagacity seemed to seep into her soul. She'd spent years in Samarcand and found its gaudy scale ridiculous.

Venice was where she should be, with its labyrinth of streets, buildings and squares hidden in ambush, its endless smell of comfortable decay. It was a city as elusive as its faith, as opaque as its lagoon, as slippery as its streets after rainfall.

She heard voices outside the room, voices she recognised, one of them loud. The door opened and Carlo Malatesta walked in with her slave Yusuf behind him.

'He did his best,' said the condottiere, throwing his hat on to a chair, 'but I'm difficult to stop.'

Yusuf was standing at the door with his arms raised, shaking his head.

Zoe pulled the edges of her gown together, tightening the belt. 'It's all right,' she said to the janissary. She turned to Malatesta. 'I would offer you wine, sir, but you appear to have had some. Would you like more?'

Carlo Malatesta sat on the couch she'd just left. He had his hands flat on his knees. 'Of course. Good wine too. The stuff in the tavern was piss.'

Zoe signalled to Yusuf who left, closing the door behind him.

Malatesta looked around the room. 'You like martyrdom?'

Zoe had bought the last Pope's paintings, the Pope who had never been pope, erased from history. St Catherine and all the other bloodied martyrs were enjoying their torture in her apartment now. It was why she preferred to receive guests downstairs.

Carlo rose unsteadily and walked to a cabinet, the smell of wet velvet following him. He opened its door. 'What are these?'

'They are eyeglasses from my factory on Murano,' she said. 'The different-coloured tassels denote their various strengths.'

Malatesta had put some on and was blinking at her. He burped and waved the smell away. 'You look better without them.'

Zoe remained silent. She'd never liked Carlo Malatesta,

finding him stupid and brutish in equal measure. She certainly didn't want him inspecting her apartment. It was filled with the story of her life: Tamerlane's chess board, his *Kama Sutra* arranged on its lectern, a jade bowl given to her by Suleyman. It raised too many questions she wasn't inclined to answer. Certainly not to this man.

Malatesta removed the glasses and tossed them to the couch. 'You'll want to know why the Prince of Rimini favours you with his visit.'

She said: 'I didn't know you were in Venice. Did you wish to discuss your deposits?'

Malatesta had much to be grateful to Zoe for. He'd removed his money from the Magoris Bank before the Pope's fall, and he'd be enriched by his share in the plunder of Mistra since he was to lead Venice's army. 'Will Magoris's gold get to Mistra?' he asked.

Zoe paused. How much should she tell this man? She decided. 'The Mamluk Sultan has sent a fleet down the Red Sea to intercept it. If it ever reaches Basra, every road west will be watched by Venice's agents. We will stop it.' She looked at the man. He'd not come to talk about the gold. 'What else did you want to discuss?'

Carlo was silent for a while. He said: 'I thought you might like to congratulate me,' he said. 'Over Bedreddin.'

Bedreddin?

Of course. Venice had sent its generalissimo to Bedreddin to refuse his request for ships to cross the straits. It had been thought sensible that someone not native to Venice should go.

'It was neatly done,' conceded Zoe, dipping her head. 'You suggested he go to Egypt to ask the Mamluk Sultan for ships, then arranged for him to be arrested. Has his army dispersed?'

'Like the snow in May. Like your servant. Where's the wine?'

Yusuf had entered unheard. He set down a pitcher and full glass on the table beside the couch. He hesitated, waiting for Zoe's eye. He got it and left.

Carlo picked up the glass and turned it, closing one eye. It was a tulip ribbed with gold leaf and he had not seen anything so fine before. He drank the wine in three gulps and stretched his arm towards the light to admire it empty. He put down the glass and poured more, then sat on the couch and patted the place beside him. 'Why don't you sit?'

Zoe remained standing. 'What did you want to talk to me about?'

Carlo summoned a frown from the rucked black of his doublet. He leant back on the couch, his arm across its back. 'You'd fuck an emperor but not a common condottiere. Is that accurate?'

Zoe walked to the door and put her hand on its handle.

He raised his hand. 'Don't.'

The door stayed shut. She waited.

'I've come to talk about Giovanni Giustiniani Longo,' he said. 'Whom you nearly killed in Constance.'

'With your help.'

Zoe was silent. She was looking at the ceiling with no expression on her face. 'I didn't expect you to nearly kill him.'

Malatesta shrugged. 'He humiliated the house of Malatesta and it had to be answered. Now, he's done it again. When we get to Mistra, I want him delivered to me.'

'So you can do what you failed to do in Constance? No.'

Zoe watched him from the door, one hand on its handle, the other holding the neckline of her robe together above her breasts. Why did it matter to her if he killed Giovanni? It just did.

416

Luke is dead. Not Giovanni too.

Carlo Malatesta had moved to the window. He unbuttoned the top of his doublet, lifting his face to whatever breeze the canal might provide. He closed his eyes. 'The Pope will want it too,' he said. 'Cleope is Pope Martin's niece and was once useful.'

'By which you mean she's unmarriagable now?'

Carlo turned to her, an eyebrow poised. 'Oh, she's still marriageable, just less so. Once the boy's dead, she'll marry where she's told. Come here.'

Zoe didn't move.

He sighed, his eyes closed. 'If you want Giovanni to live, come here.'

Zoe walked slowly over to him, holding the gown tight to her. As she came near, she smelt the wine all around him. She stood at the window and looked out while he went to the table and poured wine. When he came back, he stood behind her so that he was looking over her shoulder.

'Giovanni can either be killed or imprisoned in Rimini,' he said. 'It's up to you.'

Zoe didn't answer. Her disgust was overwhelming. She wanted him outside her house, outside her city. She began to move but his hands were on her hips. She felt his beard on her shoulder. She said: 'There are guards in the house. One shout.'

'Which you'll not make,' he said, his voice unsteady, 'because you would like Giovanni to stay alive.' She pulled her head away as his lips brushed her neck. The smell of wine was making her nauseous. She felt him press himself against her back, moving his hardness from side to side.

'I think', he said, forcing his hand under the silk to her breast, his lips moving to her ear, 'that I'd like you to play the whore, Zoe. Which is what you are.'

417

His hand went to the back of her neck and he forced her head down to the window frame. She felt her gown being pulled up, then held while buttons were undone behind. She felt sick.

'I want you to imagine I'm Tamerlane,' he said.

CHAPTER THIRTY-FOUR

AFRICAN COAST, SUMMER 1418

Nikolas and Admiral Zheng stood on the high stern deck of the treasure ship and watched a surf boat lurch over the breakers towards them, speculating as to whether it held baskets of pepper or something more valuable.

For two weeks, they had sat at anchor watching an African coastline very different from the one at Berbera. Beyond the breakers were estuary swamps covered in mangrove forest, roots reaching for air above brackish water, white-plumed egrets and wading birds grubbing between. Steam rose from the jungle to meet a low, oppressive sky and the air was full of insects that slid in men's sweat, then bit. The admiral had ordered braziers lit but still the mosquitoes came and the ship's doctors had searched the diadan for the treatment of fever.

Throughout the restless days and nights they had heard the sound of the drums. They had come from deep in the jungle and their beat had been slow and fast, faint and loud, never silent. Their throb had been the constant background to their conversation, then their sleep. They had been the reminder that, at every moment, they were being watched.

The boat disappeared from view and they felt the faint bump

of it coming alongside. They leant over the side and saw a tall black man sitting at the stern who looked different from those that had come out to sell them fruit. He wore the thoub of the Muslim and a white *taqiya* skullcap on his head. He was smiling at something they couldn't see. They watched him rise and walk towards the front of the boat, his arm held by an oarsman.

Nikolas straightened up and took a deep breath. He walked across to the steps to the deck below, feeling sick with apprehension. His hands stuck to the rail as he descended. On the main deck were gathered other passengers who'd made the journey round the southernmost tip of Africa: scholars, soldiers, concubines. He heard footsteps behind him and felt the big hand of the admiral on his shoulder.

The admiral squeezed. 'Let us hope,' he murmured.

The first thing Nikolas saw emerge above the ship's side was a straw hat, battered and frayed. Next came hair and a face he knew. He stepped forward to help the man on to the deck.

'Luke Magoris,' he said, his voice hollow with relief, 'you are late but most welcome.'

If Luke was late to the coast, then N'gara shared some of the blame. What had begun as journey had turned into odyssey; what had started as friendship had ended as love.

Months ago, they'd started at the place of silent trade, first taking the gold upstream by the Joliba River. Then, with eight hundred porters, they had carried it across bush and rolling savanna to another river, hauling it two hundred miles through fields of sorghum, millet and ground nuts, watched by bushbuck, warthog and mambas in the tall grass. They had passed villages behind thorn walls, been stared at by boys herding goats and shamans hung with clattering charms with straw at their ankles.

They walked side by side, their strides one to everyone else's two. They rested under the shade of forests of silk cotton and acacia. At every opportunity, they talked and Luke had discovered a man born to the wilderness but shaped by the city of Timbuktu, a man who had fused the certainties of the wild to the subtler study of Islam. He found a man more noble than any he'd met before.

Early on they talked of N'gara's clan, a people so rich in gold they were immune to its influence.

'The trade is secret to protect not just the mines, but ourselves as well,' N'gara had said. 'We have seen how it changes people. Salt we value because it preserves. But gold just destroys. Be sure it does not destroy you.'

Sometimes they talked of the future.

'Men from the north will come in their ships,' N'gara said once. 'They'll torture us for the secret of the gold but won't find it, so they'll go west. Our men will go with them, but as slaves.'

And sometimes, when it was night and the great stillness of Africa was all around them, they had sat beside a fire and talked of Anna and Shulen and an impossible choice.

'They are both you, Luke,' he'd said softly, his deep voice part of the night. 'They are your sun and moon, your light and shade. They will decide, not you. But you know this. It is why you sent Shulen to Mistra.'

And Luke had pondered this. Was that what he'd done?

They'd visited N'gara's home. It was in the land between the two rivers, a village set among the savannah grass. They came in the evening, leaving the caravan somewhere else, entering a circle of huts with a giant baobab tree at its centre. When the

421

moon rose, the men had brought out a cauldron and filled it with water from the tree, then stood around it.

N'gara had said to Luke: 'Bring your sword.'

And so he joined another brotherhood. When the moon was over the baobab tree, poised above its infinite branches, its reflection perfectly clasped within the rim of the cauldron, he had held out his arm and cut it with his dragon sword. He had seen his blood drip into the water and settle among the mountains of the moon, mingling with the blood of others. A blood pact.

N'gara had turned to him then, his obsidian grace the very matter of this spare and beautiful land, and he had said words that would change Luke's life.

Only you will we trade with from now. Only the Lion, or those he sends to us.

Afterwards, they had put the gold in boats and begun their long journey down the Senagana River to the coast, watched every inch of the way by lizards fifteen feet long, by tree geckos and always the Wangara, drumming their message down a thousand miles of water to the sea. They passed the green, dripping tunnels of choked and mysterious creeks, paddled to the chatter and screams of baboons and colobus monkeys, the singing, croaking, rustling life of the forest on either side. At night, they had been buzzed by the leafy membranes of fruit bats and woken by the shrill of cicadas and bullfrogs, the cries of night birds and the sudden swish of broken water.

Nearing the coast, they had come to falls and carried the boats past them to wider stretches of river where elephants bathed in the shallows between the backs and snouts of water horses while crocodiles lay still as logs on the muddy banks.

They had arrived at the swampy mouth of the river, cumbered by shoals and mudflats and a tidal stream of two knots on the ebb, the water suddenly filled with the traffic of green sea turtles, bottlenose dolphins and monk seals, the sky clustered with birds: giant fish eagles above darting snipe, pelicans, spoonbills, yellow-billed storks and bee-eaters.

Other boats had joined them then, pulling out from the shore with drums at their prows, shouting and waving. They had been expecting the boats for days; their children hadn't slept for the excitement.

Now Luke was confronted by an older kinship. He and Nikolas embraced each other, their knuckles white in the clutch. They pulled back and laughed and embraced again and kissed and ran their fingers through the other's hair. They'd not seen each other since Abyssinia and made journeys no white men had ever travelled. It was a miracle they were there together, alive.

Admiral Zheng watched with approval, wishing his countrymen would display such affection. He took Luke's hand. 'You are thin.'

Luke looked down at his filthy clothes, then turned to the tall black man behind him. 'Nikolas, Admiral Zheng, may I present to you the man who has saved me, and possibly Mistra. This is N'gara.'

That night, Luke was almost sick from the food. It was partly the snipe and turtle soup and roasted warthog dressed with mango, partly the speed of his eating. Never had food been welcomed to his belly in such haste. The only thing that gave him pause was the conversation. First he asked about their voyage around the southernmost tip of Africa.

'I had to come myself,' said Admiral Zheng, 'since I was the only man to have done it before.'

Luke smiled. 'And the Portuguese still wonder if it can be done at all. Did you have storms?'

'Some,' replied Zheng, 'but the ship rode them well. Its size makes it difficult to sink.' He lifted the bowl and poured soup into his mouth, blinking through the steam. He wiped his lips with his sleeve.

Luke tasted his own. 'Did the qilin leave as planned?'

'Qilins,' corrected the admiral.

'Zhu Chou took more than one?'

He nodded. 'To be safe, in case one died. They'll be with the Emperor by now.'

Nikolas said: 'And with this proof of heaven's mandate, we may expect more gold.' He paused and looked down. 'That is, if they made it.'

Luke glanced at his friend. He'd be missing Zhu Chou. He said: 'It was her maps from the diadan that made me decide.'

'To go west with the gold?'

Luke nodded. 'They showed the Senagana River.'

'And you thought the way east would be too difficult?'

'I didn't trust al-Tabingha from the start,' Luke replied. 'I knew he'd somehow get word back to Cairo, and from there it would get to Venice.'

He told them then of what had happened at Timbuktu and at the silent trade. 'The worst were the snakes. They weren't poisonous but they bit.' Luke rolled up his sleeve. 'Look.'

N'gara spoke then. 'We gave him a drug that would keep him still. Al-Tabingha was fooled.'

Nikolas looked at Luke. 'But how did you know you'd be

allowed to go west? You'd not have known you would save Timbuktu or meet N'gara.'

Luke drank wine. 'I didn't. But the diadan map told me the gold had always come to Timbuktu from the west. The Carthaginians had written about it. I thought I would find a way using the river.' He paused and turned to N'gara. 'Meeting this man was good fortune.'

Luke put his hand on N'gara's arm and kept it there. The Wangara chief had been by his side every mile of the way from Timbuktu and he loved him as well as he did his Varangian brothers. Their blood had mingled.

N'gara rose. He bowed, his hand to his heart. 'It is time for me to leave. There is a boat waiting for me.'

Luke rose as well and took N'gara from the cabin. Outside, the moon washed the decks white and grey and the crew moved between its shadows like ghosts. The murmur of their conversation, the gentle slap of water below, the creak of wood: all were strange to him after the fetid frenzy of the forest. He looked over to the shore. 'The drums have stopped.'

He'd only just noticed. For months the incessant throb of the drums had told them they were watched and protected. Now they'd gone.

N'gara turned to the coast and his hair became silver fleece. His voice was deep and quiet and tired. 'The last message has been sent back to Timbuktu: we have arrived and are safe.'

Luke nodded. 'And the gold will be loaded tomorrow. We will be gone by sunset.' He embraced the chief. 'My world will be empty without you, N'gara.'

They stayed like that for a while, neither of them speaking. Then N'gara gently pulled away, turned and walked to the side

425

of the ship. His body, then his head disappeared. He didn't say goodbye.

The treasure ship left before sunset the next day, its giant sails turned to catch every meagre gust of wind from the south-west, bamboo plaits screeching to the effort of gathering momentum. The sun had fallen to the horizon like something speared, its blood turning the ocean red. Monstrous oars, each worked by twenty men, had sprung from the ship's sides like legs, to help it on its way. The crouching dragon at its prow dipped and rose in the swell, its fire quenched and relit, then quenched again.

Luke saw the coastline draw away and disappear into night. Somewhere on it, N'gara would be watching him sail away. Soon he smelt salt in place of rotting mangrove and turned to the vast ocean before them, filling his lungs with its infinite air. Admiral Zheng stood on one side of him, Nikolas on the other, and beneath their feet was more gold than any ship had ever carried.

Luke said: 'It is now August. We have four months to reach Mistra before the Doge's truce runs out. We may not be a caravel, but that should be enough.'

Admiral Zheng leant forward over the rail, watching the oars being shipped as wind filled the sails. 'We might not have the speed but we have the size. And you'd miss our cannon on a caravel,' he said, straightening up. 'We are impregnable.'

It seemed likely. And, because of Benedo Barbi, the world would be watching to the east.

Nikolas said: 'All those empty boxes. What a waste. Will Barbi stay with them to Berbera?'

'No,' replied Luke. 'He's gone north to Cairo with a message for the Mamluk Sultan. He should be there by now.'

'And Shulen? Where will she be now?'

Luke thought about Shulen, of a memory so vivid that it had filled whole days of his journey west. His deception had been very great and she wouldn't have forgiven him. Had it been necessary? Yes, because N'gara had insisted she leave for Timbuktu thinking him dead, otherwise she might stay and be seen by the Wangara. They had agreed it between them as they had sat at the end of the raft late at night, whispering the plan into existence. She would only have learnt the truth later, reading Luke's will.

He watched the crescent of red sink into the sea, then turned to Nikolas. 'She will be in Mistra soon,' he said quietly, 'where she will not be welcome.'

A week later, the treasure ship creaked its way round Cape Bojador, beyond which no Portuguese caravel had yet ventured. The wind remained favourable and the sails, taut as drums, hardly turned on their nine masts. Admiral Zheng set his compass fast and let the coastline fade into nothing.

So it was with some surprise that he awoke one afternoon to be told that a sail had been seen to the north. He came on to the deck to find Nikolas and Luke already there, both shading their eyes from the sun.

'It's a caravel,' said Luke. 'It's further south than I thought they'd been. Can we signal?'

Admiral Zheng joined them at the rail. 'We can send a pigeon. There will be someone who speaks Portuguese on board.'

The man was sent for and Luke wrote the message to be translated. Soon the bird was in the air.

An hour later, the caravel was alongside, the top of its mast little higher than the deck on which Luke stood. Two Portuguese sailors sat on the spar furling the sail, their mouths open in wonder at the leviathan now joined to their ship.

The caravel's captain was named Dias, a man of weathered face and small eyes lost beneath a heavy brow. He had watched something he thought to be an island become a ship bigger than any he'd imagined. Now he was sitting in its admiral's cabin, a room as big as his ship. Around him were Luke, Nikolas, Admiral Zheng, and a man he was astonished to find could speak his language. He didn't need him.

'Where have you come from?' he asked in Greek.

'We have come up from Cape Bojador,' replied Luke.

'You came round Africa?'

'We came from China to the Red Sea, then crossed to the Nile by canal. We sailed west along the top of Africa, then south to find a way home. We did not find it. Now we go back the way we have come.'

The Portuguese captain frowned. It was not the answer he'd wanted to hear. He took a fig from the bowl before him and turned to Luke. He spoke. 'Which country do you come from?'

Luke answered.

Dias's eyes opened enough to reveal themselves. 'Mistra? Then you'll soon be part of Venice. Did you know that your country's been sold?'

CHAPTER THIRTY-FIVE

VENICE, SUMMER 1418

The play was a version of Helen of Troy, with Cleope for Helen. On the stage were little camels joined head to tail, the children stooped beneath cushion-humps, gold bars knocking their hessian sides. Luke was a man on stilts: Varangian, fair and impossibly tall. His coal-black murderer chased him with snakes and a ladder. How they laughed.

Zoe had stopped to watch. Where was Carlo? Ah, there. Menelaus. Of course.

She'd never hated any man as much as the one who'd raped her against the open window of her apartment. She'd washed and rewashed every part of herself since, but his hot wine-breath wouldn't leave her neck, and the imprint of his clammy palms stayed on her breasts. She'd been used by many men in many ways but this usage was different. Somehow, somewhere, some day, she would find the means to hurt him very badly. But not now.

She watched the play surge to its riotous climax with clash of cymbal and bang of gong. Venice had come to Troy and delivered Helen back to Menelaus. Luke lay dead beside his stilts, Giovanni caged. The double-headed eagle of the Palaiologoi was trampled underfoot and the gold was where it should be: beneath the arse of a saintly doge. Some of the audience laughed so much they'd stay for the next performance.

She turned from the stage and resumed her walk across the piazza. It was not easy. The square was even more crowded than at La Senza, people of every dress and colour, Moors to Norsemen, pressed around stalls or standing between the pillars at the waterfront to watch the fleet assemble. In a week it would carry Pope and Doge south to admit another jewel into La Serenissima's diadem. It would be their most fabulous armada yet.

She looked up at the face of St Mark's Cathedral, at the four bronze horses that had once looked out over the hippodrome at Constantinople. Only yesterday she had walked beneath them to hear mass and witness the blessing of the many servants of Venice who would take possession of her birthplace in six weeks' time.

She approached the Doge's palace to find a queue formed at its gate: young noblemen waiting to hear if they would be part of the expedition. She saw that many had ribbons pinned to their doublets, the colours of Cleope of Rimini, their pledge to bring Helen of Troy home.

She entered the gate and mounted the staircase, passing monks with scrolls under their arms. She found the Doge in a room full of tables with paper on them.

'So many monks.'

The Doge looked up. 'They do the maps and the lists. Our quartermasters rely on them.'

Mocenigo was seated at a table with the plan of a port in front of him. Zoe came to stand behind him.

'Modone,' he said, 'where we'll land. It's four days' march to Mistra.'

Zoe put her hand on the old man's shoulder. 'March? Do we take an army with us? I thought they'd surrendered.'

'Two thousand only. The young knights demand it and they say the Maniots may take time to subdue. They're wild down there.'

Zoe had never been to the Mani Peninsula, her father warning her that it was full of pirates. It was the very end of Europe, the last place to run when you'd run from everywhere else. It was mountainous land with no water where nothing grew. No wonder its people took to the sea.

Mocenigo said: 'The Prince of Rimini has asked that you accompany him in his galley.'

'No.'

The Doge looked up, surprised. 'No? It is an honour.'

Zoe recovered herself. 'Of course. Let me consider. What is this?'

The Doge leant across to the map she was pointing to, pulling it to him. 'You should check this. It is the record of the Mamonas estates that will be restored to you.'

Zoe cast her eyes over the map. Different coloured inks had been used to show the buildings, the vineyards, the olive groves, the stud. The vineyards covered most of the land from Monemvasia to Geraki. She could almost taste their grape.

'What about the Laskaris Palace at Mistra?' she asked. 'Is that not forfeit too?'

The Doge frowned. 'You'd deny his wife a home?'

Zoe turned her cold eyes to his. 'As she denied me mine.'

Mocenigo chose another subject. 'Malatesta tells me you've agreed that Giovanni Giustiniani Longo should be brought back to Rimini. He has a cage for the purpose.'

Zoe looked away. She could hide most things, but perhaps

431

not this anger. 'A cage seems excessive,' she said carefully. 'Do we wish to make such an enemy of Chios? We buy its mastic.'

Mocenigo said: 'The Malatestas have cause to seek punishment; they've been publicly humiliated. And Rimini is more important to us than Chios.'

The Doge rose, put on his hat, took her arm, and led her to the window and out on to its balcony. The morning sun shone down on St Mark's Basin, washing every kind of craft with its hard and even light. From the mouth of the Grand Canal to the gates of the Arsenale were lighters and skiffs and *barchette* moving to and fro across the water to provision the great galleys that rode out at anchor. It was a ferment of colour and noise and the Doge leant on his balcony and admired it in silence. Then he pointed. 'You see the one with the black awning on its stern deck? That's for the Pope. He arrives tomorrow.'

Zoe had heard. She was to attend the banquet to be held in his honour. Seventeen courses, they said, but no wine. She turned to the Doge. 'You asked to see me.'

Mocenigo straightened up. 'I have news from Cairo. Al-Tabingha reports seeing the Genoese engineer there.'

Zoe stared at him. 'Benedo Barbi?'

The Doge nodded. 'He was granted an audience with the Sultan. He doesn't know what about.'

Zoe turned her back to the lagoon and leant against the stone palisade, her hand to her lips. The sun was on her neck but she had no sense of it. Barbi should be in Berbera. Or at the bottom of the Red Sea. 'Was he sure?'

'He was certain. And he had no caravan with him, just one camel carrying a single box.'

Zoe tapped her lips with her fingers.

Mocenigo had moved beside her. He said: 'There's more.

432

We've had word from the Mamluk fleet sent down the Red Sea. There were no Chinese junks at Berbera.'

Zoe arranged these facts for inspection in her mind. They were not where they should be and would need to be looked at from a new perspective. She did it all in silence. The Doge watched and waited.

At last she said: 'Barbi must have sent the caravan north. He must have waited until they were out of Songhai lands and out of danger, then sent it north. He knew al-Tabingha would no longer be watching.'

The Doge nodded slowly. 'And meanwhile he himself went to Cairo? Why?'

Zoe glanced at the old man. It occurred to her that he was brave and shrewd but not very clever. Wasn't it obvious? 'The Ark never went by junk from Berbera. Barbi has brought it up to Cairo instead.' She paused. 'That's what was in the box.'

Mocenigo dipped his head again. 'But where has the gold been taken to?'

Zoe shrugged. 'There are a dozen ports it could have gone to outside the Mamluks' domains. And most of the emirs and kings of the Maghreb will be allied to Timbuktu. The gold will be safe until it reaches water.'

'Which is where we can intercept it. But our ships are watching the east.'

'So you need to send them west. What is available?'

The Doge pulled at his beard. 'The nearest ships would be at Negroponte.'

It hurt him to mention the place. Luke's fireship had struck more than the ships there. It had dealt a blow to Venice's pride that still ached to the touch. It was the biggest calamity the republic had suffered since losing Choggia.

433

'So send the fleet from there to watch the Maghreb. Stop anything that leaves it.'

Mocenigo considered this. 'And if something gets through?'

'Then it will land somewhere on the coast of Mistra. Does Negroponte have a garrison?'

The Doge nodded.

'It must be sent out to watch every part of that coastline.'

She was speaking quickly, but there was something more. 'Alexandria,' she said. 'The engineer will try and bring the Ark from there to Mistra. You've alerted the bailo, I suppose?'

'Of course. He will be stopped.'

Zoe straightened up and turned back to the view. A new galley was being towed through the gates of the Arsenale, its rigging beribboned. The *arsenalotti* were crowding the ramparts above, waving their helmets in the air. Women stood beside them throwing flowers and ribbons down to its deck. In a week, the shipyards would be empty and every galley would be rowing its way to Mistra, with a pope to protect them from storms. And Zoe would be with them.

Going home.

The caravel was making good progress. With the coastline of Africa never far from view, it was bent low before a south-westerly, its lateen sail puffed out as hard as a condottiere's breastplate, pennants above snapped straight as the wake behind it.

Captain Dias was at the prow watching for whales. In the hold beneath his feet was a small part of the gold Luke had brought out of Africa. It was half of what he would get if they reached Mistra in time. Beside him stood the man who had bribed him.

'Could we capsize?' shouted Luke. He had one hand up against the spray, the other clamped to the ship's side. The boat was rising and falling as it cleaved its way through the swell, each slap of wave a little earthquake.

'We would explode!' yelled the Portuguese. 'That's why I watch!'

Luke ducked to avoid another drenching. He had been aboard the caravel for three days now and seldom been dry. The news that Mistra had been sold had struck him hard. Dias had not known much; just that the despotate would be handed to Venice at the end of September: in six weeks' time. Luke had made his offer immediately, going below decks to bring up gold to show him. Dias had agreed and Luke had gone to Nikolas to explain.

'Can you trust him?' his friend had asked.

Luke had shrugged. 'What choice do I have? We'll not reach Mistra in time in this junk.'

And Nikolas had hugged him hard in the farewell. 'Be careful,' he'd said.

It was only after they had set sail that Luke had discovered the caravel's cargo. He had gone below to sleep among the crew, peering into the gloom to find some space to spread his mat. He had heard groans from the back of the ship and felt his way towards them. Then he heard the clink of chain.

He had found Dias in his cabin, drinking.

'Of course they're slaves!' the captain had shouted. 'Why else would we be on this cursed coast? We'll drop them at Ceuta after we've got through the Gibraltar Straits.'

'But you said we'd sail directly to Mistra.'

'They'll not last that long. We've lost three already. Would you have more die? Anyway, we'll need to take on water.'

That night Luke had beaten a man senseless. He had woken

to the sounds of violence and seen through the first strands of dawn a woman slave being raped, her body pinned. He scrambled over to find her gagged as well as chained, her eyes white with fear. He almost killed the man.

From then on he slept in Dias's cabin, his mat next to the captain's hammock, knowing he would not survive long among the crew. One morning, the slave he had saved had been found dead. She had struck her head against a beam until the wood had reached her brain. Her body was thrown to the sharks.

The days had passed, the sea unfurling like an unending carpet, foam at its curve, flying fish skimming its surface like pebbles. More slaves died and were tossed over the side and mass was heard on Sunday by all the crew, a crude statue of the Virgin brought from Dias's cabin. The slaves had been hauled on deck to kneel, then splashed with water and made to dance in their chains. Luke had stayed at the prow, watching for whales amidst the spray, hating himself more than the crew.

Now he was there again with Dias, wanting to talk about more than whales. He asked: 'When do we reach Ceuta?'

'Two weeks at most with this wind.'

'And how long will we stay there?'

Dias wiped spray from his eyes. His fingers were corded with rings, mainly gold. 'No more than a day,' he said. He turned to Luke and there was more gold in his teeth. 'Then no slaves! You can sleep easy, my friend.' He paused. 'You've not told me your name.'

Luke hadn't for good reason. The less Dias knew about him the better. He said: 'I am a merchant anxious to get back to my home before Venice gets there. I do not want to be disadvantaged.'

The captain nodded, not much interested. 'And you'll have the rest of the gold ready in Mistra?'

436

'If we get there in time, you'll get your gold. I promise.'

Dias glanced back to the ship, then up at the sail, the red cross stitched to its front. 'You went up the River of Gold, didn't you?'

Luke looked ahead. 'The Chinese carry their own gold. That junk wouldn't get far up any river.'

Dias shook his head. 'I don't believe you. We know about the river.'

Luke thought about the Christian map he'd seen, that everyone had seen. It had the Senagana in the wrong place and Mensa Musa at the end of it, holding a nugget. How many dreams had taken flight from that map? He shrugged. 'You must believe what you like.'

Later, lying on his back beside the snoring Dias, watching a moonstruck sea rise and fall through the window, he thought of Shulen. Usually when he thought of her, he thought of a night of joy and sadness, a night of fear and longing expressed in fevered coupling. Now he thought of her anger.

She'd have thought him dead until she'd read the will and her rage would have been very terrible. But she'd have done what he asked: deliver the instruction to Barbi and go north herself as fast as possible. But what then?

There had been an alternative put forward in the will, one that should be enacted if the gold never got to Mistra. Would she have followed it?

CHAPTER THIRTY-SIX

MONEMVASIA, AUTUMN 1418

Shulen was one of three sons of Abu Kabul and, at that moment, the one that most smelt of dates. She was dressed identically to her brothers in white thoub and patterned headscarf, but had added charcoal to her chin to match their stubble. She'd sailed with them in their father's dhow from Africa before a steady wind, their only pause the one they'd just endured. A line of Venetian galleys was stopping everything entering the Monemvasia roads to search their cargoes for cannon. On Abu Kabul's dhow they'd found only sacks of palm dates and a boy asleep on top of them, his headscarf pulled down against the light. They'd not thought to wake him.

Now Shulen was staring up at a place she'd only seen in her dreams. The Goulas was as impressive as Luke had described it, a giant anvil of rock washed amber by the evening sun. She saw the muddle of tiny houses embraced by the walls of the lower town; she saw the zigzag steps up to the towers and domes of the palaces and churches above. She had come at last to Monemvasia: city on the edge of the world.

Where you were born.

She saw swimmers in the sea before the walls, boys hurling

sponges at one another: jumping, diving, ducking, throwing back their heads to laugh beneath clouds of spray, loving the weightless freedom of the Mirtoon Sea. Their sea. His sea.

She looked back to the walls. There were men all along them, carrying and shaping stone, fitting it into place. There were braziers with irons in them. The city's defences were being made stronger and it was happening in a hurry. She wondered if Matthew was there somewhere.

The dhow had passed the city now and was turning in towards its port. A bridge appeared in front of them with towers at either end and warehouses behind. The smell of the tanning yard came to her across the water with the smell of fish. There were wagons lined up on the quayside being filled with what might keep a population fed under siege.

She heard a cannon fired behind her and turned to see smoke above a Venetian galley, perhaps a warning to a round ship objecting to being searched. The smoke drifted back so that only its mast and oars could be seen. Abu Kabul said something; he was pointing to a vacant berth.

They pulled themselves into it and Shulen jumped to the quay with a bundle in one hand. She turned and waved to the three men, one hand to her heart. She had said goodbye earlier.

She walked up the road to the city, the rolled cloth that held Luke's sword clutched to her side. It was busy with wagons going to or from the city gate, empty or full. At the gate she saw piles of produce waiting to be taken into the city's warehouses. She went under the arch and into the maze Luke had described to her. The main street was hardly wider than two men abreast and the alleys that joined it were steep and stepped. It was a place of endless brush and touch, of proximity and forced intimacy. It was more crowded than anywhere she'd been and she held the sword close to her front.

She turned up some steps that might lead to the Goulas. The way was less crowded and the view, as she rose, exhilarating. The sea below was a sieve, the necklace of Venetian galleys its filter. Ships were bunched outside it, waiting to be let through, one by one. She sat on the wall.

She had seen Samarcand and Bokhara, Tabriz and Edirne: giant cities of giant empires. Next to them, Monemvasia was little more than a village, yet, to a man faraway, it had inspired an idea larger than them all combined. It had taken a fever in Timbuktu to understand the towering goodness of it.

She rose from the wall and picked up the bundle. Above lay Luke's palace, which had once been Zoe's, that might be Zoe's yet. And sixty miles to the west lay another home with a wife and son in it. She began to climb, the familiar dread stealing up to walk beside her. She would have to go there. With the sword.

At the top, she came to a square full of men, most of them bare to the waist. The walls of the upper town were being mended too and piles of stone were waiting to take their place. A trestle table stood in the middle with two men bent over it, their naked backs to her. She watched them for a while, seeing their easy conversation, the touch of their arms.

She called: 'Matthew, Arcadius.'

They looked at each other, then turned. The shock of seeing them almost made her cry out. They were gaunt, thinner than she'd ever seen them, their eyes empty of laughter as they'd never been. She left the bundle on the wall and walked over to them.

'He's not dead,' she said quietly, taking their hands, holding them tight in hers. 'He's not dead.'

They kept her at arm's length, not daring to believe what they'd heard. There was fear in their eyes, fear of a chasm they were just learning to leave behind them. She looked around her. There was no one within earshot. She said again, more forcefully: 'Luke lives. It was all the plan.' She paused, seeing something new in their look. 'Yes, you'll be as angry as I was, angrier perhaps. But it's true.'

Later, they sat on the terrace of Luke's palace. The sun had just left the day, leaving behind a halo and, beyond, a band of violet. The moon was up and barely visible among the first of the stars. The place where they sat, beneath vines, was full of shadow and the whisper of evening breeze. The air smelt of jasmine.

They had not seen Shulen for eleven years and couldn't believe they were seeing her now. She had changed little: the smooth curve of her face still unlined, the long veil of her hair, tied up to pass as the son of Abu Kabul, now let down to her waist. She was as mysterious as when they had first met her in Kütahya, but now they loved her mystery. She was the sister in their brotherhood and they held her hands across the table.

They had just been told of what happened in Timbuktu.

'He was lucky to have you there,' said Matthew quietly. 'He'd have died otherwise. You saved his life.'

'And Barbi saved us all with his exploding dykes.' She smiled, remembering. 'You should have seen them.'

'I wish we had,' said Arcadius, turning her hand and looking at it. It had the slender fingers of touch and healing. 'Our lives have been dull; waiting for attacks that never came.'

'Until now.'

'Until now.' He shook his head and drank. 'And now that it's going to be far from dull, where is he? Cruising on a Chinese junk too slow to get here in time. We'll all be Venetian by the time he arrives.' He paused. 'One thing I still don't understand. When did he come up with the plan to get gold from Timbuktu?'

'When he realised that the Chinese gold would not get to Mistra in time. He persuaded King Yeshaq to give him salt as his price for reopening the trade route to Timbuktu. He knew Mali needed salt because the Songhai had taken its mines.'

Arcadius was nodding into his cup, turning it by its stem. He looked up. 'And he rescued this chief . . .'

'N'gara, who agreed to take him west to the coast, leaving Barbi to go east with empty boxes.'

'So when did Luke tell Nikolas to leave Berbera and sail round Africa to meet him?'

'When they parted in Axum.' Shulen waved away a moth.

'And neither you nor Barbi knew of it until you opened his will. Why didn't he tell you?'

Shulen frowned. 'He must have felt that the fewer people who knew . . .' She let the sentence fade back into silence.

Arcadius glanced at Matthew. He said: 'Tell us about Nikolas. Is he all merchant now?'

'He is a merchant in love.' She smiled. 'He loves a concubine from the Ming Emperor's harem. She came with us.'

Matthew laughed. 'Nikolas in love! Has it changed him?'

Shulen thought for a while. Had love changed Nikolas? She saw him suddenly, huddled over the diadan with Zhu Chou. 'He is more serious,' she said. 'And he wears glasses.'

Matthew poured wine into a cup and got to his feet. 'Well, I suppose we should toast them both.' He raised his cup and waited for Arcadius and Shulen to stand. He faced each in turn.

'To Nikolas in love and to the most secretive, conniving bastard alive.' He drank. 'Thank God he's alive.'

They drank and sat and were silent for some time. Shulen looked out at the city below. 'You don't seem to be giving in very easily. You're preparing for a siege.'

'We're taking no chances, that's all,' said Matthew. 'The kingdom is set to ignite. Any spark could do it, especially here.'

Shulen waited for more.

'The two cities have always been wary of each other,' said Arcadius. 'Now it's worse. Mistra is full of nobles from Constantinople and Monemvasia full of the people who grew up with Luke.'

Shulen pondered this. 'What about the army?'

'The army is mainly Albanian, two thousand at most. They've been bribed by Venice and withdrawn from the wall to keep order in Mistra.'

'And your Varangians?'

'Are here,' said Matthew. 'I'm taking my time to obey the order to return them to the wall.'

Shulen nodded. She could see how the stage was set for civil war: nobles, army and Venice against the people. She didn't see how the people could win. She said quietly: 'You know that Luke would not want war, don't you?'

Matthew glanced at her. 'Did he say so?'

'Well, no. But you know him better than I do. He'd not want Mistra torn apart.'

Matthew shrugged. 'I'm not sure we could stop it, Shulen, even if we wanted to. The people are very angry.'

'But you needn't encourage it. Keeping your Varangians in Monemvasia does so. Preparing your city for siege does so. You must see that.'

443

The two men traded glances. They'd discussed it many times. 'It might just buy us time,' Arcadius said quietly. 'A lot could happen.'

They fell silent again. Servants appeared with food and more wine and they waited while it was served. Shulen looked at the door through which they had left.

'No one,' she said softly, 'no one at all must know that Luke is alive. He was very clear on that.'

Matthew nodded as he broke bread. 'What about Anna?'

Shulen looked at the *garon* in front of her, her bread poised above it. Dread had entered the room to sit beside her. She said: 'I will go to Mistra.'

Matthew frowned. 'To see her? Is that wise?' He glanced again at his friend. 'They won't let you see her alone anyway,' he said.

'I have to hand over his sword and his will,' she said. 'No one in Mistra must suspect he is still alive if we are to stand any chance of saving it from Venice.'

Arcadius leant forward. 'But you said it yourself, Shulen. It's too late.'

'Perhaps,' she replied. 'I must still go.'

'Then I'll go with you,' said Matthew.

'No you won't. I want to be discreet and you've often told me how safe these roads are.' Shulen took his hand, then Arcadius's. 'You'll wish me luck and stay here, where you're needed.'

In Mistra, the sullen citizenry were sweeping the streets, watched by Albanian soldiers at every corner. They had been told to decorate their balconies, though any call for them to do so with crossed keys or lions had been abandoned and they were clad throughout in the double-headed eagle of the Palaiologoi. Mistra would remain Byzantine until the very last moment.

Down at the metropolis, the new Archbishop's palace was being prepared. It had once been a monastery but its monks had been moved and the Patriarch, who lived opposite, had threatened to move with them. He had refused all pleas for him to attend the mass to be celebrated by the Pope when he arrived.

The news that the Doge and Pope had set sail from Venice in an enormous fleet had been known for days. It seemed they were making their way south at their leisure, stopping at all the smaller Venices that lined the Dalmatian coast. The Emperor Manuel would come later from Constantinople and not stay long. He had been warned of the despotate's mood.

Plethon had been put under house arrest. If the people were to look to anyone for salvation, it would be him. The news had shocked everyone and crowds had gathered every morning beneath his window, hoping for the philosopher to appear to tell them what to do. He had not been allowed to show himself.

Giovanni and Cleope had been imprisoned too, Cleope in a bedroom high in the palace, Giovanni in its dungeon. A message had come from Venice requesting it. Her generalissimo would take no chances over them escaping again.

Anna, meanwhile, sat on her terrace and waited for Shulen to arrive.

Shulen was closer than Anna knew. She had just left her horse and her small Varangian Guard at the lower city gate and was being escorted up through the streets to the Despot's palace, the bundle in her hand. She reached the square where men stood on ladders pruning trees while women swept beneath. She came to the palace gate and a small room to its side where she was invited to sit. The guards sat opposite, staring at her. She waited there, the sword on her knee, wrapped as something else. She wondered what she would do if they tried to take it from her. She heard the swish of dress approaching and looked through the open door to glimpse red hair passing.

She felt sick. He had asked her to do it but it was a monstrous request. Anna must hate her with every nerve in her being. A man appeared at the door and nodded to the soldiers. They stood and led her out into the palace courtyard, across and into a lobby. There were voices, raised, from beyond big doors. They opened.

Shulen entered a hall with tapestries on the walls between tall windows that looked over the city. The sun shone directly into her eyes and for a moment she couldn't see the people gathered there. Then she did. Seated around a large table, as if for dinner, were four people, only one of whom she knew: Anna. She heard the doors close behind her.

Shulen sat, placing the bundle on the table before her, and looked from one to the other of the men. The youngest would be the Despot. He seemed too young to rule at such a time. The other two were old and richly dressed and must be ministers. Her eyes came to Anna and the dread crept up and held her fast within its claws. She had last seen her twenty years ago, before setting off to find Tamerlane with Luke. Anna had been a torch then, a curved vessel of energy rising to flame beneath bright, emerald eyes. She had been her very opposite: her pale, freckled skin the outcome of a more northern climate. Then, her eyes had shown unease. Now, they held cold fury and nothing else.

The Despot brought his hands together on the table and glanced at the bundle. He said: 'You have sought an audience with Anna that you might have wanted alone. But these are difficult times and we are obliged to attend.' He gestured to the other men present. 'Can you still deliver your message?'

'Yes.'

'Which is what?'

Shulen took a rolled manuscript from her sleeve. 'I have here the will of Luke Magoris, made in Cairo by jurists prepared to swear its truth by their Koran.' She placed it on the table, then pushed it towards Anna.

Anna continued to stare at Shulen. A strand of her hair had fallen across an eye but she didn't move it. She said: 'You know what it says. Tell us.'

Shulen glanced at the men. The Despot was watching Anna with his head slightly to one side. He began to say something but Anna raised her hand. 'Tell us.'

Shulen looked down. 'I have read it because it contains instructions for me to carry out, including the one to bring it to you.' Her eyes came back to Anna's. 'It's very simple. All of the estates here and on Chios, the stud, the bank – it's all left to you, then Hilarion.'

Anna didn't blink. 'Most of which will now go to Zoe Mamonas. But you knew that.'

Shulen didn't speak.

'Why were you in Africa?'

The dread had tightened its grip; it was at her throat now. She wondered if she'd be able to speak. She tried. 'I was seeking an animal for the Emperor of China.' It sounded feeble. She continued: 'We found it in Abyssinia.'

We.

'Why did you go on to look for the gold?'

Why had she? She'd not known then and didn't know now. She said: 'I saved his life. In Timbuktu, he had a fever and I saved him.'

Anna leant forward, her fingers spread over the table like

447

knives. 'You saved his life? You persuaded him to follow you to Africa, as you did to Samarcand, and you dare to talk of saving him?'

'He told me to give you a message.'

More hair had fallen across Anna's brow and stayed. 'What was his message to me?'

Shulen took a deep breath. 'He said to tell you that he loved you and was sorry.'

That was when Anna's eyes moved. They moved with the rest of her face as its banks gave way, as a torrent of grief swept away the rage. She brought her palms to her face to hold it back, but still it came.

The Despot watched her. Then he pointed at the bundle. He asked quietly: 'What is it you have there?'

'Something for another.'

Anna had heard. She looked up through red eyes. 'What for another? What have you brought?' She was rising, choking, the Despot's hand on her arm. 'What have you brought?'

Shulen unwrapped the sword, her hands shaking as they revealed the scaled neck, the curved head, the maw of the dragon head. It was old, old silver, bent into shape long before Mistra had even been thought of, yet it shone like new, seeming to draw all light to its blade.

The only sound in the room was that of Anna's breathing. She half stood, still held by the Despot, her eyes moving from the sword back to Shulen. 'Who is it for?'

'Giovanni.'

'No,' Anna said softly. 'It is Hilarion's. Give it to me and leave. Never return.'

The two women stared at each other while the others watched. Then Anna's head dropped and fell forward on to the table.

The Despot spoke quietly. 'I know what you have done for us, as do others, but now is not the time to talk of it. Give me the sword and go.'

Shulen stayed seated, looking at the unbrushed cascade of hair before her, seeing the same misery that she'd known on a riverbank in Africa.

'Go,' said the Despot. 'Please.'

Shulen looked down at the sword. She pushed it towards the Despot. Then she rose to leave.

CHAPTER THIRTY-SEVEN

ALEXANDRIA, AUTUMN 1418

Matteo Zeno, bailo of Alexandria, was perhaps second only to the Doge in importance in the Venetian world, his task to keep the Mamluk Sultan more or less friendly to the Serenissima. With the monopoly soon to be renewed, he was especially alert to disturbance of any kind and the engineer Benedo Barbi, Genoese to his fingertips, presented disturbance of the worst kind. Zeno was watching him from the walls of the bailate and not liking what he saw.

'Why is he attempting disguise?' he asked the man beside him. 'He must know we watch him.'

One of the bailo's jobs was to recruit and maintain a network of paid informers throughout the sultanate, the most important being al-Tabingha, special envoy to the Sultan. Through them, he had been informed of every move Barbi had made since coming to Egypt.

Next to him stood his treasurer Tommaso Tordi, a man very aware of the network because he paid for it. He said: 'He is trying to buy a boat, or hire one. Look, there's the cargo.'

Barbi, cloaked and hooded, was talking to a man on a dhow via an interpreter who stood between them. A donkey had just come into view with a large box strapped to its back. Two men with knives in their belts walked on either side of it, steering it towards the dhow.

It was evening and the port of Alexandria was busier than usual beneath a sky of cloud. One of its two harbours was closed for dredging and war galleys were moored alongside commercial shipping on the quay. Beside Barbi's dhow were ten galleys being prepared in a hurry. Slaves, most of them naked, sat on their benches waiting for a bald man to lock their chains. Amphorae of water were being carried up the gangplank and, on the fighting deck, *ballestieri* were oiling the leather of their slings beside Mamluk soldiers. The captain sat on a pile of coconut rope studying his inventory.

Zeno watched them. 'That is not a sea-faring people,' he said with some satisfaction. 'I suppose they sail in our galleys?'

Tordi nodded. 'Old ones we've sold to them. They'd not know the difference.'

The two men were leaning over the high wall of the bailate, which looked over the waterfront. Behind them was Venice in Egypt: the complex of warehouses, stables, barracks, audience rooms and chapel that allowed the republic to conduct the business of extracting profit from the land of the Pharos. The Lion of St Mark looked out from its Egyptian plinth with a jealous eye.

'Isn't that al-Tabingha?' Zeno asked, pointing to a man who seemed to be directing the loading of the galleys. 'Has he told us where they're going?'

Tordi had just asked al-Tabingha that same question and not received a satisfactory reply. 'He said he didn't know.'

Zeno looked at him. 'Really? That doesn't seem likely. Should we be worried?'

'That the Mamluks are trying to take the gold for themselves?'

Tordi shrugged. 'I don't think so. We have the Negroponte fleet strung out between Greece and Candia. They'd never get away with it.'

Matteo Zeno nodded slowly. He was one of the Serenissima's more gifted sons. Admitted to the Golden Book on his eighteenth birthday, he had taken his seat in the Grand Council at twenty-five. He had chosen the life of bailo because he liked to travel and he'd done much of that in recent months. He crossed the ocean to meet the Sultans of Calicut and Cambay and the Indian Princes of Cochin and Cananor. He had seen for himself how the ancient Arab monopoly in trading spices from the Maluku Islands was now challenged by the Ming. It seemed to him that Venice should welcome China's intervention and that Luke's plan to involve Abyssinia was a sound one, particularly since King Yeshaq now controlled access to the Red Sea. He just wished he'd thought of it.

Now his considerable mind was focused on a single box. 'The Ark of the Covenant,' he said, as much to himself as Tordi. 'It seems too small.'

He looked beyond the dhow where two Venetian galleys were riding at anchor amidst the round ships. Their oars were half-shipped. 'They're ready?'

Tordi followed his gaze. He nodded. 'Ready and awaiting your signal. They'll let it leave, reach open water, then intercept.'

An hour later, al-Tabingha watched the dhow row through the harbour shipping, the box on its deck hidden beneath tarpaulin, Benedo Barbi, still hooded and cloaked, sitting on it. He saw it reach open water, hoist its lateen sail and heel over as it slowly made its way past the Pharos lighthouse, its good Kerala timber protesting all the way.

He looked up at the wall of the Venetian bailate.

There.

The glass flashed twice from its ramparts and he heard the sound of wood meeting water as two galleys splashed their oars into the harbour's water. He saw men at their prows pulling up the anchors. He looked back at the bailate wall and saw that Matteo Zeno and the annoying Tordi creature had disappeared. A man coughed behind him and he turned.

'We are ready to sail,' said the captain.

Al-Tabingha nodded. 'Is he aboard?'

'In your cabin.'

The Mamluk walked past the man and up the gangplank of the nearest galley. He was dressed for riding and, like all Mamluks, despised the water. Sailing was slow and subject to the weather. He would rather a horse every time.

He reached his cabin and opened the door. Little of the breeze that had helped the dhow reached this close to the shore and the room was stuffy and smelt of fish. There was a man sitting at the table.

'Did it leave?' asked the man.

Al-Tabingha nodded. He had removed his turban and was pouring water from a jug. 'And the *galeras* followed. As you said.'

Benedo Barbi smiled. He was a man of science unused to the messy business of subterfuge, but the thought of Venetians chasing a man in a cloak and an empty box was pleasing. 'Good,' he said. 'Now, to Monemvasia.'

Far to the west, the caravel *Santa Vitória* was sailing before an untiring *ponente* wind straight out of Gibraltar, or the arse of a Barbary ape as Captain Dias had put it. Day and night, it kept the little ship to seven or eight knots so that the brown coast of the Maghreb flashed past their starboard rail like a distant smear.

'Just as well,' Dias had said more than once, usually spitting. 'The Barbary corsairs plague these waters like sharks, taking slaves from poor Christian families.'

Luke said nothing. He knew that the pirates who preyed on the Spanish and French coastal villages were as often Catalan as Berber. He was just glad that the caravel could outsail anything sent against it. Even galleys, wind permitting.

Dias glanced at him. 'We may just make Monemvasia in time for your ceremony. We are a week away.'

Luke had been thinking about the possibility of meeting Venetian galleys out of Candia or Negroponte. 'I'd rather you dropped me at Pilos on the west coast. It will cut three days from the journey.'

Dias had shrugged. 'As long as you have gold there.' He'd patted the rail on which they leant. 'She'll get us there in good time, you'll see.'

That conversation had taken place one evening as the first stars were emerging, one by one, above the racing mast. Now it was deeper into the night and Luke was alone beneath a brilliant moon that turned night into day. He could hear Dias's snores from beneath the planks below.

Out on the deck, he could see two crewmen sitting on either side of the bowsprit. From time to time they glanced up at him and he didn't need moonlight to know what they were thinking. They should be with the whores of Lagos by now, not scudding across the Middle Sea.

He thought of his sword, now in the hands of Giovanni. He thought of his son's face as he held the blade up to the light.

Luke had been given the sword when he was sixteen. It was time to pass it on to Giovanni. But Hilarion? He and Anna must think him dead. How would she have greeted Shulen? Was N'gara right?

They will decide.

He forced himself to think of other things. He thought of the treasure ship, perhaps three weeks behind. Would Admiral Zheng and Nikolas be through the Gibraltar Straits yet? Would they be staring up at the same stars? He had few fears of Venetian galleys intercepting them. Zheng's flagship had weapons on board that Venetian admirals would have seen only in their worst nightmares: gunpowder missiles, rockets that sent sprays of burning paper to set fire to sails, grenades soaked in poison, shells filled with iron bolts to scythe men to pieces, mortars packed with human excrement – he had seen them all in the part of the diadan that had been on board the treasure ship.

Luke kept his door locked that night, a knife by his side and a pillow over his head against the captain's snoring. As always, he slept against the side to stop himself from rolling.

He was surprised, therefore, to wake to silence and calm. There was knocking on the cabin door.

'Unlock it, curse you,' said Dias from his hammock. Luke rose, went to the door, and opened it to find a sailor with a frown.

'The wind has dropped,' said the man in Portuguese. 'We're becalmed and there is a fleet approaching.'

Dias tipped himself on to the floor and pulled on his boots. 'Stay hidden,' he said, buckling his sword belt. He took his hat and left.

Luke heard footsteps above him and shouts to the crow's nest. A lot of people were speaking at the same time. He had to see what they saw. He went to the stern and lifted a window hatch.

There was nothing to see but horizon. He went to the door. It was locked from the outside.

He remembered another ship, long ago: a galley sailing out of Chios. He remembered a Venetian called Vetriano who'd betrayed him to the Turks. He went back to the stern window and shouted. 'Dias! My door is locked!'

The air outside was very still, the sea even stiller. He heard footsteps and a voice from above. He looked up to see Dias bent over the taffrail, looking down at him. He had his finger to his lips. 'Shhh! It's for your own good. They mustn't see you.'

Luke leant as far out of the window as he could. 'How can I know you won't betray me?'

The Portuguese frowned. 'How? Because I want your gold. Do you think they won't search the ship if I hand you over? They'll take the gold.'

Luke saw this, but he still felt vulnerable. 'There must be somewhere better than here to hide. I need to get there before they get too close.'

The fleet was a mile away and it was running late.

Zoe stood at the prow of the first galley beside the fleet's generalissimo, Prince Carlo Malatesta of Rimini, who was leaning forward, holding up his hand to shield the sun and sucking his teeth. He said: 'It's a Portuguese caravel. We should stop. It might have seen something.'

'Seen what?'

Carlo turned to her. 'You said the gold may be leaving from a port on the North African coast. It might have seen it.'

Zoe nodded. They were late but the ceremony was hardly likely to start without them. She'd been icily civil to Malatesta throughout the journey so far. Their cabins were adjacent but hers had a nun in it and a prie-dieu propped against the door at night, both there for her daily devotions. But the condottiere had been politeness itself. Only the cage on the quarterdeck reminded her of how much she still hated every part of him.

The delays had started at Zadar. The city had arranged such magnificent celebrations that it had been impossible to leave. There had been banquets and balls and a papal mass in the main square. The same had happened at Trogir, Korčula and Corfu: church bells and choirs and entertainments to mark the crusade to bring Mistra into the Catholic fold. Now they were late.

Malatesta turned and asked for someone who spoke Portuguese to be brought to him. One of the rowers arrived on deck. A signal was sent to the rest of the fleet.

Zoe looked behind her. The Venetian armada was strung out across the sea in a giant arrowhead, its starboard tip only a mile from the shore. The westerly that had accompanied them south and kept their pennants stretched had vanished, and in its place was blue serenity disturbed only by the dip of eight thousand oars. It was a magnificent sight.

The order was given and the galley's rowers slowed, then stopped, turning the ship so that the caravel would come alongside. The caravel's sail was hanging limp from its mast, its crew lined up at the rail to see the armada approach. Malatesta spoke to the man beside him. 'Ask them what ships they've seen sailing north from Africa.'

The question was answered by a man standing alone on the aft-deck.

'He says they've seen no ships.'

Malatesta frowned. He put his fingers to his beard and scratched. 'Ask them why they're here.'

The question was asked. The reply came back after some delay.

'He says they are bound for Pilos. They have cargo to discharge there.'

Zoe was staring at the caravel, running her eyes along the crew. They stopped at the man speaking from the upper deck. He looked uncomfortable.

She said: 'Ask him what their cargo is.'

There was another pause before the man spoke again.

'They have ivory from Africa.'

Malatesta turned to Zoe. 'Why would they bring ivory here? They should be in Lagos.' He looked back at the caravel. 'I think we should search them.'

It didn't take long. The caravel was a simple affair: a single deck, crew quarters, hold and captain's cabin. Zoe watched it all from the rembata, her chin in her hand and elbow on the rail, Carlo beside her. The search party reappeared, one of them holding a gold bar.

Malatesta said: 'Ask him where he got it.'

Dias chose to answer directly. 'From Africa,' he said in Greek. 'I lied to you because I thought you'd take it.'

Malatesta nodded. 'Very likely.'

The galley's captain had come to stand beside the condottiere. His voice was low. 'Venice is friendly to Portugal, lord.'

'But if it's the gold from Africa, this is a direct challenge to Venice's monopoly. We should look at it.'

Malatesta walked over to the side of the galley and climbed over to the caravel. He took the gold bar from the man and lifted it to the sun, studying its surface.

Zoe was still watching, her eyes travelling back and forth

along the caravel's deck. They came to rest on the rolled sail at the bow. She stared at it, her head to one side. 'Wait.'

She climbed down from the rembata and was helped over the galley's side. She went over to the rolled canvas. 'What is this for?'

Dias glanced at the sail and shrugged. 'For different weather.'

She nodded again. 'Unroll it.'

The search party moved but Zoe raised her hand. 'No, not you. The caravel's crew.'

The translator gave the order. A Portuguese sailor stepped forward and said something. He was the man that Luke had found raping the slave.

'He says there is a man wrapped in the sail with a knife,' said the translator. 'He fears he'll hurt the man who finds him.'

Zoe smiled. 'I don't think so.'

She walked over to Malatesta and put her hand on his sword hilt. 'May I?' She drew the sword and returned to the sail. She poked it with the tip of the sword.

'You should come out,' she said.

The sail stirred. A voice she knew came from within. 'I'll need help. It's heavy.'

Zoe felt sick with unexpected joy. She found herself laughing. She turned to the search party. 'Help him. He won't hurt you.'

It took some time for the sail to be unrolled. Eventually Luke was revealed, blinking in the sunlight.

'I'm surprised it fitted you,' said Zoe, helping him to his feet. 'You don't look very dead.'

Luke looked far from dead. His hair was on end and his sunburnt features coated in fine dust. He looked thinner than when she'd seen him last but very much alive. The urge to laugh was still upon her. She controlled it.

459

There was a shout and she remembered who was with her.

Luke glanced behind her, wiping the dust from his face. 'Ah, you have Malatesta with you. A friend?'

'He commands the fleet. Don't provoke him.'

Two of Malatesta's men were on either side of him now, steering him to the side of the caravel. Luke looked back at Zoe. 'I take it you're on your way to Mistra?'

Malatesta came to the rail in front of him. His eyes held the same hate he'd seen at Constance. 'I've a cage for you up there, Magoris,' he said, using his thumb. 'Just like Bayezid's. It was meant for Giovanni but it will work just as well for you. Until we get him.'

Luke was being held by the arms. 'And my crime?'

Malatesta shrugged. 'Smuggling gold will do for now. We'll think of something better later, I'm sure. Take him up.'

Zoe came to stand beside Luke. She felt his elbow against her arm, smelt the salt on him. 'We cannot cage him,' she said. 'He is the Protostrator of Mistra.'

'And I', said Malatesta, turning away, 'am general of this army. We should properly torture him to find out where the rest of the gold is but I don't think he'd tell us, so we'll have to make do with the cage. Bring him up.'

Zoe felt Luke's eyes on her. 'It would seem a lot of ships to fetch one boy,' he said quietly. 'What will you do with him?'

'Not I, Malatesta. He will be imprisoned in Rimini.'

'And you believe that?'

She turned to him. 'I have his word.'

They looked at each other, both of them knowing how that word had been won. She thought back to a time, long ago in

460

Monemvasia, when their word, hers and Luke's, would have been given for nothing, as generous as the friendship that had bound them. She felt the same ache she'd felt on hearing of his death. She turned away.

CHAPTER THIRTY-EIGHT

MISTRA, AUTUMN 1418

Hilarion stood on the balcony of the Laskaris house and watched the plain below flash into day through sheets of rain. Lightning lit the farmsteads and stubbled fields, then thunder shook them apart, and the silver snake of the Evrotas River crept closer every time.

In Hilarion's hand was Luke's sword, the dragon sword.

The storm had been raging since midnight and showed no sign of abating. He had watched it from his bedroom, then from the terrace, awed by a wind that could topple trees and fling rain hard enough to blind. He had seen scaffolding ripped from walls and cranes crash on to tiles. He had seen cats rolled down the streets and shutters torn from their hinges. And always there had been the shriek of the wind above, the heavy rattle of rain on rooftops.

And a thought had cleaved its way through all the chaos, again and again.

He is alive.

The news had come up from Modone where an army from Venice had landed that morning, a cage among their baggage. It had come by courier and arrived just ahead of the storm. He'd not stopped smiling since.

He is alive.

He looked up at the city behind as more lightning clawed the sky, seeing the Despot's palace tied to heaven by sudden veins of fire. He heard a sound and turned. Anna was there, a cloak wrapped around her, pulling the door shut with both hands. She came over to him and held him.

'You have the sword.'

He nodded. 'Theodore gave it to me but it should be Giovanni's,' he said. 'You know that.'

They stood like that for some time, seeking comfort against the chaos of nature, finding strength in human embrace, in what they could understand. 'Did you believe in dragons once?' he asked.

He'd drawn his cloak around his mother and she looked up from it, strands of hair crossing her face. She looked old. 'Yes. And tonight every one of them is abroad,' she replied. 'What are you going to do?'

'Go to him. Giovanni would have done the same but he's in prison.'

'No.'

'The garrison will all be at their barracks in this storm. I should leave now.'

'No. I won't let you.'

Hilarion moved gently away from his mother, still holding her hands. He looked down at them, then at her face.

'I'm going to him.'

The same storm was raging over Edirne. Mehmed's capital was bigger and less exposed than Mistra but its minarets reached high into the sky and the people living around them had looked up and left their houses. No attempt was made to call the faithful to evening prayer that night; the muezzin wouldn't have been heard anyway.

The streets were empty even of dogs, and the offal they might have eaten flew freely. They kept to the sheltered places, cowering in doorways, whining and howling and barking at the rain that danced like imps on the cobbles and bubbled past them in the gutters. It was denser than fog, harder than nails, and no one saw the poor mule tied beside high walls, its cargo still not unloaded.

Certainly no one from the harem within. Beyond the walls lay the gardens, courtyards and rooms where hundreds of women existed only to please their sultan. At that time, many of them were in a single room. They'd brought their mattresses and cushions up from their bedrooms to the main audience chamber where the Valide Sultan was telling them stories to the light of flickering candles. She was Devlet Hatun, mother to Mehmed and, in the harem, all-powerful. She'd decided that stories might distract from the terror of the night outside.

Among her audience were two men: the Kislar Ağasi, and her brother Yakub of the Germiyans, only admitted by her express permission. Both were listening to a story about a concubine who became an empress. It was the sort of story the girls liked, and the *kadins, ikbals* and *cariyes* held their mastic breaths and hardly heard the storm outside.

Watching from the shadow of an arch, unseen and unheard, was Shulen. She'd ridden up from Mistra, visiting certain places on the way in accordance with Luke's will. She had arrived at Edirne that evening, wanting to speak to Yakub but finding her father had been summoned to the harem. She sent a message to the Valide Sultan asking to be admitted through the Gate of Felicity. The answer had come back only an hour ago.

The story ended and the Valide Sultan clapped her hands. The girls clung to each other and Devlet Hatun turned to the man sitting beside her. 'Kislar Ağasi, tell us about Timbuktu where you were born.'

Some said that the Chief Black Eunuch had survived Gülçiçek, Bayezid's mother and the last Valide Sultan, by poisoning her. Since then, and with Anna's help, he'd become a gentler creature, a giant father and mountain of comfort to the girls. His voice was deep.

'In Timbuktu,' he said, 'the women walk naked in the streets and every one of them wears gold on her arms.' The lightning struck, turning him into an ebony god atop cushions, his great bald head turning slowly from side to side as he spoke. 'There are churches shaped like pyramids and libraries where people of both sexes bathe. And everywhere there is gold. Even the dogs wear it.'

The girls had heard the story before but still loved it, the fantasy of a rich desert city a good substitute for this night of wind and rain. They glanced at each other and smiled.

'It's true,' came a voice. Shulen walked out from the shadows. 'It's all true. I've been there.'

Yakub rose and came over to her, his arms open. He took his daughter's hands in his. 'Did you find your qilin?'

Shulen kissed her father. 'We found two and sent both back to China. Then I went to Timbuktu and saw more gold than you can imagine.' She looked up and smiled at the Kislar Ağasi. 'Some of it is on its way to Mistra.'

Devlet Hatun spoke from the cushions. 'We had heard.' She turned to the eunuch. 'Take the girls to another room. I will join you afterwards.'

There was a thunderclap louder than cannon and one of the

girls screamed. The Kislar Ağasi rose and shooed them from the room.

The Valide Sultan patted a cushion. 'Sit, niece. Tell us about your journey.'

Shulen took off her shoes and climbed the cushions to sit next to her aunt. She tucked her feet underneath her. 'I'd rather speak of Luke Magoris.'

Yakub had come to sit on his sister's other side. He straightened up, his eyes wide. 'Luke? I'd thought him dead.'

'It was a ruse to stop Venice looking for him,' said Shulen. 'Now he's on his way to Mistra with gold to pay back his debts but he'll be too late.'

Yakub laughed out loud and the sound came back to them against the noise of the storm. He shook his head in disbelief. 'Luke is alive.'

Devlet Hatun asked: 'Have the Venetians landed with their pope?'

Shulen nodded. 'At Modone with an army of two thousand knights. The ceremony is in a week.'

The Valide Sultan raised her eyebrows. She was a small woman, usually veiled. Her hair was as black as Shulen's, the hair of women of the steppe. 'So soon?'

'Yes, which is why we must find a way to delay it.'

The Valide Sultan frowned. 'Why "we", niece?' she asked. 'What business is it of ours who owns Mistra?' She put her hands in her lap. 'Or yours, for that matter?'

There it was: the question she'd put to herself so often.

Yakub helped her. 'It is our duty to help those who have helped us.' He turned to his daughter. 'But I don't know what we can do. Mehmed's court is split and his hold on power is not what it was. Murad has gathered to him all those who admired Bedreddin, all the fanatics who see Christendom as the only enemy. Mehmed can't be seen to support one Christian faction over another.'

Devlet Hatun nodded. 'And Murad hates Mistra and its protostrator with every nerve in his being. Luke should not have struck him.'

Shulen looked down at her hands. The lightning came into the room and lit her fingers as if they held magic. But no magic could make her aunt wrong. Luke could expect no help from Edirne.

The Valide Sultan put her hand on Shulen's arm and leant forward. 'But he will always be welcome here,' she said, 'at least while Mehmed lives. If Luke, or anyone he loves, needs sanctuary, they can come to us.'

Yakub raised himself from the cushions. He stretched out his arm. 'Come,' he said. 'I will find you somewhere to sleep.' He helped Shulen to her feet. 'And tomorrow we will speak to Mehmed.'

Yakub led his daughter from the room and down the long corridor that connected the harem to the rest of the palace. As the lightning flashed, they walked from night into day into night again, and all the while the wind and rain assaulted the ancient stone around them as no army had done for years.

They came to a circular room with torches on the walls but no windows. There was a round table and two chairs. Yakub closed the door and turned to his daughter. 'You're not sleeping here, don't worry,' he said, sitting down and gesturing to the other chair, 'but we can hear ourselves speak. Shulen, what will you do now?'

She put her head on one side, watching him. She didn't sit. 'You worry that I will stay with the Protostrator when he's been turned out of Mistra by the Venetians.'

Yakub didn't answer.

Shulen shook her head. 'I am tired, Father, and would like my bed. You needn't worry.' She walked to the door, opened it and turned. 'I have seen Anna and know what to do.'

CHAPTER THIRTY-NINE

MONEMVASIA, AUTUMN 1418

Twenty-one years earlier Benedo Barbi had sailed into Monem-vasia to help Plethon with a nativity play and distract Anna from knowing that Luke was preparing to go to Tamerlane. Now he was sailing towards the Goulas on a Mamluk galley with the black lion of Baybars flapping at its masthead. The day was blustery and the lion skipped from point to point while white horses cavorted in the waves. In the sky, clouds rolled like chariots, some with the sun for passenger, while birds bounced between them like chaff. The rowers worked to an ever-faster tempo, then stopped. The sail would take them in now.

They came through the Venetian blockade and not a galley stopped them. No sopracomito would risk his livelihood by offending the Serenissima's most important friend. Now, with its oars shipped, the galley was approaching a quayside lashed by spray on which stood a hundred Varangians with axes by their sides. Their whipping cloaks were the only part of them that moved.

Watching them from the deck, beside the engineer, was a sullen al-Tabingha. The Mamluk liked neither the sea nor his companion, finding both beyond his control. But his orders from the Sultan had left no doubt: his past loyalties would have to change. He would deliver Benedo Barbi safely to Monemvasia without a word to Venice, or he would die.

The ship docked and ropes secured it to land. The gangplank was lowered and Benedo Barbi walked down it to meet the Akolouthos of Byzantium and another beside him. He'd last seen them nine years ago at an ambush in Anatolia.

'You've grown,' he said, embracing first Matthew, then Arcadius. 'Both of you, if that were possible. I thought age was supposed to reduce us.'

Matthew smiled and patted Barbi's head. 'We'll give you a mounting block to talk to us, old man.'

Barbi pulled his head away. 'How did you know I was coming? Has Shulen arrived?'

'And left,' said Arcadius. He pointed beyond Barbi. 'Don't let your galley leave. Can it take a hundred Varangians? We need it to take us up to Corinth.'

Barbi looked from one to the other of them. 'To the wall?'

'Yes. We have news of Luke.'

'What news?'

'That he's alive, caged and coming to Mistra. We are to meet Shulen at the wall, then march to Mistra.'

The engineer walked back up the gangway. He spoke to the captain, then turned and shouted to them. 'Bring the men aboard. They'll have to split themselves between the fore- and aft-decks. It'll take two days to get there.'

Matthew summoned Peter of Norfolk and the Varangian Company filed up the gangplank, each with a bundle and axe over his shoulder. Last to board were himself and Arcadius. The ropes were cast off, the ship turned round under oar and, quite soon, they were on their way beneath a full sail, their decks crowded with giants.

'We'll have to hide them,' said the captain, coming to stand beside Matthew. 'We'll hug the shore north, then cross to the island of Spetses at the Gulf of Argos. Venetian galleys come out of Nauplion there, so your men will have to go below.'

'They won't stop us?'

The captain laughed. 'They wouldn't dare.'

In Modone, the day was full of the same sun and bluster that had welcomed Barbi to Monemvasia. Pope Martin stood on a balcony of the castle with one hand to his tiara, the other on his vestments. He looked down on to its courtyard, the Doge beside him. There, an army of two thousand was being paraded.

Watching from a window opposite was Luke Magoris. He'd spent the night in a castle dungeon and now stood with his wrists chained before him. He was alone.

He had been mostly alone since his capture. Unwrapped from the sail like Cleopatra, he had been put aboard the Venetian galley and locked in the generalissimo's cabin. He had not spoken a word to Carlo Malatesta, nor seen him since the Prince had waved goodbye at the cabin door, one hand patting the cage behind. The condottiere's delight at taking Luke had been tempered by leaving behind his gold. But the Doge had insisted: Portugal was not to be offended.

Now the cage was the centrepiece of the parade below, strung between two heavy horses and empty for now. Around it was a riot of colour and flashing armour. There were the militias from the six city parishes, the Provisionati di San Marco in their red-and-white striped jerkins to their front. There was the gaudily hosed Company of Noble Bowmen, recruited only from the young aristocracy. There were the scarlet *arsenalotti* next to the Friulani men-at-arms, a lion on every chest. And behind, on their seasick destriers, stood a thousand knights in their crested great helms and emblazoned surcoats, three squires to a man. All of them looked up at the Pope as he blessed their flags of saints and lions and crocodiles. Even the bombards had their barrels raised to him.

Luke saw it all and frowned. He watched Carlo Malatesta take his position before the ranks, his horse skittish in the breeze. He was wearing black armour studded with gold and carried a baton. His head was bare and his thin hair fluttered with the flags.

He heard a sound behind him and turned. Zoe had walked into the room. She came to stand next to him at the window. They watched together in silence for a while.

She glanced at him, seeing the white in his hair, the lines in his sunburnt face, the eyes still as clear and blue as when she'd first seen them forty years ago. She said: 'He's going to take you to Mistra in that cage.'

He turned to her. 'And then?'

'Perhaps torture you to tell him where the gold is.'

'There's no need. I can tell you now and you can tell him. It's on a Chinese junk coming to Mistra from the west.' He paused. 'You know that he'll kill Giovanni, don't you?'

She didn't answer.

Luke looked out at the parade. The Pope was intoning some long prayer, his hand raised. 'In Constance I suppose you had some part in what happened. Was that just to hurt me?'

'Not hurt, bankrupt. And it wasn't you but Mistra I was interested in. Such conceit.'

Conceit.

The word hung between them as cold as winter breath and they let it evaporate slowly. There was the sound of metal outside as two thousand men donned their helmets. Luke asked: 'Why are you here?'

She turned so that her back was to the window, the breeze on her neck. She was dressed for riding, the long black tunic split for the saddle, black boots to her knees. She looked sober and seductive and younger than her years. 'I wanted to tell you something,' she said. 'I wanted you to know that whatever happens to Giovanni is not of my wishing.' It was said without emphasis or meeting his eye.

Luke glanced at her. She was studying her boots, their tips lifted for inspection. He said quietly: 'But you've done nothing to stop it.'

'I've tried but without success.' She turned her head away. 'It doesn't matter to me if you believe it.'

The parade outside was over and there was the shuffle of men dismissed. They would leave for Mistra within the hour. Luke turned so that he leant beside her. 'No, of course not. But then I'm interested in why you want me to know this.'

She walked away from the window to stand before the fireplace, her hands clasped. With a shock, he saw that they were trembling.

'We get older,' she said, glancing at him. 'You, me. And age brings memory and reflection. Isn't it so?'

Luke didn't answer. He watched her hands disappear behind her back. Then she turned her back to him, warming herself at a fire that wasn't there. 'Perhaps it does matter to me that you believe I tried to save Giovanni.'

He waited for her to continue.

'Did you know that Byzantine law allows sons and daughters

473

both to inherit?' she asked. 'But my father found a way to leave everything to my twin brother, a worthless drunk. So when we were thrown out of Mistra, I was forced to go to Suleyman, then Tamerlane, then Suleyman again and finally Musa. All that enslavement before my father had to die to set me free.' She turned abruptly. 'Tell me, Luke, what have I done to deserve such hatred from men?'

Luke stared at her. What had this to do with Giovanni? He said: 'I don't know. Was it that you always won?'

Zoe came to stand before him. There was something in her eyes he had not seen before. She said quietly: 'Did I always win? I don't think so.'

Luke held her gaze for a moment, then looked down at his chained wrists. He said: 'Well, you certainly won this time.'

She took a step backwards. Her dark eyes were less certain than he'd ever seen them. 'Did I?' There was a chair next to the window with lions' forelegs for arms. She walked over and sat, her hands over the paws. She closed her eyes. 'I thought I had, until I heard that you'd died.' She paused. 'I cried that night.'

Luke frowned. It had not been said with any trace of sentiment but rather as a curious discovery. After so much enslavement, so much *usage*, she'd believed herself empty of emotion. Then she'd found some, hidden somewhere deep. He remembered her face when she'd found him in the sail.

'So you see,' she went on, 'you won in the end. You may be ruined and in chains, and you'll very probably be killed, but it doesn't change the fact that you've won.'

'Why?' he asked, only half understanding. 'Because you won't enjoy it when I die?'

She shook her head, sighing. 'Luke, Luke: always so obvious. It must be lovely to see the world as you do.'

He ignored her. 'What about Giovanni? What has this to do with him?'

'I was trying to explain,' she replied. 'He's you, Luke; actually more interesting than you, I expect.' She paused. 'I thought I'd already killed you and it hurt, so I didn't want you to die again.'

Luke nodded slowly, watching her move her hands in her lap, watching them wind and unwind. She was as cold as ever, but she was bewildered too.

'No, that's unfair,' she continued, almost to herself. 'You must have been interesting otherwise I wouldn't have cared.' She put her hands back on the claws and slid her fingers between them. 'You've always felt the need for both light *and* darkness in your life, Luke, you've just not known it.' She straightened up, her arms stretched out. 'Once, Anna was the light and I the dark. Now it's the shaman's daughter, though hers is a different kind of dark. And you love her, of course.'

It was said with the same detachment as everything else. She rose and walked to the door. She turned, her hand on the handle.

'Which of them will you choose, Luke?'

From the upper deck of the treasure ship, Admiral Zheng looked down with satisfaction on the vessel below. Beside him stood Nikolas.

They were crossing the waters between Sicily and the place where Carthage had once stood until Scipio sowed salt into its ruined fields. The sea was busy with merchantmen, mainly round ships making their ponderous way from coast to coast. The breeze was brisk and the junk's sails were turned to catch every breath of it. Nikolas glanced behind at the surf in their wake. 'How long to Mistra?' he asked.

Zheng had his arms behind his back and his great chest spread out like the canvas above. He was wearing a sleeveless jacket embroidered with dragons that strained at its buttons. 'Ten days at most.'

'Luke will be there by now. The caravel was fast.'

Zheng nodded. 'But it may have stopped at Ceuta, so perhaps he's two weeks ahead. Will that be in time?'

It was approaching the end of the month which meant that if Luke was in Mistra, he'd be there for the ceremony. But what could he do against a crusade?

'I don't know.'

Nikolas looked out to sea. He and Luke had discussed the consequence of failure many times with Admiral Zheng. Apart from their certain banishment from Mistra, they had understood that they would also lose the trade with China. The Middle Kingdom cared about rank and it was Luke's position as protostrator that had largely made it all possible. For Nikolas, it would be a catastrophe. He would not see Zhu Chou again.

He turned to the admiral. 'Will the fleet have got back by now, do you think?'

Zheng smiled his enormous smile and his eyes disappeared. He liked Nikolas and approved of his love for the concubine. 'Oh yes. The Emperor will have been presented with his qilin and the mandarins will be gnashing their teeth.' His smile grew even bigger. 'The people will see heaven's favour heaped upon its son at last.'

'And the new trade route into Africa?'

'That will be welcomed by the Emperor. It will justify all of the expense of the fleets.'

Nikolas looked back at the sea and saw something on the horizon. He walked over to the rail and leant forward. 'Do you see those ships?' he asked, pointing. 'Galleys, I think.'

476

The admiral joined him and raised a hand to his forehead. 'They're coming towards us. Venetian?'

Nikolas narrowed his eyes. 'It's too far to see. Either Venetian or Barbary pirates. Probably pirates.'

They watched the ships get larger, until they could see the skirts of the galleys' oars rising and falling, until they could hear distant drumbeats carried to them over the wind. The pennants were still unreadable.

'Will they try and stop us?' asked the admiral.

They both knew what weapons they had on board and Nikolas, for one, would have quite liked to see them used. But if the galleys were Venetian, they'd be commanded by *sopracomiti* with sensible orders.

Nikolas said: 'Well, if they can't board us, they might try to ram or burn us, I suppose. They may have fire-throwers aboard.'

Zheng turned to a line of men standing behind him and issued a string of orders. The treasure ship was to be prepared for battle.

There was an explosion from in front of them. Smoke was rising from the leading galley in a little puff. A cannon had fired.

'I think we have pirates,' said Zheng.

Long rolls of leather were brought up on deck and dropped over the sides of the ship. Seawater was pulled up in buckets and splashed over them. Catapults were assembled and piles of grenades and other explosives piled next to them. Cannons on wheels were pushed to the sides where hatches were opened for their barrels. Extra oars were laid out in case the wind dropped. The decks were alive with well-rehearsed activity.

Nikolas peered out at the galleys, his eyes shadowed by his hand. He had spent a month in Venice during his preparation for trade and spent much of it in the Arsenale looking at how they made ships. He said: 'They're Venetian.'

'How can you tell?'

'The shape of the galleys. They're Venetian.'

Zheng frowned. Pirates would have been more straightforward. He asked: 'So what will they do?'

Nikolas turned to him. The two were nearly the same height and liked not looking down to talk. 'They shouldn't be here,' he said. 'They should be watching the eastern approaches.' He looked back at the ships, thinking. 'Unless ...'

'Unless what?'

'Unless they've calculated that the gold would come from the west instead of the east.'

Admiral Zheng put his hands on the rail and looked out. 'I count ten of them,' he said.

Nikolas thought hard. The Venetian galleys would not try to board them and they'd not consider sinking a ship full of gold. They'd do something much wiser. 'They'll follow us,' he said.

'Follow us?'

'Yes. They know we're bound for the Mistra coast so they'll wait for us to land, then take the gold once it's ashore.'

Zheng nodded. 'So we must land somewhere else.'

'How many soldiers do we have on board? Two hundred?'

The admiral nodded.

'Ten Venetian galleys will be able to land a thousand. All they have to do is wait.'

It was true, and what they both knew was that Zheng could not protect the gold once it was ashore. The Middle Kingdom wasn't yet ready to declare war on Venice. They looked out at the ships, close enough now for them to see that they carried no flags.

Within the hour, the galleys had encircled the treasure ship and had no difficulty in matching its speed. They were too far away for Nikolas see the men on their decks but it made little difference. The treasure ship was trapped.

The admiral watched it all with no smile on his face. He turned to Nikolas and asked the same question: 'What do we do?'

And Nikolas answered. 'Head for Monemvasia, then hope.'

CHAPTER FORTY

MISTRA, AUTUMN 1418

Hilarion rose three hours before dawn and took the road west to Modone. Inspired by Giovanni, he went as a dyer's apprentice, with ink in his pocket for his fingers. In his belt was the dragon sword. He had argued with his mother until he could argue no more, so, in the end, he left without her knowing.

He took the best horse in the Laskaris stables. It was seventy miles to Modone and he would have to cross the Taygetos Mountains to get there. He'd need a strong horse.

By dawn, he had reached halfway up the climb to the pass that, in winter, would be deep in snow. He had ridden through thick pine forest, darker than pitch, its floor scattered with limbs torn off by the storm. From either side had come the creak and rustle and sudden shriek of the night. Above him had been the only path he could see: a path bordered by treetops and pebbled by stars. When dawn came, he was above the forest and the sun exploded at his back, turning to steaming orange the shale and scrub all around, raising the hairs on his neck and sending pleasure down his spine. The heat seeped into him and he closed his eyes.

Three hours later, he reached the pass and could see the

road ahead disappear into folds of mountain and reappear, far beyond, in a gentler world of hill and valley and plain, lit up like heaven.

He kicked his horse into a trot. He wanted to be on the plain by noon and at the coast by nightfall. But the land this side was different: steep and dangerous, with silent rock and noisy water rushing through ravines below. The road twisted and turned and Hilarion kept to its inside, edging out only to skirt around the rock falls. When the horse neighed its fright, the sound came back to him. He could do no more than walk.

So it was evening when he reached the Messinian plain and the sun was painting its gentle landscape in long shadow, turning olive trees into cypresses, walls into ramparts, men into monsters. He was thirty miles from the coast and a strong horse could cover the distance in three hours.

When he saw the sea it was mottled by dark cloud sweeping in from the west. The rain began to fall, gently at first, then harder. The water trampled the hair to his skull, then ran down his back, making his clothes stick to the saddle and the insides of his legs chafe. His horse slowed to a walk as the road below melted into river.

Long after nightfall, he came at last to the sea and the town of Pilos. On its outskirts he found stabling for the horse and went in on foot, cloaked and hooded against the rain. He walked across a field where he stumbled on the remnants of fires with piles of sodden wood beside them. He stopped a man and asked him what had been here.

'Venetians,' said the man. He was old and bent and wanted to be inside, away from the weather. 'The first lot. They came and camped and left. Now we have more.'

'The first lot?'

'From Negroponte, they said.'

Hilarion took his arm. 'How long ago did they leave?'

'A week, no more.' The man pointed north. 'They went up the coast.'

Hilarion entered Pilos to find it full of Venetian soldiers. He had not heard them before because most of them were indoors, billeted on families who couldn't understand what they said. He came across a tavern where horses were tethered outside and standards propped against the wall. Two men came out to piss, shouting to each other.

The men went back in and Hilarion looked up and down the street and blessed the rain that made it empty. There was an army in this town, come up from Modone, but where was Luke? He put his hand inside the cloak and closed his fingers around the scaled neck of the dragon. Where would they have put him?

He needed somewhere to think. He smelt the tang of salt waft in from the sea and made his way towards it. The rain fell harder and he felt invisible behind its screen, but there was no one to see him anyway. He came into a big square in front of the harbour. There were soldiers here, hurrying from house to house with their heads down. There was a group talking in the middle. On one side stood an impressive building, a palace of some kind. There were guards outside it.

Surely that was where Carlo Malatesta would be housed and, quite likely, Luke with him, if he had been let out of his cage. He heard laughter from the square and saw the group break apart and disperse. There was a cage where they had stood, a shadow inside it.

Hilarion looked around. The square was emptying now, little

knots of soldiers going off to find their reluctant hosts, the rain muffling their shouts. He moved away from the wall and, crouching low, ran over.

It was too dark to see who it was inside it, but he knew. He brought his face to the bars, smelling the filth that had been pelted against them.

'Father?'

He heard someone turn, then rise from sodden straw and move towards him. He felt hands over his and saw a face he loved pressed against the bars.

'Hilarion! You shouldn't be here.'

Hilarion pulled his hand away and it disappeared into his cloak. 'I brought you this.'

He passed the sword between the bars and Luke was silent for a while, running his palm over the dragon's head. Then he found Hilarion's hand again. 'Where is Giovanni?'

'He's imprisoned in Mistra. Malatesta is taking him back to Rimini.' He paused. 'I know the sword is his. He is the older son.'

Luke dropped his head. So he knew now. He thought of Anna and the anger she'd have felt when Hilarion was told.

Hilarion brought his other hand to Luke's, holding it through the bars. 'It makes no difference,' he said. 'I've always loved him as a brother.'

Luke felt tears prick the rims of his eyes. Relief and shame washed over him with the rain. He looked up. 'I love you, Hilarion.'

They stayed like that until a sound came from across the square. Luke pushed the sword back through the bars. 'You must take it back. I can't get out of this cage and they'll find it.' He glanced beyond the boy. 'You must go. Someone is coming.'

'But I can find the keys.'

483

'There aren't any keys. The cage is soldered. Malatesta wants me humiliated. That's why I'm here.'

They heard voices and Hilarion glanced behind. There were people approaching from the other side of the rain. He tucked the sword back into his belt. Luke asked: 'Have you got a horse?'

Hilarion nodded. 'It's good.'

Luke had taken his hands again. 'Hilarion, listen carefully. I want you to ride to the wall. You'll find Shulen there and I want you to tell her this: go to Mehmed in Edirne. He can help.'

The voices were louder now and there was laughter: drunk men on their way to bed, coming for a final taunt. Luke brought his palms to his son's cheeks and his lips to his forehead, just reaching skin between the metal. But it was enough.

'I love you, Hilarion,' he said again. 'Whatever has happened or will happen, remember that. Now go.'

Hilarion rode from one end of the kingdom to the other in less than sixteen hours, stopping only once to change horses at Tripoli. He took the ancient road north, through valleys that cut through mountains. The rain had stopped and he rode into a day of shimmering heat, of trembling olive groves and orchards beside the road, the sky above washed of everything but blue.

As evening closed in, he arrived at the wall to find no Shulen but a hundred Varangians who had disembarked from a Mamluk galley that afternoon. They were all seated together, some trying to eat their supper. He greeted them, then climbed to the battlements.

'Hilarion!' Matthew was the first to see him. He drew him apart. 'Should you be here?'

The boy hadn't slept for two days and could hardly stand for exhaustion. He put his hand to the wall. 'I've come from Luke.'

'From Modone?'

Hilarion shook his head. 'Pilos. He's in a cage there. In the town square.'

'Who . . .?'

'Carlo Malatesta. He wants to put Giovanni in it too.' He glanced at Barbi. He'd not met the engineer but had guessed who he was. 'Signor Barbi.' He dipped his head. 'Do you know where Shulen is?'

'Coming from Edirne, we suppose,' said Barbi. 'I'm honoured to meet you, Hilarion.'

'You're tired,' said Matthew. 'You must sleep.'

Hilarion slept well that night, and woke to the news that Shulen had arrived. His bed had been straw laid out on the guard-room floor and his limbs ached as he rose. He found water and splashed it on to his face and walked out into mid-morning sunshine to find double the army he'd seen the night before. There were gazi horse archers now among the Varangians.

Peter of Norfolk saw him and came over. He put his arm around his shoulders and led him towards some steps where people were talking. 'You're up at last. We are to leave for Mistra within the hour.'

A woman turned as they approached. He'd heard much about Shulen, even dreamt of her, and now she was before him. She was taller than he'd imagined, her face thinner. He wasn't sure how to think of her. He knew she'd met Luke long ago in the Germiyan camp; that she'd turned from shaman's daughter into the daughter of Yakub and Khan-zada. She was half-royal, half-wild, and his mother hated her. But now she came forward and smiled as a friend. 'Hilarion.'

He said: 'Lady, have you seen Prince Mehmed in Edirne?'

'I have just come from him.' She took his hand. 'Come and join us.'

He followed her over to the others.

'This is Amasyali Pasha, vizier to the Sultan Mehmed, who I saw in Edirne,' said Shulen. 'He has brought gazi horse archers.'

'A hundred of them,' said Arcadius, 'which means we're only outnumbered ten to one now.'

'Or twenty to one if you count the Despot's Albanians.' This was Barbi.

Matthew looked up from the map. 'We've faced greater odds before. Remember Çamurlu? Anyway, we're not going to Mistra to fight. We are taking a letter brought to us by the vizier pleading Luke's cause. It is from Mehmed. We won't save Mistra but we might save Luke.'

'And Giovanni,' said Hilarion.

Matthew turned to him. 'And Giovanni,' he said. 'Now, are you ready to ride again to Mistra?'

CHAPTER FORTY-ONE

MISTRA, AUTUMN 1418

When Luke had seen Bayezid after Ankara, he'd pitied him. Nothing, he felt, could justify making an animal of a man; nothing could justify putting him in a cage. Now he was seeing the rich Messinian landscape, its fields and orchards mellowed by autumn sun, from behind bars. And he was flanked by a Venetian army that jeered as it marched.

They had left Pilos at first light and marched through villages where the people stayed indoors, frightened faces staring at their new masters from windows. The country was rich and recently harvested and full of pigs, eating its scraps and churning it back into fruitfulness. The air rang with grunts.

Soon the people became bolder. Word had passed that their protostrator was in a cage and they forgot their fear, picked up sons and daughters and came out to see for themselves. They muttered at first, then put down their children to pick up other things. By mid-morning, a rotten vegetable had been thrown at a knight. By noon, the people of Mistra were lining the road between the villages, their hands full of produce. Venetian jeers had been replaced by Greek ones, and the finest Milanese armour was spattered with filth.

The Doge rode next to Carlo Malatesta at the front of the army, the Pope and Zoe behind in a carriage. No one had yet dared throw anything at them.

Mocenigo looked behind him, then at Carlo. 'Should we release him?'

'And show weakness? No.' Carlo Malatesta was dressed in his black armour and wore a red cloak patterned with gold fleur-de-lys over the shoulder. 'We'll release him when we get to Mistra the day after tomorrow, no sooner.'

The Doge turned again, his fist on the back of the saddle. The cage was far behind but he could hear the anger. A woman ran out to pass something to Luke and a knight's horse reared, nearly throwing its rider. He saw the knight draw his sword and hit the woman with the flat of the blade. He swore, turned his horse and kicked it into a trot, reaching the cage. 'No violence!' he shouted. 'These are the people we are to rule.' He glanced down at Luke. 'You'll be released at Mistra.'

A day later, and eighty miles to the north, a smaller army was being greeted differently by the villages it marched through. There was some confusion at first. A hundred Varangians riding through in their blue *chlamydes*, axe and longbow strung across the backs of their saddles, was usual. The gazi horsemen who followed them, sometimes fanning out ahead to check for ambush, were not. Was this rescue or invasion?

But the word went out that the Akolouthos Matthew was at their head, best friend to their protostrator, who, they'd heard, had landed in the south but been caged by the Venetians. So they cheered them through the villages, then began to follow. Men picked up old weapons and fell in behind the gazis so that the little army of two hundred grew bigger by the hour.

At its head were four riders: Matthew, Shulen, Barbi and al-Tabingha. They'd just left a village and the last applause was fading.

Arcadius rode up from the rear and drew up his horse next to Matthew's. 'We have over four hundred following us now. But they're not soldiers.'

Matthew asked: 'Did you tell them to go home?'

Arcadius nodded. 'I told them but they won't listen. They want to come with us.'

The next day, Plethon was standing outside Mistra's upper gate beside the Despot and Emperor Manuel II Palaiologos. Behind them were perhaps a dozen of Byzantium's most senior nobles, some of whom had arrived from Constantinople with Manuel a week ago. The Empress Helena Dragaš had stayed behind. She had fought hard with her husband to stop the sale of Mistra and could not be persuaded to attend the shameful ceremony.

Manuel had been more shamed to hear of Luke's humiliation when he'd arrived in Mistra. He wanted to send a message to Modone demanding the Protostrator's immediate release. But the nobles had murmured in his ear, glad that Helena Dragaš was somewhere else. He had insisted, though, on Plethon being set free.

Beside the nobles stood a citizen of Venice, covered in dust. He'd arrived two hours earlier, having ridden fast from the north. He had a message for his doge.

The day was almost over and the road should have been full of men and women with nets, returning from harvesting olives in the fields above the city. Now, it had a pope, a doge and the Prince of Rimini filling it, ahead of an army that included a cage. The Pope and Doge rode in front, Carlo Malatesta next to Zoe behind.

Manuel was dressed in the heavy gilded robes of the Basileus, and his temper was sour. Plethon, in his toga, was cooler and happy to be free.

The calvacade stopped and the Pope and Doge rode forward alone, dismounting in front of Manuel and Theodore. The four embraced but no one knelt. The Emperor and his son would kiss the ring of the Patriarch in Constantinople but not the Pope of Rome.

Pope Martin stared over Manuel's shoulder. 'I am surprised to see an excommunicated man among the welcoming party.'

'As I am to see my protostrator in a cage,' replied Manuel. 'What is his crime?'

Pope Martin was wearing the full papal regalia and the triple crown was heavy on his head. He wiped his brow with his glove, still staring at Plethon. 'Magoris's crime was to attempt to break a monopoly granted to Venice by my predecessors. Plethon's crime is worse: heresy.'

Plethon stepped forward. He bowed and straightened up. 'I am interested in ancient wisdom,' he said, patting a fold of toga to his shoulder, 'as are many scholars in your own country. Have you even read the Lucretius?'

'Of course not. It's heretical.'

'No, it's just full of new ideas,' said Plethon. 'You are threatened.'

Pope Martin coloured. 'As you are excommunicated, I will not debate with you.'

The Doge intervened. 'Come, this is no way for us to start. The Holy Father knows that excommunication can only affect those in his own Church.' He turned to Manuel. 'And you should know that the Protostrator will be released from his cage once we get inside the city.' He paused and looked at them both. 'Shall we go in?'

An hour later, the dusty messenger had delivered his message to the Doge and the Venetian army had gone.

Mocenigo had received badly the news that an Ottoman army was marching on Negroponte with Prince Mehmed at its head. With Candia, it was Venice's most valuable colony and now its garrison and fleet were somewhere else. At first, he had just stared at the messenger. Then he walked back to his general-issimo and summoned the captains. When he came back to join the Pope and Manuel, he was grave. 'The army must leave immediately for Negroponte,' he'd said.

So Plethon was humming as he walked down the streets towards the palace. As soon as he arrived, he spoke to the Doge about Luke. Mocenigo listened, nodded, and went over to Malatesta. 'Break open the cage. No more of this. We've lost our army.'

The condottiere said: 'But there is an army already here.' He gestured to the men lining the square. 'The Despot has two thousand men. I'll release Magoris from his cage but we must keep him under lock and key. There's too much at stake.'

The Doge looked around him at the Albanian mercenaries. He nodded. 'Free him now.'

Plethon walked over to the cage and watched as the bars were pulled apart and Luke crawled out and got to his feet. They embraced and then Luke asked: 'Where's Anna?'

Plethon said: 'At her house, and Hilarion is with her. He arrived this morning.' He looked hard at Luke. 'Should I bring it now, do you think?'

491

'Perhaps.'

'I thought so too. Hilarion can help me.'

The journey to the chapel was slow, too slow for Hilarion, who was far ahead of his mother and Plethon.

They had left the city by the wall of the Peribleptos Monastery, helped over by monks to the horses waiting below while others kept watch for soldiers patrolling the ramparts. The night was still and a half-moon dressed everything in grey, merging objects into their shadows. An owl called from deep within the forest and was answered by one closer.

Hilarion was the last over. He had arrived at Mistra earlier and gone straight to the Laskaris house to see his mother. Plethon had come later and told them that they were to bring the Varangian treasure into the city after dark.

'The three of us?'

'There's no one else who can know of it. We can manage.'

'But I don't know of it.'

Then Anna had taken Hilarion's hands between hers and kissed them. 'And nor can you. Yet.'

He had not argued. He had been told that Giovanni knew of it but he didn't mind. After all, Giovanni was the elder son, the heir. What mattered was that the treasure, whatever it was, was coming into the city that night and he would be one of those that brought it. At last, after centuries in hiding, the Varangian treasure might be revealed. He felt giddy with excitement.

He supposed they were taking the same path that Giovanni had taken to see it. He looked back to see his mother glancing from side to side, Plethon hidden behind. Of course. This must have been the very path Anna had ridden all those years ago when she'd escaped from the besieged city to get help from Monemvasia.

Somewhere along this path would be the place where she'd first met Suleyman. Was she remembering that meeting?

The owl hooted again and Hilarion's horse snorted. The forest around was blacker than pitch. A branch cracked above him and he looked up. The moon was hidden by the trees and the sky he could see was freckled with stars. He breathed deeply and closed his eyes.

The treasure.

He opened them to see that they were coming to the clearing with the chapel in it. He had not been there before, kept away by the story every child of Mistra knew.

As they emerged from from the trees, the moon appeared and he took comfort from its glow. He stopped and waited for the others to arrive.

'We will need to be quick,' said Plethon as he rode up. 'Take the spade.'

They entered the chapel and Hilarion began to dig, his young body bare to the waist and glistening in the candlelight, earth on his hands. He hit metal and looked up. 'I've found it.'

Plethon rose. 'Well, let's bring it up.'

He got into the trench and helped Hilarion lift the casket to the floor of the chapel. They didn't open it but wrapped it in hessian and carried it to the mule. When it was tied on, Anna checked the straps. 'They're tight.'

Hilarion led the animal back to the path and stayed with them this time, Plethon walking behind. He watched the casket as it swayed. He glanced down at the dragon sword in his belt. Suddenly he felt a little afraid. He looked at Anna across the back of the mule. She was staring straight ahead. The treasure was released at last.

*

As the Varangian treasure was being brought down to the city, Luke was lying awake in a cell beneath the Despot's palace. He'd tried to sleep but the two guards outside his bars had talked without ceasing since he'd arrived. Now there was one and he was snoring loudly. The only light came from the oil lamp at the man's feet. He heard a whisper.

'Luke!'

It was Giovanni's voice and it came from the adjoining cell. He got up from the bed and came to the bars, crouching and pressing his cheek to the wall that divided them. The guard's snores faltered, then resumed.

'Giovanni, can you hear me?'

'Yes.' He heard the scrape of shoulder on stone. 'But we must talk fast. The guards change soon and the other one doesn't sleep. I always knew you were alive.'

Luke tried to put his hand through the bars. His son's face was so close, his breath mingling with his own, but he couldn't see him, couldn't touch him. He wanted so much to touch him. 'How long have you been here?'

'Not long.' He paused. 'I am your son.'

The silence was heavy between them, the weight of what had been said thickening the darkness around. Hilarion knew it so Giovanni must know it. Of course.

'I've always known,' Giovanni continued. 'As has Marchese Longo, I think.'

Silence again. Then: 'Probably. He is wise. A good father.'

'Which is what Plethon said.' There was the soft sound of breath released. 'Well, he need never know that I know.' Another pause, longer this time. 'Have you heard anything of Cleope?'

'No more than you, I expect. She's held somewhere else.'

494

The guard's snores were suddenly loud. 'Did Anna tell you that I was dead?'

'She told us both: me and Hilarion. I feared for her mind.' Giovanni paused. 'I must hope that Cleope will love me like that.'

Luke closed his eyes, rocked by the waves of guilt that rose up about him. He asked: 'Have you seen Anna?'

The guard shifted in his seat and grunted. Giovanni paused, watching him. He said: 'She's angry. It is to be expected.'

Luke nodded to himself. Would she recover from such anger? Probably not. But there was his son's life to think of. 'Carlo Malatesta is planning to take you to Rimini.'

'Where he'll kill me. To tell the truth, I deserve it. I've brought ruin on Mistra by bringing Cleope here.'

Luke stretched his fingers between the last two bars. 'No!' he said. 'You must never think that. This is Pope Martin's crusade against Plethon's heresy, backed by Venice's greed. It has little to do with Cleope.'

'So why does Carlo Malatesta lead it?' asked his son.

Luke spoke quickly. 'Venice has always wanted Mistra. Zoe has provided the excuse to seize it. She's brought together Malatesta vengeance, Venetian avarice, and Pope Martin's wish to expand his flock. Cleope is just a small part of it.'

There came no answer from the adjacent cell, just breathing.

Luke said: 'It would have happened without you taking Cleope.'

'But why has Zoe done this?'

Luke thought for a while. There were likely to be so many reasons. He tried one. 'It's about how she's been treated by men, by her father, her brother . . . by me. It's that and other things.' He paused. 'She spoke to me a few days ago. She tried to help us.'

'So might she help us now?'

495

Luke's mind wandered through the battlefield that had been his shared life with Zoe. It was a field strewn with dead. He thought of his father kneeling on a rain-swept jetty with a crossbow bolt through his heart. 'Giovanni, she tried to bury Anna alive.' He paused again. 'Some crimes can never be forgiven.'

They heard a sound from along the corridor, footsteps on stone. Giovanni's voice came closer. 'The guards are changing. Tell me quickly, is there hope?'

Luke frowned. Was there hope? Probably not, but his son needed hope. He said: 'The Pope and Doge have come far to get Mistra and it will take a miracle to stop them. But the Doge's army has left.'

'Where have they gone?'

'To defend Negroponte. The Sultan Mehmed is repaying a debt.'

The footsteps were nearing and they heard the jangle of keys. Giovanni asked: 'What about Matthew?'

'The Varangians number a hundred,' said Luke. 'And Matthew is oath-bound to obey the Emperor.'

The guard was a few steps away. He shouted something in Albanian, and the other woke with a start. He rose and banged his sword against Giovanni's bars.

Luke lay back, his head against the cell wall. There was another bit of hope he'd not shared with his son: the treasure. Would Plethon have brought it into Mistra?

And how would he use it if he had?

CHAPTER FORTY-TWO

MISTRA, AUTUMN 1418

The following morning, Luke awoke to murmur and the percussion of many feet above. He opened his eyes just enough to see dust shake free from the ceiling. He could guess why. It was the day of the ceremony and the Albanian army would be forming up in the square to escort the Pope, Doge and Emperor down to the cathedral at the bottom of the town. He didn't imagine he would be in the party.

He had seen the mood of the people on the journey up from Pilos. He had been handed flowers and food and even children to bless through the bars of his cage. He had seen the knights around him pummelled with dirt. He would not be put back in the cage.

He heard movement in the cell next door and moved towards it but the guard saw and banged on his bars. Not long afterwards, another man brought food and stayed to watch him eat.

And all the while the murmur and shuffle above grew louder.

Later that morning, Luke was taken from his cell, chained at the wrists and led upstairs into a room he knew well. It was Theodore's throne room, the biggest in the palace. It had tall windows on either side, half overlooking the city, half the courtyard, with a balcony from where the Despot could address his people. It was the room from which he and Plethon and Theodore had ruled Mistra. He remembered them sitting at the long table, looking over a map or inventory, their heads as close as their minds. They'd ruled well between them, hadn't they? How had it come to this?

He looked around him. There were shields on the walls with the Byzantine eagle on them looking both ways, east and west: two ways to empire. In between were the flags of Venice and St Peter. He felt something fall on to his hair and looked up. High above, the room's rafters were garlanded with flowers and petals floated down in the sunlight, dancing their way to his feet.

His eyes travelled over the people in the room, most of whom were looking out of the windows on to the square. He saw Pope Martin and two cardinals. He saw Manuel and Theodore. He saw the Doge, Zoe and Carlo Malatesta. He saw tense people, angry people, some afraid. Then came relief: the man he most wanted to see was looking at him.

He stared at the philosopher and received an undetectable nod in return. He had got the treasure. He looked around the room again. No Anna, and no Hilarion.

Carlo Malatesta was halfway on to the balcony, the Doge peering over his shoulder. The condottiere was speaking. 'We'll have to do it here; we'll never get across that square.'

'And the Patriarch?' This was Manuel, who stood at the next window.

'I'll send some of my men to bring him up.'

Luke glanced around the walls of the room. There were soldiers lining it, all Carlo's men. He looked through the window nearest to him. He couldn't see below the trees but could hear the growl of the crowd. It rose and fell with the shouts of individuals, and the shouts were mostly about him.

He looked back into the room to find Zoe watching him. She appeared calmer than the men and a little amused, her head to one side.

Now the Doge saw Luke. He came forward and looked down at his chains, then turned. 'Malatesta, have we not learnt from the cage?' He gestured to the window. 'From the crowd outside?'

Carlo shrugged. He was wearing armour and had a big sword strapped to his front. 'As you wish.'

'I do wish,' said the Doge. He fixed his gaze on Luke. 'The people like you.'

Luke glanced again at the window. He saw one of the treetops shaking. A man appeared on a branch, saw Luke and yelled something down to the square. A louder roar came up to them.

'For God's sake, get rid of his chains!' said the Doge.

A man appeared with a key and the chains were removed. Luke massaged his wrists.

Carlo Malatesta turned to the Doge. 'So they know he's here and they're angry.' He had his arms folded as far as his armour allowed. 'But we have an agreement to sign and two thousand soldiers to enforce it. What do you suggest? Do I bring up the Patriarch and shall we have the ceremony here?'

The Doge looked at Manuel. 'Should you talk to the people perhaps?'

Manuel was staring at Luke. 'It's not me they want to hear.'

Carlo Malatesta returned to the balcony. He said: 'We should wait for my man to return. He'll tell us how things are in the rest of the city.' He turned his eyes to Luke. 'And we shouldn't let this man speak to anyone without some insurance in place. We should bring Giovanni Longo.' He paused and looked back to the square. 'And my niece.'

The Doge glanced at Pope Martin, then Manuel. He nodded. 'Fetch them.'

They waited in silence. The crowd outside had begun chanting Luke's name and the branches of the trees were now full of people. Whatever soldiers were outside were not keeping order.

The Pope had moved to the window. 'Prince Malatesta, your soldiers are not held in awe.'

'Holy Father, my soldiers are inside this room. Outside are the Despot's.'

The door at the end of the room opened and one of Carlo's officers entered. He looked as if he had been jostled and his plume was on end. He walked over to his general and whispered in his ear. The condottiere bowed his head to hear it again. He looked up.

'It seems there are Varangians outside the city,' he said. 'And they have gazi horse archers with them. They've come up from Monemvasia and have brought peasants who are now within the walls.' He looked at Manuel. 'We should close the gates.'

The Emperor shook his head. 'Against our own people? No.' He glanced at Luke. 'The Varangians will not enter the city, will they?'

'Not if you order them not to, majesty.'

Malatesta was walking towards the door. 'Their akolouthos has entered the city, however, and is outside. We should make sure he understands his orders.'

He reached the door and opened it and Luke saw people he knew enter one by one. First came Matthew with Benedo Barbi and al-Tabingha. Behind came Giovanni, then Cleope. Giovanni was chained at the wrists. They filed in between Carlo's men and stood side by side at the end of the room, most of them directing their gaze on Luke. Giovanni and Cleope looked at each other.

Luke glanced at the Doge who was staring at al-Tabingha in amazement. He saw him go over to Zoe and whisper in her ear.

The door was still open and Anna walked into the room. She was dressed in black and her hair was gathered up like an autumn crown. She was pale and thin but her back was straight and her eyes never left Luke's face. She passed Carlo, Matthew and the others and came up to him. She put her hand to his cheek. She whispered: 'I love you.'

'And I you.' He kissed her forehead. 'Where is Hilarion?'

'At home. He is safe.'

Carlo Malatesta closed the door. He walked up to Cleope and bent to kiss her but she pulled away and slapped him. He stepped back, holding his cheek, his head moving from side to side, his jaw working over his burn. Then he straightened up and dropped his hand to his side, still staring at Cleope. He moved over to Giovanni, took hold of his chain and dragged him to Luke's side.

'You will tell the Akolouthos that he is to obey the orders of his emperor,' he said, his face very close to Luke's. 'Then you'll go on to the balcony and tell the crowd to disperse.' He drew a dagger and pointed it at Giovanni. 'And if you say anything I don't like, I'll kill this boy.'

The Doge said: 'Malatesta, you go too far.'

The Prince of Rimini rounded on him. 'Do you *want* this kingdom?' He pointed his dagger towards the window. 'There's a crowd of unarmed citizens out there who need to be told where their loyalties now lie. The Protostrator will do it.'

Luke raised a hand, the other holding Anna's. He looked at Matthew and spoke calmly. 'You will obey our emperor in all things,' he said. He turned to the Doge. 'I will speak to the people as the Prince suggests.'

He let go of Anna's hand and walked out on to the balcony. The crowd roared. He looked around the square. It was choked with people. There were thousands of them, some waving their arms, some weapons. They thronged the open spaces, the walls, the roofs, the trees. Children sat on their parents' shoulders. Where yesterday he had seen three flags hanging side by side, now there was one: the double-headed eagle of the Palaiologoi. There were no soldiers to be seen.

He scanned the crowd below, seeing faces he knew turned up to him with hope in their eyes. He saw Shulen among them; she nodded. He saw Arcadius next to her. Luke put his fists on to the balcony rail and leant forward. The crowd fell quiet.

'Citizens of Mistra,' he said, turning his head slowly so that all could hear him. 'You know me.'

A roar that continued for some time. Gradually the crowd fell quiet again. Luke looked around the square again, up in the trees and on the roofs, his eyes moving from face to face, seeing many he knew, seeing only trust.

'Your emperor has judged that the best way of preserving our freedom is to give our city to Venice.' He raised his hand as the first shout came and went. 'And who are we to say he is wrong?' Silence. 'Twenty-five years ago, this city had a Turkish army at its gates, ten years ago another. Had they prevailed, they would have enslaved you, and our churches would now be mosques.' He paused, waiting for his words to settle in the oldest and youngest mind. 'Venice is Christian. Venice is free. Venice is strong.'

The silence was universal now, both below and behind him. People in the square were frowning and shaking their heads. Luke turned into the room and his eyes met Anna's. He extended his arm; she came over to him and took his hand and stood by his side on the balcony.

'You know this woman. She was daughter to your last pro-tostrator and is now my wife. She is Anna Laskaris.' There was some murmur below. 'When she and I met, this kingdom was at war.' He paused. 'Would you have us go back to those days? Or would you have us united against a greater foe?'

A voice shouted up from the square. 'But you have gold coming to pay back these crows!'

'Yes, I do,' said Luke. 'And no one will stop it because it is guarded by ten Mamluk triremes sent out from Alexandria.' He waited for the news to be absorbed behind him. 'But it will arrive too late. Behind me are the Pope and the Doge of Venice. They're here to accept Mistra's surrender *today*.'

Luke glanced at Anna. She was watching him with the merest thread of a frown tracing her brow like a new vein. Like everyone else, she was waiting. He turned back to the square. 'Above all, you must obey our emperor and our emperor calls on you to disperse.'

The murmur that had been partial became general. It rose as a blend of anger and bewilderment, frayed at the edges, bits parting to form ragged shouts. Luke raised his hand. It might be the last time he would be able to command silence. He glanced behind him through the window and saw Carlo watching him with his dagger drawn, a grim smile on his lips, his hand on Giovanni's shoulder. He saw that Matthew had moved to stand behind him.

He turned once more to the square, one hand raised, the other holding Anna's.

'However,' he said, louder because the murmur had risen, 'Venice may decide that it does not want Mistra after all.' He turned his head to the side so that people could see that he addressed two audiences now. 'The Doge's office is not as old as our emperor's but it is wise.' He glanced inside to see Mocenigo staring at him. '*It may be*', he continued, louder, 'that Venice prizes its friendship with Egypt, its monopoly over trade through Alexandria, more than it covets our despotate.'

The crowd below had fallen silent again, its many eyes no longer on one another but on Luke. Most had no idea of any monopoly but they could hear the change in Luke's tone. This was hope.

'You will know', said Luke, 'that I have come from Africa. I received gold there from people called the Wangara. They mine the gold that comes into Venice from Egypt.' He paused, waiting for the silence to be complete. 'They have said that, from now on, they will trade only with *me*, or those I send to them.' He paused again, longer this time. 'In other words, without me, Venice gets no gold.' He gestured into the room. 'There is a man here with a letter that confirms the truth of what I say.'

Luke heard movement behind him and turned. Matthew was now standing between Carlo Malatesta and Giovanni, his sword drawn. He saw the Doge walk over to the condottiere and place a hand on his arm. He looked down at Anna and saw she was smiling at him, her green eyes clearer than they'd been before. She squeezed his hand and nodded. He turned back to the square where now there was some noise: the noise of people confused.

He said: 'I have asked you to disperse and you will not do it. You want to know the fate of your kingdom, I too. So I ask of you this instead: sit. Sit and wait for the men in this room behind me to decide what to do. And sit in silence. I myself will come back on to this balcony to tell you their answer.'

Luke turned and, with Anna beside him, walked back into the room.

He saw a rearrangement of the people there. He saw the Doge reading a letter with al-Tabingha beside him. He saw Carlo Malatesta addressing Pope Martin, the dagger still in his hand; he saw Matthew with his arm around Giovanni, still chained. He saw Cleope rise on tiptoes to kiss his son on his lips. He waited.

At length, the Doge looked up from the Sultan's letter. He said: 'Some silence, please.' He turned to Luke. 'The Mamluk Sultan confirms what you say,' he went on. 'This changes things.'

Luke inclined his head. 'To your advantage, lord, if you would only see it. The world is changing. Your trade with the East, Egypt's too, is threatened by Portugal. The key to unlocking a future where both of you prosper lies with China. I can not only deliver gold, I can deliver China.'

'And your price is Mistra.'

It wasn't a question, but Luke nodded. His price had always been Mistra. He said: 'I have a ship arriving under the command of the second most powerful man in China. It has enough gold in it to repay your debt, give money to my emperor, and build this kingdom into a prosperous trading nation that will be friends with Christian Venice.'

'Enough!' A jewelled crozier struck the floor. At last, Pope Martin had decided to speak. 'This is a sordid business,' he said, striding forward and stopping before the Doge. 'When does the expediency of *trade* rank before the will of God?' He looked around the room, his crozier held like a spear. 'Listen to what is being said! I have proclaimed a crusade to gather this kingdom into the bosom of Christ. Will you now deny me this?'

Mocenigo said: 'Holy Father, we have two great powers expressing their will: the Sultan by this letter; Mehmed by attacking Negroponte. Neither of them wants us to have Mistra.'

Pope Martin rounded on him. 'And are we now to be dictated

to by the heathen?' He moved close to the Doge. 'Is Venice ready for another excommunication? Is the Pope to transfer God's favour to the Portuguese?'

Luke watched all this, happy to let the discussion broaden to more parties. He saw a man who hadn't spoken catch his eye and he nodded to him. Plethon stepped forward.

'Holiness, I am excommunicated so I may be said to have the honesty of the damned.' He had his hands joined as he did when making a delicate point. 'I have something to show you that may inform your decision.'

Pope Martin stared at him. 'I know what you want to show me.'

Plethon looked surprised. 'Do you, Holy Father? What is it?'

The Pope straightened up. 'It is a casket.'

There was silence in the room. A petal landed on Pope Martin's beard and he brushed it away. He continued: 'Inside it are the tablets brought down from Mount Sinai by Moses. When they are put inside what was brought up from Abyssinia, they will form the Ark of the Covenant. But you have a problem: we have the chest.'

'Not so.'

Luke's head, like everyone else's, turned to Benedo Barbi, who'd spoken from the other end of the room.

Barbi continued: 'What you have is an empty box.' He gestured to al-Tabingha. 'This man will verify it.'

'So,' resumed Plethon, turning to Pope Martin, 'you may assume that what I will show you is not the Ark of the Covenant but something else. Will you follow me?'

Carlo Malatesta walked over to the Pope, still holding the dagger. 'Holy Father, the man is excommunicated. You cannot go with him.'

Manuel intervened. 'I can go.'

'No,' said Plethon. 'We go alone or not at all.'

Pope Martin glared around the room, both hands to his crozier. His eyes came back to Plethon. He nodded.

The two men walked the length of the room. The guards opened the door and they passed through it. The door closed behind them.

There was more silence in the room: the silence of those waiting for revelation. Inside, people stood apart, some looking at shields, others at their feet, some down at the crowd seated below in the square, also silent. Luke closed his eyes. His heart was beating loud enough to drive a galley. At this very moment, God's Vicar on earth would be learning that the central belief of his ministry was a lie. He'd be shown a body, a ring, and ancient manuscripts that said that Jesus Christ had been only a man after all, and that, as a man, he had not risen from the dead.

He opened his eyes to see a butterfly that had somehow flown in through a window. He watched it shimmer its way through sunbeams, past people standing like statues, past one pacing the floor with a squeak at each turn. He heard a dog bark far below, then another. He thought that eternity was being stretched out in that tall room, the only rhythm of time in the pounding of his heart.

At last, the door opened and the Pope entered, Plethon behind him. Martin was stooped, as if a heavy and invisible load had been placed on his back. He came up to the Doge and stopped. He looked up. Luke saw a face fractured with grief.

'There are things I need to think about,' he said quietly. 'Not here, but in Rome. This crusade is over.'

'No!' It was Carlo Malatesta who had shouted. He strode up

to the Pope. 'What is there to think about, Holy Father? What has changed?'

The Pope turned to him, his crozier now his crutch. He looked broken and ready to fall. 'Everything,' he said simply.

Malatesta's sword, already drawn, was pointing at Giovanni. 'But his sin hasn't changed. If I go home, he comes with me, as does my niece.'

Luke said: 'Malatesta, it is over. You'd never get them away.'

'Oh, but I will,' said the condottiere, swinging round to him. 'I have your other son held at the citadel.'

Anna gasped. She put her hand to her mouth, her eyes wide with horror. Luke said: 'Hilarion is at my house.'

'No he's not.' Malatesta signalled to the officer who'd whispered in his ear. 'Bring it.' The man came over and placed the dragon sword in his hand. 'Is this proof enough? My men have him in the citadel. When they see me leave this city, he'll be released.'

'You will not get across the square.'

'I think I will' – Malatesta pointed his sword at the balcony – 'because you'll go on to the balcony and tell them to let me pass.'

Luke considered this. He said: 'I'll need you there with me, so they can recognise you.' He looked at Giovanni. 'You and Giovanni.'

Malatesta nodded. He walked over to Giovanni and yanked his chains.

Cleope put her hand on her uncle's arm. 'If you take him back to Rimini with us,' she said, her voice forced into calm, 'you'll lose me forever. Understand that.'

The condottiere shrugged and pulled away. 'So be it.' He dragged Giovanni towards the balcony.

The three of them walked out together and the people rose to greet them. There was a sound of push and shuffle and it took time to subside. When all was silent again, Luke spoke.

'Our emperor, the Doge of Venice and His Holiness the Pope have decided, in their wisdom, that Mistra should remain free.'

The shout was so great and sudden that the square seemed to erupt. Flagstones trembled and trees shook as a lava of joy rose up, flowed over the palace roof and fell down on the city. Ripples of noise swept down through the streets, getting louder as they went. Mistra was free.

Luke held up one hand, then two, for silence but none came for a long time. People were too busy embracing their neighbours to look at the balcony. But eventually the square became quiet. Luke searched the crowd for a face. There.

Shulen.

He stared at her, making sure that she knew he was addressing only her.

'The Prince of Rimini will be leaving the palace with his niece and my former page, Giovanni.' He gestured to them. 'I ask that no man' – he nodded his head to the word – 'no *man* should try and stop them. They will be leaving the city for Modone.' He paused. 'Let this be understood.'

Luke saw Shulen turn.

Carlo Malatesta dragged Giovanni back into the hall. Zoe was waiting for him.

'Take me with you.'

The condottiere stopped in front of her. He looked surprised. 'Why?'

'I'm not popular here. I'd rather leave with your men around me.'

He thought for a moment, watching her with curiosity. Then he nodded. 'Very well. I may need your bribes.'

It took Shulen ten minutes to push her way through the square and run up the street to the city gate. Arcadius was waiting there with the Varangians.

'Malatesta is leaving with Giovanni. He's done something to make Luke agree. What?'

Arcadius looked hard at her, concentrating. 'He'd take someone hostage. Anna?'

Shulen shook her head. 'She's with Luke.' She looked at Arcadius. The same thought had entered both their minds. 'Hilarion?'

Arcadius frowned. 'But where would he take him?' He glanced up at the citadel. 'That's where I would take him. The Albanians are there.' He nodded. 'I'll take half the company up there to look for him. You and Peter take the rest to watch the road west.'

They divided the men and Shulen led her party up the road, Peter of Norfolk beside her. They reached the forest and found places to hide on either side of the road.

'How many of them?' asked Peter, when they were lying among the trees, the pine needles soft beneath them.

'Twenty perhaps. But they'll be good.'

'How do we stop Giovanni from getting hurt?'

Shulen hadn't considered this in her rush to be ahead of Malatesta. They had fifty bowmen who would not miss their targets, but what if Malatesta used Giovanni as a shield?

They heard the sound of horses on the road behind them, horses being pushed hard.

'It's them,' said Shulen. 'Get the men ready.'

The riders appeared, Carlo with Giovanni on the saddle before him, still chained. The condottiere had the dragon sword in his belt. Cleope and Zoe came next. Shulen's mind raced. They could kill most of the men but Carlo might still escape with Giovanni. The Varangians' horses were stabled half a mile away. By the time they got to them, Malatesta would be beyond reach. What to do?

She decided. She rose and walked out into the road. She was unarmed.

Malatesta brought his horse to a halt, raising his hand to stop the others. He was fifty paces from her.

'Who are you?' he yelled, his horse wheeling on the rein. He held Giovanni close to him on the saddle, his arm around his middle.

'I am someone with fifty arrows aimed at you,' said Shulen. 'Release your prisoner and they'll stay on their strings.'

Malatesta glanced at the men on either side of the road who'd risen with their bows aimed. He drew a knife and placed its blade at Giovanni's throat.

'And if a single arrow flies, I'll cut his throat.'

Cleope shouted: 'Don't let them shoot!'

Shulen's stomach lurched. She had been mad to think it would work. She turned to Peter of Norfolk. 'Lower the bows.' She looked back at Carlo. 'Even if you get back to Modone, what ship will take you?'

The condottiere gestured at Zoe. 'She'll buy one for me.'

Shulen hadn't seen Zoe until that point. She was cloaked and next to Cleope. She had a crossbow across her lap, aimed straight at her.

'So,' Carlo said, his head beside Giovanni's again, the knife still at his neck, 'you'll favour me by stepping aside and allowing us on our way. Otherwise Zoe will shoot you.' He kicked his horse. 'That is, if I haven't already ridden you down.'

Malatesta's horse reared, then started forward. Shulen stayed where she was. She shouted: 'Varangians, don't shoot!'

The horse came on, gathering speed, its rider making no attempt to change its course. Shulen was unable to move. She closed her eyes.

There was a cry, then a thud. She opened them and saw Carlo on the ground, a crossbow bolt in his shoulder. Giovanni lay next to him. Carlo tried to reach for Giovanni, but he rolled away.

Shulen glanced at Zoe. The crossbow was still aimed but had no bolt on it.

Giovanni got to his knees, his wrists still joined. He rose and staggered over to Cleope. The Varangians aimed their bows again, this time at Malatesta.

Shulen walked over and crouched beside the condottiere. She looked at the bolt in his shoulder. 'You'll live,' she said. She took the dragon sword from his belt. 'Now, let's return to the palace.'

CHAPTER FORTY-THREE

MONEMVASIA, AUTUMN 1418

Nine years ealier, the people of Monemvasia had been surprised to see a treasure ship sail into their waters. This time, they were expecting it.

In the streets and squares and trees and bell towers, on the walls and rocks below, they stood and waited throughout the day, talking of gold. They were still there in the evening when the ebbing sun joined in, splashing the heavens with the metal, hurling its colour across the sky like a careless apprentice.

At last, a horn. The sound was deep, carried over the water in waves by the swell, and the bell of the Elkomenos Church answered. Then a ship bigger than anything they'd seen before hove into view, twelve giant sails turned for the wind, dragons pointing its direction above. Around it swam sea otters, let out to play and, above, birds dived and rose for the fishes they left.

The horn sounded again and the birds scattered like seed.

Luke was in the square, standing next to the Emperor Manuel; Theodore, Plethon and Anna a little behind. He watched the treasure ship approach with relief; the Mamluk galleys had left to collect al-Tabingha from Pilos and Admiral Zheng had made the last of his journey unguarded. But here it was, the dragon at its bow nudging aside the waves, bringing its gold to Mistra.

On the quayside, a younger and less patient party watched the ship heave to and then drop anchor. The ship's decks were crowded with people: dignitaries at the top, scholars in the middle and, below, giggling courtesans in their silks under parasols. The main deck was full of soldiers with flags of every shade but yellow.

A barge was lowered over the side and the rowers took up their oars. Then two men walked down the steps and got into it. Ten minutes later, they were at the quayside.

'Nikolas.'

The Varangians embraced each other as they always did, this time with Giovanni and Hilarion instead of their father. Heads down, arms interlocked, they marked the passing of the years with whispers and laughter. Cleope looked on and smiled, her hand in Shulen's.

When it was finished, the party set off for the city gate, Admiral Zheng in front with Hilarion, the Varangians, Shulen, Cleope and Giovanni behind, arm in arm. The barge, meanwhile, returned to bring the crew and passengers ashore. Nine years ago they'd have frightened the barbarians; now they'd entertain them.

Nikolas said: 'We'll double the population, did you realise that?'

'So we've doubled the city. Look.' Matthew pointed to fields beyond the bridge, which were covered with tents of every size. The despotate had been emptied of canvas. 'We thought your passengers might like some firm ground.'

Nikolas laughed. 'You hoped the concubines might.'

514

Arcadius said: 'Shulen says you have one for yourself.'

'Whom I plan to marry when I return. Her name is Zhu Chou.'

He'd told his friends he would not be staying. They'd always thought it likely; now it was certain. They didn't speak for a while.

Arcadius turned. 'And you, Shulen?'

She was walking beside Cleope. 'I'll go back to make sure he marries her.'

Matthew saw Admiral Zheng stop to look out over the sea, his hands on his hips. Hilarion was pointing out the different ships, explaining where they'd come from. Matthew stopped as well. 'Did you pass a fleet?'

Nikolas nodded. 'A Venetian one with a pope in the middle of it. They were going fast.'

'And won't be stopping on the way, I'd guess,' said Arcadius. 'Their generalissimo will be keen to have his shoulder seen to.'

Nikolas turned to him. 'And you say that Zoe fired the shot. Why?'

Arcadius shrugged. 'Who knows? But she may have saved Giovanni's life. Anyway, she's gone with the Venetian fleet.'

Nikolas turned to Cleope. 'And Malatesta left without you. How did that happen?'

Cleope smiled. 'That', she said, 'you'll discover tonight.'

They reached the city gate and saw banners hung with dragons on them with Chinese words of welcome, dictated by Shulen. They walked into a street criss-crossed with pennants and dammed by people who fell back before them. The channelled noise was deafening. They arrived at the square.

Luke came forward and embraced Nikolas. Then he bowed to

Zheng. He turned and presented them to the Emperor. When it was done, Plethon stepped forward and took Nikolas by the arm, drawing him aside.

'Have you anything for me?' he asked.

Nikolas had given Plethon a scroll, tied up with Chinese silk, and the philosopher had not been seen since. Wherever he was, Shulen was with him.

Darkness had fallen on Monemvasia but the city was a galaxy of fire, the light carried, beacon by beacon, to Mistra. The wine stored for a siege would be drunk in a single night and the steep and cobbled streets soon ran Malvasie red. People slipped as they danced, singing as they fell. In the main square, tables had been set for a more formal feast and Admiral Zheng, his ambassadors and the loveliest of the concubines sat between Greeks with interpreters at their backs. Far above them was a night full of stars and, closer to, paper lanterns strung tree-to-tree, a gift from the Ming. Out at sea a big ship rode at anchor, also lit by lanterns, a river of silver joining it to the city. Tomorrow, gold would come down that river, more gold than any had ever seen.

The feast had many courses with entertainments in between. But the viol-players, jugglers and acrobats were no match for the fireworks that erupted from the treasure ship at the end. Monemvasia had heard of Mistra's gardens in the sky. Now they saw their own night explode into flower, saw showers of light, heard bangs loud enough to wake the city cemeteries. They cowered at first, then cheered.

Luke sat next to Anna at a table raised by a dais and studied her as she watched the fireworks end. As the last dribble of fire fell into the sea, he saw the calm she herself had reached. He had been told of an anger that had nearly destroyed her, then seen how it had changed to relief, then guilt, then the thing that had never really left: love. Tonight he had seen her take Shulen away to talk. N'gara had been right.

They will decide, not you.

The Emperor rose to speak. 'I have an announcement to make that will gladden the hearts of all who wish peace upon this despotate.' Manuel looked at Theodore and the woman beside him. 'My son is to marry Cleope Malatesta of Rimini, niece to Pope Martin.'

Luke looked at Giovanni. Since he'd had the idea, they'd discussed it often. It wasn't perfect but it was nearly so. The Despot wasn't interested in women but liked Cleope and needed a wife; Giovanni wanted Cleope to stay in Mistra. The Pope had blessed the match and Carlo Malatesta, his shoulder bandaged and sore, had been forced to agree.

'This marriage will bind our empire to Rome. Pope Martin has agreed to hold a council there to promote union between our two Churches. From such union can come help, should we need it in the future.' He raised his glass. 'To Theodore, Cleope and peace.'

Chairs were pushed back and people rose, Chinese next to Greek. They lifted their glasses to the couple and drank.

Now Manuel was facing Luke. 'We should also drink to our protostrator,' he said, raising his glass again. 'There is a ship out there with gold enough to enrich this kingdom.'

The guests drank and sat down. More toasts were made, some serious, some less so. The feast went on and no one went to bed. The treasure ship would leave on the morrow, as soon as the gold had been unloaded. Everyone wanted to remember that night for the rest of their lives.

Much later, Plethon appeared. Luke made room for him on the bench between him and Anna. He looked tired.

'You should come,' Plethon said. 'I need to show you something.'

Luke glanced at Anna. 'Both of us?'

The philosopher shook his head. 'Just you. And Giovanni.'

Luke saw Giovanni standing behind Plethon. He was holding the dragon sword.

Anna leant across and said to Luke: 'Go and say goodbye to her. I'll stay.' She smiled. 'Go.'

Luke rose and kissed his wife on the forehead, holding her face in his hands until she pulled them gently away. He followed Plethon and Giovanni out of the square and down several streets, stopping for embraces at every corner. They came to a church, the same church he'd taken Anna to on the night they'd tried to flee Monemvasia all those years ago. It was lit by candles at the windows and inside were Nikolas and Shulen, sitting together on the altar steps. Nikolas was holding the scroll he had given to Plethon.

Plethon took the scroll and turned to Luke. 'This', he said, holding it up, 'is the last testament of Nestorius, Patriarch of Constantinople, who was expelled from the city and took his heresy east. It is part of the Ming diadan and was brought here on the treasure ship, sent to me by Chen Cheng.' He paused. 'You'll know that Nestorius's heresy concerns the humanity of Jesus Christ. He'd seen the casket that contained the body, as some of us have done.'

He lifted the scroll higher. 'Except that it never was the body of Jesus Christ. The Patriarch lied. He abused another's skeleton and even created a ring. He did it to support his heresy and this' – he waved the scroll – 'is his confession.'

Luke stared at him. He shook his head slowly, thinking of a sacred oath, sworn by each of his ancestors. He thought of generations of Varangians who had offered their lives to protect something that had been a lie all along. He thought of his father who had died on a jetty not far from there. Suddenly he felt very tired. It was the same feeling he'd had when it it seemed that all his sacrifices for Tamerlane had been in vain, that oceans of blood had drowned the cities of Asia for no purpose. He sat down in a pew and put his head in his hands.

Giovanni came and sat down next to him. He rested the sword across both their knees so that the dragon stared up at Luke. He put his arm around his father's shoulders. 'It's not been for nothing,' he said quietly.

They both stared down at the sword in silence, oblivious to the others in the church. Luke lifted the dragon head and turned it in the candlelight, watching the silver scales become a river. He nodded. 'Perhaps this has been the treasure all along,' he said softly. 'An ideal to unite people to do noble things.' He turned to Giovanni. 'As you have done. As you will do.'

'With Hilarion.'

'With Hilarion.'

They heard movement. Plethon walked over and put his hand on Luke's shoulder. 'We'll leave you.'

Giovanni rose and he, Plethon and Nikolas walked towards the church door.

Luke thought of something. He looked up. 'Will you tell the Pope?'

Plethon stopped. 'Perhaps.' He opened the door and turned. 'Perhaps not.'

They left.

Luke and Shulen were alone in the church. He took her hand and led her out of the church and up on to the city walls, then along until they reached a tower. They climbed to its battlements and looked out over a sea lit only by the moon and the lights of the city. The treasure ship was a black island on its surface.

He turned to her. 'You're going back to China,' he said. 'Tomorrow.'

She nodded, still looking out. 'With Nikolas.'

The noise of celebration was less now, for the hour was late. He heard snatches of song and the crash of a table overturned, then laughter. He took her hand. 'Did you ever think you'd stay?'

She looked at him. 'Perhaps. When you were ill in Timbuktu. But then you died.'

'Shulen, I had to lie to you. It was N'gara's condition.'

She put her head to one side. 'And you thought I might betray you? After everything?'

He looked at her in silence for a while. Then he said what he'd said before.

'I'm sorry.'

She put her finger to his lips. 'Hush. Don't be. I have forgiven you.'

He asked: 'Does Anna know?'

'We talked tonight. She knows.'

He nodded.

They will decide.

'Will you come back?' he asked.

She looked up at him and the moon made her hair as silver as the sea. Her eyes locked on to his and were as mysterious as they'd been when he'd first seen her on the steppe.

'No, I won't come back,' she said. 'But, one day, you'll come to me. You will come to China as part of the empire you will build around the world, Luke Magoris, uniting people to do noble things.' She smiled. 'Until then, I'll wait.'

HISTORICAL NOTE

The Rise of Empires span the end of the fourteenth and first half of the fifteenth centuries, the last decades of the Byzantine Empire and a time of extraordinary global change: change that would determine the nature of our world today.

The series began with Byzantium in peril. In the first book, *The Walls of Byzantium,* a crusade from the West to relieve Constantinople was annihilated by the Turks at Nicopolis on the Danube (1396) and the Sultan Bayezid boasted that he would 'water his horses at the altar of St Peter's in Rome'. But in the second, *The Towers of Samarcand*, Tamerlane, a successor to Genghis Khan, was persuaded to come west to decisively beat Bayezid at the Battle of Ankara (1402). Bayezid was captured and put in a cage, but his eldest son Suleyman escaped with half of the army and crossed to Europe. Two other brothers, Mehmed and Musa, were captured and imprisoned.

This third novel, *The Lion of Mistra*, opens with Tamerlane's death as he prepares to invade Ming China. Mehmed has been released to rule the Ottoman lands in Tamerlane's name but his brother Suleyman has invaded Anatolia, taken Bursa and forced Mehmed back into his fortress at Amasya. Suleyman now looks set to threaten the Byzantine Empire again and the third brother, Musa, is sent into Europe to open a second front against him. Musa finally defeats and kills Suleyman and proclaims himself sultan, thus triggering a second civil war, which his brother Mehmed wins.

At the start of the fifteenth century, there were six important empires in the discovered world. Richest by far was the Ming Empire of China. The Ming dynasty had swept aside a hundred years of Mongol rule and in 1402 the third 'Yongle' Emperor, Zhu Di, had ascended the throne. He was perhaps the greatest of all the Chinese emperors, a man of towering drive and ambition who embarked on a series of huge projects: rebuilding the Great Wall, constructing a new palace in Beijing (the Forbidden City), extending the vast canal system to the south, and collecting all world knowledge into an eleven-thousand-volume encyclopaedia: the diadan. Perhaps his greatest project was to build the treasure fleets. He sent six of these enormous fleets out into the world to trade and exchange knowledge; the diadan went with them. They were commanded by the eunuch Zheng He and comprised ships over four hundred feet in length, with state rooms for scholars, envoys and concubines. But the Yongle Emperor faced opposition from the traditional 'Confucian scholar' class who had always ruled China and believed that foreign contact upset the *tao*. They disapproved of Zhu Di's ambitious plans and resented the eunuchs who'd brought him to power. In order to prove a heavenly mandate for his rule, the Yongle Emperor ordered a qilin be brought to China. The qilin was a mythical beast to the Chinese, but bore a close resemblance to a giraffe. One was brought to his court in 1414.

The second biggest empire was that of Tamerlane, built in twenty short years through slaughter and destruction on a scale never before seen. By 1400, from India to Syria, the great cities of Delhi, Herat, Kabul, Aleppo, Damascus and Baghdad had been reduced to ruins and towers of skulls. When Tamerlane's successor and grandson Pir Mohammed died, his son Shahrukh took the throne and was followed by his son Ulugh Beg, a scholar, man of peace and astronomer, who would build a great observatory outside Samarcand which can still be seen today. Without Tamerlane, the Timurid Empire gradually dissolved, but it remained a great power until the sixteenth century (and would provide the basis for the Mughal Empire of India thereafter).

Third of the empires, in wealth if not in size, was the Mamluk Empire of Egypt. The Mamluks were a slave warrior caste that had seized power from the Fatimids in the thirteenth century and consolidated their power by driving the crusaders from the Holy Land and the Mongols from Syria. But having lost Syria to Tamerlane, the Mamluks began the fifteenth century rich but fearful. Their wealth was based not just on the fertility of the Nile delta region but also on Egypt's status as the link between western and eastern trade. The port of Alexandria was the largest in the world and most of the world's gold supply, mined in the Empire of Mali, came through it on the way to Venice.

The West African Empire of Mali, though not a world power, was certainly rich, and its city of Timbuktu was a centre of Islamic culture and learning. The Emperor Mensa Musa had, in the fourteenth century, taken the hajj to Mecca and, on the way, spent so much gold in Cairo that the price of the metal was depressed for a decade. Until the discovery of America, most of the world's gold came from the mines of the Wangara, a Malian tribe who'd insisted on the 'silent trade' for their gold since the days of Carthage, whereby the exchange (usually for salt) happened via holes dug side by side and smoke signals sent to engage the other party.

The Ottoman Empire was born in the early fourteenth century in Anatolia, one of the many Turkic tribes snapping at the frayed frontiers of the Byzantine Empire. The Ottomans crossed into Europe in 1354 and, by 1402, under the leadership of the fourth in the line of Osman, Bayezid (known as 'Yildirim' or 'Thunderbolt'), were on the point of taking Constantinople. Their defeat at Ankara at the hands of Tamerlane meant a critical respite for Byzantium and led to a ten-year Ottoman civil war between the sons of Bayezid from which the second, Mehmed, emerged victorious at the Battle of Çamurlu (1413). Although Mehmed was a friend to Byzantium, it would not be long before Constantinople was threatened again by his son Murad.

The Byzantine Empire was the eastern half of the Roman Empire, the part that survived after German tribes overran much of the western half in the late fifth century. The Byzantines rightly considered themselves the heirs to Romulus and Remus and called themselves Rhomaioi, not Byzantine. Once a great world power, by the early fifteenth century the Empire had been reduced to just Constantinople and the Greek Peloponnese. This was partly the result of the great Arab conquests and the spread of Islam, and partly the perfidy of the Fourth Crusade when the crusaders, at the instigation of Venice, had been diverted to assault and plunder Constantinople. The Byzantine Empire never recovered from that.

By the time of these books, the Empire had practically no army or navy and the Varangian Guard, once its elite force, had almost ceased to exist. The Varangians had originally come from England, refugees from the Norman Conquest of 1066, and were famed for their height and use of the axe. The Emperor Manuel travelled to England as part of a European tour to raise money for the defence of Constantinople. Manuel spent Christmas 1400 at Henry IV's palace at Eltham, when a joust was organised in his honour. He was the only Emperor of Byzantium to visit England. In 1413, Henry IV was succeeded by his son Henry V who resumed the Hundred Years War with France and won the remarkable victory of Agincourt in 1415.

Finally, we come to where this series begins and ends: Mistra. The Peloponnese was called the Despotate of Mistra and invariably ruled by the brother or son of the Emperor in Constantinople. Mistra's capital was also called Mistra (or Mystras), and had been founded in the thirteenth century near the ancient site of Sparta. Its main trading port was the city of Monemvasia, sixty miles to the east, its fierce rival for wealth and influence. With Constantinople under siege from Sultan Bayezid (1396–1402), and thereafter by his son Musa, many of the city's rich fled to the safety of the Peloponnese. Because of this, Mistra enjoyed a renaissance of art and learning and the renowned philosopher Plethon made his home there. Plethon believed that Mistra could survive the fall of Constantinople if it reached back into its ancient Greek past. Much of his teaching was considered heretical.

Finally, there is the Venetian Empire. Of all the city states of northern Italy, the richest and most powerful was Venice. Its empire, developed to protect its trade routes, included most of the Dalmatian coast as well as the islands of Candia (Crete) and Negroponte (today's Evia). Its most important trade route was that to Alexandria where Venice enjoyed a monopoly, granted by the Pope, to trade with the heathen Mamluks. It is entirely true that Venice coveted the Greek Peloponnese as a vital stepping stone to Alexandria and in fact came close to buying it from cash-strapped Byzantium in the early fifteenth century.

Meanwhile, this period saw the Renaissance gathering momentum in Europe with new 'humanist' thinking, based on the rediscovery of ancient texts, challenging some of the Church's authority. In northern Italy, the riches from trade and banking had turned city states like Venice, Florence, Genoa and Milan into powerful centres of art and culture, each jealous of the others' wealth. Little wars were constantly being fought between them using the services of mercenary armies led by condottieri. The Papal States joined in these wars with enthusiasm although the papacy itself was in schism, with one pope in Avignon and the other in Italy, each claiming obedience from different European nations. Councils were arranged in Pisa (1409), then Constance (1414–18), to resolve the issue. Pisa succeeded only in creating a third pope while Constance managed finally, in 1417, to secure a single pope, Martin V.

The Council of Constance was the biggest Church council in history and was attended by thousands of temporal and ecclesiastical rulers. It had been called by Pope John XXIII, who had been born Baldassare Cossa on the island of Ischia. He was brilliant but deeply flawed and had been sponsored for the papacy by the Medici family of Florence, who'd bought him his cardinal's hat for ten thousand florins, hoping to receive the Curia's banking in return. At the Council of Pisa, Alexander V had emerged as one of three popes but was found dead soon afterwards while staying at Cossa's palace in Bologna. Succeeding him as pope, Cossa spent prodigiously and outraged everyone with his scandalous behaviour. At Constance he was charged with everything from heresy to incest. He fled, was caught and brought back to be defrocked and imprisoned. His papacy was erased from all records, which explains why another pope was able to take the name of John XXIII in the twentieth century.

At the start of the fifteenth century, Venice and Egypt were at the centre of world trade, while the Ming Chinese, through their treasure fleets, were challenging Arab control of the spice trade in the East. In the West, the Portuguese were taking their first tentative steps down the west coast of Africa, capturing Ceuta from the Moors in 1415. It was a new design of ship, the caravel, that allowed them to do this, given its ability to sail into the wind. However, it wouldn't be until 1497 that Vasco da Gama would round the Cape of Good Hope. A big motivation for finding new trade routes had come from the destruction of the old land routes first by Genghis Khan and then by Tamerlane.

The tension between Christianity and Islam was at the root of the West's fear of Ottoman territorial ambition and the reason for crusades like the one that ended on the field of Nicopolis. But the Ottomans didn't possess the Arabs' fanaticism; and while the Mongol Tamerlane may have called himself the 'Sword of Islam', he was as happy to destroy Muslim Baghdad as Christian Smyrna. The truth is that a great deal of the fire had gone out of the Arab spread of Islam seen between the seventh and ninth centuries, and much of this was due to the Mongol destruction of the East over the thirteenth and fourteenth centuries.

There are some interesting historical characters in *The Lion of Mistra* that are worthy of further mention.

Manuel II Palaiologos was one of the greatest of Byzantine emperors and it was his genius for diplomacy that helped keep the Empire alive until 1453. He spent much of his reign trying to get money or arms from the West to save Constantinople, even seeking ways to unify the Churches of East and West to allow the Pope to sanction another crusade.

His son Theodore II came young to the throne of Mistra. He was a learned, private and somewhat austere man who married Cleope Malatesta of Rimini and then ignored her. It was a childless marriage.

Cleope's father was the condottiere Malatesta dei Sonnetti and her cousin (not uncle as in this book) was the ruthless Carlo Malatesta. Her uncle was the man who succeeded Baldassare Cossa, Pope Martin V.

Braccio da Montone was, with Malatesta, one of the great condottieri of his time. They were great rivals and fought each other at the Battle of Sant'Egidio. Braccio's victory allowed him to take Perugia, the city that had previously expelled his family.

Giovanni and Cosimo de' Medici were the first two important members of that extraordinary family. Giovanni founded the bank and Cosimo built it, in large part through his advantageous connection with the papacy and, in particular, Baldassare Cossa. Their financial innovations led to global expansion. Cosimo de' Medici was a humanist and patron of learning and the arts. He was later to befriend Plethon and bring him to Florence to teach Platonic philosophy.

Poggio Bracciolini was secretary to five popes and a great hunter of classical manuscripts held in the libraries of Europe's monasteries. His greatest find was the Lucretius poem *De Rerum Natura* (*On the Nature of Things*), which he discovered in the monastery of Fulda in Germany in 1417. The poem expounded the teaching of the Greek philosopher Epicurus and put forward revolutionary ideas about the nature of matter.

Jan Hus was the forerunner to Martin Luther and can be said to have initiated the Reformation. He was a Bohemian priest who denounced the corruption of the Church and in particular its sale of indulgences. The King of Hungary, Sigismund, promised him safe conduct to the Council of Constance to put his case to the seniors of the Church but then reneged. Hus was imprisoned and burnt at the stake in the square of Constance.

Marchese Giustiniani Longo was the leader of the Genoese Mahona joint stock company that leased the island of Chios from the Byzantines for the purpose of trading mastic and alum. His son Giovanni was a true historical figure; Marchese's wife, Fiorenza, Princess of Trebizond, is fictional.

The Laskaris family – that of Luke's wife, Anna – were indeed Protostrators (chief ministers) of Mistra. There was frequently great rivalry between the cities of Mistra and Monemvasia where the Archons ruled, supposedly in the name of the Despot. The Mamonas family were Archons of Monemvasia in the fourteenth century.

Finally, two aspects of Christianity feature heavily in this book: the Nestorian heresy and the Ark of the Covenant. Nestorius was Patriarch of Constantinople from 428 to 431 and believed that Jesus Christ existed as two persons: the divine and the human. His teachings were condemned as heretical in the Council of Ephesus (431), leading to the Nestorian Schism, in which churches supporting Nestorius broke away and largely went east, spreading widely across Asia. It is known that many of the Mongol leaders were Nestorians. The Ark of the Covenant is a chest, described in the Book of Exodus, containing the Tablets of Stone on which the Ten Commandments are inscribed. The gold-plated acacia chest was carried ahead of the Israelites, causing waters to part and the walls of Jericho to fall. Today, Ethiopia claims to house it in the Church of St Mary of Zion in the ancient city of Askum (Axum in this book), brought there by Solomon's illegitimate son by the Queen of Sheba.

RISE of EMPIRES

Greece and Turkey, the gateways between Europe and the eastern world, the cradle of so much history, the fount of so many ideas, are full of places we all know and love.

It is here that, back in the fourteenth and early fifteenth centuries, a great struggle took place between the Byzantine Empire, the remnant of the once great Roman empire, and the powerful Ottoman Turks, the Islamic force rising from the Anatolian plains.

Constantinople had a famous harbour for the safety of its ships and formidable walls and Byzantium had great armies. The finest of its warriors were the Varangian Guards, elite fighters who had originally come to Constantinople from England as refugees from the Norman Conquest. One of these Varangians, whose destiny is to save the Byzantine Empire, is the hero of THE RISE OF EMPIRES.

The story of Constantinople, of the heroic struggle to keep the invaders out of Europe and the richness that this brought with it comes to a triumphant conclusion in the next and final book in the series, to be published in 2017.